D1528104

1

SHOWMANCE

Author of the Hearts Series

L.H. COSWAY

For anyone who's ever been terrified of something, but went ahead and did it anyway.

"The power of a glance has been so much abused in love stories, that it has come to be disbelieved in. Few people dare now to say that two beings have fallen in love because they have looked at each other. Yet it is in this way that love begins, and in this way only."

— Victor Hugo, *Les Misérables*

One.
Rose

All actors are sluts.

Okay, so maybe not *all* actors, but whatever. I was in love with an actor, or at least I thought I was, and he was about as oblivious as those little old ladies who used to swoon over Liberace. So oblivious that, even though we'd been sleeping together, he had the gall to ask me to pop to the shop and grab him a pack of johnnies. But not for us, oh, no. Apparently he planned on banging the leading lady after the show.

I stood there, gobsmacked, my bleeding heart dripping all over the floor as I tried to maintain some dignity.

"Excuse me?"

"Johnnies, condoms, prophylactics. You've heard of them, yes?" Blake elaborated.

"Y-yes, of course I've heard of them, but what about — "

He cut me off. "These past few weeks have been great, Rose, but I'm just not in the market for a relationship. Best if we both move on now, eh?"

My head moved slowly from side to side in disbelief. "So it all meant nothing to you?"

"Of course it meant something. It meant I got you in my bed. We had a nice time. Let's leave it at that."

There was an odd, disconnected look in his eyes that I couldn't quite decipher. Then it hit me. He didn't care about me at all. Probably never had. It was my own hopelessly romantic heart concocting a very lovely but very misleading illusion. I must've looked pissed beyond belief, because Blake swallowed and braced himself as though about to take a punch.

I wanted to punch him. Maybe I should have. Instead I told him angrily, "Buy your own johnnies, you whore." And then I stomped out of the room, tears catching in my throat.

I arrived home just after eleven to find my flatmate, Julian, entertaining a few friends in the living room of our spacious London flat. And before you wonder, no, I couldn't afford spacious, not on a choreographer's assistant's salary. Julian was the one who could afford it, and that was because he was a big ol' gigolo.

And before you wonder, yes, he was an actual gigolo. I wasn't adopting that oh-so-modern habit of affectionately referring to my BFF as a whore. Not my style. When I'd called Blake one earlier in the evening, I'd meant it in the traditional sense.

"Cheer up, Rose!" Julian called to me, draped across the lap of a blonde wearing a purple blouse. "If you keep up that face, it might get stuck."

I glared at him, hung up my coat, and went into my bedroom. The door slam was satisfying, but it was all I had left. Flopping down onto my bed, I buried my face in the pillows.

My heart ached as I finally let the tears flow. God, why did this shit have to hurt so bad? What was the point? I wished I'd been born asexual. That way I could just focus on my career and not get sidetracked by pretty men with wandering penises...penii?

"Okay, let's be having it," Julian declared as he flounced into my room and shut the door. "What happened this time?"

I turned over to scowl at him. "Get out. You're all...sexed up. I don't want sexed-up sympathy."

He smirked. "Olivia's put me in a cheery disposition. You should be glad. It means I'm in a mood to indulge this episode, whatever it's about."

I assumed Olivia was the blonde in the purple blouse, though I knew she wasn't a client because he never brought his work home. No, she was purely for enjoyment. Julian cocked an eyebrow, waiting for me to spill. He often refused to talk about my love life because I chose the worst men to fall for, even though I knew better. And I did know better. Nevertheless, I always went for actors. When you worked in theatres throughout the West End, they made up ninety percent of the dating pool.

"I've been sleeping with Blake," I blurted before burying my face in the pillows once more. I couldn't take the judgement that was sure to follow. When I was met with stony silence, I chanced a peek at him. Julian stared at me, his luscious lips drawn into a thin line.

"What are you looking at me like that for? Say something."

"Anything I have to say you're not going to like."

"Just hit me with it. I can take it."

Another long silence, followed by a breathy sigh. "Of all the men you could have slept with, you chose Blake Winters, West London's very own public bicycle. Everybody's had a ride."

Well, you couldn't accuse Julian of mincing his words. I exhaled heavily, my throat clogged with emotion. "But he was so beautiful, and charming, and he made me feel special. Every day for three whole months we'd meet for tea and biscuits on the roof of the theatre at eleven fifteen. We used to talk about *everything* -- our fears, our hopes and dreams. I felt like we had this…connection. Then last month after we'd been out drinking with the cast, he took me back to his place and we had sex. It went on for two weeks, until one morning he got distant on me, couldn't get me out of there fast enough. And today when I saw him on set he was just *awful*. I trusted him, Julian. He was the first person I'd been with in a whole year, and now my heart feels like it's breaking."

He came closer and wrapped his arm around me, smelling of perfume. Olivia's, I presumed. "Well, of course it does. You're not a casual-fling girl. You're a forever girl. But the likes of Blake Winters doesn't want forever, nor does he deserve it."

"He might want it…someday."

"No, he won't, and I'm telling you this because *I'm* a Blake Winters, so take it from somebody who knows. Our attention spans are as short as our list of conquests are long."

"You're not helping." I groaned as I imagined a different woman gracing Blake's bed every night. My breast bone ached with misery.

"I'm sorry, love. Maybe this will make you feel better. Did you know his real name is Oswald?"

I grimaced. "As in Cobblepot?"

"The very same. I had a romp with one of his exes several moons ago, and she had a big mouth. Doesn't have quite the same ring to it as Blake Winters, eh?"

"No, definitely not." I almost smiled. Julian gave my shoulders a squeeze, his embrace a small comfort to me.

"Tomorrow's closing night, isn't it?"

"Yes. At least after that I won't have to see him again. Iggy's been contracted to work on a stage adaption of *Moulin Rouge*. We start rehearsals in a fortnight."

"Well, that sounds exciting."

"Yeah, I think so, too. Anything to take my mind off Blake."

Julian gave me a stern look. "Don't let this get you down, Rose. You're too good for him, far too good. Look at that rack and those legs, look how gorgeous you are and how talented. You just need to learn your worth. As soon as you do, you'll see that Blake was never worthy of you and you'll finally find someone who is."

His words hit home. I was certain Blake couldn't see the real me, not after how he'd acted tonight. But perhaps I couldn't see the real me, either. I smiled at Julian grimly. "Sounds like a fairy tale."

His eyes softened. "If anybody deserves one, it's you."

"And you," I said quietly, my voice tender.

He grew uncomfortable and glanced away, clearing his throat. "Yes well, you get some sleep, beautiful. First thing on tomorrow morning's agenda is a trip to the STD clinic."

As he turned to leave, I launched a pillow that went sailing through the air and hit him square on the back of the head. But damn, he was right. He always was.

Two.

Rose

For two whole weeks I wallowed. The first few days were particularly unpleasant and consisted of me going through several boxes of Kleenex, not washing my hair and letting out dejected sighs that I was sure were driving Julian up the wall.

In the end his patience ran out, and he firmly escorted me to the shower, still in my PJs, and shoved me under the water.

It was COLD.

"Fuck! Julian!" I swore loudly, struggling to get out of his hold.

"Finally, a sign of life," he exclaimed glibly, and I scowled at him hard.

The icy liquid slithered down my body, and somehow the shock of it drew me out of my stupor. Julian was right. I'd been acting like a zombie, and it was ridiculous. Blake didn't warrant such broken-heartedness, especially not after how easily he'd tossed me aside.

After my cold shower intervention, I threw myself into work, spending hours with my boss, Iggy, as we put the finishing touches to the *Moulin Rouge* choreography. It wasn't long before the first morning of rehearsals arrived.

Iggy pulled me excitedly inside his office the moment I walked into the studio. His eyes glittered with untold gossip as he closed the door behind us. "Have you heard that Jacob's hired Damon Atwood to play the male lead?"

I gave him a perplexed look. "Who in the what now?"

Jacob Anthony was one of several directors who kept Iggy and me employed on London stages. He also had a reputation for being something of a diva, but he was so good at what he did that most people chose to overlook it. "Damon Atwood," Iggy repeated. "Don't you remember him? He won the Oscar when he was thirteen for that Holocaust flick where he played a little boy in a concentration camp. Riveting stuff."

"Oh, yeah," I said, memories surfacing. "I saw that one. It was amazing. Didn't he retire from acting, though?"

Iggy nodded. "Yes, when he was seventeen. His career was riddled with bad luck, truth be told. His mother died of cancer when he was fourteen, and afterwards his dad crawled out of the woodwork, looking to cash in on his success. He made sure Damon only took the big money roles, a right bastard, if you ask me."

I eyed him. "You're well informed."

"Of course I am. Spent the morning on Wikipedia after I heard the news." Iggy grinned. "Anyway, there was a very high-profile court case when Atwood won emancipation from his father. He hasn't been heard of since, but apparently he's been living on the Isle of Skye in Scotland."

"From Hollywood to the Isle of Skye. That's quite a long way to go. His dad really must've been a bastard," I said sadly.

"Yes, well, it was a long time ago. Actually, he's probably about your age now, twenty-six or so. I for one am eager to see how the years have treated him," said Iggy just as the door swung open.

"Hahaha! That's the most hilarious thing I've heard all week, Jacob!" a syrupy-sweet voice crooned.

Jacob Anthony walked into the office with Alicia Davidson on his arm. Iggy shot me a cynical look at her sugary fake tone, and I tried to stifle a grin. I loved my boss. He was nicknamed for his distinct resemblance to Iggy Pop, and I'd known him since I was a scruffy teenager, hovering outside his dance studio, penniless and eager to learn.

Alicia was tall, red-haired, voluptuous, and probably the most beautiful woman I'd ever seen in real life. She was an actress from L.A. making her West End debut in the lead role of Satine. If the rumours were true about Atwood, she'd be playing his love interest as the glamorous, ailing courtesan.

Alicia and Jacob barely acknowledged that Iggy and I were in the room with them.

"So tell me about Damon," Alicia went on. "How on earth did you manage to lure him out of obscurity for this? I mean, can he even sing?"

Jacob shrugged. "To be perfectly honest with you, hon, I haven't met with him in person yet. All our correspondence has been through email. He's supposed to be arriving today so that we can audition him properly, but for I all I know this could be a very elaborate catfish scam. As for if he can sing, who's to say. If he can't, we'll get him lessons. Can you imagine the sort of attention we'll attract from the press with Damon Atwood on the roster? Alongside your good self, of course."

Alicia glowed and shot him a flirtatious smile while Jacob ushered her further into the office. "Miss Davidson, might I introduce you to our choreographer, the wonderful Iggy Thomas."

"Very pleased to meet you, Mr Thomas," said Alicia.

Iggy took her hand and gave it a gentlemanly peck. "Likewise, and please, call me Iggy. Rose and I are really looking forward to working with you."

Alicia's bright green eyes landed on me, and she gave me a wide, pretty smile as she reached over to shake my hand. "It's lovely to meet you, too, Rose."

"And you." I grinned, momentarily dazzled by her beauty. Note to self: stop falling in love with every new actor you meet, male or female.

Jacob quickly whisked Alicia away, leaving me and Iggy alone once more.

When they were out of earshot, Iggy asked dryly, "Do you think the carpet matches the drapes?"

I snort-laughed and sat down, pulling my dance shoes from my bag to unravel the laces. Mustering a surprisingly accurate impression of Jacob, I lazily waved a hand through the air. "Who's to say."

Iggy snickered and took the shoes from me, unknotting the laces within seconds.

***

We spent the morning with the chorus line, teaching them preliminary sequences for the big club scene. Jacob, Alicia, the choral director, and a number of assistants sat at a long table, watching our progress and taking notes.

It was after lunch that the tension in the building heightened, whispers cascading from ear to ear as news spread that Mr Atwood had finally arrived. Iggy's studio took up the entire top floor of a large Victorian building in central London; it included one large practice room, several smaller ones, dressing rooms with showers, and a few offices. I wondered where they'd sequestered Damon Atwood.

I summoned up an image from the movies of his that I'd seen. He'd been young, but I remembered he was tall, with dark hair and deep, soulful brown eyes. Though who knew what he was looking like these days.

I often found that child actors looked odd when they got older. Not because their appearances were particularly unusual, but more because you were so used to seeing their faces as children that it was strange when their features transformed into adulthood.

Case in point: Macaulay Culkin.

"I heard he lives in a tiny little cottage and works on the fishing boats that operate out of the island for no pay. Why anyone would want to work on a stinky fishing trawler when they've got millions sitting in the bank is beyond me," said a woman sitting a few feet away from me as we took our break. I recognised her from the chorus line.

"But can you imagine him working?" said another. "I saw him arrive out front a half hour ago. Boy has grown up good."

I shamelessly continued listening to them gossip for the next ten minutes as I chomped on some Bombay mix. Then Jacob flounced into the room once more, several assistants heavy on his heels, and took a seat at the long table.

There was some frenzied chatting between him and the choral director, an older woman named Maura. Turning to one of his assistants, he gave some instructions and the girl hurried from the room. When she returned, a hush fell over the studio as she escorted a tall man inside. His brown hair was long and came to just below his ears. Some heavy stubble dusted his face, and he wore scuffed, workman's clothes: a long grey coat and steel toe–capped boots. Despite his distinctly laid-back appearance, I sensed a special aura from him, that certain *je ne sais quoi* they called star quality.

This was Damon Atwood, and he was entirely unexpected.

He didn't look weird to me, like grown child actors normally did. No, he looked like his previous incarnation had been a costume and this was his true self come to fruition.

"Well, then, Mr Atwood, let's see what we have to work with," said Jacob, a pad of paper in his lap and a pen poised at his lips. "Have you prepared a song?" Damon nodded but didn't speak. There was a stoicism about him, his dark brows drawing a distinctive line across his forehead. He stood at the front of the studio and shot a look to the assistant as she hit a button on the sound system. Music began to play, the intro to "Nature Boy."

When he opened his mouth to sing, he didn't sound how I thought he would. His voice was a revelation, more Nat King Cole than Ewan McGregor, and the tiny hairs on my arms stood on end as I suddenly found myself leaning forward to listen. He had my undivided attention.

Man, his singing was like aural caramel, smooth, thick, and undeniably sultry. The entire room was held rapt by his performance, barely an intake of breath to be heard. Damon stared at his feet half the time, almost as though he was too shy to face us. Still, it felt like somebody so large, somebody with such a strikingly masculine appearance, couldn't possibly be self-conscious. It was only as he sang the last line that he finally looked up, and somehow his eyes locked on mine, like he sensed my spellbound attention.

The greatest thing you'll ever learn is just to love and be loved in return.

Goosebumps rose on my skin.

When he finished there was a beat of silence, like everyone had been struck speechless.

Jacob cleared his throat. "Well, you definitely won't need a voice coach," he said, eyeing Maura with a pleased expression. I was slightly annoyed that he hadn't taken a moment to compliment Damon on his performance. Describing it as life-altering wasn't even an exaggeration. Directors, unfortunately, were often desensitised to greatness, spending their lives amid the highly talented and beautiful as they did.

I, on the other hand, wanted to leap from my seat, run up to Damon Atwood, and wax lyrical about the cadence of his voice and the depth and quality of his tone.

"We will, however, have to make some alterations to your…look. Jenny here" — he gestured to one of his assistants — "will pencil you in for a barber's appointment in the morning."

"Pardon?" said Damon, his brow furrowing. It was slightly hilarious, like someone had just told Sean Connery he'd have to do an accent.

But speaking of accents…hearing him speak for the first time was an experience in itself. He sounded mildly Northern, sort of Sean Bean-esque. *Hello*. It was a little diluted, though, probably because he'd spent so many years in L.A. during his youth.

"Your character, Christian, is a clean-cut young man," Jacob explained. "And you look like you just stepped off the set of *Vikings*, no offence."

Damon didn't say a word, just continued staring at Jacob like he was mildly confused by him.

As though suddenly aware of the tension, Jacob sprang up from his seat and hurried across the room, throwing his arm around Damon's broad shoulders and speaking to him animatedly as he led him back out the door.

"Well, that wasn't awkward," said Iggy as he came to sit next to me. "How about a wager on how long Atwood will last? I'm not sure he'll even make it to opening night."

I shot him a glance. "That's mean."

He raised his hands. "Hey, I know people. Jacob and Damon are about as suited as Britney and that bloke she married for twenty-four hours."

"It was actually fifty-five, you big cynic."

"And they say romance is dead." He grinned and pulled me up with him. "Come on, practice until four and then home."

Two hours later, I was leaving the studio and scanning the road for approaching taxis when I caught sight of Damon standing by the kerb. There were two moderately sized suitcases at his feet as he stared down at a piece of paper in one hand and his phone in the other. His attractive brows were knit together in consternation.

Now, I wasn't normally the type to approach strangers and offer unsolicited assistance, but there was something about him in that moment that seemed oddly helpless, despite his size.

"Hey, uh, are you all right?" I asked, my voice snagging his attention.

He looked up, a few moments passing as he took me in, and I wondered if he remembered our brief moment of eye contact earlier that day. After a minute he looked back down at the items he was holding. "I'm fine, thanks."

His response was dismissive, but not in a rude way, more in a way that said he just wanted to be left alone. I should have gone then, but for some reason my feet wouldn't move.

I gestured to his suitcases. "Have you just arrived in London?"

His attention flicked from me and then back to the paper he held. He seemed tired. "Aye." God, I really loved how he spoke. His words weren't too thickly accented, but they held just the right amount of gravel to make my femininity aware of his masculinity. He looked at me again, this time pressing his lips together and glancing inside for a second. "You work in there?"

So he did remember. The thought had my pulse racing for some reason. I offered a friendly smile. "That's right. I'm Rose, the choreographer's assistant."

Damon grimaced. "I can't dance."

His honest response solicited a light chuckle from me. "In that case, you picked a stellar gig."

He didn't say anything then, just stared at me as though trying to figure out my game. I took a step closer and glanced at the paper he held. It contained an address, and I recognised the street because it was only a few minutes away from my and Julian's apartment.

"Is this where you're staying?" I asked.

He withdrew the paper, tucking it firmly back in his pocket like it contained information on breaking the Enigma code rather than a simple address.

"Aye," he answered, still wary.

I motioned to his phone. "If you're looking for directions, I live close by. We can even share a cab if you'd like."

Again, he eyed me warily, like maybe I was a thief trying to steal his luggage. "No thanks, I'll make do."

"It's really no problem," I went on.

Now he frowned, growing agitated as he grunted forcefully, "I said *no*."

I jumped in surprise and took a step backward. There was a catch in my throat as I raised my hands and relented. "Okay, no worries. See you around."

As I turned to leave, I heard a frustrated sigh. "Hang on," he called.

Hesitantly, I turned back to him and waited.

"I'm sorry. I'm no good with people these days." There was remorse in his voice, and it made my pulse stammer.

I looked at the ground, toeing a loose stone with my Sketchers. "It's okay. All this must be a big change for you."

He nodded, his brown eyes studying me a moment before glancing over my shoulder. "Here's a taxi." Holding a hand out, he flagged it down, and it pulled to a stop. He didn't say a word as we both climbed inside, but I could tell he felt bad for snapping at me. Sharing the cab he'd previously refused must have been his way of apologising without words.

We began our journey in quiet, and I was suddenly floundering for conversation, perhaps because Damon felt so imposing. He was Hollywood handsome, but rough around the edges. He was also very large, looming almost, and he seemed uncomfortable with his size. I kept glancing at the thigh that was closest to me, noticing he held it rigid so it wouldn't invade my personal space or knock against mine.

When I pulled out my phone to check my messages, I began to sense him looking at me. Trying to ignore his stare, I scrolled through some old texts, pretending they were new. When I couldn't take much more, I chanced a peek at him. He was blatantly staring, but not in a cocky or creepy way, more in the way a child stares at something new and unusual.

21

"What?" I asked, self-consciously tucking some hair behind my ear.

Damon shook his head but didn't turn away. "Pardon?"

"Why are you staring at me?"

It took him several beats to answer. "You've got a kind face." He sounded surprised, like kindness from a stranger was the last thing he'd expected when he got to London.

"Oh," I breathed, my lungs filling. "Well…thanks."

At long last Damon cast his gaze out the window, and I felt a tingling sensation just below the surface of my skin. When the cabbie stopped outside the house he was staying in, Damon seemed hesitant to get out. We both spoke at the same time.

"Looks like a nice place."

"Come in with me."

Something about his request made my heart skip a beat, but he obviously didn't mean it in *that* way. "What?"

"You seem good with people. I'm not. There's going to be someone in there looking to show me around, and I don't want to deal with them."

I stared at him in disbelief. "So, you want me to deal with them for you?"

"Please," he said, his tone begging me not to make a fuss.

I looked at the driver, who seemed just as perplexed by the situation as I was. However, there was something about Damon Atwood that I couldn't bring myself to say no to, so I shrugged and nodded.

"Okay, let's go."

Damon exhaled and shot me a grateful look. Then he shoved a fifty through the pay slot – way too much for the journey we'd taken – and hurried outside with his luggage.

I followed him to the gate. It really was a very nice house, refurbished Edwardian with a bright red door.

Damon lifted the knocker, and a moment later it flew open, a young, eager-looking man welcoming us in. He was from the letting agents. Damon stepped right past him, walked upstairs, and shut himself inside the bathroom.

Weird.

I, on the other hand, was left to deal with the aftermath.

"Is Mr Atwood quite well?" the young man asked.

"He had a bit of a dodgy curry for lunch. He's not feeling the best," I lied, and he seemed relieved that he hadn't somehow inadvertently offended a client. I let him go through the motions as he showed me where everything was and how the central heating worked, etc. By the time he left, Damon was still in the bathroom. I hesitantly went upstairs and gently knocked.

The door opened slowly, and Damon peeked his head out, asking, "Is he gone?"

"Yes."

He exhaled in relief, and I cocked a questioning brow at him. He seemed hesitant to explain. "City types stress me out. Thanks for…well, just thanks."

"It was no problem," I replied, not mentioning the fact that I myself was a city type. Thrusting forward an envelope and two sets of keys, I said, "These are for you."

Damon accepted them without question, and I turned to leave. "Wait," he called, almost desperately. I turned back around. His mouth opened, then shut, then opened again. "I don't have food."

It was the last thing I'd expected him to say. "There's a Waitrose around the corner."

He shook his head, as though annoyed with himself. "Waitrose, right, sorry."

I paused, eyeing him, but not spending too much time thinking about what I said next. "Do you want to come have dinner at mine? I'm making chili con..."

"Yes," he said eagerly, before I even had a chance to finish the sentence. This was odd, to say the least. First he adamantly refused my help, and now he was latching on for dear life. I didn't understand it, but I decided to just go with the flow.

I gave him a sceptical look. "I have to warn you -- my flatmate, Julian, will be there, and he's about as 'city type' as you can get."

"Oh." He suddenly seemed less enthusiastic.

"He's harmless, though," I offered. *Yeah, about as harmless as a honey badger.*

Damon scratched at his stubble, a thoughtful expression on his face. "I *should* make an effort be sociable."

"You're coming, then?"

Damon's face nodded while his eyes shook their head...or at least, that's how it seemed to me. I cleared my throat.

"Okay, that's, um, that's good. Let's get going."

It was a mildly chilly day, so I zipped my coat all the way to the top and shoved my hands in my pockets, my bag hanging over my shoulder as we walked. It was quiet for a minute or two, and I had between one and twenty pent-up questions just burning to be asked. In the end, I went with the most obvious.

"I hope you don't mind me asking, but if you don't like city types and you can't dance, then why on earth did you sign up to be in a musical on the West End?"

Damon's handsome brown eyes slid to mine. "How much do you know about me?"

I inhaled a quick breath. "Well, I didn't know much until this morning, when everyone bar the cleaning lady was gossiping about you being cast like it was Christmas come early."

He winced, seeming uncomfortable with this titbit, but soldiered on. "After I retired from film, I went to live with my maternal grandmother on the Isle of Skye. She died just over a month ago."

"I'm sorry," I said gently.

Damon shrugged. "She was ninety-four. She had a good innings. On her death bed, she asked me to revive my art. The next day I got a voicemail from Jacob Anthony, asking if I'd audition for his musical. Felt like kismet. I love singing, and I admit I do miss acting. Gran had been hopeful that I'd perform again, so impulsively, I said yes."

"And now you're regretting it," I added.

He just stared at me, but didn't answer. His gaze wandered over my features, sharpening momentarily on my mouth. His expression was indecisive. A minute later, we reached my apartment, and I dug in my bag for my keys.

"So," I began as I led him up the stairs to the top floor, "Julian can be kind of full-on when you first meet him, but really, all you have to do is let him yammer on about himself, and he'll be quite happy to do all the talking."

"I'm not a big talker," Damon admitted as I slotted my key in and turned it.

I almost got a crick in my neck as I bent my head to look up and give him a kind smile. "Yeah, I noticed that."

He appeared momentarily self-conscious, so I reached out and gave his hand a soft squeeze of encouragement. He jumped slightly at my touch, like he wasn't used to it. I felt a little shot of adrenaline shoot through my chest at the sensation of his skin on mine. Something both old and new awoke inside me but I couldn't say exactly what it was.

Then I let go, and it faded.

Three.

"Well, now, who's this?" Julian asked as he slid up off the couch, where he'd been lazily scrolling through his tablet. I chanced a quick, reassuring peek at Damon before answering my friend. "This is Damon. He's in the cast." Julian groaned as he approached, his chestnut hair sitting messily atop his head. "Oh, please, Rose, not another actor."

I glared at him, trying to channel as much "shut the hell up" into my eyes as possible. My flatmate didn't really have a censor. A moment of quiet ensued while Julian circled Damon, taking his measure. "You don't look like an actor."

The edges of Damon's mouth twitched for the briefest second. "Thanks."

"He's got a sense of humour, too. He'll go far." Julian grinned in my direction, then sauntered into the kitchen. "I'm starving. Are you cooking dinner?"

"Aren't I always," I sighed, and then asked Damon if I could take his coat. He shrugged out of it, his eyes not leaving me all the while, and then I went to hang it on the rack by the door. On my return he bent to ask curiously, "Another actor?"

I took a moment to absorb the sensation of his breath hitting my skin. It was...not unpleasant. Julian, who I swear had the hearing of a bat, didn't miss a beat as he let out an amused chuckle. "Rose has a weakness for those in your profession."

Damon looked at me in question. I strode over to the breakfast bar, again glaring at my friend. "Yes, well, I've sworn off all thespians after the last disaster, so Damon here is safe."

"What disaster?"

For someone who claimed not to be a big talker, he sure had a lot of questions.

"Ever heard of Blake Winters?" Julian chirped, plucking an apple from the fruit bowl and taking a big bite. Damon shook his head. Julian scrunched his brows.

"Have you been living under a rock?"

"No, I've been living on an island," said Damon.

Julian cocked his head to the side, as though trying to figure out if he was being sarcastic. "Well, he's an actor, like you, and he sleeps around. Rose had the great misfortune to have her head turned by the young Mr Winters. He seduced her and then left her in the lurch, the swine." Julian pouted his lips, affecting a disapproving expression.

"Sounds like an arse," Damon put in, and both Julian and I began laughing.

"I like this one," said Julian.

I grinned as I thought, *yeah, me too,* and found myself suddenly blushing.

I was sure that if I'd met Damon a month ago, I'd already be head over heels, especially considering the whole brooding, antisocial thing he had going on. However, though my Blake wounds had scabbed over, they were still fresh, so I wasn't really feeling anything more for him than friendship.

Damon took a stool and sat as I began gathering the ingredients for dinner. At the same time, Julian's phone started ringing, and I knew it was his work number because it rang to the tune of "Roxanne" by The Police. Yes, my friend had a dark sense of humour to go with his inability to censor.

And yes, I was aware it was odd how normal it had become for him to be taking a call from someone who wanted to hire him for sex, but Julian and I had both had a very non-traditional upbringing. What was surreal to others was ordinary to us. And the sad fact of the matter was, if Julian hadn't been working in the sex industry, he'd probably be strung out in a heroin den somewhere, waiting to die.

Experiences had moulded him in such a way that he needed constant stimulation.

It was the lesser of two evils, and I'd grown to accept that. In life, you often had to reshape your square edges to accommodate the plethora of difference that existed in the corners of our individualities.

"Yes, all right, I'll see you in a half an hour, then," said Julian, and he hung up. He had that little thrill of excitement in his voice that told me this was a client he liked.

"I'll have to take a rain check on dinner," he went on, striding back over to the kitchen. "Duty calls."

"I'll leave a plate in the oven, just in case you're hungry when you get home."

"Thanks, you're a doll. It was a pleasure to meet you, Damon," he said with a smile before grabbing his coat and scarf and hurrying out the door.

Damon watched him go before his attention returned to me. "Quite the character, isn't he?" I said as I chopped some garlic.

"Are you two — "

"Oh, God, no," I interrupted, immediately knowing the direction of this thoughts. "Julian's like a brother. Actually, he sort of was my brother for a little while."

"Ah," said Damon, before glancing at his watch. "What does he do?"

I pursed my lips, wondering if I should just get the matter of Julian's profession out of the way sooner rather than later. My friend made no secret of what he did for a living, but at the same time, he didn't go shouting it from the rooftops, either. If anyone were to ask, those women were simply paying him for his company, nothing more. In fact, every once in a while that really was the truth. There were lots of very wealthy, very lonely women out there who just wanted someone to take them out for dinner and dancing.

"Yeah, um, Julian's job runs somewhat unconventional hours."

"Oh?"

"He's an escort."

Damon's mouth fell open slightly. "An escort as in...."

"Women pay him for the pleasure of his company."

He cleared his throat and shifted uncomfortably in place as his brows drew together in consternation. Staring at the countertop, he seemed lost for words to the point that he looked like he was in physical pain. I felt bad. Maybe I should've waited a little longer before laying it on him.

"It's okay. I wouldn't know how to respond to that information, either," I told him with a reassuring smile. "Julian and I, well, we didn't have the most conventional childhood."

I watched as Damon swallowed and shook his head. A long moment passed as he appeared to be experiencing some kind of internal struggle. I didn't know how to take it.

I mean, people were usually surprised when they discovered Julian's job, but they didn't look like it pained them inside.

"No," he said finally. "It's not that, I just…I don't have the best memories of sex workers, but I'm sure Julian is different." He paused to clear his throat. "What kind of childhood did you have?"

He sounded genuinely curious, but I was still stuck on his comment about sex workers. What the hell did that mean? I didn't want to pry, though, so I answered his question instead.

"Up until the age of ten I lived alone with my mum. I was an only child, and my dad left when I was little. Then she met a man named Elijah. He had that kind of small-town charisma, and Mum fell for it hook, line, and sinker. He also had two other women in his life, Julian's mum, Kimberly, and Joanna, who had two daughters from a previous marriage. The four of them quickly fell into a polyamorous relationship, and I suddenly found myself moving into a new home with a bunch of new siblings, Julian being one of them."

I paused to let Damon absorb all that, because I knew it was a lot to take in. "Well, that's uh, not something you hear every day," he said finally.

"No," I replied, exhaling as I continued to prepare dinner. "It was unusual, to say the least. What about you, though, any brothers or sisters?"

"None. Mum died when I was fourteen, and then the only real family I had left was Gran. I cut my dad off a long time ago." He paused to glance up at me, and there was something terribly sad in his expression. "Now there's just me left."

I wanted to ask what his father had done to warrant being cut from his life, but I didn't.

"Well, Julian and I know all about losing family," I said softly. "My mum passed when I was twenty, and his mum's been living in a psychiatric ward for the past few years. She's there but...not there, you know?"

Damon nodded but, like me, he didn't ask questions. I poured some oil into the pan and began cooking the meat. The next time I looked up, he was gone. My eyes travelled across the flat to find him standing by the shelves in our living room, where we kept all of our books and DVDs.

I watched as he scanned the titles before calling over his shoulder, "Gene Kelly?"

"I'm kind of obsessed," I admitted sheepishly.

"You must have his entire back catalogue here," he commented. There was something in his voice that hinted at amusement, but I couldn't be sure. He didn't seem to smile very often, so it was hard to tell what he was thinking.

"He's my idol, like, the greatest dancer who ever lived, in my opinion. I even went to a talk given by one of his wives a few years ago and got to meet her afterwards. God, I was such a fangirl. The whole time I had this internal dialogue that was all, *this woman TOUCHED Gene Kelly. This woman HAD SEX with Gene Kelly. She probably even did his laundry.* I hugged her way longer than was appropriate and may have freaked her out a little. You'd swear I was a thirteen-year-old meeting Zane Malik," I confessed.

Damon returned to the kitchen, his eyes finding mine. "I was a little like that when I met Gary Oldman. I idolised him for years." He paused to wince. "We were working on a film together, and when we were first introduced my hands got all sweaty and I stammered through half my sentences. He probably thought there was something wrong with me."

I chuckled. "Man, I'm glad I'm not the only one. Nice name drop, by the way."

Damon's cheeks reddened the tiniest bit. "I didn't mean to."

I smiled warmly as I stirred some chili sauce into the meat. "I'm pulling your leg, but speaking of idols, you could find yourself in the running to becoming one of mine. Where on earth did you get those pipes? Your singing is just incredible."

A new expression took shape on his face, one that made my belly flutter. It was intense. His eyes met mine and held them. "Thanks," he murmured.

"You're welcome," I replied, and a strange ticklish sensation whispered across my chest.

A few moments of quiet fell as I served up the food. Damon ate quietly, like a well-behaved St. Bernard chowing down in the corner. I found myself studying him. The man was such a contradiction, with the rugged looks of a heartthrob and the personality of a hermit just coming out of hibernation. I could tell that quietness was natural to him. It made me wonder how he ever got into acting, though they did say that to act was a shy man's revenge on the world.

"What?" said Damon, drawing me from my thoughts as I realized I was staring – quite like he'd been staring at me in the cab earlier.

I scooped some rice up onto my fork and gave him a small smile. "I was just thinking how you're the most unlikely person to be an actor, particularly a stage actor. Have you ever done a play before?"

Damon frowned as he glanced down at his plate. "No, this will be my first."

"Are you frightened?"

Now he looked back up. "Terrified."

There was something about his candour and his unveiled expression that had me reaching across the table to squeeze his hand again. "Would having a friend make it easier?"

He seemed surprised by my question. "You'd like to be my friend?"

"Well, I'll admit I'm not offering for entirely selfless reasons. I'm still broken-hearted over Blake. I could use a friend, too."

He squeezed my hand back, his gaze intent on mine. I smiled at him, and he seemed fascinated by the expression. His attention moved over my features, from my eyelashes to the tip of my nose and then finally to my lips. Slowly, his mouth started to curve, and I suddenly realised he was smiling back at me. It was startling because it was so unexpected, the expression transforming his face into something powerfully beautiful. It practically knocked the air from my lungs.

"Friends, then," he said finally, and I tried to steady my rapidly beating heart.

Four.

Damon

Stop staring at her. She'll think you're a creep. Farrah, one of the women from the costume department, was measuring me up for a suit, while various cast members hurried around us. I would have found it more stressful if I wasn't so focused on Rose. She sat on the floor in one corner of the dance studio, earphones in, eyes downcast, an iPod in one hand and a sandwich in the other.

A couple of days had passed since we shared dinner at her flat, and I noticed this was her routine every lunch time. I hadn't yet summoned the courage to approach her. Our only real contact was to say hello when we passed each other by. Nothing really.

Yesterday she gave me a secret little smile when our eyes met across the studio. I didn't know how to take it, so I just turned away. It was fucking awful. The disappointed look on her face afterwards almost killed me.

Why was it so hard to just smile at people? I'd managed it when we shared dinner in her flat, but maybe that was a fluke. Sometimes I felt like I was made from stone, solid and unmoving, only ever free when I delved into a role and became someone else.

Still, the way I trusted Rose was unforeseen. I didn't easily let people in, but there'd been something in her eyes, something guileless that made me feel like I could give her a glimpse of the man behind the mask.

"For someone so wonderfully tall, you slouch way too much," said Farrah. Work was starting on designing costumes for the show, so she was visiting today to take measurements from all the lead actors.

I glanced down at her. When you were my height, you were forever glancing downward. "Sorry."

"Just." She pursed her lips and reached up, grabbing my shoulders and straightening them out. "Stand like this. That way, we'll be done quicker. You clearly hate this."

I did. I hated people touching me, especially strangers. Briefly, I remembered Rose taking my hand and squeezing it the other day. I hadn't hated that, not at all. Not knowing what else to say, I simply repeated myself. "Sorry."

Farrah snickered. "A man of few words, I see."

I shrugged because again she was right. I was far more eloquent and articulate inside my own head than I ever was when I spoke. Being quiet was my nature, even when I was a young lad. Perhaps that was why acting suited me; the words came pre-prepared.

My childhood tutor, Mr Gilroy, had held a devout passion for extending the vocabulary. This passion worked on me to a certain extent. I could write endlessly wordy and expressive essays and short stories, but when it came to speaking out loud, the words fled. There was this strange block that prevented them from travelling from my mind to my mouth. There still was, probably always would be.

I returned my attention to Rose as Farrah stretched a measuring tape down my right arm. Her friend, Julian, had said she'd been burned by some actor, and she'd told me herself she'd sworn off them, so it was a waste of time being so curious about her. Unfortunately, I found myself noticing *everything*.

Her dark brown hair was never out of its chaotic, messy knot, and she always wore leggings and tops that were too big for her. They had a habit of falling off one shoulder, or dipping down at the front as she demonstrated a dance move. She had no idea how sexy she was, completely unaware of my perverted ogling or the dirty thoughts I found myself succumbing to. But perhaps that was part of the allure, her complete and utter lack of self-awareness.

There was this freckle on the underside of her jaw that I found myself studying like I was going to be tested on the bloody thing.

"Damon, I need you over here," Jacob called, and Farrah let out a sigh.

"Go on. I've just finished anyway."

She hurried off. Alicia, the lead actress, walked into the studio alongside Eddie, who was playing Harold Zidler, and Bob, who was playing the Duke. We had a read-through of the entire script on Tuesday, but I still wasn't sure what to make of my costars. It'd been a long time since I'd experienced showbiz types. These days I was used to ordinary, down-to-earth people.

"Where's the bathroom?" Bob asked as he stumbled up to Jacob, a little unsteady on his feet. The bloke was addled.

Jacob's lips firmed as he took him in, clearly coming to the same conclusion.

"First," said Jacob, "the bathroom is down the hall and to the left. Second, I don't tolerate the consumption of alcohol in my productions, so get sober and keep your drinking for your day off. Now please, go use the facilities so that we can begin rehearsing this sequence."

Bob scrunched up his brow and Jacob sighed, motioning for his assistant to show Bob to the bathroom. I stood holding my pages, running the song lyrics through my head. I didn't have the entire show off by heart yet, but I'd get there.

"I don't know what I was thinking casting him. The man's got an alcohol problem," said Jacob flippantly as he approached me. He moved his shoulders as though shaking off the unpleasantness. "Anyway, how are you today, Damon?" He reached up and ran his fingers through my hair. I shifted backward, finding him way too overfamiliar. "Have you given any more consideration to having these locks chopped? Lovely though they are, they don't exactly match your character."

"I'll do it this weekend," I told him, and he seemed pleased by this. As far as I was concerned, hair was just hair. I didn't have any kind of emotional attachment to it, but for some reason, Jacob had interpreted my social awkwardness for aggression, surmising I was pissed at the idea of changing my appearance.

"Marvellous! In that case, I'll look forward to your transformation."

Iggy, the choreographer, entered the room just then, and I saw him wave Rose over. He was a strange-looking man, with long, fine brown hair and sinewy muscles. Rose pulled out her earphones, stuffed the last of her sandwich in her mouth, and wiped her hands off on her leggings. I smiled at her lack of femininity, because ironically it was captivatingly feminine.

She glanced at me as she approached the group and shot a friendly smile my way. *Smile back,* I urged myself. *For fuck's sake, do something!* In the end, all I managed was a slight grimace, but maybe that was because I had to start dancing in a minute.

"Okay, this is the scene of The Pitch. Today we'll practice the dance routine for 'Spectacular Spectacular.'" Jacob paused and glanced over his shoulder to his second assistant. "Is Bob back yet?"

"I'll go get him," said the woman before scurrying off. Jacob let out a dissatisfied breath. "Probably throwing his guts up as we speak."

Alicia, who stood just next to Eddie, appeared disgusted at the description. A minute later Bob was back, and he looked decidedly less bleary-eyed. I wondered if Jacob's assistant had rammed her fingers down the man's gullet and forced him to vomit just to sober him up a bit.

Jacob eyed him narrowly before turning back to the rest of us. "As I was saying, this scene is The Pitch. The Duke has just walked in on Christian and Satine" -- he paused to motion between me and Alicia -- "in a compromising position. In order to cover up what they were doing, the two, alongside Harold, Toulouse, and the rest of the gang, pretend they were rehearsing, and proceed to make up a fictitious play which they would like the Duke to bankroll. We won't worry too much about vocals. Right now I just want to see how you all do with the choreography."

And cue my nausea. I hated dancing and had been fumbling my way through routines for days now. I was beginning to wonder if I should just chuck it all in and find a job that didn't involve this kind of daily humiliation. Unfortunately, I was a stubborn git and hated quitting anything once I'd started. That meant I was in this for the long haul.

I didn't see her approach, but I felt someone tug on my sleeve and glanced down to see Rose at my side.

"Relax. This is one of the easier sequences. You basically get to crawl around on your knees and bounce up and down like a toddler. So long as you can coordinate with the others you'll be fine."

She was trying to make me feel better, but it wasn't working. I'd been born with two left feet.

"All right, everybody, let's limber up, shall we?" said Iggy, and he began doing scissors jumps. Soon everyone was joining in, and Rose gave my sleeve another little tug as if to say, *go on*. I joined in, and she went off to stand by Iggy.

When we'd completed the warm-up, Iggy began demonstrating the routine. "A one, a two, a one, two, three," he instructed as he glided across the stage like some kind of muscular gazelle. The others mimicked his movements, all of them experienced with dancing.

I, on the other hand, was completely lost. Rose walked through, giving guidance where it was needed, and then finally she came to me. Without a word she began fixing my posture, one hand going to the base of my spine and pushing it forward, the other to the backs of my knees to straighten my legs. She touched me without hesitancy, but with a keen eye and near scientific precision, a little like a nurse or a doctor might. Still, her warm hands soothed me, and I inhaled the scent of her citrusy perfume.

"Can't dance indeed," she said with warmth in her eyes. There was no criticism in her voice, just a mild, friendly hint of teasing. The next half hour was pure agony, but less so because Rose helped me step by step. Once it was time to practice the song, I was confident I could at least complete the dance routine without injuring myself.

Maura, the choral director, played the opening chords on the piano as Rose stepped away, and I took my position next to Eddie.

Bob stood before us, assuming the role of the Duke, as Eddie began to sing. Alicia laughed when Henry, who was playing Toulouse, accidentally shoved an elbow in her side.

I hadn't spoken to her much, but she seemed nice, not too high maintenance like you'd usually get with film stars. When I sang to her toward the end of the routine, she fluttered her eyelashes, her green eyes turning doe-like, as she played her part. Satine and Christian were supposed to be falling in love. I tried to convey that when I sang, and caught a quick glimpse of Rose, who wore a strange, captivated expression.

In fact, when I looked around, I noticed most of the others were looking at me in the same way, even Jacob. The song we'd been practicing came to a stop.

"What?" I asked.

Jacob blinked and stepped forward, clearing his throat. "Oh, Damon, if only you could dance as well as you sing." He turned to the others. "Okay, everybody, from the top."

And that was all anyone said about it. I still wasn't quite sure why they'd all been staring like they had.

"Let's take fifteen," said Iggy after we practiced the song with the dance routine several times. "Then we'll do a few more run-throughs before the end of the day."

I watched Rose return to her coveted corner, sticking her earphones back in and hitting "play" on her iPod as she chugged on some water. I wanted to go over there, talk to her. Already my feet were on the move, and it was completely out of character. I never approached people. They approached me.

Taking a seat beside her, I pulled a bud from her ear and stuck it in mine. A prim voice spoke, and I realised she wasn't listening to music. She was listening to a book.

"What's this?" I asked, and she smiled a little sheepishly.

"It's a novel called *Outlander*, you know, like the TV show. I'm a bit of an audiobook junkie," she explained, and

41

there was something about how she said it, with a hint of embarrassment, that I found endearing.

I listened for a minute, unexpectedly falling into the story. Rose poked me in the arm. "You should consider doing one. I'd listen to a story narrated by you any day of the week."

I stared at her, unsure how to reply to that. After a moment I leaned in, my shoulder brushing hers as I spoke low. "And what book would you have me narrate?"

She paused to consider her answer, tapping her lower lip with her middle finger. "Hmm, if only Elizabeth Gaskell had written *North and South* from the male point of view. You'd make a fantastic Mr Thornton."

I affected a brooding frown. "That's how you see me? All moody and tortured?"

She eyed me, seeming surprised that I knew who Mr Thornton was. "Maybe add 'shy' to that list. You've barely spoken a word to me all week."

I rubbed at my jaw and looked across the studio to where Iggy stood with Jacob, both men talking, their eyes on us. "Yeah, sorry about that."

Seeming to notice my self-consciousness, she nudged me with her elbow. "Did you know you sound like Sean Bean? I could listen to him recite the phone book," she said on a sigh. Did that mean she could listen to me recite the phone book, too? For a second her blue eyes widened, like she just realised what she'd said. I didn't want her to feel uncomfortable, so I changed the subject.

"Do you remember earlier when I was singing my part of the song for the first time?"

Rose nodded and took another gulp of water. My attention wandered to the delicate curve of her throat as she swallowed and then back up to her bright eyes. My brow furrowed. It was becoming disconcerting how closely I watched her sometimes.

"Everybody got weird for a second, just...staring at me. What was that about?"

She turned her body to look me dead in the eye. "You have no idea, have you?

"No idea of what?"

"Of how good you are. When you sing, I swear, even the straight guys in the cast get stiffys."

I sputtered a laugh, surprised by her unexpected bluntness. "You're lying."

"And you're oblivious, Damon. You're a fantastic actor and an amazing singer. It's hard for people not to go all googly-eyed when you perform. I guess that's why you're a star." She shrugged like it was simple.

"I haven't been a star for a very long time, and even then it wasn't all it was cracked up to be," I said. What I really wanted to say was, "Do you get a stiffy when I sing?" Or, uh, the female equivalent.

Do you get wet when I sing, Rose?

The question filled my head with images. In my mind she was spread wide and naked on my bed, begging, pleading.... My gaze wandered from her curious expression to her exposed shoulder. Her oversized T-shirt was hanging off again, revealing a tight tank top beneath. The rise and fall of her breathing led my attention to her tits, which were round and full, but frustratingly hidden beneath the bagginess of the top.

"Hey, guys," came a sweet voice, and I looked up to see Alicia approaching us. "That was a tough wake-up call, huh? I think I need to start working out more."

"Oh, stop, you did great," Rose replied. "You're a natural dancer."

43

"Unlike me," I added, and Rose elbowed me in the side.

"You'll be a natural by the time Iggy and I are done with you. Don't worry." She smiled, and I almost believed her. Alicia edged closer and lowered her voice. "So, uh, what's the deal with Bob? Is he, like, some kind of lush or something?"

Rose let out a slow breath. "Poor old Bob. He's been a regular on the circuit for years, but his wife left him a couple of months ago, and he's hit the bottle pretty hard."

"Oh, no, really?" said Alicia with affected concern.

"Yeah, it's sad. Heartbreak can fuck with the best of us at times," Rose replied.

I wondered if she was thinking of Blake, how he broke her heart. I wanted to know what had happened between them, and it surprised me. Being around all these people after spending the last eight years of my life in near-solitude was overwhelming. I was eager to know them. Well, maybe not all of them. Maybe just Rose.

What was it about her?

"Right, back to the grindstone, everyone," Iggy called, clapping his hands to gather everybody's attention. Alicia gave us each a little finger wave and strode off. I dropped my head forward and rubbed at my temples before glancing up to see Rose giving me a sympathetic look.

"This is torture for you, isn't it?" she said, blue eyes taking me in.

I nodded. "I'm not sure I'll ever take to this dancing lark. I'm too big and awkward."

"Big is good," she replied, and then paled. A moment of quiet ensued, and it was leaden with tension. I let my eyes drop to the freckle on her jaw as she fumbled for words to continue.

"I mean, for a male dancer, because you have to be able to lift your partner and whatnot. The awkward part we can get around." She paused and pursed her lips, tilting her head as she considered me. When she spoke again, she leaned close, her voice low. "I can give you lessons, if you like. After hours, that is. Not to brag, but I'm very good at what I do, and you seem more comfortable around me than other people. If we're alone, you'll be less self-conscious. You can just relax and let me guide you. What do you think?"

"Sounds like a good idea," I answered, perhaps a little too quickly.

I couldn't deny that the thought of spending more time with Rose appealed to me. She was right — I was more comfortable around her than others. She was a sea of calm to my troubled thoughts, and I wanted to feel more of that. I wasn't used to it.

"Hey, you two, chop chop," Iggy called, shooting us an impatient look.

"I'll let you know when we can start our lessons," Rose whispered, and hurried over to her boss's side.

Five.
Rose

Props were so much fun. I sat on a sparkly, diamond-encrusted swing in the theatre as Iggy paced from left to right, his hand on his chin as he pondered me. Okay, so maybe it was more cubic zirconia encrusted than diamond, but you know what I mean.

The swing was for Alicia's big "Diamonds Are a Girl's Best Friend" number. Though rehearsals were still ongoing at the dance studio, the set for the show was in the process of being built, and Iggy and I were trying to figure out some logistics for the choreography. I relished the freedom of the empty theatre as I swung back and forth in various seductive poses, pretending to be Satine.

No audience. No fear.

There was one reason why I'd never aspired to dance in front of an audience, and that was a severe case of stage fright. For years Iggy tried to encourage me to fight my phobia, but in the end he accepted I was a lost cause, destined to forever linger behind the curtains.

I didn't mind. I liked my job. It was comfortable and safe. And though I sometimes mourned for what might've been, I knew I could live with it. After all, not performing on stage was hardly the end of the world. I still got to do the thing I loved. I still got to dance.

My friend Farrah happened by and shot me a grin. I'd worked with her on my last production and was delighted to discover she'd been hired to do wardrobe for *Moulin Rouge*.

"You should get a load of the corset I'm designing for this scene," she called over. "It's going to be a fucking masterpiece."

"How very modest of you to say," Iggy replied dryly, and she flipped him off before sauntering away. Those two always had a sort of bitchy love/hate friendship. I was sure if Iggy wasn't gay, the both of them would've started having uber-hot hate sex a long time ago. I loved Farrah because she was one of those no-nonsense older women who kicked arse at living life, who you sort of wished you could become one day.

A couple of minutes later, the lead actors arrived for a preliminary stage rehearsal. I locked eyes with Damon, and a tiny shiver of awareness trickled down my spine. He stared up at me, his eyes zeroing in on the curve of my waist before running down the length of my body. I remembered our little conversation from yesterday. I'd embarrassed myself twice, first admitting how I'd love to hear him narrate an audiobook, and then with the whole "big is good" comment. Somebody needed to put a leash on my mouth, seriously.

Alicia approached me. "So, this is the swing, huh? Jacob's been waxing lyrical to me about it all morning. I have to admit, it's pretty impressive."

I nodded, and Iggy came over. "Rose is going to teach you how to use it. We want to make sure there's no chance of you falling off and breaking your coccyx, or you know, anything else. Sorry, I just like saying the word 'coccyx.'"
He chuckled, and Alicia shot him a weird look. Iggy was the kind of man you either got or you didn't.

I cleared my throat and nodded up to the rafters, where Paul the props guy was finishing his coffee break. "We're going to practice with Paul lowering you down. During the performances, your outfit will be harnessed to the swing and then released once you hit the stage. I'll demonstrate first."

Sitting back down on the swing, Iggy hooked the harness around my waist, and I gripped a tight hold as I shouted to Paul, "Beam me up, Scotty!"

I just about made out his eye roll. Like Farrah, I already knew Paul from previous shows. We'd practiced the lowering of the swing a few times earlier in the morning, so I was an old pro at it now as everybody watched me rise up to the ceiling. A small jolt of stage fright hit me, but I rejected it just as quickly. There were ten people here, tops. Nothing, really. It was Damon's attention that I felt the most, and I was beginning to realise that he watched me more closely than the others.

As I was lowered back down, my eyes found his once more, but I couldn't decipher his expression. His gaze was so...consuming. I used the ropes as reins and swung in a circle, kicking my legs out and raising an elegant hand in the air to show Alicia how we wanted her to do it. Damon's attention never left me all the while.

Once I was back on the stage, I got off and began instructing Alicia further. She perched herself on the diamond-esque swing, arching her spine in a delicately seductive pose. It didn't take long for her to seriously impress me. She'd trained as a dancer in her teens, so she picked everything up fairly quickly, even joking to me at one point, "Forget about diamonds — a Visa Infinite card is a girl's best friend."

I grinned in return, probably because it reminded me of something Julian would say. Iggy busied himself with showing the lead actors their positions, while Jacob described what he wanted from them for the scene.

It was about twenty minutes later that Bob finally showed his face, looking dishevelled and hungover. *Oh, Bob.* I wished I was on friendlier terms with him so maybe I could offer some help, but I only really knew him in passing.

Jacob looked like he wanted to drown a bag of kittens when he clapped eyes on the man. He left the others and quickly pulled Bob backstage, I presumed to exchange a few harsh words. I shot Iggy a concerned expression, which he returned, and then tried to get on with showing Alicia her final moves.

Jacob and Bob returned a few minutes later, with Bob looking suitably shamefaced. It was as we were running through the last of the choreography for the scene that I noticed Bob get up from his seat.

His grey complexion concerned me, so I left Alicia and went to see if he was all right. Unfortunately, no good deed goes unpunished, and when I reached him, he pushed me violently out of the way, mumbling that he was going to be sick. I slipped and would've fallen if it weren't for Damon.

He moved fast, catching me in his arms before I hit the floor. I sucked in a breath, my chest heaving as I stared up at him.

"Close call," he said, frowning as he stared down at me. I nodded, unable to find my voice for a second. His quick reflexes were impressive.

"You okay, Rose?" he asked, his mouth caressing my name. I swallowed and tried to ignore how nice his arms felt around me, how good he smelled this close.

"I'm fine. Thank you. I might've been out of action if you hadn't been so quick on the mark."

His lips firmed, and a moment passed between us before he pulled me upright. My chest brushed against his forearm, and I shivered at the contact before stepping away from him.

"Did I just see what I think I did?" came Jacob's shrill voice. Both Damon and I turned to look at the director, his expression furious. He didn't wait for us to confirm that Bob had pushed me, but simply straightened his spine and strode after him.

"Shit," I whispered, biting my lip in worry as I watched him go. "I hope Bob doesn't get fired over this."

Damon's firm hand gripped my shoulder, and he stared down at me, his eyes sincere. "He's out of sorts and probably will be for a long time. Maybe it's for the best."

I glanced away, my gut churning, because I knew what it was like to be Bob, too heart-broken to care about life's priorities anymore. Sure, what had happened with Blake was nothing like having your wife of twenty years leave you for another man, but I dunno, I still felt a kinship towards him. All my life I'd been so eager to love, which seemed to attract the wrong sort of attention and inevitably left me lovesick and alone. Perhaps it was because I knew how it felt that allowed me to empathise with Bob.

Maybe Damon had never had his heart broken. Maybe that was why he didn't understand Bob like I did.

"We'd better get back to work," I said curtly before returning to Alicia. I didn't look at him directly, but I felt him watching me leave.

***

Later that day I felt bad about being so short with Damon. After being told by an assistant that he'd gone inside his dressing room a little while ago, I decided to seek him out. I'd ask if he'd like to begin our private dance lessons tomorrow evening. See if he was up for it.

When I reached his dressing room, I found the door slightly ajar, and before entering I could hear voices coming from within. Recognising one of them as Alicia's, I peeked through the crack in the door and saw her perched in the seat by Damon's dressing table while he stood off to one side.

"I've always wanted to visit Scotland, you know," she said in the sweet, flirtatious voice she always seemed to use with men. "That's where you've been living all this time, right?"

"Not on the mainland. My home is on the Isle of Skye, where my grandmother was born."

"Oh, is that where you grew up, too?"

I rolled my eyes. Couldn't she tell the difference between a Scottish and a Yorkshire accent? As soon as the question entered my head, I realised I was being jealous and possessive of Damon's friendship. It became clear that I quite liked being the only person he made an effort to talk to, and I didn't enjoy the idea of being usurped by Alicia.

"No, my mam was Scottish, but she left when she was a teen. A lot of young people leave, wanting something more than the simple island life. She met my dad and settled down close to Sheffield. That's where I spent my early childhood."

"And did you miss acting? Is that why you decided to do this show?"

"Yes and no. If acting could be just acting, then I never would've quit."

A quiet elapsed, and I guessed Alicia didn't know how to respond to what Damon had said. I heard a soft feminine sigh.

"I understand. Your life is no longer your own. Sometimes I think about how everything was before I got famous, and I feel sort of envious of that girl. There was so much she was better off not knowing."

If Alicia was putting this on, then she really was a good actress. And that was the thing — she was so good at what she did that I couldn't tell if she was being real or not. I heard a floorboard creak, like Damon had taken a step closer to her.

"Did you want to be famous back then?" he asked.

"More than anything else in the world."

"Why?" He sounded genuinely perplexed, which made me wonder why he got into acting if he never wanted the fame. I hated that he sounded fascinated by Alicia's reply, like he was getting to see a side of her no one else did.

"Because I wanted everyone to love me," she answered, and then let out a sad laugh. "The thing I didn't know was that if ten thousand people love you, there are always going to be a thousand who hate you, and even though the love far outweighs the hate, you'll feel it so intensely that the love might as well not exist at all."

Oh, wow. I didn't expect this. She was being real, and I couldn't compete with it, not in a million years.

"We all fixate on criticism," said Damon. "And those that say they don't are fucking liars."

Alicia let out a surprised laugh and I turned away from the door, deciding to leave them both to it. They were costars, and it sounded like they were bonding. Far be it from me to interrupt. And yes, okay, I was jealous. It was ridiculous, but I couldn't seem to help it.

As I walked down the pale magnolia corridor, I remembered Damon smiling at me in my flat, and a sharpness struck my chest. It was the only smile he'd given me, and I held it close, like a gift. The fact of the matter was, I didn't want Alicia stealing smiles that were meant for me. They were so rare, so fleeting, that it almost felt like a challenge to get another one. He was so closed off, never showing much, but still just enough to leave you dying for another glimpse.

Six.

Rose

I was listening to *Outlander* again. Jamie was being particularly swoon-worthy towards Claire, and I was enjoying the excitement of their growing relationship. Truthfully, it caused a thrilling little sensation to fizzle in my stomach.

The next thing I knew, someone tugged a bud out of my ear and silently placed it in their own. I knew it was Damon without even having to look, because it was the exact same thing he'd done the other day. Plus, I recognised his woodsy cologne.

Shut up, it wasn't obsessive that I already knew his scent off by heart.

I was still feeling a bit funny after my unexpected bout of jealousy yesterday, and I knew if I looked at him, the feeling would return. So instead I stifled a smile around a bite of my sandwich and continued to quietly listen. He was being brazen in a way only Damon knew how, and I quite liked the contrast to his normally reserved demeanour.

We sat on the studio floor, staring ahead, the story in our ears painting a picture on the wall of mirrors before us. Iggy and I had spent the day working out some kinks in the choreography, while the cast were busy rehearsing songs with the choral director in one of the smaller practice rooms.

The stark emptiness of the studio only functioned to amplify the intensity of Damon's presence. Of course, I was certain the intensity was one-sided. The man clearly liked me as a friend and nothing more. I was a reliable candidate for friendship, loyal and trustworthy, always around when needed. The likes of Damon Atwood didn't date women like me. They dated mysterious and ethereally beautiful models from Eastern Europe. Or you know, curvaceous red-headed bombshells from L.A.

I was desperate to know how his conversation with Alicia had ended, but I was determined to battle my own curiosity and let it forever go unknown. After all, if things had heated up between the two of them, then it would only make me feel worse. On the bright side, I hadn't thought about Blake in almost twenty-four hours. There was always a silver lining.

"Do you think Claire and Jamie are going to get together?" Damon asked, nudging me with his shoulder. He had no idea how appealing I found it, the simple touch.

Hitting "pause" on the iPod, I turned to face him. "If they don't, then I'll have a serious bone to pick with the author. I feel like I've been waiting forever for it to happen," I blurted, and then glanced shyly at my lap. What was it about my obsession with romance that always made me feel embarrassed? Like it was a silly, girlish thing to obsess about. In reality, it was what we all wanted, right?

I could still remember being ten years old, sitting on my living room floor, my face so close to the TV screen it was a surprise I didn't need glasses. Some old romance flick would be on, and I'd watch how the hero looked at the heroine, realising he loved her. I'd been fascinated by every tiny facial muscle as it moved, forming an expression I wanted to see reflected back at me one day. In my mind I called it "the look," but I'd yet to ever receive it.

I know, I was an idealistic little fool. Still am, apparently.

I'd thought Blake had given me "the look," but it'd all been an act. And now I was thinking about Blake again. Thanks, brain.

Damon studied me with a thoughtful expression. "What about her husband? You know, back in 1946."

"Well, don't you have an ear for the details," I replied, and shrugged. "I don't know. I mean, it's possible to marry someone and then meet your true love afterward, isn't it? Not that I'd wish such a fate on anyone, but it is possible. I don't feel the love between Claire and her husband like I feel it between Claire and Jamie. Or, you know, the potential for it."

"It's still cheating," said Damon.

"Shut up," I complained, and shoved him in the arm. "I don't want to think about that. I just want to enjoy the love, and you're ruining it for me."

He raised his hands in apology. "My bad. I'm in a bit of a mood today. It's the anniversary of my mam's passing. Talking about other things, fictional things, helps keep my mind off it."

"Oh," I said, inhaling a deep breath, my eyes wandering to how his hands fidgeted in his lap. The confession made my stomach flip, like it always did when Damon revealed something new about himself. "I'm sorry. We can talk about the book. I'll even let you ruin the love for me if you want."

That almost got a smile out of him. *Almost.* His lips twitched, but then nothing. This man was locked up tighter than a bank vault. "Nah, it's okay. Far be it from me to ruin love," he teased. His mouth still looked sad, but his teasing heartened me.

"If it's any consolation, I know exactly how you're feeling. I have to live this day every year, too."

"How did your mother die?" he inquired quietly. "If you don't mind me asking."

I shook my head. "I don't mind. She threw herself in front of an oncoming train." The fact had become custom to me over the years, and I tended to forget just how awful it sounded to new ears. Damon look horrified. "Wow, this conversation just took a turn for the morbid," I went on, apologetic.

"Don't be sorry. I'm the one who asked."

"She, um, she was heartsick over Elijah. You remember the man I told you about? The one she'd been having a polyamorous relationship with?"

Damon nodded, his dark eyes intent on me.

"Well, everything was great between the four of them in the beginning, but then jealousy started to rear its ugly head. My mum, Joanna, and Kimberly were all involved, but Elijah, being the only man, was sort of the focal point. After a while things got messy, and they wanted him to pick one of them. Push came to shove, and he chose Joanna. Both my mum and Julian's were devastated. Kimberly fell into a deep depression and was admitted to a psychiatric hospital. Seems extreme, but she'd always been unhinged, even before she met Elijah. Poor Julian had a terrible time of it growing up. Then there was my mum. She took a more final approach to ending her heartbreak, I guess."

My hand suddenly felt warm, and I glanced down to see Damon's palm spread out over my knuckles. My heart beat fast. "She must have really loved him to do something so terrible just to end the pain."

I nodded, struck by his unexpectedly eloquent and meaningful sentiment. "Some people love too much. My mother was one of them. Not that Elijah ever deserved how she felt for him. Sometimes I hate her, because she clearly loved him more than me, but then, I was grown up. She thought I didn't need her anymore."

"And that's the ridiculous thing," Damon added, as though my words were his own and he was just finishing a thought that belonged to him. "No matter how old we get, we always need them."

I glanced at him from under my lashes and asked quietly, "What was your mum like?"

He didn't answer right away, just stared dead ahead as though thinking about her. "She was strong and incredibly loyal. When I started to get famous, she protected me from all the people who might have tried to exploit it. Then she grew ill, and I didn't have that protection anymore. My dad showed up at her funeral. They'd separated when I was little and I hadn't seen him in years, but I was relieved, because I was just a lad and I didn't want to be alone. I went to live with him, but he wasn't Mam. He didn't care about protecting me. Instead he used the money I earned to throw constant parties and live the high life. I went from being completely sheltered to being exposed to everything a child shouldn't be around, alcohol, drugs, prostitutes, you name it."

The abundance of his words went to show how strongly he felt for his mother and how badly what came after her death had affected him. I didn't know what to say, but I suddenly understood why he'd turned his back on acting, if only to get away from a life that terrified him. People were starting to trickle in for the afternoon rehearsal, and it felt odd that we were discussing such personal things over our lunch break.

"Where is he now?" I asked.

Damon frowned. "Still in the States. Any road, I haven't seen him since the day I was granted my emancipation. If I never do again, it'll be too soon."

The ferocity in his voice made me think that what he'd told me was just the tip of the iceberg. This wasn't the first time I'd heard of showbiz parents taking advantage of their children's success, and my gut twisted to think of Damon in a situation like that.

"I feel the same way about Elijah. It just seems so unfair that he gets to keep on living his life when he ruined my mother's."

Damon's eyes met mine in understanding. We were silent for a moment, and then Farrah hurried by, probably on her way to a meeting. She waved and shot me a knowing look as I sat with Damon, and I realised that his hand was still on mine. I hastily pulled away and cleared my throat.

"We both should be getting back," I said.

"Scared you off, did I?"

I shook my head. "No, of course not. The things I told you about Mum were just as personal...." I paused, hesitating over what to say next.

"Rose?"

Oh, hell. I really should just tell him. "People are starting to talk about us spending so much time together," I blurted.

It was true. I hadn't heard anything *per se*, but I'd stepped into my fair share of conversations lately where everybody just went quiet. That only ever happened when people were gossiping about you.

"We spend time together because we're friends," he stated plainly, like it was that simple.

"Yes, but, I've got a bit of a tendency toward developing show crushes, and Farrah knows it." I fiddled awkwardly with the hem of my top.

"'Show crushes'?" Damon appeared perplexed, and I couldn't blame him. I was babbling like an idiot.

"You know, crushing on the people you work with during a show. They all probably think I'm some sort of gold digger. I don't want anybody spreading rumours."

This made him let out a hard, disbelieving laugh. "I live in a two-bedroom cottage and my car is a fifteen-year-old Volvo. Are you going to stop being my friend just because people are talking? Let them. I could give two fucks what they think."

I watched his posture stiffen and began to feel guilty. "No, I'm not going to stop being your friend. Don't mind me. I care too much about what other people think. I need to stop."

Damon's eyes flickered between mine as he studied me. I felt a little like I was under a microscope and grew self-conscious. Finally, he said, "Good, because I still need you to help me find a decent barber."

What was this? Humour from Damon Atwood? He wasn't smiling but his voice held a hint of teasing.

I shot him a look of mock horror. "But I like your hair how it is. Don't listen to Jacob — you can easily just slick it back when you're on stage."

He ran a hand through his long locks. "Nah, it's a bother this long, any road. I could do with getting the chop."

"Yeah?"

The tiniest, most minuscule smile tugged at the edges of his lips, and my heart leapt. His eyes were warm as he responded, "Aye."

"Well, okay then, meet me out front after rehearsals, and I'll take you to the place Julian gets his hair done."

"Sounds like a plan," said Damon, leaving me to finish the last of my sandwich.

Seven.
Damon

Rehearsals ended half an hour ago. I took a shower and currently stood outside in the cold, waiting for Rose. I rubbed my palms together, my breath visible in the chilly evening air. Several members of the cast passed me by, sending curious glances my way. They were probably all wondering what I was doing, waiting around on my tod.

Aside from a surprisingly interesting conversation with Alicia yesterday, I hadn't really made much of an effort to befriend anyone. The only person I really spoke to was Rose, and when she wasn't around — for instance, when we were running lines from the script — I felt oddly alone. All day I couldn't get the phrase "show crush" out of my head. I'd never heard of it before, but it made sense. Lots of celebrity couples met through working together.

Sure, when being interviewed they all gave the same answer about acting out love scenes.

No, I didn't enjoy it. We're like brother and sister.

Or....

It was more awkward than sexy, especially when you have twenty pairs of eyes watching your every move.

Often these things were true, but other times they weren't. I hadn't ever filmed a love scene; however, I was sure that if I had to do one with a woman I was attracted to, I'd feel something other than awkwardness. If I had to touch her, pretend to be aroused and listen to her laboured breathing, even if it was fake, I'd feel...oh, bloody hell. I'd be horny as fuck, let's put it that way.

"You shouldn't be out here with damp hair. You'll catch your death," said Rose as she approached me. "Sorry I'm late, by the way. I got held up talking with Iggy."

I shrugged. "No worries."

"The barber's isn't too far from here. Do you want to walk?" she asked.

"Sure," I replied, and held out my arm. She linked hers through it, and I let her lead the way. Glancing down, I saw she'd let her hair out of its knot. The long, wavy strands framed her face and disappeared inside her thick winter coat.

"I don't suppose Iggy held you back to discuss what a lost cause of a dancer I am," I said self-deprecatingly.

Rose grinned, her pretty lips curving at the edges, and shook her head. "Nope. One of the backing dancers was in a minor car accident this morning and will need to be replaced. He was asking my opinion on who to call. I know a lot of people in the biz."

"Ah, I see." I wanted to ask her why she couldn't do it. In fact, I'd been wondering why she wasn't a part of the cast for a while now. She was certainly good enough.

"And stop being so down on yourself," she went on. "You're not as bad as you were five days ago, and that's saying something. If you want, we can go back to the studio after your haircut and have our first private lesson."

I tilted my head at her. "I wondered if you'd forgotten."

"Of course I hadn't. I actually went to find you yesterday to set a time, but you were in your dressing room with Alicia and I didn't want to interrupt."

My brow furrowed. "Why not?"

Her shoulders rose and fell on a sigh as she glanced away. The tip of her nose was beginning to redden from the cold. I couldn't say why exactly, but it made me want to offer my coat, or, I don't know, warm her up somehow. "It sounded like you were both having a serious talk and it would've been rude to just...barge in."

Had she been listening? The idea of her being curious enough to do such a thing brought forth a swell of pleasure. "What did you hear?"

Now she focused on the toes of her shoes as we walked. "Something about wanting to be famous. I don't know."

"She was telling me about her upbringing. Apparently she was born on a farm in Kansas," I said, and stared ahead at the approaching cars out on the road.

Rose's eyes flicked to mine. "Really? I never would've guessed that. She seems so polished. I mean, the only thing that's Dorothy about her is the hair."

I shrugged. "She's showbiz, but not in a way that's intimidating."

Rose poked me in the arm. "Yeah, well, of course she wouldn't seem that way to you. You're both on the same level of beauty. You don't know what it's like being an outsider trying to handle all that...charisma coming at you full force."

Her admission took me completely by surprise. I stopped in my stride to stand in front of her and ask low, "You think I'm beautiful?"

She blushed at my question, then answered defensively, "Well, there's clearly a reason you used to be famous."

"Are you saying I'm all looks and no talent?" I feigned offence.

"Oh, shut up." She scowled. "You know it was both. Now can we please keep walking? I need to get out of this cold before my toes freeze off."

I kept up the pace with her but didn't let it go. "Just out of curiosity, what exactly is it like to deal with full-force charisma? Because it sounds terrifying."

Rose shook her head, trying to hold back a smile as she stopped in front of a shop door and pulled it open. "Completely horrific," she deadpanned, and I barked a laugh. She stared at me a moment, as though stunned by the sound. Blinking once, twice, three times, she shook her head and continued inside. I wanted to ask her what I'd done to warrant such a reaction, but pushed back the impulse. If I had an odd laugh, then I didn't really want to know.

The barber shop was small, with navy walls and red leather upholstery. A blond man had his back turned to us as he swept the floor. Rose let out a low whistle and he swung around, smiling widely at the sight of her.

"Rose! Long time no see! How's Julian? It's been a couple weeks since he's been in for a haircut."

"He's good. Rocking the long-haired look at the moment. I'm sure he'll get sick of it soon and be in for a trim."

"Well, you tell him I'll be more than happy to see his pretty face," he replied before his attention fell on me. He winked. "Speaking of which, hello there."

"Don't be a flirt, Graham," Rose chided. "This is Damon. He's playing the lead in a new show of *Moulin Rouge*, so if you can summon your best Ewan McGregor circa 2001, we'll be forever in your debt."

"Oh, I can do better than that. It's a pleasure to meet you, Damon," he said, offering his hand. We shook, and he leaned close to whisper, "You're far hotter than Ewan anyway."

I wasn't sure what to say to that, so I simply shook my head in good humour.

Rose was already taking off her coat and hanging it up on a rack by the door. "Hush. You'll leave the poor man traumatised," she told him playfully. I loved the easy way she had with people, so naturally friendly and warm. She couldn't see me staring at her since she was looking at Graham. It was a good thing, too, because if she had, she might have realised that if anyone had a show crush, it was me.

Graham went to prepare his workstation then and Rose approached me, silently helping me out of my coat. I was quiet, enjoying her closeness as she ran her hand over the sleeve of my woollen jumper.

"This is nice," she murmured, and my eyes instinctively wandered to the cream silk blouse she wore. It was the first time I'd seen her out of her regulation dance clothes. She must've changed before coming to meet me.

"Yours is nice also," I said, a frog in my throat.

What the fuck? *Yours is nice also*? Why did putting "also" at the end of a sentence automatically make a person sound stiff? Living on an island for the last eight years had seriously fucked with my game.

Rose smiled, her blue eyes twinkling. "Well, aren't we both full of compliments today."

Her hands were still smoothing down the sleeve of my jumper, and my eyes grew hooded as I watched their descent. When was the last time a woman had touched me skin to skin? My ex-girlfriend, Lizzy, felt like a lifetime ago. We'd both been lonely and had filled a void in each other's lives. In the end, it was she who'd pushed me away, telling me I needed to deal with my issues, that she wasn't the one for me.

"Hey, are you all right?" Rose asked gently.

I swallowed and nodded before turning to sit in the chair Graham gestured to. It'd been a while since I'd thought of Lizzy, and it still hurt to remember how alone I'd felt when she told me I needed to go, that I was just filling time with her, and simply "settling" wasn't what either one of us deserved.

When I looked at Rose through the mirror, she lifted a brow, her eyes wide with concern, like she thought she'd done something wrong. I returned her look with one of my own, one that said everything was fine. She seemed content with that and went to sit on a bench, flicking through a magazine while Graham set to work on my hair.

After a while Rose lost interest in what she was reading and simply sat back to watch me. I met her gaze through the mirror once more, my eyes travelling over her form. Her dark brown hair was twisted along one shoulder, her blouse tight over her full chest but flaring out at her hips. Her dark jeans outlined her shapely thighs, and my mind began to wander as I imagined how she might look stripped bare.

There were so many details to a woman that the imagination just couldn't do justice. I wanted to know if she had freckles anywhere other than the sparse few that dusted her cheeks. Would she feel soft underneath me? How would she smell with my scent all over her? How would she taste? Would she be tight and wet if we fucked?

Jesus.

The direction of my thoughts must have showed on my face, because Rose tensed up, folding her arms over her chest as she focused on the floor for a time. I couldn't tell if she was embarrassed or if my attention was simply unwanted. I hated the lack of certainty, wished I was better at reading women and their subtle cues.

When Graham was done with me, he pulled the coverall off and held a mirror up to the back of my head so that I could see.

"Well, what do you think?"

"It's great. You've outdone yourself," said Rose before I could answer. In truth, I had no opinion other than it didn't look like someone had gone to work on me with a hacksaw. Right then I only really valued my looks in relation to how they affected Rose. I wanted her to be attracted to me. No, I *needed* her to be, needed her to look into my eyes and tell me to fuck her until she couldn't stand straight.

I stood and walked over to the counter to pay Graham, while Rose went to gather our coats. When we were standing outside, she stuck her thumb out for a taxi to take us back to the studio, saying it was too cold to walk this time. I caught sight of a few men standing on the other side of the street, watching us, and it struck me as odd. They looked like press, but they couldn't be. Nobody cared about me anymore. I was certain that most people had completely forgotten who I was since I'd been out of the public eye for so long.

"Did you see those men?" Rose asked once we were seated in the taxi, and I swore inwardly. I hadn't been the only one to notice them.

"Aye," I said, exhaling a gruff breath.

"I think they were photographing you from outside when you were getting your hair done. I didn't want to say anything at first because I thought it might freak you out."

"Let them take pictures. They'll get bored eventually."

"Hmm, well, maybe you should think about hiring a PR rep, just in case. People still remember you, Damon. I know you probably thought you could just come back and fly under the radar, but I'm not sure it's going to work out that way."

I nodded, posture stiff. "I'll look into it."

Rose's expression turned sympathetic. "I know this is the last thing you wanted." She paused, studying me for a moment before lifting her hand and running her fingers through the freshly cut strands of my hair. "This style really suits you, you know. I like it," she murmured, and I relished her touch. The more contact I had with her, the more I seemed to crave it.

When she moved to withdraw her hand, I reacted purely on instinct. Reaching up, I pressed her fingers to my scalp, the warmth of them seeping into me like a soothing balm. Time slowed down. I heard her exhale a tiny breath as our eyes locked. In reality it only lasted a moment, but it felt like longer. When I let go, her hand fell into her lap and I muttered an apology.

"Sorry. Didn't realise how much I missed being touched."

Rose nodded like she understood, staring at the glass screen in front of her. "It's okay. It must be lonely living so far away from people." She went quiet then, like she was considering whether or not to say more. Then she asked, "Do you have anyone waiting for you back in Skye? I know your grandmother passed, but was there a woman?"

Her question piqued my curiosity. Did she care if there was a woman? A deep, possessive feeling struck me, because I liked the idea of her caring.

"There was someone for a few years, but she ended it. She thought I was settling for her, that because our part of

69

the island was less populated than others, she was my only option." She also thought I needed vast amounts of therapy to deal with my trust issues, but I wasn't quite ready to tell Rose about those yet.

"And were you settling?" she asked quietly.

I glanced out the window. It was starting to rain. "I don't know. Maybe. I didn't love her, and Lizzy was a woman who deserved to be loved."

When I looked back at Rose, she seemed fascinated by what I was saying. Blinking, she sat back and began brushing nonexistent lint off her jeans. "You're not like other men," she said, still focusing on her jeans.

"No?"

She shook her head. "You're very honest. I haven't had a lot of experience with honest men lately."

The idea of some prick being dishonest with Rose made me want to break something. She was beautiful and talented, sexy as fuck. How could any man not feel like the luckiest bastard in the world to be with her?

The taxi stopped, and I leaned forward to pay the driver before Rose got the chance. She was going out of her way to help me, and I didn't plan on letting her spend a penny while we were in each other's company. God knew I had more than enough to go around. Perhaps it was seeing how obsessed my dad had been with spending that made me the opposite. He couldn't go a day without splashing the cash. It was like an addiction. I, on the other hand, had been wearing the same boots for the last five years.

Was the fear of spending money a real phobia? I just didn't see the point in having ten things when one would do.

Iggy's studio was all locked up when we got there, everybody gone home for the evening. Luckily, Rose had a key. I followed her up the stairs, where she began turning on lights and fiddling around with the thermostat.

"I know we're going to be roasting once we start dancing, but I'm just so cold right now. I feel like I want to press my entire body up against a radiator." She chuckled and removed her coat and scarf.

I wished she'd press her entire body up against me and we could warm each other, I thought to myself.

"January is one of the coldest months," I said.

Jesus Christ. I was coming out with some truly awful lines tonight. Like always, Rose didn't tease me for my awkwardness; she just smiled and went to hook her iPod up to the sound system. I took off my coat, glancing around. I peered at myself in the wall of mirrors that stretched from floor to ceiling. Back home my cottage had one mirror in the bathroom and that was it. I probably looked at myself once in an entire day. Some days not at all. Staring at my reflection now was like having a tattoo on your shoulder that you forgot was there. It was like, *huh, so that's what my face looks like.*

I ran a hand through my new haircut. It felt different, like I was touching somebody else's hair. Rose came and stood beside me, placing a hand on her hip.

"Not too shabby, eh?" she said, her eyes meeting mine through the mirror.

I tensed up as though I'd been caught doing something unseemly. "It's hair."

"You never told Graham if you liked it. You do realise that's the ultimate insult for a barber, right?"

I frowned. She shook her head and laughed. "I'm messing with you. To be honest, I think you made his day just by walking into his shop. Come on, let's get started."

I followed her over to the middle of the dance floor as she went on, "I'm going to teach you a basic foxtrot. There's a scene or two where you're going to need to ballroom dance with Alicia, and this is a good place to start."

Leaving me standing there, she went to turn on some music, and a minute later "Fly Me to the Moon" by Frank Sinatra came on. Rose returned to stand in front of me, holding her arms out as though about to dance with an invisible partner.

"Okay, so watch my feet. It's really easy. You do two slow steps forward, one quick step to the side and then back."

I studied her feet like my life depended on it. She said it was simple, but there was still a good chance I'd fuck up.

"Damon," she said, drawing my attention to her. "You're biting your lip. Stop it. You won't learn if you're too tense."

I nodded and released my lip. I didn't even realise I was biting it, but now I tasted blood on my tongue. Rose let out a slow breath and demonstrated the steps for me again.

"All right, I think I have it."

She eyed me sceptically. "Are you sure?"

"Aye."

"Come here, then."

I stepped closer to her and she took my hands, placing one on her back just below her armpit and the other she laced her fingers through. Her blouse was cool and silky under my touch. I thought I saw a tiny tremble go through her, and my cock reacted. I silently urged it to fuck off. I didn't need Rose noticing my stiffy and thinking I was some kind of sexual deviant.

"Don't worry about trying to lead," she said. "I'll do that until you get the hang of it."

"Two steps forward and one to the side."

"And then back," she smiled.

"Let's do this."

Laughing, she shook her head, her smile widening. "You'd swear we were about to bungee jump off a skyscraper."

I grimaced, because she was right. I was acting daft. "I don't want to fuck up."

"You won't. Relax."

It turned out she was right. Well, almost. I stepped on her toes a couple of times, apologising profusely, because I knew it had to have hurt even though she pretended it didn't. I had big clumsy fucking clown feet. Finally, on the fifth try, I managed to pull it off.

"I told you that you could do this," she said triumphantly. "Look at you, you're even starting to lead and you don't even realise it." We danced our way across the room until Rose's back hit the wall. My chest bumped hers, a small *oomph* of breath escaping her as my mouth crashed against the top of her head. I could feel her tits this close. Fuck, they were full and soft, and I knew they'd feel incredible bare. Her hair was silky and smelled like flowers. I wanted to bunch it in my hand, pull her head to the side, and taste her neck.

"Shit, sorry."

"It's fine," she replied, unfazed. We broke apart, and I willed my cock to fuck off once more as I followed her back to the middle of the room.

"Now I'm going to teach you how to change direction so that doesn't happen. This is a corner step." She took my hands again, placing them back where they had been. I inhaled deeply, eyes on the delicate curve of her collarbone until her voice demanded my attention. "Imagine we're on a crowded dance floor. We don't want to go bumping into other couples, so we need to corner step to avoid them. When I take a step back with my right foot, you take a step forward with your left, and then we do a little turn like this," she said, moving our bodies before continuing, "until we're facing a new direction. See."

I completed the steps without thinking. I just followed the movement of her body, not over-concentrating like before. I'd never been a great dancer, but with Rose it felt natural. All I had to do was lose myself in her voice, and my body responded. It probably had a lot to do with the fact that I wanted to fuck her until she couldn't walk, but shit, at least my horn-dog urges were good for something.

"Look at you, you're doing it," she enthused.

My gaze warmed on her and we continued dancing until one song bled to another and another. Before I knew it, we'd been practicing for an hour, but it felt like we'd only just begun. Rose didn't even realise that I was enjoying being near her on a level that had nothing to do with learning how to dance. And it wasn't just sexual. I liked being around her, having the feel of her body beneath my fingers. She made my head feel clear and untroubled. When a vibration sounded, interrupting us, she let go of my hand and went to pull her phone from her bag.

"Hey, Iggy, what's up?" she answered, her voice a little breathless. I knew it must've been from all the dancing, but it made me think of sex again. I wanted to make her breathless in so many different ways. She tugged at the end of her top, and my eyes followed the movement.

"Yeah, uh-huh, okay. Sounds good. See you tomorrow," she said cheerily before hanging up. I watched as she placed her phone back in her bag and turned to face me. "Apparently, Alicia's organising for everyone to have drinks tomorrow night to celebrate the first week of rehearsals. It's a little early to be celebrating anything, if you ask me, but it could be fun. Do you want to go? I'm sure Alicia will ask you when you see her tomorrow either way."

"Are you going?" I asked, stepping closer so there was less than a foot of space between us.

"Yep, it'll be good to blow off some steam."

"Then I'll go, but…I don't really know anyone."

She began putting on her coat and handed me mine. "Well, maybe you could use this as an opportunity to get acquainted with the rest of the cast. Alcohol is a fantastic social lubricant, you know."

I grimaced. "I'm a horrible drunk."

Rose grinned. "Oh, really? Do you start spouting insults and telling everyone what you really think of them?"

"Something like that."

It was a lie, but fuck if I was telling her the truth. Ale turned me into a horny teenager, and I was certain that if I got drunk around Rose, I'd try doing all the things I'd thus far only been picturing in my head. Best to only have one or two pints tomorrow, then.

"I get really giddy when I'm drunk, laughing at stuff that isn't even funny. You'll see. It's irritating as hell."

I bet it was more cute than irritating, but I let her think I believed her all the same. Rose locked up and we left the studio, sharing a taxi home since we lived so close to one another. It had been a real stroke of luck, actually. Jacob had rented out the house for me, and though it was way bigger than what I was used to or needed, I liked that it meant Rose was within reach.

We got to her place first, and she grabbed her bag, then opened the door. Before she got out, she turned back to me. "You did great tonight, really. I'll see you tomorrow," she said, and smiled warmly.

"See you tomorrow, Rose," I replied, and made a concerted effort to return her smile. It was awkward and stilted, but her eyes still lit up. She must've thought I was a right grumpy old bastard with the way I went around frowning all the time. The trouble was that a smile made you vulnerable. It showed a person you liked them, gave them a strange power over you. Or maybe I was just a freak to think it did. After a moment Rose shook her head.

"Not a single bloody clue," she muttered to herself, getting out and closing the door behind her. Twisting in my seat, I watched her climb the steps to her flat and wondered what she meant.

Eight.
Rose

Damon was really starting to learn how to dance. I had to admit, despite my confidence, there had been a small part of me that wondered if he would. It was the morning after our lesson, and though I was supposed to be concentrating on work, my mind kept wandering to the night before. I'd definitely felt something more than friendship when his warm palm flattened out on my back while we danced. And when his fingers interlocked with mine, I couldn't help fixating on how big and masculine they were.

God.

It was happening again.

I was developing feelings for an actor, and it had to stop now before it got out of hand. I was the first person to admit I had a problem, that I fell for people too quickly. It was the sort of thing that had doomed my mother to a life half lived, and I wasn't going to let myself go down the same path.

Damon, of course, was different. He wasn't like the other actors I'd fallen for. He was introverted, unsure of himself, and completely oblivious as to just how earth-shatteringly handsome he was. The men I'd liked in the past had been vain, egotistical, and knew exactly the effect their looks had on women.

Nevertheless, sometimes the good ones could break your heart even worse than the bad.

"I once had a client who wanted us to use a sex swing. She brought me back to her place, where she had the thing rigged up in her spare bedroom," said Julian as he stared ponderously at the swing for Alicia's "Sparkling

Diamonds" bit. He'd found himself at a loose end today, so I invited him to come to work with me. Iggy was busy at a meeting for a potential show we'd be choreographing next year, which left me in charge.

I cocked an eyebrow at my friend, noticing the first few buttons on his shirt were carelessly undone. "And did you have a good time?"

"It allows for deeper penetration," he answered, as though discussing the sandwich he planned to eat for lunch. "Motion sickness can become an issue, though."

"I'll keep that in mind if a man ever suggests using one," I said, a hint of a smile in my voice. I'd long since gotten used to the way Julian spoke so openly of things other people might find uncomfortable. There was no room for embarrassment when you shared an apartment with a male escort.

"Just so long as it isn't Oswald, then I say go for it," he replied. "You could do with some deep fucking. It might ward off all that sexual frustration you wear like an old frock that doesn't fit you anymore."

"His name is Blake. And I have no intention of ever seeing him again, so you don't have to worry. Also, don't be a bitch. Some of us lack the tenacity to simply go out and get sex whenever we feel the urge. There's this little thing call self-consciousness, perhaps you should try a dash of it sometime. Too much confidence can be just as off-putting as too little, Julian."

"Meow. Saucer of milk for table five."

I sighed. "Look, I'm taking a break from romance right now anyway, so can we change the subject?"

"Sex doesn't have to be romantic."

"It does for me. You know this."

Julian looked at me sympathetically, like he felt sorry for my need for love as a prerequisite to sex. "So," he went on, changing the topic like I'd requested, "what are we doing today?"

I glanced at my watch. "Alicia should be here soon. She's playing the lead. We have to do a dress rehearsal for one of her songs."

"Isn't it a little early for that?"

"Usually, yes, but Farrah's designed a special outfit with a corset that's very constricting, so we need to make sure the routine's doable with it on. Otherwise, Iggy will have to adjust the choreography or Farrah will have to redesign the costume."

Julian was already pulling his phone out to Google Alicia and see what she looked like. "*Well*," he murmured as the image results popped up on the screen. I left him to his browsing as Farrah motioned me up onto the stage. Alicia waited in the wings, all kitted out in her costume. My mouth opened slightly, because if I were a man, I was sure I'd be staring at my own personal wet dream right then. The corset hugged tight to her curves before flaring out into an ostrich feather bustle at the back and lacy hold-up stockings at the front.

"I know what you're going to say. I'm a genius," said Farrah, and I grinned at her.

"Yeah, pretty much."

"Let's wait to see if she can manage the swing in that frou-frou construction before we have any claims to genius," Jacob butted in.

"Yes, well, there's been an issue at one of my shops that I need to go deal with, so let me know how everything goes. If any adjustments are needed, I'll take care of them when I get back," said Farrah.

Jacob sighed and shooed her away. "Okay fine, just go."

She left, and I approached Alicia, noticing that she seemed a little nervous. "Do you remember the steps we went through before?"

She nodded, glancing at Jacob for a second, and then answered quietly, "Yes, but I swear that man is getting on my last nerve. It's like he expects perfection at every turn."

I was surprised by her statement, because I'd thought those two worshipped the ground the other walked on. Then again, Jacob Anthony did have a reputation for being a perfectionist, and there was a definite prickly side to his personality. I guessed the Alicia/Jacob honeymoon was over.

"Just ignore him. If a director doesn't get on your nerves every once in a while, then he's not doing his job," I said lightheartedly. It almost got a smile out of her.

Walking back down the steps, I took a seat in the audience. I needed to watch Alicia from a distance so I could pick out any mistakes. Julian quickly came and silently sat down beside me.

Alicia would begin from above the stage. We waited a moment or two for Jacob to take a seat, and then Alicia appeared from up high, seductively singing the opening lines a capella as the swing slowly lowered. As soon as she appeared, Julian's attention was rapt, and his full, almost feminine lips curved into a seductive smile. I knew that look. It was his "okay, now I'm interested" face.

Alicia wore the sparkling outfit that Farrah had designed especially for her voluptuous form with grace, every curve sculpted to perfection. When she started singing, Julian's smile widened, his eyes gleaming at the sight of a shiny new toy.

Alicia's vocals were on point, but she was being too rigid with the swing. Jacob must have noticed, too, because he motioned for the music to be cut just when the song reached the "Material Girl" interlude. "She's stiff as a board up there. Fix it, Rose," he ordered.

I hurried to the stage, and Alicia shot me an irritable look. Julian had come with me, and her attention wandered to him briefly before returning to me.

She pursed her lips and threw up her hands. "What?"

"The corset's too tight, isn't it?" I asked, and she let out a sigh before nodding.

"It's literally suffocating the life out of me. How did you know?"

I tapped the side of my head. "Dancer's intuition. Here, turn around and I'll loosen it up a little."

She did as I asked, her green eyes going to Julian again as I located the laces on the corset.

"And you are?"

"Julian Fairchild," he replied, and though my attention was focused on the corset, I just knew the expression he was wearing, all sexy confidence. "It's a pleasure to meet you."

"Do you work here?" Alicia inquired further.

"I can, if you'd like me to."

I cast Julian a censoring look as I told her, "He's my friend. He's just here to hang out for a while." For a second I shuddered at the idea of him offering her his "services" before being momentarily struck by the irony of a real-life "courtesan" meeting the actress who was playing one. Or, well, whatever the male version of a courtesan was...courtier?

81

"Oh," said Alicia. She paused to look him up and down as though taking his measure. Something in her eyes told me that whatever she saw, she didn't like it. It annoyed me a little, and I couldn't exactly pinpoint why. Perhaps I just didn't like people prematurely judging my friends.

Julian cast his gaze over to the where my hands were struggling with the infernal laces. They just didn't want to play ball. I heaved a frustrated sigh.

"What did Farrah make this thing with, steel wires or something?"

Julian raised an eyebrow. "Can I try?"

Alicia reared back, as though appalled by the very idea. "I'm sure Rose can manage."

"Oh, come on, I won't bite. Removal of undergarments is my forté," Julian answered flirtatiously.

She shot him an unimpressed look. "I'm sure it is, but you'll be going nowhere near mine, thank you very much."

"Can he try?" I hedged, knowing I was getting nowhere. "I really can't get the strings loose. It's too bad Farrah had to rush off so soon."

Alicia was quiet for a moment, and Jacob grew impatient as he called up from the audience. "What's taking so long?"

"We're trying to loosen the corset. It'll just be another minute," I called back, and cast a pleading look in Alicia's direction.

"Oh, just get it over with," she said, resigned, as she threw her eyes up to the heavens.

Julian grinned and gently pushed me aside before reaching for the back of the corset. I noticed him run his knuckles over Alicia's bare skin, and she jumped ever so slightly before endeavouring to ignore him.

"You're good friends with Damon, aren't you, Rose?" she asked, her voice friendly.

"Yes," I replied hesitantly. "Well, if 'good friends' denotes being the only person brave enough to break down his walls of introversion."

She didn't seem to get my joke, but that was probably because Julian was distracting her as he seductively loosened her corset.

"I was wondering if you have his number? I'd like to invite him for drinks tonight with the cast."

"Oh, there's no need. I already invited him. Iggy called last night to ask if I wanted to go, and Damon was there," I replied, then realised how it sounded.

Julian glanced at me, a smirk touching his lips. Alicia appeared unconcerned, and it didn't surprise me. I was no competition to the likes of her, and, judging by the dreamy way she said Damon's name, I could tell she'd set her sights on him.

"Was he now," Julian purred.

I narrowed my gaze at my friend. "We were at the studio. I'm giving him extra dance lessons because he's been having trouble with the routines."

"Ah, that makes sense," said Alicia. "The guy has zero coordination."

I wanted to argue with her, because he'd come on leaps and bounds after only one lesson, but I kept it to myself.

"Totally forgivable with a face like that, though," she went on, and Julian cocked a brow once more, this time in Alicia's direction.

"All done," he told her, and she sat up, running her hands down her sides.

"That's much better," she said and stood, not even bothering to thank him.

We left the stage, and Alicia returned to her place on the swing.

"All right, from the top, everyone," Jacob announced, and the song began again.

"It appears Miss Davidson has her heart set on your Mr Atwood," Julian murmured as he took the seat beside mine.

"He's not *my* Mr Atwood. He's my friend. And let's not gloss over the fact that you were practically salivating all over her." I wholeheartedly ignored the twist of discomfort in my gut at the idea of Alicia and Damon becoming an item.

"Uh-huh. And tell me, you two having private little dance lessons, was that his idea or yours?"

"It was mine. But I was only trying to help him," I huffed defensively.

"But of course."

"There's nothing going on, Julian. I mean it."

"So you don't want me to come along tonight and distract Alicia while you spend time with Damon?" he probed, all sly.

"If you want to come I'm not going to stop you, but you don't need to distract anyone on my behalf."

"Sure," he said with a roguish grin, and I was two seconds away from slapping him upside the head.

"Can we talk about something else?" I asked, folding my arms.

Now his grin widened. "I just think it might be a good idea for us to band together to stop their potential relationship. That way we can both get what we want."

I snorted a disdainful laugh. "No way under God."

"I bet he shags like wild man. Are you sure you want to pass that up?"

This time I did slap him.

"Ow," he complained, and it was my turn to grin.

***

I didn't see Damon all day. He and a few of the other actors were taking part in a dialogue workshop. I wondered if he still planned on coming out for drinks that night, but tried not to get too excited. My "actors" ban meant I could only enjoy Damon's company in a platonic fashion, and that would just have to do.

After finishing up Alicia's dress rehearsal, Julian and I took the tube home to grab a quick shower and a bite to eat. I emerged from my room at eight, kitted out in a dark purple wrap dress and black Louboutins. Julian got them for me as a Christmas gift, and I'd been dying to give them an outing for weeks. I left my hair down in its natural wavy state and put on a touch of makeup.

"Somebody's out to impress," Julian commented as he adjusted his cufflinks in the living room mirror.

"Hey! I wear dance pants five days a week. A girl needs to get dolled up every once in a while, you know."

"Especially when there's a tall, dark, and handsome ex-film star to be seduced," he taunted, but I didn't take the bait. Instead, I eyed him pointedly.

"You Googled Damon."

"I most certainly did. Made for some very interesting reading."

I frowned. "What do you mean?"

"Well," said Julian, "according to an inside source, his father took him on these crazy week-long benders when he was underage, encouraging him to drink and do drugs."

Now I frowned even harder, because, going by what Damon told me of his dad, I imagined it was true. "That's awful. And you of all people should know not to be judgey about stuff like that."

"I'm not being judgey. In fact, I feel bad for the poor bloke. Things must have pretty shit with his old man for him to give up his entire career just to get away from him."

"To be honest with you, I don't think that was the only reason. He wasn't cut out for the fame. There were some paps following him last night, and he got real edgy."

"Well, if he doesn't like being papped, then he picked the wrong city to start working in," Julian commented glibly, and disappeared inside his bedroom. When he emerged, he was sliding a slim black tie around his neck, and I had to admit he looked good. With tousled golden-brown hair, hazel eyes, and perfect lips, Julian wasn't a man left wanting in the looks department. It made me wonder why Alicia had been so frosty with him when they met today.

What had she seen that she didn't like?

When I heard a car horn beep outside, I knew our taxi had arrived. I quickly grabbed my coat and purse before Julian slid on his suit jacket and offered his arm.

"You should count yourself lucky that your best friend is an escort who can offer you free services whenever you need a male companion," he teased as we went downstairs and into the lobby.

"Not to mention unsolicited tales about sex swings," I added, and he shot me a playful smile.

When we arrived at Club 49, a hip and stylish bar in Soho, I noticed a few familiar faces among the smokers outside. I waved a quick hello before Julian ushered me in. Not once in my life had I been stopped by a bouncer when accompanied by Julian. He simply exuded a worldly confidence that made other people want to bend to his will.

That annoying "What Do You Mean?" song was playing, and I spotted Iggy over by the bar with Farrah. We went to join them, and, since my boss had a soft spot for Julian, he smiled flirtatiously.

"Long time no see, Jules. How've you been?"

Julian bristled slightly. It irritated him when people called him Jules because it made him sound like a woman. Iggy knew this and always played on it. I never mentioned to my boss the reason for Julian's prickliness. He'd been bullied pretty harshly at school for looking like a girl, and he hated any reminders of that time.

He didn't look like a girl anymore, of course. Puberty had worked its magic, and his pretty face had grown into a masculine sort of beauty over the years.

"I've been good," he answered curtly, leaning casually against the bar and lifting a hand to get the bartender's attention. "A glass of pinot grigio and a tonic water and lime, please."

The wine was for me, the tonic water for him. Due to a history with drug abuse, Julian had been teetotal for years. Don't get me wrong, he liked to party with the best of them, but he tended to steer clear of alcohol.

"I heard there were some problems with the corset," said Farrah, sipping on a glass of red.

I nodded. "I had to loosen it a little because she couldn't breathe. It means there won't be as much boob lift as before, but at least she won't look so stiff."

"In that case, I'll have to make a few adjustments."

"Did you hear that Bob got the sack?" Iggy butted in, and I frowned gloomily.

"Oh, no, poor Bob."

Iggy nodded. "Jacob's been up in arms because he has to find a replacement. I wonder who they'll go with."

"Let's just hope it's someone who doesn't have such a penchant for liquid lunches," said Farrah.

My gaze wandered about the club. Almost as though my eyes had been drawn to him, they fell on Damon. He sat at the other end of the long bar, holding a bottle of Bud. Beside him was Alicia, and they appeared to be deep in conversation. I tried not to let the bubble of disappointment in my belly affect me too much.

They were costars. Of course they were going to want to spend time getting to know one another. Not to mention the fact that I wasn't in the market for a relationship. I was supposed to be enjoying the single life for a while.

Sigh.

In an effort to fix my attention elsewhere, I chatted with Iggy and Farrah some more. A few minutes went by before I noticed Julian was missing, and I had a sneaking suspicion where he'd gone. Casting my gaze to where Damon and Alicia were sitting, I sure enough found my friend insinuating himself into their conversation. He occupied a stool on the other side of Damon. Alicia's expression was frosty, but Damon didn't seem too bothered by the third party.

Deciding I needed to extract Julian from whatever game he had planned, I told Farrah I'd be right back and made my way to the other end of the bar.

"Hey, guys," I said, doing a little wave.

"Rose," said Damon, taking me in. His eyes wandered over my dress, lingering for a second on my shoes. His gaze darkened, and I felt a momentary buzz of awareness before I forced my attention back to Julian.

"Sorry to interrupt, but I need to borrow my friend," I said, tugging on his arm.

"You're not interrupting. Sit down," Damon urged me, and his lovely accent gave me shivers.

"Yes, Rose," Julian added with emphasis. "*Sit down.*"

Before I could respond, Damon pulled up an extra stool and ushered me onto it. Alicia remained quiet, watching the interaction in her champagne-coloured cocktail dress, her hair styled in waves like a fifties pinup. Damon wore a navy shirt and jeans, and I noticed how good his hair looked clipped short. He'd even used some product. I must have been caught up in staring at him because he cleared his throat and looked at me curiously. I studiously glanced away.

God, what was wrong with me? It was like "One" from *A Chorus Line* started playing in my head every time I was in the same room with him these days.

Julian stood and held an arm out to Alicia, asking her to dance. I could see it was on the tip of her tongue to refuse, but she didn't want to come across as bitchy in front of Damon.

"Sure," she replied stiffly, and allowed him to lead her onto the dance floor.

"Something on your mind?" Damon asked quietly as I watched them leave.

I blinked and looked to him, feeling flustered for some reason. "*A Chorus Line*," I blurted.

"Pardon?"

"I, uh, was just thinking of when Iggy and I worked on that show together. It was a lot of fun," I told him. Could I be any more random right now?

I was relieved when he didn't comment on my tangent and instead said, "I like your shoes."

My breath caught at the simple compliment. I knew he was telling the truth because I remembered how he'd stared at them just a moment ago. Another shiver had the skin on my arms beading into pimples.

"Thanks," I replied.

"Can I buy you a drink?"

"Oh, no, you don't have to do that."

"I want to. White, right?"

"Yes, but you really don't…." Before I could finish the sentence, Damon had the attention of the barman. A minute later, there was a fresh glass of wine in front of me. I couldn't think of an appropriate topic of conversation, so I looked across at Julian and Alicia again.

"He dances better than me," Damon commented, seeing where my gaze was fixed.

"That's because I taught him everything he knows," I answered, smiling. "But anyway, stick with me and I'll have you strutting the boards like a pro in no time."

"I never considered not sticking with you, Rose." He spoke low, and I blushed. What was with him tonight? He was acting more forward than usual. Perhaps it was the beer. I wondered how many he'd had.

"Well, that's good to know." I swallowed and lifted my wine glass, knocking back a long gulp. A second later I felt a warm hand on my arm, and glanced down to see Damon's fingers gently gripping me.

"Rose," he began, but was immediately interrupted by Jacob.

"Oh, my God, you two would not believe the day I've had," he complained as he called to the barman. "A double shot of whiskey, and make it snappy."

"I heard about Bob," I said, pretending to empathise. It was hard to feel bad for someone as self-centred as Jacob Anthony. Don't get me wrong — the man was a fantastic director, just not a fantastic person. Damon lifted a brow in my direction, and I noticed he'd withdrawn his hand. I mouthed the words "they sacked him," and he nodded in comprehension.

"Now I'm going to have to spend my entire weekend auditioning replacements. Bloody nightmare," he complained, picking up the whiskey and downing it in one long gulp. "Again," he told the barman. It was difficult not to chuckle at his drama-queen antics, especially when I made eye contact with Damon and saw he was having the same problem.

"Well, I'd better go do the rounds. Show this one how to have a good time, won't you, Rose?" said Jacob, patting Damon on the shoulder.

"I will," I replied as he disappeared into the crowds. Once he was gone I could finally let my laughter out. "My God, he's such a diva."

Damon shot me a simmering look. "So you're going to show me a good time?"

"I'm going to show you *how* to have one. Don't go getting any ideas," I answered, waggling my finger at him. Man, he was being sassy tonight. Tipsy Damon equalled flirty Damon.

"All right, show me how, then," he taunted, so I stood and presented my hand to him.

"Come with me." I smirked, and he eyed my hand for a moment before taking it.

I led him toward the dance floor, where Julian was trying his hardest to win Alicia over. I might have been mistaken, but I thought she appeared a little flustered by his sexy moves.

I felt a tug on my hand before Damon leaned down to shout in my ear over the music. "I'm not dancing."

Shuddering slightly at how his breath washed across my skin, I turned to face him. "And why not? This is the perfect opportunity for you to practice in front of people."

"You can't dance a foxtrot to this," he grumbled, and I laughed because it was true. The "Cheerleader" song was playing.

"Let's try something a little more modern, then," I suggested. "Just follow my lead. This song has a great drumbeat."

Once we reached the dance floor, I began doing some pseudo-Jamaican dance-hall moves, and Damon looked a little transfixed by my hips. It wasn't a pointedly sexy dance, more cool and funky, but it did require a lot of hip rotations. "Watch my feet," I told him as I took his hands. "Iggy and I teach this routine to the teens club we do at the studio once a month. It's easy."

"Easy, right," Damon deadpanned, and I chuckled.

"Seriously, just move with me. You'll pick it up," I assured him.

Suddenly, he let go of my hands and instead slid them around my waist. "I like this better," he said, bringing his mouth to my ear. "Teach me like this."

"Um," I said, fumbling for words. Our bodies shifted against each other as Damon moved to the beat. It was nothing like the dance I'd been trying to show him. That dance had been playful, this one was intimate...sensual. His closeness caused every nerve ending in my body to spark with electricity.

"Okay, so, when I move my left shoulder back, you move your right shoulder forward and vice versa," I instructed, my voice dry and scratchy.

"Aye," he murmured, but it didn't sound like he was really listening. He sounded distracted, and that made two of us, because I could barely breathe with him so close.

As we began to dance, Damon's hands travelled up my back, sending tingles radiating all along my spine. The song ended and cut into another, this one slower. He stopped moving his shoulders and instead just held me, dancing slowly as his fingers found the nape of my neck and sank into my hair.

"Damon," I began earnestly.

"Rose," he said, his voice a low rumble. I felt it vibrate right through me.

"You're being very tactile."

"I told you I'm not a good drunk."

"Are you drunk?" I asked.

"My inhibitions fly out the window," he went on. "I do all the things I normally just think about doing but never act on."

"Oh."

"Say that again. I like it. Your lips go all round and pretty."

Before I could respond, Alicia appeared in front of us.

"Mind if I cut in?" she asked.

I wasn't sure why, probably because I felt awkward and embarrassed by what Damon had just said, but I decided to make a joke. "Admit it, you've been dying to dance with me all night."

I had to give her credit — Alicia didn't miss a beat. "As tempting as that sounds, Rose, I meant Damon."

Pulling away from his arms, I gestured with my hands and spoke louder than was necessary. "He's all yours."

When I left the dance floor, I found Julian waiting for me with a glass of wine. "I thought you might need this."

"You thought right," I said, taking a sip. "I guess your attempt at wooing Alicia through dance failed, then."

"She's a tough nut to crack, but that only makes the challenge greater," he answered, unfazed.

"I can't believe I'm saying this, because all women adore you, but I just don't think you're her type. She wants Damon." Even saying the words was painful.

"No need to sound so glum, my darling. She *thinks* she wants Damon because he's safe and loyal like a puppy. Before long she'll come to realise that puppy dogs don't have eyes for vixens." At this he cast me a sidelong glance. "They have eyes for sweet blossoming flowers."

I snickered. "Is that a reference to my name?"

"It is."

"Well, it was corny as fuck, and it looks like we've both lost our dance partners for the night. Want to watch me get drunk?"

Julian smiled around his glass of tonic and lime. "But of course. Once you're good and sloshed, I'll coax out all your secrets."

"The trouble with that plan is you already know them all," I said, and downed a long gulp.

***

I was on my fifth glass of wine when I felt the sudden and uncontrollable urge to pee. Hurrying to the ladies' room, I hopped from anxiously from foot to foot, willing the queue to move quicker.

When I finally got into a cubicle, I sighed with relief before emerging to wash my hands. Alicia had skilfully kept Damon and me apart ever since she took him for her dance partner. I tried not to be bothered by it, because it was for the best if I was going to stick to my "no more actors" rule.

Let them have each other, my drunken, unhappy brain grumped.

All these gloomy thoughts had me gumming for a cigarette, and though I'd given up socially smoking years ago, I found myself wandering down the corridor that led to the bathrooms, searching for a way to the club's smoking area so I could bum one off somebody.

I hadn't gotten far when I bumped into a rock-hard chest and glanced up to find Damon staring down at me.

"Been looking for you," he said, the shine of intoxication in his eyes.

Maybe it was the wine, or maybe it was sour grapes, but I replied somewhat curtly, "I was sitting at the bar with Julian all night."

Damon's brows furrowed. "I meant just now."

"Of course you did."

"Are you pissed at me?"

I folded my arms and cocked a hip, which looked much sassier when you were wearing five-inch heels. I liked how they also made it so there was less of a height difference between us. "Nooo."

Okay, so the sasstastic posturing was ruined by the worst comeback ever.

"You are. You've got a right stroppy look on your face," he said, and I noticed he was moving us now so that my back became flush with the wall.

"I'm just drunk."

"You said you were a giddy drunk. You don't look giddy."

I didn't know how to respond to that, so I simply lowered my gaze and hoped he'd let the subject drop. He didn't.

"I'm sorry about Alicia. She won't leave off. It's starting to grate."

"You didn't seem very bothered," I retorted, and his features darkened.

"I was bothered," he stated firmly.

I just scoffed and looked away. Damon caught my chin and pulled my face back to him a little roughly. "You're the only one I want to spend time with, Rose."

I shivered as a moment of intense quiet passed between us. Our gazes locked, and I inhaled shakily. His eyes were hooded, sharpening when they focused in on my lips. I swallowed unconsciously, and my breathing grew deeper. The loud club music was slightly muted out here, and all I could hear was my own heartbeat drumming in my ears.

"That's the beer talking," I muttered.

"Aye. I only tell the truth when I'm drunk."

Damn, he had me there. His gaze held me captive, and I felt like I was sinking into a pool of quicksand, completely lost in his deep, impassioned brown eyes.

"You're very close."

"Need to be to do this," he grunted, and dipped his head. His lips brushed against my neck. I gasped and trembled when I felt his tongue flick out to lick a line across my skin. Shivers encapsulated my entire body as I grew hot and flushed. His crotch pushed against my stomach, his hardness pressing into me and giving me a very clear idea of what he was packing. His hips rocked back and forth, rutting, seeking, wanting.

Wow.

Perhaps Julian was right about him fucking like a wild man.

A low moan escaped me when his hands found my neck, his thumbs pressing gently into the hollow of my throat. His hips pushed forward once more, his cock hard and ready. My hands gripped tightly to his shoulders, too shocked by what was happening to do anything else. A raspy growl emanated from deep in his throat as he licked me once more.

"Tell me what your pussy tastes like," he rasped, the blunt eroticism of the request bringing me back to my senses. What was I doing? I was drunk and acting crazy. Breaking away from him, I fell against the wall, my chest heaving as I tried to catch my breath. Arousal made my head feel dizzy.

"I have to go," I blurted.

"Rose," he called after me, but I didn't look back.

Nine.
Rose

The entire weekend I was in a lust-filled haze. I replayed what happened with Damon at the club over and over again, using it as material to get myself off. I had to. He'd turned me on so much that I felt like I might burst if I didn't find some relief.

Even though I'd been drunk, I remembered every detail, from the hot, wet press of his tongue to the delicious way his body felt pushed urgently into mine. His erotic, dirty words. I hated how I'd left things and wished I had the balls to call him and explain why I'd run off.

He texted me Friday night just as the taxi pulled up to my apartment. One word.

Sorry.

He had no reason to apologise. After all, I'd hardly found what he'd done unpleasant. I didn't respond to the text, because it felt too impersonal. I wanted to find him at rehearsals on Monday and properly explain why I'd run, why he didn't want a clingy mess like me latching onto him anyway.

When the weekend finally came to a close, I selected my favourite Nike yoga pants and a wraparound cotton top to wear to the dance studio. We had a big day ahead of us, and Iggy wanted to get the choreography for the club scene perfected before we moved on.

I constantly scanned the room for Damon, but there was no sign of him. I only spotted him arriving a moment before Jacob strode in, and then my attention was all on our director. Or rather, the person he'd just ushered into the dance studio.

Fuck. My. Life.

There in all his perfectly imperfect glory was Blake. With shaggy dark brown hair and light blue eyes, he wore carelessly ripped jeans and a rumpled white T-shirt. A cigarette was tucked behind his ear, and he had that perennially tired "I've just been shagging" look on his face. Ugh.

"Gather 'round, everyone, I have an announcement," said Jacob, clapping his hands for attention. I watched the scene unfold with suddenly dawning horror. "As you may have heard, we've had to let Bob go, and here to fill the role of the Duke is none other than Blake Winters. I hope you'll all give him a very warm welcome."

Everybody clapped, some approaching Blake and introducing themselves. Well, he wouldn't be getting any warm welcomes from me. I had nothing but frost in my bones for that man. When my eyes met Damon's, I saw that he'd recognised the name and put two and two together. He was all the way on the other side of the room, but I could still make out his expression.

It asked, *Are you all right?*

I gave him a slight nod to say I was fine, and then quickly fled for the bathrooms to have a meltdown in private. My heart beat too quickly, and though I'd just showered an hour ago, my entire body felt clammy with sweat. I couldn't do this. I couldn't work with Blake again.

I remembered how he'd befriended me, talking to me each day during rehearsals and gaining my trust. It didn't take long for me to develop feelings for him, and although I was aware of his reputation, I convinced myself that I was different. That maybe I'd be the one he'd change his ways for.

I know, I was an idiot.

By the time we finally slept together, I was completely gone for him, lost in ideas of forever and always. It was too bad that his forever and always only lasted until he'd achieved orgasm. When he cast me aside I'd been heartbroken, but at least I'd gotten out early. And sure, I'd recovered from the hit my feelings had taken, but I was still raw. I definitely didn't want to have to see his face every day for the next several months.

Blowing my nose with a tissue and splashing some water on my face, I regained my composure and decided it was time to face the music. Just before I was about to emerge, I heard a hesitant knock on the door.

"Rose?" It was Damon.

I cleared my throat. "I'll be right out."

One final look in the mirror, a deep inhalation, and I strode toward the door. Damon stepped back when I came out to avoid a collision. His eyes flickered over my face as he studied me in concern.

"Are you okay?"

"Yes." *No.*

"That's him, isn't it, the prick who — "

I silenced him by quickly covering his mouth with my hand. "Don't say it. The walls have ears around here, and I don't want any rumours starting. But yes, that's him, and I'm fine, truly. I don't need any coddling."

His eyes flicked down, sharpening on my fingers pressed against his mouth. I felt a tingle between my thighs when his gaze turned hot, and withdrew my hand. Damon wore a very masculine expression as he surveyed me, his brows drawn together and his mouth a straight line. It took him a few moments to come to the conclusion that I wasn't about to break down in front of him.

"Okay," he said, seeming hesitant to continue. "About Friday — "

Nervous tension coiled inside me as I cut him off. "We can talk at lunch."

He frowned. "We have a few minutes."

"No, I…I'm just not in the right frame of mind to talk now, but at lunch I promise we will. I'll explain everything."

"There's nothing to explain."

"At lunch, Damon," I stated firmly, shooting him a meaningful look before heading back out into the studio. Almost the entire cast was there, and I noticed Alicia in a far corner chatting with a few of the dancers. I quickly took note of where Blake was and did my utmost to avoid him. When Damon joined us, he went to talk with Eddie, and then I saw Jacob approaching him with Blake. He began introducing them, and though I couldn't hear what was being said, I saw Damon's posture go decidedly rigid. He'd never met Blake before, but he'd already decided he didn't like him because of how he'd treated me. The thought gave me a warm feeling in my belly.

I felt like I was holding my breath the entire time they spoke, and I could have killed to know what was being said. Trying to stem my curiosity, I started stretching, and a few minutes later, Iggy was there, calling everybody to order. They all began taking their places as he came to whisper in my ear, "Have you seen Bob's replacement?"

I nodded and spoke quietly. "Yes, and I'll be doing my best to avoid him. I don't know what Jacob was thinking casting him anyway. Blake's far too suave to be the Duke. The Duke is a snivelling weasel, not to mention *old*."

"Quiet now, Rose. I might begin to think you care," Iggy chided me. "And anyway, the whole point of acting is to portray a range of characters. He's hardly going to play himself, now, is he?"

Iggy's logic peeved me off, but I didn't let it show. Jacob, his assistants and Maura, sat at their table at the head of the studio, while Iggy and I went to stand in front of the cast. Almost as though I could feel his eyes on me, my attention was unwittingly dragged toward Blake, who stared at me like he'd just noticed a friend he hadn't seen in a while. The bastard even had the gall to smile, like we were tight. Bosom buddies. Old pals.

He was in for a rude awakening.

I kept my expression blank, and his brow furrowed as he mouthed my name questioningly, *Rosie?* The nickname I'd once thought adorable now caused bile to rise in my throat.

"Take note of your places, everybody, and please stay on your marks. Eddie, I want you up here in front. We'll start with 'Lady Marmalade' and then move on to 'Because We Can.' I want you all on your toes," said Iggy loudly before he counted us down and began calling out steps. I noticed he wasn't in the best mood today, and the cast suffered a gruelling morning because of it.

"Maggie! You're about a foot off your mark. Please, we don't have time for this," he barked at one of the dancers. She looked like a rabbit caught in the headlights, so I went to help her find her footing. As I moved through the dancers, I passed by Damon and our arms grazed, setting all of my tiniest hairs on end. It was revelatory, the effect his touch had on me, and I still had no idea what I was going to say to him at lunch.

Jacob called for a fifteen-minute break, and I grabbed my coat and purse to head to the nearest coffee shop. It was as I was leaving the building that somebody caught hold of my elbow, stopping me in my stride. I turned to find Blake's clear blue eyes staring back at me, and I momentarily wanted to vomit.

"Rosie, it's me, Blake," he said, like it had been years since we'd last seen each other instead of weeks.

"Yes, I know who you are, Blake. I haven't undergone a lobotomy since the closing night of *Guys and Dolls*." He'd played the lead role of Nathan Detroit, a high-rolling gambler. His affected New York accent had been rocky at best.

"Okay," he said, eyeing me shrewdly as he pulled the cigarette from behind his ear and lit up. "You're pissed at me, I get it. I acted like a world-class prick to you before, and I'm sorry."

"It's in the past. I'd rather not discuss it," I said, and began walking again. Blake followed, easily keeping pace with my quick strides.

"I didn't know you were working on this show," he told me.

I laughed bitterly. I also found that hard to believe since rehearsals were taking place in Iggy's studio. Still, I didn't bother arguing about it. Instead I gave him as much attitude as I could muster. "Of course you didn't. I doubt you would've agreed to the role if you'd known. Wouldn't want to have to go through the bother of being nice to an old notch on your bedpost."

"I still would have taken it, Rosie. It's a good part. Admittedly, I'd prefer to play the lead, but it seems that role has already been cast."

I snickered at the idea of him even thinking about usurping Damon. Dancing aside, Blake didn't even come close to the kind of star power and charisma Damon had in his little finger.

We reached the coffee shop, and I held the door open. "Look, Blake, I have no interest in rekindling our friendship, or whatever it was we had, but I'm prepared to be civil to you if you'll be civil in return. That way we can both do our jobs and not be tiptoeing around each other for the next four months."

Blake took a drag of his smoke and exhaled. He watched me for a second, as though trying to decide if I was playing some kind of game. "All right, civility it is. And I mean it when I say it's good to see you, Rosie. You look great."

I didn't respond to his compliment, only nodded and turned to go inside. Putting in my order for a small flat white, I glanced back outside to see he'd gone. My breath whooshed out of me, and I felt relieved that the encounter was over. I wouldn't put it past him to try waiting outside to walk me back, wheedle his way into my affections again so he could fool me into another night of meaningless sex.

When I returned to the studio, I instantly spotted Damon sitting on a chair by the window. Alicia was perched on the ledge before him as she took a sip from a bottle of water. He said something, and she giggled loudly. Normally I wouldn't be so affected by the scene, but after talking with Blake, I was wired and tense. Therefore, seeing Alicia acting flirtatious with Damon made me violently jealous.

Speak of the devil, Blake stood in a group, but his eyes were on me. He seemed to notice where I was looking, and a curious expression crossed his face. I quickly went to stow away my coat and purse. The last thing I needed was Blake interfering in what was between Damon and me.

We got straight back to rehearsing, and by the time lunch came around, I was ready to collapse into bed and go to sleep. It was a good thing the cast would be running lines for the afternoon session. I could go home and relax, but not before I shared a quick lunch with Damon. I'd promised him we'd talk, and I'd never be mean enough to stand him up.

Ten.

Damon

It was a strange morning, and it only got stranger when I went to use the bathroom and bumped into Blake the arsehole. It seemed appropriate to be standing in the shitter. I'd just zipped up my fly when he walked inside, rubbing at the scruff on his jaw in agitation. I didn't have anything to say to him, so I kept my mouth shut.

I did wish he'd quit standing there though, watching me. It was beginning to create an atmosphere, and atmospheres made me want to lash out. It was one of the main reasons why I spent so much time on my own. There was less chance of me doing irritating fuckers a mischief.

"So, Rose, eh?" he said, looking at me through the mirror as I washed my hands.

I only cocked a brow in response and turned off the tap. The bloke had been nothing but friendly when Jacob introduced us earlier, but now there was an air of hostility about him, and he could fuck right off if he thought I was gonna bite.

He let out a low chuckle at my continued silence and went on, "You might not know this, but we used to have a thing, Rosie and me."

"Good for you," I muttered, and turned to leave.

"Ah, he speaks," Blake declared, and I suddenly wanted to punch the sod. "Look, I'm not trying to a dick —"

"No?" I interrupted, and he laughed.

"No. In fact, I'd like us to be mates. It'll be a long old three-month stint when this thing finally goes to stage if we're both hating on each other."

"I don't hate you. I don't know you," I replied evenly.

He let out a long, over-exaggerated sigh. "Let's cut the bullshit, shall we? I've been asking around, and apparently you and Rose are tight. And since I know her so well, I know she wears her heart on her sleeve and has probably told you all about what happened between us."

When I didn't respond, he barked another amused laugh. "So that's how it's gonna be, eh? Look, I just wanted to tell you that I'm not here to cause upset. In fact, I've had a lot of time to think these past few weeks, and I want to make things up to Rose."

"Fair dues, mate," I said, mildly sarcastic. I didn't believe his bullshit for a second. Sometimes you just met people who made your hackles rise. Blake was one of those people. I moved to leave again, but he sidestepped into my path for the second time. I lost my patience. He opened his mouth to speak, but I glowered at him, taking a step forward into his space. I was a few inches taller, which made it easy to glare down as I crowded him.

"Move," I grunted.

Blake raised his hands in the air but did as I ordered.

"I know you don't like me, Damon, but you'll change your mind, you mark my words," he said in a sincere voice before finally letting me pass. I very much doubted that, but I let him have the final say all the same.

I really didn't know what to make of him, and couldn't be sure if he was trying to tell me he wanted to win Rose back, or if he genuinely wanted to be buddies. I was so preoccupied with these thoughts that I left the studio and was sitting on a park bench ten minutes away when I remembered I was supposed to meet her for lunch. *Fuck.*

Pulling my phone from my pocket, I quickly dialled her number. It rang out with no answer, so I called again. This time she picked up on the third ring.

"Damon," she said, sounding breathless. "I'm just leaving now, but I can't find you."

Lifting a hand, I scratched at my chin and answered. "Yeah, I'm a bloody space cadet. I've already left. I forgot — "

"No, no, don't worry. It's fine." She cut me off, sounding relieved, if I was being honest. "We can do lunch some other time. Iggy's offered to drive me home and I'm wrecked, so I'll see you tomorrow, okay?"

I half-smiled. "This a brush-off?"

"No, of course not," she hurried to answer. She sounded like she was afraid she'd hurt my feelings. "I just...I guess I'm just trying to delay the inevitable."

"You really know how to make a bloke feel wanted," I joked, and I could imagine her fluster on the other end of the line.

"Oh, God, I'm saying all the wrong things today. It's Blake. I'm certain of it. The moment he showed his face this morning, my wiring got scrambled."

I tried to ease her embarrassment as I assured her gently, "Hey, you can handle Blake, Rose."

"Yeah, well," she sighed. "Tell that to the turmoil in my tummy. The idea of working with him on this show makes me want to vomit."

Frowning, I shifted the phone into my other hand and said, "I don't want you to feel cornered. I can talk to Jacob, ask that he cast someone else."

"You'd do that for me?" she whispered, taken aback.

"Aye. Remember the first day I got here and you helped me even though I was a rude old git?"

"Yes." She was still whispering.

"Well, I don't forget kindnesses like that, petal. You've got a friend in me whenever you need one."

A pregnant silence fell between us, and I could almost hear her thoughts churning.

"Don't talk to Jacob, just…if I ever need a friend during rehearsals, be there. You're surprisingly good at bolstering my confidence, Damon Atwood."

The tone of her voice told me she was smiling, and my chest puffed up with pride that I'd made her feel better.

"I'm here whenever you need me," I promised.

"Thank you," she replied. "I'll see you tomorrow."

She was about to hang up when I said, "Wait."

"Yes?"

I coughed, uncertainty making me hesitate. "Come over for a brew later."

Her voice showed I'd taken her by surprise. "Oh, um, over to your place?"

"Aye."

"Ah, okay, sure. I'll text and let you know when I can make it."

"'Bye, Rose."

"Goodbye, Damon."

She ended the call, and I slid my phone back in my pocket. Nearby movement caught my attention, and I looked across the park to see the same gaggle of photographers from the other night, the ones who'd been snapping shots of me at the barber's. I was seeing them around more and more, and it was beginning to get on my goat.

I didn't want this kind of attention.

Getting up, I shoved my hands in my coat pockets and left the park. I ate a quiet lunch in a nearby café before returning to the studio for the afternoon session. The second I walked inside Alicia was there, sliding her arm through mine and leading me into one of the practice rooms. It was starting to become clear that she had an interest in me that wasn't entirely platonic. And truthfully, I should have been over the moon, because she was beautiful, but she just wasn't Rose. She didn't calm me, nor did she make me feel like I could trust her unconditionally.

I hadn't lied on Friday when I'd told Rose she was the only person I really wanted to spend time with. I was already wishing away the next few hours so I could finally go home and see her.

"I have this piano at the apartment I'm renting, but the thing is huge," said Alicia, her arm still linked with mine. "I was wondering if you could come over later and help me move it. You've got big arms — I bet you're great at moving furniture around."

"Afraid I've got plans," I told her, and noticed Blake standing with Jacob and Eddie. His eyes were on me. He gestured to Alicia and then mouthed the word *niiiccce*, like we were pals and he was complimenting me on being arm in arm with a gorgeous bird. The bloke was living on another planet.

"Oh, no," Alicia pouted, affecting a sad expression. "How about tomorrow, then?"

"I — "

"What's happening tomorrow?" someone interrupted. Blake had come to join us.

"Hello, Blake, isn't it?" said Alicia in a pleasant voice. "I'm Alicia, and Damon here has kindly offered to help me move the piano in my apartment tomorrow, haven't you, Damon?"

"I'm not sure…."

"How very kind of you," said Blake, and I gritted my teeth. I could barely get a word in with these two, and it was difficult not to just grunt something rude and walk off. I wasn't out on a boat and these people weren't foulmouthed fishermen. This was a completely different world, full of urbanity and false pleasantries. There was a small part of me that truly hated it.

Now Blake winked. "I bet you'll move her piano real good."

Fucking prick.

Alicia tittered a laugh, and I was sure I must have looked unimpressed. Before I could say more, Jacob was rounding everybody up. The rest of the afternoon passed quickly, and I was happy not to have to talk to Blake again, aside from when we had dialogue together. Acting was easy for me, real-life conversations less so. And that was before you even added the fact that I had cause to dislike him. The guy had been with Rose. He'd put his hands on her. I just couldn't seem to look at him and not want to punch him for it.

By the time I got home that evening, I felt like I could breathe again. I'd changed into some comfortable jeans and a loose jumper when my phone buzzed with a text.

Rose: *Are you home yet? I can come over now if you're not too tired...*

Damon: *I'm home. Come over. I'll put the kettle on.*

Rose: *Okay. See you in a few :-)*

The hazy drunken memory of my tongue on her neck entered my head, and I groaned. I should have kissed her then while I had the chance, but I'd been too preoccupied with her skin; it had felt so *soft*. The problem with me was that when alcohol was involved, all my inhibitions flew out the window, and they certainly had on Friday night.

111

Fuck, what had I even said to her?

She'd tasted like sunshine, and the sound of her gasping, the subtle intake of breath, made me harder than I'd ever been. My balls tightened just remembering it. The second I arrived home that night, I'd had to take a long, hot shower while relieving myself of my need.

Christ, I really had to think of something else right now or I'd be sporting a massive stiffy when I answered the door. Some of my things were lying around, so I did a quick clean-up. About ten minutes later there was a tentative knock, and I'd thankfully calmed down from wanting to shag her silly.

Opening the door, I found Rose in her light brown pea coat, her hair windswept and her cheeks reddened from the cold.

"Come in," I said, and she stepped inside. "It's biting out there."

"Tell me about it," she agreed, unwinding the purple knit scarf from around her neck. "The entire walk here I was fantasising about cosy open fires."

I led her into the kitchen, suddenly struck by a vision of her sitting by the fire in my cottage back in Skye, wearing a shirt of mine and nothing else.

Okay. I really had to get a handle on this fantasy business.

Rose took a seat at the small table by the window while I went about making the tea. Every couple of seconds my eyes went to her. She sat back in the chair, emitted a tired breath, and began fiddling with her hair. Pulling it out of its knot, she ran her fingers through the strands, then fixed it back up again. She must have sensed me looking because her attention flicked to me, and I almost scalded myself with hot water as I quickly pretended I hadn't been ogling.

"How did the afternoon rehearsals go?" she asked. "I hope Blake didn't give you any trouble."

I affected a bland expression. "Why would he?"

She grew flustered. "I don't know. Never mind."

Bringing the pot and two teacups over to the table, I set them down and took the seat across from her. Gran had always been a big tea fanatic, and the proper way to serve it had been bred into me since I was a teen. I'd already put out milk and sugar before Rose arrived.

"I did talk with him," I admitted, and her eyes flicked quickly to mine.

"Oh?"

I scratched at my stubble. "He said he'd like us to be friends."

"Huh." She wore a thoughtful look.

"What does 'huh' mean?" I cocked my head.

"I'm not sure. It just feels like he's up to something."

"Maybe he wants you back," I ventured.

At this she snickered derisively. "I don't think so. I was just an amusement for him, a way to pass the time. The only reason he'd want to make amends would be to use me some more, and I have enough self-respect not to let that happen. Fool me once, and all that."

"You don't think he's changed?" I asked.

"People don't change in a matter of weeks, Damon. At least not as much as Blake would've needed to. I was aware of his reputation for being a ladies' man when we first met, but he'd been so kind to me, so chivalrous, that I thought perhaps it was all just rumours. I found out the hard way that it wasn't."

I was frowning again as she reached out to pick up the pot and pour some tea for us. "It's his loss," I said, my voice unexpectedly gruff. Bastard didn't know how lucky he'd been.

She lifted a shoulder, then let it fall. "Maybe. Maybe not. I'm horrible at relationships. I get so clingy and paranoid, always needing to know what the other person is thinking, needing to be with them twenty-four seven. Mum was like that, too, and we both know how badly that ended. It's probably for the best that I stay single," she said, her eyes on her teacup before she looked at me pointedly. "If not for me, then for the sake of the poor sod who gets stuck with me." A small, self-deprecating laugh escaped her.

I tried to read between the lines of what she was saying. This was clearly her roundabout way of telling me I was better off not being interested in her. She had no clue how appealing I found the idea of her clinginess. In fact, she could cling to me all she wanted, preferably while naked.

The real take-home message though, was that she didn't want to talk about what happened on Friday, and I couldn't blame her. After the way I'd spoken and how I touched her, I was surprised she wasn't ignoring me completely. I'd way overstepped the mark.

I stared at her for a long moment, so long she began to grow self-conscious as she clasped her fingers around her cup, her eyes on the table as she blew off the steam. My eyes were drawn to how her lips shaped themselves, forming a seductive "O" that she was entirely unaware of.

"Some men aren't so immature that they can't handle the love of a good woman," I said, and she glanced up. "Blake is a fuckwit for how he treated you."

She let out a shaky laugh. "You're probably right."

114

She skirted around the fact that I was talking about myself, how I'd never treat her like he treated her. However, I could tell she was nervous about me broaching the topic, so I let it lie. She was trying to be single for a while, and I was willing to accept that. It wasn't like I was going anywhere.

"Can I ask a question?"

"Of course," she said, and took a sip of tea.

"Why don't you dance on stage? You're so much better than half the women in the show. I don't understand."

She smiled wanly. "Some of us don't crave the limelight the way others do."

"Don't you?"

She shook her head. "No. Well, it's perhaps a little more complicated than that. I love to dance, but I've got terrible stage fright. I wish I could do it, but I just don't have it in me. For some reason, audiences take all the fun out of it for me. It's ironic, because dance is a visual art form designed to be seen by others, but I've always been more comfortable creating rather than portraying. It's sort of like how writers write and actors say the lines. I create the routine for dancers to perform."

"Artistry without applause," I said. "A noble pursuit."

"Well," she ventured sheepishly, "perhaps not so noble. Sometimes I stand behind the curtains and close my eyes, pretending the clapping is for me. That way I can enjoy the reward without the fear of being on stage."

I gave her a warm look. "There's no shame in wanting acclamation. We all need it every now and again."

She leaned forward, hands still cupping her mug. "Do you ever get nervous before a performance?"

"Nervous, yes, but not afraid. It's easy to be someone else. Being myself is the problem."

115

"When did you first know you wanted to be an actor?" she asked. "It's fine if you don't want to talk about it, but I have to admit, I find you a fascinating study. When you're Christian during rehearsals, you're so animated, but then when you go back to being Damon, you're like a closed book."

Her question made me self-conscious, but at the same time I wanted to answer it. I wanted her to know me. "I was always a shy lad, never had a lot of friends at school. When I was eight, I had a teacher who was determined to draw me out of my shell. She gave me the lead in our school play of *James and the Giant Peach*. It was like" — I paused, trying to find the right words — "wanting to be an artist all your life and then finally finding paint for the first time. If I wasn't myself, I could be anyone. I didn't have to hold back. I was…free."

Rose ate up everything I told her. This was probably the most open I'd been with her since we'd met. "And then it just took over."

"How did you know?"

She blushed. "Because I felt exactly the same way when I discovered dancing. I saw a film when I was little with Fred Astaire and Ginger Rogers, and just felt like my heart was going to explode. I knew right then and there what I wanted to do with my life."

I studied her, my eyes focusing on the flush of her cheeks and the delicate shape of her mouth, before whispering, "What a pair we make, eh?"

She glanced up. "Quite the pair." A moment elapsed and she cleared her throat, twirling a strand of hair around her finger. "I heard a couple of the girls in the show say you were working on a fishing trawler back in Skye. Is that true?"

"It is. No idea how word got around, though. We certainly don't use Twitter out at sea."

She grinned. "Oh, I don't know. Maybe some of the men on your boat enjoy posting pictures of all the fish they've caught, like, 'Hey, everyone, check out the size of my pollacks.'"

Her eyes glittered when I laughed at her joke. "Nah, we're all too exhausted half the time for any of that faffing about."

"Why do you do it, though?" she asked, her expression turning curious. "I mean, unless you lost all your money in a Ponzi scheme, then you must have enough to keep you living comfortably."

Exhaling a breath, I answered, "I like the harshness of it, keeps me grounded. During my film career I was given anything I wanted, especially after Mum passed and Dad came on the scene. I quickly discovered that spending money and indulging in luxuries made me miserable. That sort of life just isn't for me. I like working hard for things, appreciating simple stuff like a cup of tea shared with a friend." I paused to gesture between the two of us. "Or a hot meal at the end of a long gruelling day of labour. I feel like I've earned it. Not to mention I don't really see the value of gold-plated iPods or watches worth as much as houses."

Rose leaned her elbows on the table as she studied me. "You're very interesting to me, do you know that?"

"I am?"

"Yes. I've never known someone to be so enlightened yet completely uncertain of who they are at the same time."

I stared at her intensely, because she'd hit the nail right on the head. I was an actor. Even if we did know who we were at the beginning, after a while sometimes we played so many roles that we forgot.

"Perhaps you being here, getting offered the part right after your grandmother passed, really is kismet. Maybe you're supposed to do this to find yourself."

"Enlightenment on London's West End?" I asked, amused.

"Enlightenment is often found in the most unexpected places," she replied, lifting the cup to her mouth again with a teasing smile.

My eyes traced the curve of her lips and the feminine line of her jaw, and I thought, *If I could find myself anywhere, it would be inside you, Rose Taylor.*

"Have you been practicing the dance moves I taught you?" she went on, and my attention was drawn away from the swell of her breasts. I sat up a little straighter, like she'd caught me doing something I shouldn't.

"Uh, not exactly."

She shot me a playful scowl. "Well, how about we have another lesson now? This room should be big enough."

"I, ah — "

"No excuses. I promised I'd turn you into a dancer, Damon, and I won't give up until I succeed. Now, is there an iPod dock or anything we can play music on in this place?"

I stood and walked over to the kitchen to turn on the radio that was built into the wall. "Only this, I'm afraid."

Some awful hip-hop song came on, and I winced. Frank Sinatra I could deal with. Whatever this was, not so much.

"I can't dance to this."

Rose was already up and pulling our chairs into the middle of the room, placing them side by side. "Of course you can. This is Jason Derulo. If you can't dance to Jason, then you really are a lost cause. Besides, the great thing about *Moulin Rouge* is that the music is completely anachronistic. Any genre or era will work."

I watched as she sat on her chair, then patted the seat of the other. "Come on," she urged me. "Mirror what I do."

Reluctantly, I did as she asked, watching as she gripped the edge of her chair, then began to move her legs. She pushed up, then swung around so she was sitting on it backwards. The movement caused her top to rise up, revealing an inch of smooth stomach.

I changed my mind. I could definitely dance to this song. More precisely, I could watch Rose dance to this song. I could watch her dance to it forever. She was in complete control of her body, and it was one of the sexiest things I'd ever seen.

"You're not doing it," she complained and I blinked, realising I'd been so transfixed that I hadn't mirrored a single one of her dance moves.

I cleared my throat. "Could we, ah, start over?"

She stared at me for a second and nodded. "Sure, watch my feet. First you slide from side to side, then you take a step with to the right, a step to the left, and push up off the chair with your right hand."

This time she watched me while she gave instructions. For a moment her eyes seemed to glaze over, her attention wandering to my waist. I briefly wondered if she enjoyed watching me as much I enjoyed watching her.

She clapped then, and I glanced at her. "You've got it. Okay, now I want to show you how to step onto the chair and lower the front to the floor before stepping off."

"Won't that damage the chairs?"

She shook her head. "Nah…well, probably not. They look like pretty standard Ikea numbers, so if they break, I promise I'll replace them."

She held her hand out to me, and we both stepped up onto the chairs at the same time. Letting go, she lifted one foot, placed it on the chair back, then slowly lowered it to the floor while keeping a steady balance. She made it look way too easy. When I attempted to copy her, I wobbled and almost lost my footing. She smiled.

"It's hard at first, but once you get the hang of it, you can make it look smooth as fuck. This move is especially sexy when men do it."

At that I smirked. She flushed for speaking for so openly, but Christ, I hoped she found me sexy.

"I mean, like, it usually is, anyway."

For some reason I felt like teasing her. "Do you think I will?"

Her eyes widened, and she coughed nervously. "Um…."

"Relax, Rose. I'm messing with you."

She grew flustered. "You're mean."

I concentrated on what I was doing, and placed my right foot on the chair back again and thrust forward. The thing went flying, bashing into the floor while I whacked my ankle off the side.

"*Fuck*," I swore, hopping away and wincing.

"Oh, crap, are you hurt?" Rose asked, hurrying to my side.

I sat on the floor, holding my ankle as I gritted my teeth. "I'll be fine."

"Let me see," she insisted, and began rolling up the end of my jeans to reveal an ugly red welt. "Oh, my God," she exclaimed and glanced at me. "Do you think we should go to the hospital?"

Now I laughed. "Rose, it's not even sprained."

She bit her lip, and my attention was transfixed by the action. "Yeah, but I feel bad. Maybe I should've taught you something easier first. I think I got a little carried away with that seductive base line." She laughed shyly.

Reaching out, I cupped her cheek in my hand. "I've been hurt a lot worse. Don't fret," I whispered, and her eyes rose to mine. Now she bit her lip even harder, and I wished I was the one doing it. Her taste came into my head again, and it was all I could do not to groan. She surprised me when she closed her eyes and sank into my touch. My heart hammered harshly in my chest, and I wanted to move my hand, sink it into her hair or run it down over her neck. Anything. But in that moment, I was too scared of breaking the connection.

If I'd learned anything from Friday night, it was that Rose could be skittish when it came to intimacy.

In the next second, her phone rang, and she exhaled. I dropped my hand and pulled us both up to standing. Rose's gaze was searching for a second, her bright eyes flickering between my dark ones, and I knew she had to have felt the intensity between us just as much as I had.

She answered the phone. "Hi, Julian, can I call you back in a minute?"

He must have agreed, because she hung up and then turned back to me. "I should get going. We've both got a full day of rehearsals in the morning."

"Of course, let me walk you to the door," I said, while on the inside it was the opposite.

Don't go. Stay. Let me kiss you. But I didn't say any of that, and a moment later I'd walked her to the door and she was gone.

Eleven.
Rose

"You have the best and worst timing in the world, do you know that?" I said as I left Damon's place and called Julian back.

"I do?" he asked with intrigue. "Pray tell, what exactly did I interrupt?"

I scrunched up my forehead. "You know, I'm not even entirely sure."

"So it was something to do with the dashing Mr Atwood, I presume," he said, and I could just imagine his giant grin on the other end of the line.

I exhaled. "Yeah, we were having a moment. At least, I think we were. Maybe it was all in my head."

"Oh, quit the modesty, Rose. The man likes you. He more than likes you. Anyone with a pair of eyeballs can see it."

His statement made me flustered, my belly tightening with a mixture of excitement and dread. The dread was down to the fact that if I let myself fall for Damon and it ended badly, I wasn't sure I'd ever recover. It was easier getting over Blake, because behind it all I knew he was a deeply flawed person, but Damon was inherently good. He was flawed, sure, but in a way that was strangely admirable.

"Yes, well, it doesn't matter, because I'm not dating actors anymore, remember? Anyway, what did you want to talk to me about?"

Julian quickly let the subject drop and moved on to other matters. "Well, you know how I'm turning thirty on Sunday?"

"Uh-huh."

"And you also know how I've been adamant I wasn't going to mark the occasion?"

"Yes...."

"Well, I've changed my mind. I want a surprise party at our place, and I want you to plan it for me."

I sputtered a laugh. "It's not a surprise if you know about it, Julian."

"Oh, hush, that's neither here nor there. I'll pretend to be completely flabbergasted when I walk through the door. I'll even practice my reactions in the mirror, maybe throw in some waterworks for good measure."

"Please don't."

"So you'll do it?"

I sighed. "Yes, Julian, I'll throw you a non-surprise surprise party. It would have been nice to have a little more time to prepare, but I'll do my best." For years Julian had paid the lion's share of our rent and utility bills without a single complaint. If he wanted a party, I'd give him a party.

"Brilliant. I'll leave my card out in the morning so you can shop for supplies. Oh, and you'll invite your friends from work, won't you?" he went on like butter wouldn't melt. The penny finally dropped.

"This is a ploy to get Alicia to our place, isn't it?" I said as I climbed the stairs to the apartment.

I had my key in the door and was stepping inside when he answered coyly, "Darling, I have absolutely no idea what you're talking about."

He was sitting in the living room when I met his eyes and hung up the phone. "She's not interested in you, Julian. It's unfathomable, I know, but she isn't. Why are you so determined to win her over?"

I took off my coat and hung it by the door before going to join him on the couch. His expression turned contemplative as he chewed on his lip. "I have this idea in my head that she'll be a *fantastic* lay and now I can't stop until I have her. You're not a man. You wouldn't understand."

I didn't think it was because I was a woman that I didn't understand, I thought it was more because I wasn't a Julian. My best friend was single-mindedly determined once he got an idea into his head. I lifted his hand and intertwined his fingers with mine.

"Even if you can get her to fall for your charms, what happens when she leaves and goes back to L.A.? You might miss her."

I cast him an intuitive glance, because sometimes I wondered if he wasn't more emotional than he let on. Don't get me wrong, I didn't think Alicia was the one or anything, far from it. But I did suspect that his pursuit of her was indicative of a change in him. He was about to turn thirty. He couldn't keep living the way he was living forever.

Julian arched an eyebrow. "When have you ever known me to wallow over a lost love, Rose? I'll pick myself up and move on to the next, just like I always do. Besides," he went on, lifting our clasped hands and bringing my knuckles to his mouth for a kiss, "you know you're the only woman I've ever really loved, and that's because I don't want to have sex with you."

I looked at him sadly. We'd had countless conversations over the years about his strange outlook on love and sex, and how for me the two went hand in hand, never separate, but for Julian, they had to be forever apart, never together.

"One day a woman will come along when you least expect her, and she'll wash away everything that came beforehand," I whispered.

He didn't reply, but he didn't have to. Though he might have argued otherwise until he was blue in the face, I knew that when it came down to it Julian wanted to find real love just as much as I did. I might have accepted his lifestyle and the choices he'd made along the way, but that didn't mean I couldn't wish for more for him. When you loved a person, you wanted them to be happy, no matter how unlikely the possibility, and you never stopped hoping they would be.

***

The following morning, I walked into Iggy's studio with a takeaway coffee in hand and a determination to spend as little time in Blake's company as possible. My head was full of plans and preparations for the party, which I was to throw on Saturday night, per Julian's instructions. His birthday was on Sunday, but apparently the whole thing would be a wash if we threw it then because nobody went out on a Sunday night – his words, not mine.

When I saw Damon standing in a group next to Alicia and a few other cast members, I decided to go over and invite them all to the party. It made my stomach twist to see how she had her arm slid through his, like they were an item or something. The only saving grace was I knew by the look on Damon's face that he was completely uncomfortable. He hated being in groups, so obviously Alicia was the one who'd forced her company on him.

She was almost as determined to win Damon as Julian was to win her. It was quite the predicament. If only some higher power could change the target of their affections.

"Hi, everyone," I said, and gave a little finger wave. "So, I need your help. I'm throwing my best friend a surprise party for his thirtieth on Saturday and need some guests to make up the numbers. This means you're all invited." I was met with lots of positive noises, but when I looked at Alicia, she appeared less than enthusiastic. She knew exactly who the party was for without even having to ask.

"I'll come," said Damon quietly, and I shot him a thankful smile. Memories of last night flooded my head, how his hand cupped my face, his eyes flashing with heat and curiosity.

"I'll come, too," Alicia put in, suddenly finding the idea a lot more appealing now that Damon was going. Of *course*.

"And me," came another voice. I instantly bristled as a warm arm slid around my shoulders. It was Blake. I stepped aside quickly, breaking the contact and eyeing him with barely concealed suspicion.

"I didn't invite you," I said stiffly. He grinned and tucked a strand of messy hair behind his ear. The gesture I'd once found sexy as hell now caused bile to rise in my stomach.

"Well, that's not very kind," he said.

I wanted to walk away, but I stood my ground. "No, it isn't. I only give kindness where it's due."

"I sense some history here," Alicia chirped with a gleam in her eye, her tone sickly sweet. I wasn't a violent person but I sort of wanted to smack her right then.

"Rosie's my ex," Blake explained, all matter-of-fact. "She doesn't like me very much." The smile on his face said he was enjoying my prickliness, and I couldn't for the life of me say why. I was also furious that he'd outed our past to at least five cast members. Everybody would know about it by the time the day was through.

"Aw, he calls her Rosie. Isn't that adorable," Alicia went on, and again, not a violent person but....

"I prefer Rose," said Damon, and I sent him a grateful look before addressing Blake.

"I'm not your ex. If I recall correctly, we were never actually a couple."

He waved a hand lazily through the air. "Semantics."

"There are no semantics about it. I wasn't your girlfriend, Blake, so stop trying to make people believe otherwise."

"Ouch, somebody got out of bed on the wrong side this morning," he said in a lilting voice, and took a step closer so that our shoulders brushed. Now he whispered, "Or are we a tad sexually frustrated? What's it been, five weeks?"

I swear, I could have decked him, but instead I clenched my fists and kept my calm. "I bloody knew you couldn't keep the act up for long."

"There was never an act. I swear I'm not here to cause a lot of trouble, Rose." He paused before amending his statement, the innuendo evident. "Well, maybe I am here to cause a *little*."

Before I could say another word a shadow fell over us. Damon had come to stand behind me, his posture protective. "Back off" were the only words he uttered, and Blake laughed like he was being ridiculous.

"We're just talking."

A hand came to rest on the base of my spine, and I shivered. I liked how it felt when Damon touched me, even though I knew I shouldn't. "Aye, well, go talk to someone else. Rose isn't interested." The territorial tone to his voice made my stomach clench. In the time I'd known him,

Damon hadn't struck me as a confrontational person, although he did have an intimidating side. But maybe that was just because he was always so stoic. The fact that he was confronting Blake on my behalf had tingling butterflies wreaking havoc on my insides. My heart wouldn't stop thrumming.

Blake's eyes turned calculating as he glanced at Alicia. "I've been meaning to ask — do you need any extra help moving your piano later, or would you prefer to have Damon come alone?" The placid look on his face was at odds with the trouble he was trying to stir. It took me a second to digest what he'd said as I turned to look at Damon, a question in my gaze.

You're going over to her place later?

Now the butterflies transformed into blades cutting at my heart. It was ridiculous, because I had no claim over Damon. So why did it hurt so much to think of him making plans to be alone with Alicia?

His lips firmed, and now he was the one who looked like he wanted to punch Blake. Reaching out, he moved to take my hand into his, but I pulled away, too many feelings bubbling up inside me. I needed to get of there.

Thankfully, Iggy provided me with the perfect escape as he called my name, needing my help with something. I stepped away from the two men and followed my boss out to his office, only exhaling when I shut the door behind me.

"What do you need?" I asked, my voice strained.

He peered at me speculatively. "Nothing. You just looked like you were stuck between a rock and a hard place out there. Thought you could do with rescuing."

I heaved a sigh. "I did. Thank you. Blake's being...difficult."

Iggy pulled a folder from one of his filing cabinets and began flicking through it. "Realised what he threw away, has he?"

Pressing my fingers to my temples to relieve the headache I could feel forming, I answered, "I don't know. He's being very forward, not to mention talkative. Everybody's going to know about what happened between us."

"Oh, honey, we're creating a West End show. There's going to be far more gossip flying around than your little fling with Blake Winters. Don't worry about it. They'll all be talking about something else come lunch time."

"Yeah, you're right," I said, my thoughts a jumble.

A moment later there was a knock on the door before Damon poked his head in. "Rose. Can we talk?"

Iggy shot me an arch look, which I ignored as I stood and went to Damon. "Sure, what's wrong?" Stepping out into the corridor, I closed the door to allow us some privacy.

Damon looked frustrated. "I didn't offer to go to her place. I got roped into it."

I placed a hand on his arm to reassure him. "Hey, you don't need to explain yourself."

His gaze fixed on the hand that was touching him, and he let out a gruff breath. "But I want to."

Now his eyes rose to meet mine meaningfully, and I swallowed at the intensity in them. It felt strange, this thing between us, because ninety-five percent of it was completely unspoken. It was just a feeling, one that drew me to him like a moth to a flame. It made me notice the little things, like how his pupils dilated when he watched me dance last night, or how his breathing deepened when he touched me, how the only times I'd ever seen him smile were at me.

"You're allowed to have friends, Damon. You said yourself that Alicia's a nice person. If you like her, you should get to know her." Every word was like swallowing glass, but this needed to be said. I didn't own him.

"I don't like her. I like you," he said, and I grew antsy.

"Let's not talk about this."

"Why not?"

"Because I told you, I'm terrible at relationships. You'll be running for the hills in the space of a week." I stared at the floor as I spoke. Damon's fingers slid against my skin as he cupped my neck.

I glanced up. His gaze was hooded and sexy. "Let me be the judge of that."

I swallowed deeply, my voice failing me. A strange expression passed over his features, like he was struggling over what to say. "You," he paused, frowned, then tried again. "You captivate me."

My heart stuttered. The clear, undeniable honesty in his words had me trembling.

"You're being crazy," I managed.

"Do I captivate you?" he asked, a vulnerability in his eyes like he honestly had no clue how I felt for him. His fingertips dug into my flesh, while a light sweat broke out all over my body. A few people stood chatting at the other end of the corridor and I grew self-conscious, wondering if they were listening to us. I stared at Damon, but I must have hesitated for too long because he looked disappointed. He stepped away, eyes on the floor.

"I should go," he said, and walked away.

My gut sank, all my energy gone as I slumped back against the wall. A minute later I dragged myself to the bathroom, splashing some water on my face and willing my heart to calm down as Damon's voice echoed in my head.

You captivate me.

Do I captivate you?

When I came back out, Jacob and Iggy had gathered everyone in the main practice room, though most of the actors were sitting on the floor to watch Damon and Alicia rehearse a scene.

"In this part, Satine still believes that Christian is the Duke. Think of it as a comedy of errors. She thinks he's come to her chamber for sex, while Christian is under the impression she knows he's a writer and they're going to discuss the play he's composing for her to star in."

I listened to Jacob go on with further instructions as I took a seat on the floor with the others, still a little disoriented. Iggy showed Damon and Alicia how they were to move. It wasn't a dance routine as such, but there was a point at which he would take her hand and twirl her in a romantic fashion.

"Now" — Jacob butted in again — "when you burst into song, I want it to really pack a punch. I want even the people sitting in the Gods to have goose pimples, so don't hold back."

The scene began, and I watched as Satine pulled Christian into her (imaginary for now) boudoir. The dialogue played out, with Satine pretending to be overly aroused by Christian's poetry. She hammed it up, but she was supposed to, and everybody chuckled at her display.

Damon was wonderful in his role, bringing a sort of masculine vulnerability and inexperience that encapsulated Christian's character. He was animated, the way he spoke vivid, and I knew it was true when he told me he felt free when he acted. Free of the shackles of his own identity.

And then, when he burst into song, I was certain the people sitting in the Gods would have goose pimples, just like Jacob wanted. There was absolutely nothing quite like Damon when he sang. My entire body tingled with energy as I sat on the floor directly in his line of sight. I couldn't see Alicia because her back was facing me, but I was certain she didn't have to use too many of her acting skills right then to portray Satine falling for the man standing before her.

He was just incredible. It was all I could do not to sigh, especially after the intense moment we'd shared outside Iggy's office. When he glanced at me, singing the line about not remembering if her eyes are green or blue, his gaze bore into mine and my entire body tensed. I felt like I was having heart palpitations, and for the rest of the song I knew he was singing to me. I could just feel it.

"Very good. You were a little stiff at first, but about midway through the number, I really started to believe you. Excellent work," said Jacob.

I swallowed, struck by his words. It had been about halfway through the song that Damon had looked at me, but I tried not to obsess too much on what that could mean.

"Now," said Jacob, ushering Blake and a few of the other lead actors forward, "we'll rehearse The Pitch again. This scene comes directly after 'Your Song,' but we haven't practiced it with our new Duke yet."

I stood to assist Iggy with the choreography, catching Blake's eye as I crossed the studio. He wore a familiar look of interest, and a small shiver trickled over me. That was the same look he used to give me when he wanted sex, and even though I had no interest in rekindling anything with him, it still made me remember. Blake had been fantastic in bed, one of the best I'd ever had.

A small smirk graced his mouth then, like he knew what I was thinking about. I plastered on a placid expression and tried not to look at him after that, focusing on directing the dancers and pointedly ignoring him from there on out.

Never. I'd never be a fool for him again.

I knew it with a keen certainty, but I couldn't be sure if it was because I had a newfound strength in myself, or if I was becoming a fool again, only this time for a different man. Once more I thought of Damon's words, a shiver encapsulating my body.

You captivate me.

Do I captivate you?

Yes, Damon, you captivate me. And it's terrifying.

Twelve.
Rose

I didn't see much of Damon over the next few days and was busy preparing for Julian's birthday. On Saturday morning I woke up with a whopper of a headache and knew for certain it was down to the stressful, tension-filled week I'd had. Blake's involvement in the production turned my work days into a minefield of avoidance, and at the same time I had my burgeoning feelings for Damon to contend with.

I was both thankful for and irritated by Alicia, who always seemed to be by his side. It made sense, of course. They were playing the leads and had a lot of scenes together, but even at lunch she managed to hog his attention, and I never really got the chance to speak with him.

Sitting in bed, I rubbed at my temples and picked up my phone. I shot off a message to Iggy, asking if he could do me a massive favour. Before I knew it, he was knocking on the door to the apartment, his arms full of shopping bags, ready to take over the party preparations.

"Go take some painkillers and get a nap," he told me. "I'll make sure this place is fit to host royalty by the time I'm done."

I said it before but I'd say it again — I really loved my boss. Sure, he had his moments, but didn't we all. Iggy had always been more like an eccentric father figure to me than an employer.

Julian was spending the day getting pampered at a health spa, so we had lots of time to transform the apartment into party central. Or at least, Iggy did. I went to bed as instructed and woke up only half an hour before the guests were supposed to arrive. I couldn't believe I'd slept most of the day.

Walking out of my bedroom still in my pyjamas, I found Iggy sharing a glass of wine with Farrah, who must have arrived while I was sleeping.

"So, how's the patient feeling?" Iggy asked as he took me in.

"Much better," I answered, mustering a smile. "Thank you so much for doing all this. The place looks amazing."

"It was no trouble at all," said Iggy, waving away my thanks as I looked around the apartment. He'd decked the place out in the gold and silver decorations I'd bought, and in the kitchen there were trays upon trays of finger foods, alongside at least two dozen bottles of wine and champagne. A second later he was at my side, ushering me back to my bedroom.

"Go shower and doll yourself up a bit. You look like crap," he said, and I had to laugh at his honesty.

Inside my *en-suite* I turned on the water, waiting for it to heat up before stepping under the spray. The hot water warmed my bones, and I spent extra time exfoliating and shaving my legs. When I got out, I could hear the party guests already starting to arrive. I felt so much better than I had that morning, so even though I was late, I took my time getting ready. After all, I knew Julian wouldn't make an appearance until an hour that could be considered fashionably late.

I wrapped myself in a towel before going to pick out something to wear. Settling on a dark blue dress that brought out the colour of my eyes, I laid it out on the bed with some underwear and hold-up stockings before going to blow-dry my hair. It was after my makeup was done that I pulled off the towel and began to put on my underwear.

I'd barely gotten the stockings on and was just about to pick up the bra when my bedroom door opened and I heard a masculine intake of breath.

Turning almost in slow motion, I found Damon standing frozen in my doorway, his eyes dark as he took me in. Tiny tendrils of awareness pricked at my skin, and I began to feel my nipples tighten from his stare alone.

My voice was barely a whisper. "What are you doing?"

He cleared his throat, his eyes still glued to me, before starting to apologise. "Fuck, sorry…." His voice trailed off, and I realised I hadn't made a single move to cover myself. I hurried over to my closet and grabbed a black robe before shrugging into it.

When I looked at Damon again, he seemed to be struggling, his gaze levelled intently on the floor.

"You can look now," I said, and he glanced up, exhaling.

"Sorry."

"You already said that."

"I should go." He turned to leave, but my voice stopped him.

"If you were going to go, you should have done it while I was still naked," I said quietly. "I'm covered now, so why don't you just come in and tell me what you wanted. And please, shut the door."

My voice was shaky and my stomach tight with nervous tension. It was arousing that he'd seen me half dressed, but at the same time incredibly embarrassing. Had he liked what he'd seen?

Damon went and closed the door, sealing us in privacy. The tension thickened, and I suddenly realised it was probably a bad idea asking him to stay.

"I've barely seen you all week," he said on a deep exhalation, still standing several feet away from me. Right then, I was thankful for the distance.

I tightened my robe and tipped my chin up. "You've been busy," I replied simply. The rest of the sentence was implied: *You've been busy – with your costar.*

As though echoing my thoughts, he went on, "I came here tonight with Alicia."

"Okay...."

"She showed up at the house, and I couldn't get rid of her."

I tried to play it cool. "Why are you telling me all this, Damon?"

He swallowed thickly before laying his dark eyes on me. So much was communicated in the silence, but then all he said was, "I didn't invite her. I don't even know how she got my address."

I turned away and picked up a bottle of perfume from my dresser, shakily spraying some on my wrists and neck. "Like I told you before, you don't need to explain yourself. We're friends, but that doesn't mean you're obliged to inform me about your romantic life."

He grew still after I said it but didn't reply. Waves of tension rolled over him, and then he took several strides across my room until he was next to me. I didn't look at him, but instead gave him my profile. The room was so quiet; I listened to him breathe as he looked at me. A flush broke out over my neck and chest under his attention.

When my gaze flicked down momentarily, I noticed he was hard. My lips parted on a small gasp. I wondered if he was aroused because of what he'd seen. The spot between my legs quivered, and I instinctively clenched my thighs to dull the ache. He took my hand, lifting it and inhaling the scent of my perfume on the inside of my wrist.

"You smell like orange blossom," he murmured, and my throat grew dry.

I stood there, frozen, as he made eye contact with me before pressing his lips to the skin he'd just inhaled. Time stood still and I closed my eyes, savouring the connection. Then he drew away, a struggle in the set of his mouth.

"I'll go get you a drink," he murmured hastily and I nodded, thankful for a reprieve.

He lowered my hand, then turned and walked out of the room. I felt like I could finally breathe again as I desperately glanced around, trying to remember what I was supposed to be doing.

Dressing. Right, I was supposed to be getting dressed. Grabbing my things, I went inside the *en-suite* and quickly put on my outfit. The dress fitted tightly to my form, outlining my curves and emphasising the swell of my chest. All of a sudden, I felt far too bare. After the way Damon had looked at me, devouring me with his eyes, I sort of wanted to cover up.

Running my fingers through the waves of my hair before topping up my lip gloss, I put on my heels and walked back out into the room. Damon stood by my dresser, a glass of white wine in hand. His gaze wandered from my face to my neck before roving down over my body. I was exposed to him in that moment in a way that caused an unbearable heat to simmer just below the surface of my skin.

"You're beautiful," he said, handing me the glass.

139

My breath caught, my throat constricting at the devastatingly simple compliment. I took the wine and quietly uttered my thanks before taking a seat on the bed. I needed a minute to just sit down and get my bearings. If only Damon weren't standing there, staring at me like he wanted to ravage me. Perhaps I should have suggested we go out and join the party.

"Julian hasn't arrived yet, has he?" I asked, looking up to find Damon's attention trained on one of my partially opened drawers. And of course, it was my underwear drawer. A couple of my lacy undergarments were on display.

He closed his eyes for a second and swallowed before answering, "No, not yet."

"That's a relief," I said, and took a sip of wine. "He would've given me hell if I missed his grand entrance."

He didn't reply, and I thought he might still be preoccupied with my underwear. Getting up, I placed my glass on the dresser and went to close the drawer. "Sorry, um, I wasn't expecting anyone to come in here."

"It's my fault. I should have waited for you to come out, but I really wanted to see you."

I glanced at him and couldn't handle how he was looking at me, so I swiftly changed the subject. "You're getting better at dancing. I've been watching you during rehearsals."

He tilted his head, his eyes calculating. "Think I could still do with a few more private lessons."

"Yeah?"

He nodded and reached down to tuck a strand of hair behind my ear, his fingers lingering at my neck. My phone, which was sitting on my dresser, buzzed with a text. I

140

picked it up while Damon continued to stroke just below my earlobe. It was from Julian.

I'll be arriving in ten minutes. Make sure everybody's ready.

Damon must have been reading the text over my shoulder, because he chuckled low.

"I thought this was supposed to be a surprise party."

I smiled. "Yeah, just wait and see. He'll put all the actors in the room to shame when he comes in."

I quickly typed out a reply.

They'll be ready. Text when you're outside.

I tried to think of somewhere to keep my phone, but my dress had no pockets. With no other choice, I slid it into the cup of my bra. Damon watched with wry interest.

"Don't laugh. I never do this, but I need my phone on me for when Julian gets here and I don't have any pockets."

"I can mind it for you," he offered.

"Oh," I said in surprise. "That'd be great, thanks. Less chance of breast cancer and all that," I went on stupidly, and was just about to take it out when Damon reached forward and I froze. He ran his knuckles over my bare collarbone, then slid his fingers inside my bra, deftly plucking out the phone. I closed my eyes and swallowed at the sensation of his warm, masculine fingers brushing my breast.

"Three, three, seven, nine," I said, eyes still closed.

Damon's voice was a husky rumble. "Pardon?"

"That's my pin code, so you can check the message when Julian texts."

"Three, three, seven, nine," he repeated, and I opened my eyes to find him staring at me with a mixture of fondness and lust. Okay, so normally I wondered a lot what went on in his head, especially since he was so closed off at times. But in that moment, I knew he desired me. It was the unexpected boob sighting. That had to be the reason.

I cleared my throat and said softly, "I'd better get out there. Poor Iggy must be run ragged with all the preparations."

He coughed, looking a tad sheepish. "Aye. I'll be out in a minute."

I looked at him quizzically and he motioned to the seat of his pants, where he was very visibly hard. My mouth formed a round "O" in realisation.

"Right, of course. Take as much time as you, uh, need," I said, awkwardly grabbing my wine glass and hurrying out the door. When I entered the living area, I exhaled heavily, my entire body tingling from the encounter in my room.

I was delighted to find a bunch of guests had already arrived, but not so delighted to find that one of those guests was Blake. His eyes trailed down my body in blatant appreciation, but his attention didn't feel the same as Damon's. With Blake it was all about sex, but with Damon there was a purity, a certain soulfulness to his appreciative looks. Perhaps the difference was that, unlike Blake, Damon actually cared about me as a person. Blake was all about his own selfish gratification.

It was jarring how clearly I could see him now, as opposed to the rose-tinted glasses I once wore. Though they did say that hindsight is twenty-twenty.

I went and gave Iggy a massive hug, thanking him again for being such a life-saver. Farrah was chatting with Alicia, and Blake had insinuated himself into the conversation. As though sensing his emergence from my room, I turned and saw Damon approach. Our eyes met, and he bent low to speak in my ear. "Julian just texted.

He's outside now and says he's waiting until he sees the lights turn off to come in."

"Thanks," I replied, and clinked my glass with a fork to address the room. "Okay, everyone, Julian will be here in just a minute. I'm going to turn the lights out, and then when he comes in, I'll switch them on and we can all shout 'surprise.'" I was met with lots of noises of agreement as I headed for the light switch. Damon followed, remaining at my side, and when the lights went out and everybody grew hushed, he whispered so that only I could hear, "You have beautiful tits, Rose."

His voice was low and gravelly, and I broke out in shivers, my palm sweaty where I held it by the light switch. My thighs trembled at his husky tone, images flooding my mind. I wished he'd touched me back in my room, taken control and not given me a chance to flee. I wanted to say something, but I couldn't seem to find my voice.

Would, *you have a very beautiful cock* suffice? At least, what I could see outlined beneath his pants looked beautiful.

A second later, the door was opening and everyone was jumping up to shout "happy birthday" to Julian as he came in, plastering an expression of surprise and glee on his face.

Everything got a little busy after that as I arranged all of Julian's gifts on the kitchen table for him. Blake seemed to always be within a few feet of me, and it was really getting on my nerves. Well, it was until Julian clocked him and declared loudly, "Ozzie, ya ol' hoebag, how're things?"

Unable to stifle my laughter, I watched as Julian slung an arm around Blake's shoulders. He didn't seem at all fazed by how Julian had addressed him, but that was Blake for you, completely self-involved.

"I'm good. Happy Birthday, by the way," Blake replied, and Julian shot me a mischievous grin.

"It'd be a lot happier if you'd sling your hook."

Alicia, who was standing nearby with a glass of champagne in hand, couldn't help but to address Julian. "Don't you think it's a little bit rude to speak to your guest like that?"

Julian's eyes shone at the challenge in her voice, dropping his arm from Blake as he approached her. "It's my party, Alicia darling, so I'll speak to my guests however I please." He was grinning, while Alicia narrowed her eyes to slits.

"If that's the case, then I'm surprised anyone bothered to show up," she replied cuttingly before turning and walking away, her hips swaying with sassy attitude. Unsurprisingly, Julian followed her. I sighed, sensing those two might end up murdering one another by the time the night was through. Well, either that or shagging each other's brains out.

"You could cut the sexual tension with a knife," Blake commented, sidling up to me, his tone friendly.

"What?" I replied stiffly.

A gleam came into his eyes. "Between Julian and Alicia."

"Oh, right. Yeah."

Turning away from him, I continued stacking the last few colourfully wrapped gifts on the table. Julian was going to have a ball opening all these. I smiled at the thought, and Blake misinterpreted it as directed at him.

"Now, was that so hard? I've missed your smiles," he purred, and this close I could smell the Issey Miyake cologne he always wore. Three things would forever remind me of Blake: Issey Miyake, Twinning's Breakfast

Blend, and custard creams. I'd had to buy a different brand of tea ever since he cast me aside, and that truly bothered me. I used to love Twinning's.

"I'm smiling at the gifts. Not at you," I said, finally meeting his gaze as I placed a hand on my hip. "By the way, did you ever manage to bed your last leading lady? I remember you being quite determined."

Blake winced. "I was despicable to you. I know that."

"As far as I can see, you're still the same person," I replied casually.

Now his lips thinned as he frowned, eyes studying me. "You do realise I was off my head on coke the entire time we were together, don't you?"

I gaped at him, my mouth opening and closing as I tried to comprehend what he'd just said. "You were…what?"

He nodded and ran a hand through his tousled locks. "I got myself into a program just last month. I'm three weeks clean," he said, and pulled his phone from his pocket to show me his sobriety app.

"But…but you never seemed like you were on drugs. I don't understand," I replied, reeling from the information.

"I'd been abusing my body for a long time, Rose. I knew how to hide it. Besides, didn't you ever wonder about all the crap I used to talk? Bullshitting on and on about the meaning of life and the size of the universe?"

My brows drew together. "That was one of the things I liked about you. I enjoyed talking about all that stuff."

Now he laughed softly. "You're way too nice for your own good. I was a piece of shit who didn't deserve the time of day from you. Now I just want to make amends."

My expression turned cynical. "How?"

145

He took a step closer, his gaze moving from my lips, then up to my eyes. "By proving to you that I'm worthy. I never should have let you go." He tried to take my hand into his, but I pulled away.

"Don't touch me."

Blake exhaled and dropped his head as though in shame. "Right, yes, I won't do that again. I'm sorry."

I didn't know what to say, and I was sure my bewilderment was written all over my face. Without another word, I left Blake standing there and went to find Julian. I needed to talk, needed my best friend to reassure me that I wasn't losing my mind. Had Blake really been high the entire time we were together? Somehow that didn't make me feel better about his behaviour. No, it made me feel worse, because what kind of dimwit doesn't notice that the man she's sleeping with is on drugs?

I searched the entire apartment but still couldn't find Julian, so I headed for his bedroom. I walked down the hall that led off from the living area and was just about to knock on his door when it opened. Alicia emerged, looking slightly less put-together than she had earlier. Her face paled momentarily, but then she plastered on a breezy smile.

"Rose," she said.

"Alicia," I replied.

Flipping her hair over one shoulder, she stepped past me and back out into the apartment. When I entered Julian's bedroom I found him leaning against the wall, his slim black tie askew and a recognisable shade of pink lipstick smeared on his mouth. It was the exact same shade Alicia had been wearing.

I let out a disbelieving laugh. "You didn't!"

Julian grinned. "I did."

I laughed some more before flopping down onto the end of his bed. "I'm not even going to ask."

"No need. She wants me. Now it's only a matter of time." The confidence in his voice told me Alicia was in for it – well and truly in for it. Retrieving a slim cigarette holder from the pocket of his slacks, Julian pulled one out and lit up.

"So, what did you come interrupting a perfectly good time for?" he asked, exhaling a billow of smoke.

"It looked like your good time was already over. And I came to tell you about the interesting conversation I just had with Blake."

Julian's eyes shone with interest. "Oh, really? Do tell."

"He said he was on drugs while we were together, and that he's three weeks clean. He even showed me this sobriety app on his phone."

My friend arched an eyebrow. "Major Tom was a junkie? Didn't see that one coming."

I sighed. "Me, neither. Am I a horrible person that I never even realised?"

Julian tutted. "Of course not. Some people are very good at hiding these things. In her day, my mother could down an entire bottle of gin and still look like she just stepped off the pages of a fashion catalogue. And let's not even get started on the kind of sneaky behaviour I could pull off during my addiction." He paused for a second to eye me while he smoked. "What was his poison?"

"Cocaine, apparently."

"That's a hard one to disguise."

"I know. I just thought he was naturally hyper."

Julian laughed. "Oh, Rose."

"Shut up. I feel terrible, but that doesn't mean I'm prepared to be his friend. Drugs or not, he hurt me."

147

"And Hell hath no fury like a woman scorned," Julian added as he eyed me perceptively.

I shook my head, silently taking the cigarette from him and inhaling a drag. "I'm not scorned, not anymore. I just don't trust him. Sure, he might be clean now, but that doesn't mean he'll stay that way. I like my life how it is, and letting someone like Blake back into it could mess with the balance."

"Not to mention there are other things holding your interest these days," Julian chirped. "Speaking of which, why did Damon have your phone?"

"Oh. I asked him to keep an eye on it for when you texted. Actually, he still has it. I should go get it from him."

I rose from the bed, handing Julian back his smoke.

"Hurry," my friend urged me humorously. "You don't want him finding all those sexy selfies you take on the sly."

I narrowed my gaze. "I'll have you know my phone is selfie free. Not all of us can't get enough of the sight of our own faces, Julian."

He chuckled, and I left his bedroom. When I entered the living area, the party seemed to be in full swing. There was a group gathered around Iggy as he sipped on a glass of wine and recounted some story they all seemed to be finding fascinating. I'd bet my last penny he was telling them about the weekend he spent with Boy George.

Both Alicia and Damon were among the group, and Alicia was standing way too close to Damon for my liking. Ugh. She thought she could kiss Julian and keep it her dirty little secret, while returning to the party and acting like Damon was the only one for her.

Excuse me while I roll my eyes.

I approached and tugged on Damon's arm. He glanced at me.

"Hey," I said quietly. "Could I get my phone back?"

"Sure," he said, moving away from Alicia to pull the phone from his pocket and hand it to me.

"Thanks."

"Your dress is very pretty, Rose," said Alicia, the compliment dripping with honey. Perhaps she thought that if she buttered me up, I wouldn't reveal her excursion in Julian's bedroom to Damon.

"Thanks. Yours is, too." I peered up at Damon, who wore a vaguely uncomfortable look. He clearly didn't know what to do about Alicia, and she was very obviously determined to stick to him like glue for the evening. I actually felt a little bad for him. Well, that and obscenely jealous.

Julian interrupted all conversations as he re-entered the room and loudly made an announcement. "Okay, everybody who wants to take part in a game of Spin the Bottle, gather round and take a seat on the living room floor. The rest of you dirty voyeurs can hang about and watch, or completely ignore us. Whatever wets your whistle."

I almost groaned, preparing to make a speedy exit, when all of a sudden Iggy grabbed my hand and pulled me down to sit on the floor.

"Let go!" I hissed, but he only smiled at me blandly.

"Rose dear, I spent the entire day slaving away for you. The least you can do to repay me is take part in a little game of Spin the Bottle." There was a sparkle in his eye that told me he was up to something, and I knew from past experience there was no end to the mischief my boss could create with when fuelled by several glasses of white wine.

In the end about fifteen of us had made a circle on the floor, the twenty or so other party guests happy to chat amongst themselves and ignore Julian's childish games. You'd swear we were attending a sweet sixteen. I caught Damon's eye directly across from me on the other side of the circle, and thought Alicia must have roped him into taking part. He looked like he'd rather be anywhere else right then – like say, dancing the Macarena naked in front of five thousand people. Still, I wished he wasn't playing. The idea of Damon kissing any of the women currently present made my stomach twist with discomfort.

Julian, who still had yet to sit down, came and placed a glass of champagne in my hand before sitting next to me. He put an empty wine bottle in the middle of the floor and spun it. It landed on a woman, one of the backing dancers from the show who I'd invited. When he spun it again, it landed on a man I didn't know, but who must've been an acquaintance of Julian's. The two crawled across to each other and kissed awkwardly at first, but then they seemed to get into it and I noticed a definite hint of tongue action.

"Get a room!" Iggy jeered loudly and they pulled apart, both looking slightly breathless.

Julian laughed with devilish glee, and a few more kisses followed. Iggy ended up kissing Farrah, and he hammed it up by licking her face first before mussing up her hair like a couple in an '80s music video. I chuckled and tucked my legs under my bottom, sipping my champagne and sort of getting into the game. It was fun, so long as that bottle never landed on me. I wholeheartedly made an effort to ignore the fact that Blake was standing just outside the circle, not taking part but watching. It struck me as odd, though, because he was usually the type to relish this sort of thing.

Sitting on the floor was giving me pins and needles in my feet, so I slipped off my heels and rubbed at the base of my foot. Feeling someone's attention, I looked up and saw Damon watching the movement of my fingers. For some reason it made me flush, so I pulled my hand back into my lap. Iggy took a turn spinning the bottle, and I was too busy wondering about the way Damon had been looking at me that I didn't immediately realise it was pointing at me.

Shit.

Iggy rubbed his hands together, preparing to spin it a second time. "Okay, Rose, let's find you a kissing partner, shall we?"

I closed my eyes, tension coiling in the pit of my stomach, and when I opened them, the first thing I noticed was the unhappy slant to Alicia's mouth. The bottle was pointing at Damon, and there was some kind of annoyance in his expression.

"Better pucker up, Christian," Iggy crooned in delight, teasing Damon as he addressed him by his character's name.

I picked up my glass and downed the rest of its contents before crawling on my hands and knees over to where Damon sat. When I reached him, I sat back and whispered, "Sorry about this." I wasn't entirely sure why I was apologising. It was probably because he still seemed annoyed for some reason.

He reached out and took my hand in his, pulling me close so he could murmur in my ear, "Don't be."

"You don't seem happy," I ventured, still quiet enough so that only he could hear.

"I'm not."

My stomach lurched. He didn't want to kiss me. But why? Back in my bedroom he seemed ready to throw me down on the bed and fuck me into oblivion. Now he looked like he'd rather kiss anyone else in the world, and it was making me nervous and unsure.

"Take your time, you two," Iggy put in sarcastically. "It's not like we haven't got all night or anything."

I turned and shot my boss a dark look. He'd been the orchestrator of this scenario to a certain extent, and I wasn't quite sure he hadn't somehow made the bottle stop on Damon. Turning back to the man in question, I leaned closer, placing my hands on his shoulders and inhaling a deep breath. This was it.

I was about to kiss Damon Atwood.

Thirteen.

Damon

This wasn't how I envisioned our first kiss playing out, not in a roomful of people, and certainly not in the middle of a fucking party where I couldn't do all the things I'd been wanting to do to her for weeks.

The memory of her tits, full and heavy with perfect rosy nipples, was branded into my skull. The way it felt when I brushed one with the back of my hand to remove the phone from her bra, so soft, made my head numb. I felt like I'd been walking around in a constant state of arousal, which was a pain when you were stuck in an apartment with forty or so virtual strangers.

Rose had both her hands braced on my shoulders, but she only stared at me. I noticed her tremble a little. She was nervous. Fuck. My irritability at the situation couldn't have helped matters. She thought I didn't want to kiss her, but bloody hell I did. I just knew that once I started, there was a good chance I wouldn't be able to stop.

I'd want to lose my hand under the skirt of her dress, feel her slickness.

I'd want to bury my face in her abundant, beautiful fucking cleavage until I couldn't breathe.

She seemed frozen in place, so I pulled her hands from my shoulders and lifted her into my lap. I took control, not giving her a choice. If this was going to be our first kiss, I was going to make it count. Fuck all the people watching us. For once in my life I was going to be unselfconscious about something. I was going to take fucking charge.

She moved onto me with ease, and her dress rode up as she levelled her thighs on either side of my hips. The edges of her lacy hold up stockings were revealed and it was all I could do not to groan at the sight. I palmed her cheek, caressed it softly, and noticed her let out the tiniest gasp.

I whispered my lips across hers first, feather light, before capturing them fiercely and sinking my hand into her hair. She let out a sexy little whimper. I tugged on her hair, adjusting her head so I could kiss her more deeply. She moved on me, as though trying to climb closer, and I felt my balls tighten as I began to harden. She was so sexy in a completely oblivious way, and when I felt the heat between her legs press into me, I had to stifle a groan.

Her arms came to wrap around my neck, her tongue moving with mine as I savoured her. She tasted like champagne and sunshine. I couldn't get enough. Her full, round chest pushed into me torturously, and I knew I had to end the kiss before I took her right there on the floor. Giving her hair one more gentle tug, I felt her shudder, like she liked it.

I fucking loved that she liked it.

Every single time she wore a ponytail to rehearsals, I'd had visions of gripping her hair in my fist as I sank into her from behind. Pulling back, I gave her bottom lip the tiniest nip. Her eyes were closed. She breathed heavily as they fluttered open, and for a second I was lost in a sea of blue.

"Hey," she whispered, her gaze unfocused.

"Hi," I whispered back.

She bit her lip, dazed. "Um…"

"Rose, I just need to…" I murmured, cupping her cheek again and moving to capture her mouth one last time. Her lips had me hypnotised. I only remembered the people watching when someone spoke.

"Well, that was fucking *hot*," Farrah exclaimed from the other side of the circle, knocking back a mouthful of wine.

"If that's what you're into," Julian commented with a wink, and Rose shot him a dark look. He raised his hands in the air. "What? I'm sure you two would have very lovely missionary sex with lots of eye contact and murmured declarations. That's not my cup of tea, is all I'm saying."

Rose was suddenly blushing beautifully. I wanted to caress her cheek again, but she moved further away from me and returned to where she'd been sitting previously. If only Julian could see the fantasies I'd been having of doggy-style sex with Rose, he might have had to rethink his prediction.

Alicia was decidedly quiet beside me, but I didn't look to see her reaction to the kiss. I'd never given her any indication I was interested, so I couldn't really be held accountable for putting her nose out of joint.

I wanted Rose. Only Rose.

In the end I didn't have to look, because she got up from the floor, brushing down her skirt and announcing, "I'm bored. I'm going to get more champagne."

Without a word Julian went after her, and everyone seemed to silently accept that the game was over. When I saw Rose making her way over to the kitchen, I stood and intercepted her.

"We okay?" I asked, studying her pretty features. She didn't say anything for a moment, and wouldn't – or maybe couldn't – meet my gaze. I tilted her chin up with the tips of my fingers. "I didn't mean to make you uncomfortable with what I said earlier, if I did…."

She shook her head as she swallowed. "No, no, you didn't. I liked…." She paused to lower her gaze again.

When she spoke, it was to the floor, and I really hated how she refused to give me her eyes. "I mean, I don't exactly find it unpleasant when you say stuff like that." When she finally looked up, her expression was meaningful, and something flipped inside me.

She enjoyed when I spoke to her explicitly? In that case, I could murmur dirty nothings to her all night long.

"So," she went on, breaking the moment and clearing her throat, "another drink?"

"Yeah, another drink," I agreed in a warm voice before bending low to whisper in her ear, "Those stockings are sexy as fuck, by the way. I can't stop thinking about how they'd look like without the dress."

She stilled, her throat bobbing as she swallowed. "D-damon."

"Rose?" I slid my hand along the curve of her spine and she went silent as she breathed heavily and closed her eyes.

"Maybe I'll show you sometime," she said shakily.

It was all I could do not to drag her into her bedroom and demand she show me now. "I'll hold you to that," I replied.

She started walking again and I followed her to the kitchen, where Julian stood a few feet away from Alicia, a look on his face like he wanted to eat her alive. She was ignoring him by chatting with some other party guests.

I still wasn't too sure what to make of Rose's flatmate. There were too many question marks hanging over his head. He seemed like a normal enough bloke, so I just didn't understand why he chose to do what he did for a living. Admittedly, I was biased, and, thanks to my father, had some fairly traumatic memories of prostitutes. This was why I was trying to reserve judgment where Julian was concerned.

"Here you go," said Rose, handing me a bottle of Budweiser.

I allowed my fingers to skim over hers, and she shivered slightly. She was still feeling the kiss, same as me. I was just about to suggest we go somewhere a little more private, like her room, for instance, when some cheers sounded from the living area. Aside from the bedrooms, the entire apartment was open plan. I looked over the top of Rose's head to see Blake seated by the piano, taking requests from the party goers.

"That slag better not be trying to steal my birthday thunder," Julian commented dryly, right before Blake burst into a rendition of "I Got it from Agnes" by Tom Lehrer.

My gran used to love Tom Lehrer. She thought he was hilarious. Rose turned to see who was singing and I saw her lips turn downward, forming a frown.

"He always has to be the centre of attention," I heard her mutter under her breath.

I stood next to her in silence. Blake pointedly levelled his gaze in her direction. Rose's lips firmed and her cheeks began to grow flushed, though I thought it was in annoyance rather than embarrassment. The party-goers laughed at the innuendo in the song, while Rose placed her glass down on the table and said, "I need the bathroom."

I nodded and knocked back a gulp of beer. Only seconds after Rose left, Alicia was in front of me, one hand on her hip as she eyed me curiously.

"You like her, don't you?"

I almost choked on the beer. "Who?"

She cast her eyes to the ceiling like it was obvious. "Rose."

I gave her a stoic look. "I might."

"You don't kiss someone you only 'might' like the way you just kissed Rose, Damon. Aren't you worried?"

"Should I be?"

"Of course you should. She's got history with Blake, and he clearly still has a thing for her. He's barely taken his eyes off her all night."

I firmed my jaw, the notion making me want to break something. I didn't enjoy the feeling.

"She doesn't want him back."

"They all say that, and then before you know it, you're walking into their trailer and finding them naked and fucking on the couch."

I stared at her, perplexed.

"Sorry. I'm letting my own experiences cloud my judgement. I'm sure Rose would never hurt you like that."

"Did that happen to you?"

She tucked a strand of her scarlet hair behind her ear and leaned back against the counter. "Yes. About two years ago I was dating another actor, and I won't name any names, but let's just say he began cheating on me with his ex. I caught them both going at it in a trailer on set one day and naturally put an end to things." She tipped her glass to her mouth, all *c'est la vie*.

"I'm sorry."

She waved away my apology. "I'm over it now. Still, I know how much that shit can hurt, and I wouldn't want the same thing to happen to you with Rose."

Alicia gave my shoulder a tender squeeze and walked away. I stood in place, contemplating the idea of Rose giving Blake another chance. It made me feel sick to my stomach. I lifted my beer and almost downed the entire contents of the bottle in one go.

Before I knew it, the party had progressed, and I'd had more drinks than I could count. I sat in the living area with Farrah and Iggy as they both recounted all manner of interesting stories from their years working on the West End.

Rose remained out of sight. In fact, I hadn't seen her since she'd disappeared to use the bathroom. I clenched my beer bottle tightly, almost smashing the thing in my hand as I imagined her in her room with Blake, patching things up. My tension faded when I saw Blake over by the window, chatting with a group of people.

But where was Rose?

I wanted to go find her, but at the same time I didn't want to suffocate her, so I tried to keep from searching the apartment for where she'd hidden herself away. The hours went by, and slowly but surely the party guests started to leave. The alcohol must've taken hold, because the next thing I knew, it was morning and I was waking up on the couch. Alicia was next to me, her head resting on my shoulder as she lightly snored. On the opposite couch were Julian, Iggy, and Farrah, all asleep, too.

Christ, I felt like death warmed up.

Memories began trickling back. We'd well and truly burned the midnight oil, having drunken discussions about all sorts of random topics. Rubbing at my eyes, I blinked a few times, peering around at the mess left over from the night before.

At first the apartment seemed silent, but then I heard voices coming from the direction of the kitchen.

"I can manage by myself, Blake. You don't need to help," said Rose quietly, probably not wanting to wake anyone.

"I'm here, aren't I? I might as well do something useful."

Rose sighed, and I heard the crinkle of a plastic bag as she cleaned up. "Just go home. It's morning. The party's over."

"I have nothing on today. Want to hang out once the apartment's clean?"

"Have you got a hearing problem? I said I don't need your help."

"Yeah, well, I'm going to help you anyway."

"Good God, fine, help me if it'll make you happy, but I'm not hanging out with you today. I have plans."

"And what would those be?"

"Washing my hair."

"You clearly just showered."

"And you clearly haven't. All the more reason for you to *go home*."

Blake laughed deeply, like he was enjoying her prickliness. It got on my nerves. The bastard needed to leave Rose the fuck alone. Remembering that Alicia's head was resting on my shoulder, but not quite remembering *how* it had gotten there, my stomach dropped. Rose would've clearly had to walk through the living area to get to the kitchen and seen us.

Fuck, this looked bad.

Shifting my body slightly, I stretched and slid away from my costar. When I stood from the couch and turned around, Rose was the first thing I saw. She was in the kitchen, wearing a pair of plastic gloves and collecting rubbish in a bin bag. Blake was just a few feet away from her, eyeing me with an indecipherable expression.

Rose gave me a weak smile. "Morning, sunshine. How's your head?"

160

I rubbed at jaw. "Thumping. Can I use your bathroom?"

She nodded. "Yes, sure. There are some new toothbrushes under the sink if you'd like to use one."

"Thank you," I said, looking at Blake and then back to her.

As I headed off down the hallway, I heard him complain, "You didn't offer me a toothbrush."

"That's because we aren't friends," Rose replied coldly. "Damon's my friend."

Her chilly response almost made my lips curve in a smile. In the bathroom I held my hands under the tap for a while, feeling grubby, before washing my face and brushing my teeth. I gave myself a sniff and found I didn't smell too funky, so I thought I'd make do until I could get back to my place. When I emerged, everyone else had woken up. Iggy called good morning to me as Julian suggested we all head out to a nearby café for some breakfast.

"I haven't finished cleaning yet," said Rose as she pulled off her rubber gloves.

"Don't worry about that. I'll have Pippa come around while we're out to spruce the place up."

"Who's Pippa?" Farrah enquired.

"His cleaning lady," Rose answered with a hint of disapproval. "I try to tell him we don't need some woman to clean the apartment when we're perfectly capable of doing it ourselves, but he won't listen."

Julian held out his hands. "These fingers were made for far more important things than scrubbing toilets."

Mostly everyone laughed, except for Alicia. She seemed determined to be cold with Julian, and I didn't really understand why. She didn't know what he did for a

161

living, at least I thought she didn't, so it couldn't be that. Maybe he just rubbed her up the wrong way.

About twenty minutes later, we all left the apartment to complete the short walk to the café down the street. Along the way, I caught hold of Rose's elbow. She glanced at me, letting some of the others pass until we were alone.

"What is it, Damon?" she asked. There was no annoyance or irritability in her voice, so maybe she already knew that my sleeping next to Alicia had been entirely innocent.

"I can't remember falling asleep last night. I was drunk," I said, hoping she got the underlying message. Christ, it felt like I was constantly trying to explain that my feelings toward Alicia were purely platonic – if that. I liked her well enough as a work colleague, but I didn't see myself staying friends with her after the show closed.

Rose tugged her coat sleeves down over her wrists. I studied her face, free of makeup, and wondered if any woman had ever seemed so pretty to me.

"Oh, right. Well, I kind of flaked out on the party early. Sorry about that. After a while I just wasn't really in the mood anymore, so I hid in my room and went to sleep."

This news surprised me. "You slept through all that noise?"

She gave a slight shrug. "Earplugs are a wonderful invention."

I nodded. "Well, just so you know, I didn't intentionally sleep next to Alicia. I just woke up, and there she was."

Rose's eyes glittered with humour. "It sounds a little creepy when you put it like that."

My lips twitched in amusement. "True."

She drew closer, putting her hand over her mouth and whispering theatrically, "Oh, my God, what if she roofied you?"

I think it shocked us both when I barked a loud laugh.

"You're daft."

"And you should consider laughing more," said Rose. "It's a wonderful sound. Also, I'm not daft, I'm hilarious. Come on, let's go get some food before we both starve to death."

At the café we were seated at a long table. I took the place next to Rose, and Iggy sat on the other side of me. It was a relief, because I really needed to distance myself from Alicia for a while. There were only so many times that Rose was going to let things slide, and I was tired of messing everything up.

We all put in our orders, and the waiter came around to serve us coffee, tea, and orange juice.

"Oh, God," Farrah complained as she pressed her fingers to her temples. "I'm so regretting all those glasses of champagne last night. I'm gonna be feeling this hangover for *days*."

Julian chuckled, and she stabbed a finger at him. "Yeah, yeah, laugh it up, pretty boy. Just you wait until you hit forty. You'll be as bad as me. I'm really not looking forward to getting up for this eight o'clock meeting I have tomorrow."

Julian eyed her pointedly. "You need to take a leaf out of my book and quit the demon drink. Also, being your own boss helps. That way if you're hung over, you can simply take the morning off."

"What is it that you do anyway?" Alicia cut in with an arched brow.

Julian smiled at her widely from across the table. "I'm a freelance children's entertainer," he lied. "You know, for parties and such."

Alicia let out a disdainful chuckle. "What, like a clown?"

"Yes," said Julian, running his thumb over his bottom lip. "Exactly like a clown. Quite similar to being an actor, I imagine."

"Easy there, Jules," said Iggy. "Half the people at this table are actors. You don't want to go down that road."

"No, I want to hear what he has to say," Alicia interjected. "What's so clown-like about being an actor? And I know you're lying about that being your job, by the way."

"How shrewd of you," Julian answered.

Alicia stood firm. "You still haven't explained yourself."

"Well, isn't it obvious? An actor performs to entertain people, sometimes even humiliating themselves, just like a clown."

Alicia slammed her hand on the table, all the humour gone from her features. "I'm not a clown."

"I didn't say you were. I said you were *like* one."

"It's the same difference. My God, has anyone ever told you how rude and disrespectful you are sometimes?" Her voice grew shrill as she picked up her napkin to dab at her mouth. "Some manners would go a long way, you know." Once she'd finished speaking, she stood from the table, glancing around at the rest of us. "I'm sorry, everybody, but I think I'm going to leave now."

When I looked at Julian, he appeared momentarily regretful for what he'd said. Then he plastered on a devil-may-care expression, while Alicia said her goodbyes, put on her coat, and walked out onto the street to flag down a taxi.

Rose frowned at her friend. "Julian, that was a bit much."

"What? She brings it out of me."

"You should go after her, Damon," Blake suggested out of nowhere. I glanced at him. "You two did spend most of the night wrapped around each other on the couch, after all. It's the gentlemanly thing to do."

Was he fucking shitting me? Now I glowered, knowing exactly the game he was playing. Rose seemed to stiffen beside me. Blake was lucky I was averse to violence, because right then I might've punched him.

"I'm sure she'll be fine," I answered coldly before Julian stood and interrupted.

"No, I'll go after her. This is my fault."

He left, and through the window I could see that she was still standing by the side of the road, waiting for a taxi to stop for her. Julian emerged, and she said something to him that didn't look very kind. We all watched the silent conversation unfold. Julian was clearly trying to apologise, while Alicia threw some obviously barbed comments back at him.

"Love-hate is the best kind of love," Iggy sighed into his coffee cup. "All that passion. I'm a little jealous."

"What about love-love?" Rose spoke up. "Isn't that better? I don't get why people should have to half hate one another just for a relationship to be passionate. It seems a little dysfunctional, if you ask me."

"It is dysfunctional, but that's what makes it so exhilarating," said Iggy.

"Is that what you feel towards me these days, Rose, love-hate?" Blake enquired.

165

"Minus the love and you're right on the money," she threw back cuttingly.

Blake pouted at her in a way I was sure he thought was attractive. Then again, I wasn't exactly his target audience. "That's harsh."

"It's the truth."

"I agree with Rose," I said, coming to her defence. "There's absolutely nothing wrong with two people being together based on attraction and mutual respect."

"Yes, I get that there's nothing wrong with it," said Iggy. "But who'd want all that lovey-dovey stuff when you could be having passionate fights and mind-blowing make-up sex?"

"Sane people who aren't deranged," Rose answered, lifting her orange juice and taking a sip.

"And those who are confident enough in their bedroom skills that they don't need to rely on emotional trauma to create desire," I added quietly before realising I'd spoken so candidly. It suddenly felt like all eyes were on me, and I wished I hadn't spoken at all.

Iggy grinned and clasped his hands around his mug. "Okay, now I'm interested. Perhaps a non-dysfunctional relationship can have its advantages."

"Especially if it involves a tall, dark, and handsome Oscar winner with the dreamiest brown eyes you've ever seen," said Farrah, shooting me a wink.

I shifted uncomfortably and looked away, a little embarrassed. Rose was quiet beside me, and I wondered if she agreed with Farrah's summation. She glanced up at me from beneath her lashes for a second, but I couldn't tell what she was thinking. We were locked in a moment, and I had this urge to tuck a fallen strand of hair behind her ear.

Instead, I curled my fingers into a fist to keep my hands to myself.

When I looked out the window again, it seemed Julian had managed to calm Alicia down a little. They were still talking back and forth, but with fewer hand gestures than before. A taxi finally pulled up, and Alicia climbed inside. Julian returned to the café, not saying a word as he reclaimed his seat. He pressed his hand to his mug as though to check the temperature, then let out an irritated sigh. "Great, now my coffee's gone cold."

Rose shot him a look. "Serves you right."

"Yeah," Blake added, siding with Rose. "Didn't your mother ever teach you how to respect women?"

"Oh, up yours, Manwhore McGee," Julian threw back with casual bluntness.

It took everything in me not to spit the mouthful of tea I'd just drunk out all over the table.

Fourteen.
Rose

His lips had been so warm and intent, and I'd adored the way he'd ever so gently tugged on my hair, causing prickles of desire to trickle all the way down my spine.

My daydreams of the kiss I shared with Damon on Saturday night were taking over my Monday morning thoughts. We'd been practicing the dance routine for "Rhythm of the Night" when Jacob called for a fifteen-minute tea break. I took the opportunity to grab a coffee and listen to a few minutes of *Outlander*. It was getting closer to the sex scene, I could tell. Amid uncontrollable circumstances, Jamie and Claire had been married, and we all knew what happened on the wedding night. Winkety-wink. Perhaps during lunch I could cloister myself away somewhere to listen in private.

Shut up, I wasn't a perv.

"Hi, Rosie," I heard someone say, and pulled out my earphones to see Blake standing over me, a friendly smile on his face.

"Hello."

He toed the edge of my dance shoe. "You look pretty today."

"Thank you," I answered stiffly.

I was still trying to get my head around everything he'd told me during Julian's birthday party. If he was truly working to get over an addiction, then I didn't want to be mean to him. In fact, I was all for him cleaning up his life. But the fact still remained that he'd carelessly brushed me off like a troublesome piece of lint. So yes, I'd be cordial towards him, but I wasn't going to start reigniting our friendship, sharing tea and chats during rehearsal breaks like before.

Jacob called for Blake's attention, and I was glad for the reprieve. On the other side of the studio, I saw Damon standing with Eddie. His eyes were on me, and he cast me a questioning look. I returned it with a tiny shrug and watched as he pulled out his phone and began tapping on the screen. A second later a message popped up on mine.

Damon: *Are you okay?*

Rose: *Yes :-)*

Damon: *Can we share lunch today?*

Rose: *Sure.*

I shoved my phone back in my pocket and stood up to stretch, still feeling Damon's attention. It did strange things to me, and all of a sudden I felt giddy, my insides aflutter. We had another hour of practice before lunch, and I was suddenly looking forward to it far more than usual.

Unfortunately, Iggy was in a terror of a mood, and we suffered a gruelling hour because of it. It wasn't really his fault, though, and I could understand why he was feeling irritable. It seemed like everybody was off their game today, their moves sloppy and uncoordinated. I tried not to feel guilty for the fact that it might've been down to some of them being in attendance at Julian's party on Saturday night.

The moment he called for lunch, Iggy pulled me aside, letting free all of his frustrations over the mess our dancers were in. I did my best to console him, and amid all this, I completely forgot I'd agreed to meet Damon for lunch. When I finally managed to calm Iggy down, all I wanted to do was find a quiet spot, eat my sandwich, and try to de-stress from the nightmare we'd just endured.

In one of the small practice rooms, I found a chair, sat down, shoved my earphones in, and dug into my lunch. A couple of minutes later the door opened, and I glanced up to see Damon step inside. I hit "pause" on the audiobook and shot him a look of apology.

"Oh, my God, I'm so sorry! I completely forgot I was supposed to meet you. Iggy chewed my ear out over all the mistakes everybody was making during rehearsals, and I've just been so frazzled."

Damon waved away my apology. "No worries. Can I sit? It's okay if you'd rather be alone." He held a packed sandwich in his hand, alongside an apple and a bottle of energy drink.

"No, not at all," I said, patting the seat beside me as I wound up my earphones to put them away. Damon eyed them.

"Are you listening to *Outlander*?"

I nodded.

"You don't have to stop. I've actually been curious to see what Jamie and Claire have been up to," he admitted.

My heart skipped a beat as I remembered what part of the book I was on. The sex hadn't started yet, but I could tell it was about to. No way could I sit here listening to a sex scene while I ate lunch with Damon.

"Oh, no, it's all right," I said, but he reached out to take the earphones from me anyway, unwinding them with his long fingers.

"I want to listen with you," he said, somewhat gruffly.

I couldn't speak as he gently placed the bud in my ear before putting the other in his. I didn't do anything for a second and then realised he was waiting for me to hit "play." Oh, God, this was actually happening. Somehow I didn't quite have it in me to say, *I'm sorry, but I'd rather listen to this part on my own.*

So, with no more time left to dawdle, I moved my finger over the screen. The narrator's posh accent came on, reciting the last few lines of one chapter before announcing the title to the next: Revelations of the Bed Chamber.

Damon stiffened for a second before his dark eyes fell on me. I glanced at him, tried not to blush, and took a too-large bite out of my sandwich. It got lodged in my throat, and I had to work hard to swallow it down. I could tell Damon probably wanted to abandon ship, but he'd made such a fuss about listening that he couldn't really back out now.

We both ate in quiet for a while, just listening, but the entire time I was overly aware of Damon's presence. His breathing seemed heavy and tense, and I listened as he inhaled and exhaled. After a few more minutes, I closed my eyes, falling into the story and at the same time wishing Damon could touch me the same way Jamie was touching Claire.

He took her hands into his, smoothing his fingers over her palms.

I wanted Damon to smooth his fingers over mine.

They talked about their past experiences, like soon-to-be-lovers do.

I wanted to talk to Damon about my past, tell him everything and hear every word he had to say about his own.

When the characters started to kiss and touch, their need palpable, I felt Damon's eyes on me again. I didn't even have to look. The heat radiating off him was almost too much to bear. My cheeks grew flushed and I shifted in place, squeezing my thighs together to dull the ache being

171

this close to him created. If I were alone, I knew I wouldn't be aroused like this — it was the words, the picture they were painting, combined with his presence, that had me teetering on a knife's edge, wishing for the courage to simply grab him and press my mouth to his.

Blessedly, the scene didn't go on for too long, and I was glad. I wasn't sure how much more I could listen to without spontaneously combusting. Warmth met my skin then, and I looked down to see Damon take my hand into his. I glanced up into his soulful brown eyes and saw a world of want and need there. To my dismay, he didn't do anything but press his fingers into the cushion of my palm, drawing lines up and down that made my spine tingle.

I inhaled a sharp breath when his thumb brushed over the inside of my wrist, his gaze flaring at my reaction. You'd swear he just shoved his fingers inside my underwear instead of simply touching my wrist. My mouth fell open as he studied me, a question in his expression.

Do you want me like I want you?

Yes.

I hoped he could see my answer. Damon's attention fell to my lips, his gaze turning dark, when a few cast members passed outside the door, chatting noisily. He dropped my hand, and a moment elapsed before Iggy entered the room, clearly having been searching for me. He stood in the doorway, glancing between the two of us, then cleared his throat.

"Rose, we just had a delivery arrive downstairs. I need your help taking it to the storage room."

"Oh, right, sure," I said, dusting the few sandwich crumbs from my lap. When I stood, my earbud fell out, and I saw Damon was holding my iPod as he pressed "pause" on the story. He wrapped everything up and handed it to me, his fingers brushing my hand again. My skin ignited at his touch, and I tried to come down from the high of whatever it was we'd just shared.

"I can help," he offered, but Iggy waved him off.

"No need. It's only a small delivery. Rose and I can handle it."

I shot Damon a hesitant smile as I left, and followed Iggy downstairs. My boss didn't ask any questions about what he'd just walked in on, but instead he put me to work carrying boxes of new stretching mats upstairs to the storage room. Once there, I began taking inventory of the old ones and organising to have them disposed of. All the while I could still feel Damon's hand on mine, still see the way his eyes had devoured me, and I wanted to be back there. It was the most arousing experience of my life, and we hadn't even been doing anything sexual.

Alone in the storage room, I began to visualise what it would be like to be naked with Damon, to have his big, strong body over mine, taking control. A tidal wave of desire washed through me and I swallowed, my throat suddenly dry.

I felt somebody's presence in the room before a hot hand landed on my shoulder. The warmth sank into me, and I knew it must be Damon. He was still feeling what had happened between us, just like I was, and I was relieved that he'd come for me. Come to give me more than just a touch on my hand.

His fingers moved from my shoulder up to my neck, his thumb skimming the sensitive skin below my ear, and I moaned. He let out a breath that sounded surprised, and I moved my bottom into him, feeling him hard as stone as I pressed back. His arm wrapped around my middle, pulling me closer to his body. Lips whispered over the back of my neck, and I moaned a second time.

"God, I've missed this."

I froze, my eyes going wide as I stood there in horror. That hadn't been Damon's voice. It was Blake's. And suddenly everything that was wrong with the situation hit me at once. He didn't smell like Damon, his lips weren't as soft, and his arms were sinewy dancer's arms, not thick workman's arms, arms that had been sculpted by labouring on a fishing boat.

"Get off me," I whispered in a barely audible voice, too shocked to start pushing. Blake didn't hear me, or perhaps he was ignoring what I said, and continued planting kisses along my neck. Finally finding some brain cells, I turned in his hold and stepped away. He stared at me, looking aroused and confused. He had no right to be confused. Where did he get off touching me without my permission like this?

I was about to give him a piece of my mind when I sensed a third presence. When I looked over Blake's head, there in the open doorway stood Damon, and I'd never seen such a furious expression on his handsome face.

Our eyes connected, his filled with anger and hurt, mine filled with guilt and confusion, and then he turned on his heel and left.

"Rosie, come here," said Blake, grabbing my hand and trying to pull me back to him. Since he was still facing me, he had no idea that Damon had been there, watching as he kissed my bare neck and I ground myself off his erection. Jesus.

I felt sick, violently ill. This was such a bloody fuck-up.

"Stop it," I said, smacking him away.

"You liked me touching you. The noises you were making, fuck, Rose...."

At this I finally lost my temper. "Oh, for crying out loud, Blake. I thought you were somebody else!"

His expression was one of astonishment, but I didn't stick around to argue with him. Instead, I brushed swiftly past him and out the door, hurrying to catch up with Damon. Out in the studio, the cast were arriving back from lunch, the place a riot of activity. I pushed past bodies, searching for a tall dark-haired man, but I couldn't find him anywhere. Had he left?

"Rose, I need you over here," said Jacob, grabbing me by the elbow and leading me into a group of dancers. "We're going over 'Rhythm of the Night' again. Satine will ask Christian to dance with her, but I need you to make sure the surrounding dancers are on point. We don't want another repeat of this morning."

"No, of course not," I said, a little breathless and still scanning the room for Damon.

Alicia made an appearance, clad in black dance pants and a flesh-coloured top that made me do a double take for a second. If you didn't look too closely, you'd almost think she was going topless, the Lycra material moulding to her skin. Also, her bra was so thin that you could see her nipples poking through. Every straight man in the room's eyes were glued to her, though in all honesty, there weren't many.

"Somebody's out to garner attention today," Iggy commented dryly as he passed me by, and I couldn't help but agree. Earlier in the day she'd had a wraparound cardigan over her top, but she must've taken it off during lunch.

There was still no sign of Damon and I started to panic, thinking he'd gone home early. The idea of him being so distraught that he simply had to leave made my heart clench with pain. It was never my intention to hurt him, *never*, and I felt physically ill at the mix-up. Pulling my phone from my pocket, I tried calling him, but it went straight to voicemail. Unable to get through, I tapped out a quick text message.

Rose: *What you just saw was not what you think AT ALL. Please come back to the studio and let me explain.*

I'd go after him, only I knew Iggy would tear me a new one if I disappeared, especially with the day we'd been having. Everybody began stretching and limbering up, and a minute or two later the door opened loudly, a gust of air rushing in. I turned my head to see Damon striding inside the dance studio, wearing his coat and scarf. He began removing them, a dark, scathing look on his face. Did he leave and then decide to come back? Had he gotten my message?

Jacob eyed him, opening his mouth as if to comment on his lateness. But then he saw his expression and seemed to think better of it. Alicia started walking in his direction, leaning casually against the wall when she reached him. I watched as I guided the dancers through their warm-up and could just about hear their conversation.

"Damon, I was supposed to be meeting with a friend of mine for dinner tonight, but she had to cancel. I have a reservation at *Chez Bruce* and was wondering if you'd like to join me instead? It's a Michelin star restaurant, and I hear the food is just incredible."

Was she serious right now? Even after kissing the face off Julian in his bedroom at the party, and even after seeing the way Damon had kissed me, she was still making a play for him. *Unbe-fucking-lievable.*

Damon appeared lost in his own head as he blinked and then finally looked at her.

"What?" He sounded gruff and irritable, like she was an annoying fly buzzing in his ear when he was trying to concentrate.

She huffed out a little laugh and smacked him playfully on the arm. "You weren't listening! My friend cancelled on me and I want to have dinner tonight. What do you say?"

My body moved on autopilot as I continued to eavesdrop, and I was more than a little relieved that Damon didn't once look down at her chest. Then my gut sank when he seemed to sense me watching them, his eyes finding mine. His entire face hardened as he stared at me for a long moment before looking back to Alicia.

"Okay," was all he said, and she smiled like he just agreed to marry her. A wave of nausea overtook me, and now I felt like I really might vomit. He was saying yes because of what he thought I'd done with Blake. That had to be the reason. This was payback.

"Right, well, I'll stop by your place around eight, then," said Alicia before skipping across the room to Jacob.

I couldn't stand this. I had to talk to Damon. Leaving the dancers to continue their warm-up without me, I approached him. He was radiating an aura that said "leave me the fuck alone," so although I wanted to touch him, to try to calm him down in some way, I didn't.

"Can we talk?" I whispered, my voice pleading.

His jaw tightened as he glanced at me briefly. "I have nothing to say to you."

"Damon, please, it's not what — "

177

"Oh, Christian, can we have you over here next to your Satine?" Jacob called, and I sighed. Bloody Jacob. Couldn't he just leave us alone for two seconds so that I could explain to Damon what had happened?

Without another word, Damon moved past me and over to where Jacob stood with Alicia. Iggy joined them a second later and began instructing them on the routine that was to follow. Satine would invite a bewildered Christian up to dance and he would accept, bemused and overwhelmed by her outlandish display.

The scene began as Damon took a seat and Alicia stood before him. He was in such a dour mood that he still hadn't noticed her nipples, which were clearly all for his benefit.

She held her hand out, "Dance with me."

Damon hesitated before Henry, who played Toulouse, gave him a push, and then he was standing in front of her. She danced for him. He took her in his arms, and they moved together while the rest of the dancers performed around them. Damon had been doing really well with the choreography lately, but right then his timing was completely off. His movements were awkward, like he wasn't even paying attention, and Alicia yelped when he stepped on her foot.

"Sorry," he said, but his voice sounded miles away.

Sweat broke out on my skin, and I wished I could press "pause" for a second. Damon was clearly having a terrible time dealing with his anger, and there was no need. Everything he'd seen me do with Blake had really been meant for him.

Speak of the devil, I caught Blake's eye and found him staring at me curiously. I felt like yelling at him for what he'd done, but I'd been just as foolish not to turn and check who'd come up behind me. Still, he had no right to try to touch me without permission, and I was mad. So fucking mad at him.

"Okay, from the top," said Iggy. "And Damon, please try not to injure Miss Davidson this time around. She does need her feet to dance with, after all."

He mumbled something that sounded like another apology, ran a hand through his hair, and they started the scene over fresh. This time Damon misplaced his footing and Alicia tripped, almost falling flat on her face. Jacob completely misread the situation, thinking Damon's sloppy moves were down to being distracted by "her top."

"Okay, I think I know what the issue is here. Alicia, you need to go and cover yourself up. Poor Mr. Atwood can hardly be expected to perform with your smuggled raisins directly in his line of sight."

A few people chuckled and Damon frowned, looking at Alicia as though finally becoming aware of her attire. Alicia did her best Marilyn Monroe as she brought her hand to her mouth and gasped, glancing down at her chest in surprise. *Pu-lease.* Like she hadn't known all along. It was bordering on ridiculous. She'd gone to put her cardigan back on when Iggy called me over.

"Rose, can you come here for a second? Damon dances well with you. I think we should practice the routine without Alicia a couple of times until he's comfortable. You know this part, don't you?"

I nodded silently and walked across the studio. I knew every routine in the entire show by heart. I had spent several weeks helping Iggy to develop it, after all. Damon's eyes fell on me, and for a moment he seemed stricken. I stared at him, trying to silently communicate everything I couldn't say in front of all these people.

179

I recited Satine's lines with practiced confidence, unfazed by those around me. They were the cast, and I was comfortable with them. It was audiences full of strangers that I feared. Damon looked at me with such vitriol as I held my hand out that I had to stifle a gasp.

"Okay, a little less anger and little more dumbstruck by the courtesan's beauty, Christian," said Jacob from a few feet away.

Damon smoothed out his expression and took my hand, but when he did, his grip was too tight. Almost forceful. Well, now I knew what it was like to be on the receiving end of Damon Atwood's temper: scary.

His silence only functioned to make me feel that much more intimidated. He stared down at me like I was a stranger and my stomach twisted into knots. I knew why he was reacting like this. He'd told me before he didn't trust easily, but he'd trusted me, and look what had happened. He thought I'd betrayed him.

The backing music played through the sound system as the cast sang the song. I danced with Damon, but he held his body as far away from mine as possible.

"That wasn't what you think," I said under my breath, quiet enough so that only he could hear.

"It looked pretty clear to me," he practically grunted, his hand still tight around mine.

"I was taking inventory in the storage room when he came up behind me. I thought he was you, Damon. Everything you saw was a mistake. I was letting him kiss me because I *thought he was you*," I said, emphasising my words. "After the lunch we shared, I thought you'd come to find me."

His eyes moved between mine as my explanation sank in, and the tightness in his body loosened slightly.

180

"Okay, a little less chitchat and a little more saying your lines," Jacob ordered, obviously noticing our whispered conversation.

Damon's expression eased a small bit, his mouth opening and then closing. He couldn't respond to what I'd told him because we were in the middle of the scene, which required dialogue. Out of the corner of my eye, I saw Alicia return to the room, her chest thankfully covered as she looked over at us.

I saw her ask Jacob a question as she folded her arms, probably wondering what I was doing dancing with Damon when it was her job. He gave her some explanation, and her mouth formed a thin, unhappy line.

My attention returned to the man in front of me. His warm hand pressed into the base of my spine, and he studied me closely. I wondered if he believed what I'd told him. Then the scene ended I stepped away, but we didn't get the chance to speak because Jacob whisked him back to Alicia.

I went to stand by the wall, and someone slinked up beside me. As soon as I smelled his cologne, I knew it was Blake. Never again would I forget to smell a man before I let him start putting his mouth all over me.

"So, you thought I was someone else," he said, voice tight. "I suppose I don't have to think too hard to figure out who you mistook me for."

"You had no right touching me like that," I hissed.

He let out a mirthless laugh. "Sorry, I kind of forgot to ask permission when you started grinding on my dick."

I glowered. "Fuck you, Blake."

"Of course you can fuck me. Any time you like."

I levelled him with a serious look. "Damon saw us, you know. He was standing in the doorway."

Something passed over Blake's features, something that almost looked like satisfaction, but it was gone in an instant. Now his voice gentled. "I'm sorry about that, but I genuinely thought you knew it was me. Don't you remember my touch, Rosie?"

"I wasn't paying the right amount of attention," I answered stiffly.

"I couldn't believe my luck when you let me kiss you. I forgot just how good you taste. I miss you."

"You don't miss me, Blake. You just think you do. You're nostalgic for me at best, and the only reason you want me is because you're lonely and I'm here."

He frowned and shook his head. "That's not true."

"It is. You've had to give up all your old friends, haven't you? That's the first part of rehabilitation, cut all the other addicts from your life. So now you're all alone and you see me here every day, the girl who was reliable and always available when your bed was too cold to sleep in alone. Well, I'm sorry, Blake, but you lost me. I'm not trying to be cruel, and I honestly wish you all the best with overcoming your addiction, but we're not getting back together. I can't make it any clearer than that."

He put his hand to his chest, inhaling a sharp breath. "Way to make a fella feel special, Rosie."

I cast him a sympathetic look. "I just want you to know where we stand, that's all. I don't want to hurt your feelings."

He eyed me for a long moment. "You're wrong, you know."

"Wrong about what?"

"About me just wanting you because I'm lonely. I want you because you're beautiful and kind, and you make me laugh. I want you because hindsight's a bitch and I can finally see all that I've lost. I've lost the only woman I ever came close to loving."

Something stabbed at my chest, my eyes widening at his words. The sad fact of the matter was that if Blake had told me this a couple of weeks ago, I probably would've forgiven him for every bit of pain he'd caused. I was a soft touch when it came to forgiveness. But not now. Now I had very real feelings for Damon, feelings far stronger than anything I'd ever felt for Blake, and I could only go forward, never back.

Right at that moment, I saw Damon turn in our direction, having just finished a conversation with Jacob. His eyes moved between Blake and me, his expression darkening again. I saw so much in his gaze: anger, betrayal, jealousy.

This day was just the worst.

"Give me another shot. I promise I won't let you down again," said Blake.

I turned and gave him my final statement. "I can't do that. I'll always care for you. Maybe that makes me naive, but it's just how I am. I don't want to be with you anymore. I'm sorry."

With that I left to go use the bathroom, needing a few minutes alone. I mouthed "toilet break" at Iggy to let him know where I was going and he nodded, half distracted by something one of the cast members was saying to him.

In the bathroom I splashed some water over my face, holding my wet hand to my neck for a moment and closing my eyes, trying to find some calm. It was no use. My heart still beat double time and my gut was all twisted up.

When I stepped back out into the hallway, I came face to face with Damon. He stopped mid-stride, standing just a couple feet away from me. I couldn't tell if he'd come in search of me or if he just needed a breather, the same as I had.

"Are you actually going to have dinner with Alicia?" I whispered. It was the first thing that popped into my head, hurt clutching at my chest at the very idea.

"What were you talking to Blake about?" he replied roughly, not answering my question.

I swallowed and rubbed at my collarbone, which was hurting for some strange reason. A physical manifestation of my emotional pain, perhaps. "I was telling him that when he came into the storage room earlier, the only reason I let him touch me was because I thought he was you. Damon, I would never, ever do anything to hurt you, and I would never be involved with two men at the same time. You have to believe me."

His posture remained rigid, his demeanour distant. "Are we involved, Rose?"

"Emotionally, yes," I said, searching his gaze. "You have to feel it, too. When we're together, the way we talk, the way you look at me, it's more than just friendship."

"I thought friendship was all you wanted. I thought you'd sworn off actors."

"I had, but then you came along…."

Damon rubbed at his jaw in agitation. "When I saw him touching you, I didn't like how it made me feel, Rose. I wanted to hurt him. I wanted to bash his fucking head in."

I gasped at his confession and stepped closer, needing to be nearer to him. "But now you know it was a mistake. None of it meant anything."

His eyes flickered between mine, and he exhaled heavily. "You have no idea the kind of betrayal I've suffered in my life," he said, so, so quiet. "For a long time I thought people only wanted me for what they could gain

184

from it. This friendship I have with you is a big deal. I haven't let someone into my life like I have you in years."

His words made me catch my breath, and I closed the distance between us, placing my hand gently on his arm. "I understand, and I value your friendship more highly than anything else in my life right now."

He cast me a pained look. "It hasn't been very long since you were with Blake. I need to know I'm not just a rebound."

"You're not, I promise you, you're not," I hurried to tell him.

"I can tell you believe that, but maybe you don't really understand what's going on in your head. I think you need more time to resolve what you felt for him before moving on to anything else," he said.

"Damon — " I interrupted, but he cut me off.

"I know I'm being hypocritical, because you told me from the start you weren't ready for a new relationship, but I pushed for us to get close anyway. This is more my fault than yours. I should have respected that you weren't ready. I should have listened, but you're just so beautiful to me, not just physically but spiritually, and I couldn't help...."

I frowned at him now, a ball of emotion clogging my throat. "What are you saying?"

"I'm saying we need some distance for a while. You need to find a balance in your heart away from Blake, because I want all of you, Rose, not a quarter or a third or a fifth. I want everything. And right now you're not in a place to give me that. Even if you think you are, I can see that you aren't. What I feel for you means I'm willing to go through the pain of staying away from you until you're ready for me."

His gaze seared into mine as his meaning sank in. He wanted me, but not right now, not until I was ready for him. But I felt ready. I felt like I was going to explode, I was so ready. The flurry and quantity of his words told me this was serious. Damon didn't speak openly very often, nor with such passion. This meant that when he did speak, you listened. You savoured every syllable because you knew he guarded them closely, only doling them out when they truly meant something.

I had to respect his wishes. He deserved that much. To this end I gave him a firm nod and whispered a single word, "Okay."

We shared one more meaningful glance before returning to rehearsals in silence.

Fifteen.

Four weeks later.

I was beginning to wonder if willpower was my greatest strength. It was a silent strength, one that didn't make its presence known physically, but it was a strength nonetheless. The willpower I expended in staying away from Rose was monumental. Every day at rehearsals I had to resist the cord that pulled between us, begging me to get close.

When she entered a room, my eyes were drawn to her against their will. I was entranced by such little, unimportant things, like how she stretched her arms up and fixed her hair into a knot, or how she rubbed at her lower lip when she was thinking about something intently, or how she massaged the outside of her thigh when she had a stitch.

And honestly, I'd thought I was being such a mature, thoughtful grown-up when I'd suggested she take some time to find her heart again. But now, well, I was beginning to regret being mature. In fact, fuck maturity. Why couldn't I just be selfish and greedy and take her? Each day the silence between us felt like a weight on my shoulders, and though we sometimes spoke, it was only ever about the show or some bland, friendly greeting. I was beginning to worry that she was having second thoughts, that her feelings for me had lessened with time.

And then there was Blake. There were very few people in the world I truly wanted to hurt, and Blake Winters was one of them. The way I'd felt that day when I saw him with his hands on Rose was maddening. I could've beaten him to a pulp if I didn't have so much of my trusty willpower at hand.

The scary part was, I didn't hate him because he was a bad person. I hated him because I saw how he looked at Rose and I knew he had real feelings for her, feelings that might've even rivalled my own. He wanted her, and I wanted to crush him for it.

"Penny for your thoughts?" came a sweet feminine voice, and I turned to find Alicia at my side.

Much to my dismay, I had gone for dinner with her that night. Mostly because I was so messed up over Rose that I'd completely forgotten about it until she'd arrived on my doorstop, all gussied up in a tight red dress. I tried to feign tiredness, but she wouldn't take no for an answer. At dinner I decided to find some balls and tell her upfront that I had feelings for Rose and I wasn't interested in a relationship with her. She'd seemed a small bit hurt at first, but she'd quickly gotten over her disappointment. In truth, her disappointment bewildered me slightly. I was an antisocial, grumpy old hermit at the best of times. Why someone as pretty and glamourous as Alicia Davidson would be interested in me was a puzzle I wasn't equipped to solve.

Over our meal I'd started to tell her about Rose, unable to stop once I started. She seemed to empathise, and told me a few tales about her own love life. Over the weeks she'd become something of an unexpected confidante, and I was more than a little surprised by the easy, platonic friendship we'd struck up.

"Just feeling a little rough today," I finally answered, and she cast me a sympathetic expression, her eyes wandering across the studio to where Rose was sitting on the floor stretching. Blake stood over her, saying something I couldn't hear.

Prick.

Alicia patted me on the shoulder, and Rose glanced up just in time to see it.

"It'll get better. Don't you worry, hon," said Alicia. "Are you excited to move into the theatre next week?"

I shrugged. Perhaps I would be excited if I wasn't so mixed up about Rose. Studio rehearsals were coming to an end, and next week we'd begin dress rehearsals at the theatre. I tried to muster some enthusiasm, but all I could see was Blake standing over Rose, staring at her with the need to possess in his eyes.

"Well, anyway, did you hear about this tradition Jacob has with his casts?" Alicia went on, interrupting my violent thoughts about the man standing in front of the woman I wanted.

I furrowed my brow. "Tradition?"

Alicia tilted her head, grabbing her foot and bending her leg to stretch her thigh muscles. "On the weekend after studio rehearsals finish up, he organises to take everybody for a day of group bonding. I hear that this time around he's chosen paintballing."

"It's true," said Iggy, unceremoniously joining our conversation as he came into the room, his hair bizarrely up in pigtails. Nobody batted an eyelash. "This weekend we're all going to spend two hours on a bus so that we can run around the woods shooting bullets of paint at one another. I for one am truly looking forward to the bruises," he deadpanned, sounding none too excited about the activity.

"I've never been paintballing before," I said.

"In that case you're lucky," said Iggy with a wry expression before striding over to speak with a few other cast members.

"Don't listen to him. It's tonnes of fun," said Alicia. "I used to go with my brothers all the time when we were kids."

"You have brothers?" I asked, wondering how this never came up before.

"Yep. Five of them, and I was the only girl." She grimaced. "My parents were so surprised I turned out to be such a girly-girl and not a tomboy. I like to think there are advantages to being able to fight off a suplex while wearing heels and a cocktail dress. My brothers were crazy about wrestling."

"Sounds impressive," I admitted.

She flicked her hair over her shoulder and grinned. "It is."

Again I looked across the room to Rose to find her watching me. I swallowed, unable to look away. Her loose top was dipping down at the front, revealing the seductive curve of her chest. I remembered walking in on her during Julian's party, her smooth, perfect skin bared to me. Fuck, I'd been wanking myself blind to the memory of that night for weeks now. My gaze trailed over her body before returning to her face. She blushed and looked away, continuing with her stretches.

It had been four weeks since our conversation, four weeks since I'd spent any real time with her outside of work. Perhaps it was time to get a little closer.

***

"Christ, it's early," Eddie complained as he climbed aboard the bus parked outside Iggy's studio. I didn't blame him for being grumpy; the man was pushing sixty. I'd just turned twenty-six a couple months ago, and even I felt exhausted with the early start. Jacob had hired a coach to take us to the paintballing centre, the downside being that it was a two-hour journey and we'd been instructed to arrive at the studio at six-forty-five a.m.

I stood outside finishing my coffee as various members of the cast and crew disappeared inside the coach. Though really I had an ulterior motive. I was waiting for Rose to arrive so I could ask her to sit with me, maybe spend the journey talking so I could see how she was feeling about us these days.

Unfortunately, my plan was shot to shit when Alicia turned up wearing a light blue velour tracksuit with the words "girl boss" written across the backside. I quirked a brow. Not that I was particularly interested in that part of her anatomy, but when somebody has something written on their arse, you look.

"Hey, Damon, come sit next to me," she said, linking her arm through mine and leading me forward.

"Actually, I — "

"Yes, yes, get on the bus," came Jacob's shrill voice, interrupting me. "We need to leave at seven sharp, and we're still several people short."

One of those people was Rose. I really hoped she was going to show up. Before I knew it, I was sitting next to Alicia in the second row, since all the other seats were already taken. It was a little like being at school again, everybody wanting to sit at the back of the bus so they could cause trouble where the teachers couldn't see.

A couple minutes later, Jacob was making noises about leaving. Rose was the only person who hadn't yet shown. I tried not to feel too disappointed.

"She might not be feeling well," Iggy suggested when Jacob inquired after her. "I'll give her a call and see what's going on."

191

Just before he pulled out his phone, there was a knock on the front window. The driver opened the door and Rose climbed aboard, her face flushed.

"Sorry I'm late," she said with an apologetic expression. "My alarm clock is on the fritz and I overslept."

"Well you're here now. That's all that matters," said Jacob, waving her forward.

The last seat left was in front of me and Alicia, right next to Blake. Of course it fucking was. I watched as Rose sat down and uttered a quiet good morning to him. She turned her head a little to cast a hesitant smile at me and Alicia.

"Morning," she said.

"Hey, Rose," Alicia replied, a little too sweetly. I didn't appreciate the veiled hostility in her tone and knew she considered Rose to be a cock tease. She just didn't understand the connection we shared.

"Morning," I said, leaning forward with concern when I saw her rubbing her shoulder. She'd pulled a muscle the other day during practice. "How's your shoulder?"

"A little achy, but I'll survive."

"Are you sure?" Blake butted in. "Can I give you a massage or anything?" His voice was gentle, caring. Those familiar violent feelings I was having all too often these days returned.

"Oh, um." Rose's eyes flared like she didn't know how to respond.

"Here," said Blake, putting his hand on her arm. "Turn around."

Don't fucking touch her, my inner voice warned angrily. Would violently assaulting my costar get me sacked from the production? Probably. When he started massaging her over the fabric of her shirt, I gritted my teeth so hard I wouldn't be surprised if I chipped a tooth.

"I once slipped a disc when I was rehearsing for *Phantom of the Opera*," Blake went on. "It was the worst pain of my life."

Rose hummed a response, her posture loosening as he rubbed between her shoulder blades. I wanted to be the one touching her, wanted it so badly my hands were fisted in my lap. Soft, cool fingers met mine, and I glanced to the side. Alicia flared her eyes at me. *Relax*, she mouthed, clearly noticing my tension.

I took a few deep breaths and stared out the window for a minute or two. If I kept looking at Blake giving Rose a massage, I was liable to lose my shit.

My attention went to Jacob, who rose from his seat at the front of the bus, bracing himself in the aisle to face everyone.

"How about a sing-along?" he suggested, and I tried not to look at the bright orange shirt he wore because it was already giving me a headache. A few people groaned, and Iggy shouted from several rows behind me.

"Give us a chance to wake up first. My body still thinks it should be asleep and dreaming of Ben Affleck in a mankini."

Lots of people laughed while Jacob shot him a pouty look. "Well, I apologise for ruining such enticing dreams, but I do think a little sing-song will help wake us all up. Who's in the mood for some *West Side Story*? I'll be Tony."

"Don't you mean Maria?" Iggy shot back. I stifled a chuckle.

"Oh, hush you! I can already tell you were the troublemaker at school, Iggy Thomas," said Jacob, a touch of flirtation in his voice.

"Please don't inflict us with your singing," Maura, the choral director, cut in, her jibe good-natured.

"I'll have you know I've been complimented on my voice by some of the greatest singers of stage and screen," Jacob replied haughtily, trying to keep from smiling. He obviously knew he couldn't sing, but he didn't seem to care. This was proven when a second later he burst into the campest off-key rendition of "Maria" I'd ever heard. Even with the tense mood I was in, I found myself laughing, and soon enough everyone was joining in with him.

Several songs later, the mood on the bus had lightened significantly, and we were on the motorway, heading out of the city. I stared at Rose through the gap in our seats. She looked tired, and I could tell from the set of her mouth that she was still in pain, even if she claimed to be fine.

God, she was beautiful. Her dark brown hair was tied up, several curly strands hanging down over her pale, elegant neck. I wanted to run my fingers through them, kiss the patch of skin between her neck and her shoulder.

I saw Blake nudge her as he leaned in to speak, "Do you remember the time we went for drinks after studio practice ended for *Guys and Dolls*?"

She stiffened and continued looking out the window. "Uh-huh."

"You wore that black French Connection dress, the one with the low neckline. I couldn't stop looking at you that night, and you knew it."

Rose furrowed her brow as she glanced at him a second time. "Why are you bringing that up?"

He's bringing it up because he knows I'm fucking listening.

There was a part of me that hated the history they shared, and I also hated that once upon a time, Rose had loved this prick. We were only half an hour into our journey, but somehow I knew the next ninety minutes were going to be torture.

"I was just wondering if you think about that night like I do," Blake said.

Now she shifted in her seat to face him properly. "I dunno, were you high that night?"

Her words surprised me, and I could tell Alicia, who was listening, too, was also surprised.

Blake cleared his throat. "Why do you ask?"

"Just wondering. You said you were high the entire time we were together. I know we hadn't gotten together properly then, but I'm guessing you were still using at the time."

"Rosie," said Blake with a wince. He appeared genuinely hurt by her words. And what the hell? He'd been a junkie when they were together?

She swallowed and fidgeted with her hands, casting sad eyes in his direction. "I'm sorry. I shouldn't have said that," she whispered, looking around to see if anyone was listening. She didn't realise she had a rapt audience of two sitting directly behind her. I glanced at Alicia, and she cast me a raised eyebrow.

A moment of silence elapsed before Rose placed her hand on Blake's. "How are you doing with your program anyway? Still good?"

He nodded, giving her a weak smile. "Yeah, still going strong. You might have been right about the loneliness, though. It's crazy, the amount of people I can't see anymore."

"Well, there are lots of good people out there. I'm sure you'll have no problem making new friends, Blake. You were always the life and soul of the party."

"You're forgetting one thing," he said with a hint of self-deprecation. "I was on coke back then."

Rose frowned. "Right. Well, it's not like you've had a complete personality transplant. You don't seem too different to me."

"Is that a compliment?" he gave a small chuckle.

Her forehead crinkled as she started to smile. "I'm not sure. God, I always say the wrong thing."

"It's okay. I always found your foot-in-mouth disease endearing."

She shook her head, still smiling, and pulled her hand away. I exhaled a breath in relief. I really couldn't handle her touching him, even if she was only trying to be kind. And now I didn't know how to feel about Blake anymore. If the bloke was battling an addiction, then I felt bad for him, but at the same time I couldn't stand how he looked at Rose.

"Hey," said Alicia, leaning forward to wiggle her fingers through the gap between our seats. "How about we all play a game of 'Have You Ever'? Maybe it'll help pass the time a little."

Rose turned her head to Alicia, worrying her lip as she considered it.

"I'm game," said Blake.

"Yeah, me too," I added. Anything for the chance to interact with Rose.

Finally, she nodded and Alicia sat back, clasping her hands together as she told us how to play the game. "Okay, so I'll start us off. Lift your hand in the air if your answer to the question is yes, or leave it down if it's no, and from then on whoever answers no has to ask the next question. But, and this is only to avoid boredom, let's keep the topic about sex. It'll keep things interesting." She grinned.

Both Rose and Blake turned fully around to face us, Rose appearing a little uncomfortable at Alicia's topic suggestion. All I could do was stare at her. This was the closest we'd been in weeks, and the sunlight drifting through the windows cast her eyes in a glittering shade of pale blue. When she saw me admiring her, she began worrying her lip again, glancing downward.

"Have you ever," Alicia began, pausing before finishing her sentence, "slept with someone whose name you didn't know?"

Both she and Blake held their hands up while mine and Rose's stayed down. The question provoked a memory I'd shoved to the back of my mind, and I grew tense as I tried to push it away once more.

"Never?" Alicia gasped, glancing between the two of us. "Oh, my God, you haven't lived. It's such a rush fucking a stranger."

"I dunno. I've never really had it in me to do that sort of thing. I'd probably end up developing feelings for the person when all they're out for is a quick shag," said Rose self-consciously.

Blake stared at her, a frown on his face.

My heart thumped, because I was the exact same. I couldn't have sex with someone I didn't have feelings for. My cock just didn't respond unless I both desired and cared for the woman.

Suddenly everyone was looking at me, waiting for an explanation as to why I'd never been with someone whose name I didn't know. I threw my head back against the seat, noticing Rose's eyes wandering over the fitted long-sleeved T-shirt I wore. Her attention made my pulse race and my body fill with heat.

"I lived on an island of only 10,000 people for nine years. It's hard to find someone whose entire family history you don't know, never mind their first name."

Alicia patted me briefly on the shoulder. "That's sort of adorable, Damon."

When I looked at Rose, I saw her eyes levelled on the spot Alicia had touched. Perhaps she found it just as maddening to see another woman with her hands on me as I found it seeing her being touched by another man, by Blake.

"So, who asks the next question?" Blake enquired.

I gestured to Rose. "Ladies first."

She smiled and pursed her lips. "Ah, I dunno, I can't think of anything. It seems wrong to be asking sex questions at this hour of the morning."

"I've got a good one," Blake butted in. "Have you ever...walked in on your parents having sex?"

Rose shot him an annoyed look while Alicia let out a sound of disgust. "Ew, Blake, just no. That question is gross."

"Hey, you picked the topic," he said, smiling widely before glancing around at each of us. "Yay or nay? I have to admit I've never had the honour myself, but then again, my old man was pushing seventy when my parents had me. Mum was his fourth wife and almost thirty years his junior, the dirty old bastard."

"Wow, that's some age gap," said Alicia. "And yes, unfortunately, that has happened to me. My brothers and I were supposed to be away all day at the county fair, but when we got there, my younger brother and his friends thought it would be hilarious to throw blue slushy all over my dress. My entire outfit was ruined, so I had to go home early. The cherry on the cake of that awful day was walking inside my living room to find my parents going at it on the couch." She paused to shake off a shudder. "Some things you just can't unsee." She turned to nudge my shoulder. "What about you, Damon?"

I scratched my head and furrowed my brow. "I was very young, probably under five. I went inside my parents' bedroom searching for one of my toys, and all I saw was them both on the bed, scrambling to cover themselves. It's only looking back that I can see what was actually happening."

Alicia gave me sad goo-goo eyes and patted my shoulder a second time as she laughed. "You poor baby."

"Yours sounds far more traumatising. At least I was too young to put two and two together," I said.

"True." Alicia cast her attention to Rose. "So, I guess you're one of the lucky ones who never walked on their parents horizontal, then?"

Rose reached up to rub at a red spot on her neck, and I noticed how uncomfortable she seemed. Then I remembered her telling me of her mother's unconventional relationship, and I realised why she was looked so ill at ease. "No, actually, I have. Too many times to mention. My, um, my mother was bisexual. When I was growing up, I lived in a house with her and her three lovers. They were polyamorous. That's how I know Julian – his mum and mine were involved."

"That's fucking hot," said Blake, the twat. Seriously, had he no tact?

"I've told you about it before." Rose frowned at him.

Blake seemed caught off guard. "Maybe I was, uh, not myself when you told me."

"Sounds pretty traumatising," said Alicia sympathetically.

Rose shrugged. "I was a kid. I just kind of accepted my reality." She looked sad, and I wanted to comfort her so badly right then that it took a physical effort not to reach between the seats and pull her close.

"Since I answered no, does this mean I get to ask the next question as well?" Blake interrupted, probably eager to change the subject.

"Go for it," Alicia told him.

"Okay, let me think," he said, and I thought I could see some hidden agenda behind his eyes. "Have you ever had sex in the shower?"

There was a pause that felt awkward, mostly because Rose was blushing as she glanced at him sideways. Ah, fuck, they'd had shower sex, hadn't they? That was clearly the reason Blake asked the question. I kept my hand down while all three of my companions raised theirs.

"Do you know what?" said Alicia. "Totally fucking over-rated. I mean, I know in the movies they get to take some measure of artistic licence, but in real life, shower sex is just awful. First, it's uncomfortable, second, there's soap everywhere, meaning you're in danger of slipping and injuring yourself, and third, well, I won't go into detail, but water *does not* make for good lubrication."

She must have been speaking a little too loudly, because at the mention of lubrication Jacob's head spun around. He sent Alicia a perplexed look, and a comical beat of silence elapsed before he turned back, continuing the conversation he was having with his assistant. I stifled a laugh, but the humour I found in the moment quickly vanished when Blake spoke huskily.

"Mine and Rosie's experience was a shared one."

Rose's posture stilled, and I didn't think I'd ever seen her look so stiff, even more so now than during the previous topic. "Yeah, well, we don't need to go there."

"Why not? It's a good memory."

"Blake," she said, her voice firm. "I said no."

He kept on staring at her. I spoke, wanting to change the subject. "Since I've never had the honour of shower sex, is the next question is mine to ask?"

"Believe me, you're not missing much, but yeah, ask away, hon," said Alicia, smiling in my direction.

I rubbed at my jaw, searching my head for a good one. Blake was being a cock asking that last question, so maybe I should be a cock right back.

"Have you ever...cheated on someone?" I asked, casting a challenging glare in Blake's direction. He moved his mouth in agitation, and I knew I had him. Shockingly, though, he kept his hand down, and Alicia was the only one to raise hers.

"Yeah, I cheated once or twice when I was younger, but I've changed my ways since then," she admitted.

I barely even heard what she said because I couldn't take my eyes off Blake. Leaning forward, I confronted him, "You sure about that one, mate?"

The prick had the gall to smile. "Perfectly sure."

"I find that hard to believe."

Now his smile fell, and his gaze turned hard. "Believe it, because it's true."

Rose began fidgeting with the hem of her shirt where she sat next to him, looking like she wanted to be anywhere else in the world right then. Guilt hit me like a punch to the gut. I was acting like an arsehole, and regretted being so aggressive with Blake. He'd hurt her, and she clearly didn't want to dredge up all that old stuff, especially the idea that he might've been with someone else at the same time he was with her.

"*Okay*," Alicia interrupted, "maybe we've all had enough of this game. How about we play some I Spy instead?"

Abruptly, Rose stood from her seat, moving past Blake and out into the aisle. "I'm going to go sit with Iggy for a bit," she said, not looking at any of us.

"Rose," I called, but she didn't turn back.

Shit, I'd fucked up, hadn't I?

Sixteen.
Rose

By the time we reached the paintballing centre, I almost felt like I could breathe again. That little game Alicia suggested had turned into one of the most torturous experiences of my life. And what the hell had Damon been thinking, asking that question about cheating?

For the last month he'd barely said two words to me outside of work stuff, and now this. It didn't feel like the Damon I'd come to have feelings for. That Damon was shy and kind. The Damon who'd asked that question, quite frankly, had been a dick.

And okay, maybe he'd been right suggesting I take some time to properly sort my head out. I'd been doing some serious soul searching these past few weeks, coming to the realisation that I hopped from one man to the next in terms of emotional attachment. Sure, I wasn't exactly a serial monogamist, but when I stopped have feelings for one person, I tended to dive straight into having feelings for another. It wasn't healthy.

My mother had been the exact same way. Loving so readily that it had ultimately been her downfall. That entire messed-up relationship between her, Elijah, Joanna, and Kimberly was the final nail in her coffin.

So yeah, I was grateful to Damon for helping me see all this, but at the same time I was mad at him. It seemed like he and Alicia were growing closer and closer, and though he might not have been interested in her romantically, she was more than interested in him. It was taking all of my strength to be polite and friendly towards her, when half the time I just wanted to tear her hair out. It wasn't like me, and I hated the turmoil my feelings were in.

"It's official. I do not look good in combat green," said Iggy, scowling down at the protective gear we'd been given to wear when we arrived. Being so slim, the clothing seemed to sag on him. We also had to wear these funny helmets to protect against the paintballs. It was a good thing I wasn't vain, because we were all going to be sporting some serious hat hair before the day was through.

"But you look fabulous in Chanel black, and that's all that matters," I told him with a smile.

"Well, there is that," he grinned, placated.

For the rest of the bus journey, I'd avoided Damon, Alicia and Blake in favour of sitting with my boss. Now we were all standing outside the activity centre as a good-looking guy in his early twenties told us how the session would play out. I suspected he recognised Alicia, because his jaw practically dropped to the floor when she strode out of the changing rooms in her paintballing gear. I imagined a lot of men reacted to her in this way. Particularly since she was most famous for a role she played in a film about sex addiction where she went full frontal. Lots of people in the industry had applauded her for her bravery.

Sensing someone watching me, I glanced to the side. Damon stood several yards away, his eyes levelled in my direction. I quickly dropped my gaze, my emotions too raw right then to maintain eye contact.

In the end it was decided we'd be divided into three teams, to be selected by Jacob, Alicia, and Damon, respectively. Jacob insisted both Damon and Alicia be team leaders, since as the lead actors they were the lifeblood of the show...or something like that. I hadn't been listening much, too lost in my own head. Alicia pouted sadly at the idea of being on an opposing team to Damon.

God, she was so bloody fake sometimes.

"Rose."

I heard my name being called and blinked, suddenly realising that almost everybody was staring at me.

"Huh?"

Jacob sighed and shook his head. "Damon's picked you for his team, silly goose. Go stand next to him."

My gaze widened as I forced my legs to move. Damon had picked me first – before anybody else. In a small way I felt flattered, but in another I felt like he was overestimating my worth. I was rubbish at paintballing. The last time I'd done this, I'd come home with more bruises than a month-old peach.

"You shouldn't have picked me. I'm terrible at this," I whispered to him while Jacob called out his selection.

Damon glanced down at me, his masculine mouth forming an attractive shape. "I'll always pick you first, petal," he said, and butterflies flooded my belly.

His words were spoken softly, and with such affection that I thought I might swoon and faint on the spot. Forgotten were my misgivings about how he'd spoken to Blake on the bus. Now all I could think about was the way he was looking at me, like we were alone instead of surrounded by people.

A couple minutes later, we all had our paintball guns strapped to our chests as the game began. I ran through the forest, finding a spot behind a thick log and crouching down. Damon came and joined me, his presence soothing like a protective shadow. Unlike Iggy, he looked way too good in combat gear, way too *manly*, and I had to make a conscious effort not to ogle.

"Good spot," he said. I nodded just as a bunch of paintballs went sailing over our heads, splattering with several loud pops on the bark of a tree a couple of feet in front of us.

"Maybe I spoke too soon," Damon whispered. "We've been spotted. Come on."

He got up and I followed suit, several of our team members joining us as more paintballs flew in our direction. I managed to avoid being hit and took cover behind a tree. When I saw Alicia's unmistakable red hair peeking out of her helmet as she moved in the distance, I smiled and took aim. I tried not to dwell too long on the satisfaction it gave me to hear her shriek when I hit her in the leg.

Chuckling quietly to myself, I shook my head just as I noticed Damon behind a tree close to mine, watching me.

You're bad, he mouthed, and I blushed at having been caught.

Blake had been picked for Jacob's team, and all of a sudden he was there, shooting paintballs at me, Damon, and the rest of our group, like bloody Rambo or something. Jacob was beside him a second later, joining in on the attack. Damon managed to peg our director in the arm, and he let out the most hilarious high-pitched shriek I'd ever heard. I would've rolled over with laughter if I wasn't so busy shooting at them.

I got Blake in the arm, the yellow paint splattering all over his combat fatigues.

"Oh, you're in for it now, Rosie," he called, grinning in challenge.

I backed away a few steps, hands clammy on my gun, as Blake advanced. Then suddenly Damon was in front of me, his broad, masculine shoulders set in a protective posture.

"Run!" he barked, then shot at Blake. He didn't have to tell me twice, and a second later I was dashing through the trees, hoping to find a place to hide. As I ran, a sharp pain shot through my shoulder and I buckled over onto my knees. Glancing around, I couldn't see anyone, so I knew whoever got me must've taken their shot from far away. Still, the paintball hurt like a bitch. I'd been hit right in the spot where I pulled a muscle during rehearsals.

A warm hand touched my arm, and I blinked. Damon crouched down in front of me, a look of concern on his face.

"You all right?"

I winced. "Not really. Someone shot me in my bad shoulder."

Damon's expression darkened as he helped me to my feet. "Come on, let's find someplace safe where we can check it out."

We were in the farther end of the woods, but I could still hear the pop and whirr of paintballs being shot in the distance. When we found an old wooden shed, Damon pushed open the door and led me inside. It smelled like wet leaves and earth. There was nowhere to sit, so I leaned against the wall for a minute, trying to catch my breath as I pulled off the helmet. Damon did the same.

"I'm beginning to wonder if I should've just stayed in bed today," I said as he came to stand in front of me, his hands going to the padded vest I wore. "Perhaps my alarm not going off was a sign."

"Whoever shot you is a fucking arsehole," he grunted, his mouth set in an annoyed slant.

"Hey, this is the name of the game," I said as Damon clipped free the vest. All of a sudden, he was turning my body and pulling my shirt away from my skin to check the damage. My pores prickled when the cool air hit me, and I swallowed at his hot touch.

He sucked in a harsh breath and swore, "Jesus Christ."

"Those paintballs leave really bad bruises," I said, trying to break the tension that was rolling off him in waves. It made my stomach coil tight in anticipation of him full-on losing his rag. Sure, Damon was always so silent and stoic, but I got the sense he could be scary if fully triggered.

"Jacob's a fuckwit. Does he want us all too injured to perform?" He sounded angry.

"I'm not sure he thought that far ahead. I can just imagine him stumbling upon paintballing in an online search, and picking it simply because he thought it'd make him seem cool."

Damon's fingers touched the area that was sore, and I inhaled sharply.

"Sorry," he apologised, moving his hand away.

"No, it's okay. Just…is it very bad?"

"Your shoulder is red and a little bit welted. The bruise won't come until tomorrow. How's the pain?"

I bit my lower lip and turned back around. "It's manageable."

His dark eyes zeroed in on my exposed shoulder and neck. "Do you want to go back to the centre? We can sit the rest of the game out."

I shook my head. "You go back and play. I think I'll just rest in here for another few minutes, then head to the centre myself."

He didn't appear to like this plan and shook his head. "I'm not leaving you on your own out here."

"Why?" I feigned terror. "Are there bears?"

Damon bit back a smirk, and I enjoyed getting a reaction out of him. "No, smartarse, there aren't bears, but this is a big forest. You could get lost."

"I can remember the way back. I'll be fine."

"I'm not leaving you, Rose." He stood firm, and I could tell from his tone that he wasn't going to budge on the matter. I busied myself fixing my clothes while Damon slid down the wall to sit on the leaf-strewn floor. A second later I joined him, and an odd silence filled the space.

"Here," said Damon, pulling me into his chest. "Lean against me. That hard wall can't be very comfortable on your shoulder."

He was right, it wasn't. His chest was a far superior surface. Unfortunately, sitting with Damon's arm draped around me brought with it a lot more feelings than sitting against the wall of the shed. This was the closest I'd been to him in what felt like forever, and my senses were on overdrive. His smell filled my nose, his warmth seeped into my body, and his touch set my nerve endings alight.

"I'm sorry for how I acted on the bus," he said, breaking another long stretch of quiet.

"It's okay. Blake started it. I wouldn't have liked hearing of yours and Alicia's sexual exploits, either."

His hand that had been rubbing my arm gently stilled. "Alicia and I are friends. Nothing more."

"Oh," I said, relief flooding me. I'd been ninety-nine-percent sure nothing had happened between them, but there had still been a tiny part of me that wondered, especially since they spent so much time together. Okay, so maybe 'wondered' was too tame a word. Violently jealous was probably a better description....

"What I said a month ago hasn't changed, Rose. I still want you," Damon murmured, his breath hitting the top of my ear.

I twisted in his hold to meet his eyes. "You were right, you know."

"About what?"

"About me needing time to resolve my feelings. And, well, I think I just needed time to be alone in general."

"Yeah?" he asked, his eyes on my lips. "I was starting to wonder."

I could barely register his words, slightly transfixed by the way he was staring at my mouth. "Wonder?"

His hand left my arm completely to go to my neck, where he gripped me firmly. "If I'd made a mistake. You don't speak to me anymore. It's hard to know what's going on in your head."

I could've laughed at that, because if anyone was difficult to read, it was him.

Instead, I whispered, "Damon, I might not have spoken to you, but I was always aware of you."

He let out a breath, his forehead dropping to mine. "And I you. Not being around you makes me miserable," he confessed.

Our breaths mingled. My chest rose and fell rapidly as my pulse picked up, a curl of desire forming inside me. The longer we stayed wrapped up like this, the bigger it grew. His fingers dug into me where he held my neck and I closed my eyes, savouring the feel of him. He moved his face closer, his lips just barely brushing mine. I trembled. He did it again, and then again, until I caught his lips in mine, not letting him retreat this time. A long, relieved sigh escaped him as we started to kiss in earnest, our mouths melding together, our tongues searching, like we were trying absorb one another whole.

I clutched at his shoulders, climbing into his lap like a needy kitten as I whimpered against his lips. Damon's hands fumbled for me, his fingers undoing a few buttons on my shirt and trying to get beneath the padded vest without much success.

"Fuck," he grunted in frustration. I felt the word rumble all the way down between my thighs.

"Here," I said breathlessly, needing his touch just as much as he needed to touch me. I took his hand and guided it inside my shirt. His fingers brushed the tops of my breasts, and I moaned at the same time a fierce, masculine rumble sounded from the back of his throat.

His hand slipped beneath the cup of my bra, palming my breast fully, and I pulled free from the kiss to bury my face in the crook of his neck. This was all too much, and I was so turned on I was just about ready to have sex with him here on the floor of this damp old shed.

His lips sought mine again as he flicked my nipple with his thumb. I gasped into his mouth, his tongue sliding leisurely along mine.

"Rose," he groaned, still palming my breast. "I could fuck you right now."

God. I shivered at his dirty words and the way he said my name. Moving my hips, I felt his erection press firm and hard between my legs. I couldn't tell how much time passed, and I wanted him to fuck me, I was that desperate for him, even out here in the middle of the woods with our colleagues nearby.

I arched my spine, and his cock moved against me in just the right spot so I cried out in pleasure. Damon broke away from the kiss, his breathing erratic as he struggled to restrain himself. I tried to calm down a little, my breathing just as unsteady as his was. He'd been right to break the kiss. We'd barely even discussed what was going on between us, and diving right into forest sex was probably a bad idea.

Probably.

Silently, he moved his hands over my clothes, fixing everything back in place. My cheeks burned bright red, and I trembled when his fingers brushed my collarbone. His mouth curved into an almost smile that very nearly did me in. "So reactive," he murmured.

"That's what happens when you kiss a girl to within an inch of her life, then leave her hanging," I griped.

His eyes flicked to mine, so dark and brown I could've gotten lost in them. And then something truly wondrous happened. Damon smiled at me, a full, beautifully masculine smile that made my knees weak.

"You're smiling at me," I breathed.

He quirked an eyebrow. "And?"

"And stop it, you can't just never smile and then suddenly lob one on me. It's disconcerting."

He chuckled in response, and I groaned. "Now you're laughing. Gah! Are you trying to kill me? Do you realise your laugh is the sexiest sound on earth, only surpassed by the noises you make when you kiss me?"

His smile started to fade, only to be replaced with a look of such fierce desire I swore a bucket of ice water wouldn't be enough to cool me down. I cleared my throat and tried not to spontaneously orgasm. "We should head back. Everybody will be wondering where we've been."

He smouldered at me, but didn't argue, only gestured for me to lead the way. We stepped out of the shed and had

212

walked in silence for a minute or two when a voice called our names. It was one of our teammates and also a dancer in the show.

"Rose! Damon! Did you two get lost?" he asked, glancing between us.

I tucked a strand of hair behind my ear as Damon answered, "Aye."

"Right, well, Jacob's team won. We're all heading back to the compound now for some lunch," he said.

"Sounds good," Damon replied, and we all started walking through the forest.

My cheeks were bright red the entire way back, and we both kept stealing glances at one another. Damon had a twinkle in his eye that hadn't been there this morning, and my chest ached with the need for him to touch me again.

I could only imagine what might've happened back there if we'd just let our bodies lead us.

Seventeen.
Damon

I'd never been more frustrated in my life. Finally, I was kissing Rose, touching her like I'd only been able to imagine in my head for weeks, and then that little voice in my head – Jiminy-fucking-cricket – urges me to slow down. Telling me I'm moving too fast when we both need to take things slow. My conscience was a motherfucking cockblocker.

In the paintball centre's dining hall, Jacob was celebrating his victory, while the other two teams licked their wounds. If this was his idea of group bonding, then I wasn't sure he knew the meaning of the term.

A few disgruntled looks were thrown my way from those who'd been on my team. It was hard not to feel bad, especially since I'd spent most of the game with Rose when I should've been out there leading them to victory.

"Damon, over here," Alicia called, waving her hand in the air. She sat at a table with Blake and a few other cast members, and appeared to be signing an autograph for one of the centre's employees. Rose moved to make a beeline for Iggy's table, but I caught her hand.

"Don't go. Sit with me," I urged her in a low voice.

Her eyes moved between mine, her throat bobbing as she swallowed. "Okay."

A minute or two later, we were taking a seat at Alicia's table. She was telling everyone how some sneaky player had shot her in the leg when she wasn't paying attention. I did my best to hide my grin, glancing sideways at Rose. We both knew that sneaky player had been her. She didn't look at me, only focused on eating her sandwich. She did, however, nudge me with her knee as a silent plea for me not to say anything.

I spread my legs wide, leaning my thigh against hers. She stilled for a second, unsure what to do, but then she simply accepted my need for contact. We'd reconnected today, and no way was I letting her go this time.

"I didn't see much of you during the game, Damon," Alicia commented from the head of the table.

I turned to her and shrugged. "Must not have crossed paths."

"Huh," she said, her sharp green eyes moving to Rose and then back to me. There was a prickliness to her posture that put me on edge. These past few weeks Alicia had been my sounding board, a sympathetic ear, a friend. Now I wasn't too sure if she'd had a hidden agenda all along.

I ate my lunch quietly, letting the others chat around me. It wasn't out of the ordinary, as I was usually the silent one in the group. Rose however, wasn't talking much, and normally she was more conversational.

I nudged her with my shoulder. "You okay?"

She swallowed down a bite of food before glancing at me and nodding. "Yeah, just tired."

"How's your shoulder?"

"Not too bad."

I watched her for a minute, wondering what she was thinking. Did she regret the kiss? I felt a tension coming from the other side of the table and several seats up. Blake sat there chewing on a piece of bread, watching us with an unhappy slant to his mouth. I wished I could just whisk Rose and myself away from all these petty jealousies and dramas. More and more these days I felt like my life was becoming some soap opera–style love triangle. Or perhaps a love square was the more accurate term.

When it was time to get on the bus again to go home, I made sure to corner Rose. We needed to talk.

"Sit with me."

Her eyes flicked to mine and then away. "Aren't we supposed to keep the same seats as before?"

"Nah, come on," I replied, standing firm as I took her hand in mine. My fingers slid through hers, fitting perfectly.

She seemed to grow nervous at the gesture as she fumbled a response. "Well, all right. If you're sure nobody will complain."

"I'm sure."

We got on the bus, and I led her to the back. I let her have the window seat and had just settled in when I saw Alicia headed in our direction.

"Guys! Aren't we all going to sit together like we did this morning?" she asked, hands on her hips.

Perhaps I'd been a little premature, thinking there wouldn't be any trouble. Thankfully, though, before I even had a chance to reply, I saw Iggy swoop in, his wise, perceptive eyes on Rose and me as he slid his arm through Alicia's.

"Come sit with me, darling. I'd like to pick your brain about that dance school you attended back in the States," he said, leaving her no room to argue.

A second later he led her to the front of the bus, and I let out a relieved breath. Feeling Rose's eyes on me, I turned my head to look at her. Her lips were curled in a hint of a smile, and she seemed amused for some reason.

"You can't blame her for being determined," she said. "Sometimes I wonder if you have any idea what you look like."

216

I leaned closer, my hand braced restlessly on my thigh. "What do I look like?"

She laughed gently. "You see? No clue at all. You're incredibly handsome, Damon, handsome in a way that doesn't come around too often. Maybe even more so because of the fact that you don't know it."

A deep sense of satisfaction hit me to be reminded that Rose found me attractive. "Should I say thank you?"

Now she laughed some more. "And you don't know how to take a compliment, either. It's kind of adorable."

"Glad you're amused. My looks are more of a hindrance when I'm being hounded by Alicia to take her out to dinner when all I'd rather be doing is staying home and reading a good book."

Rose smiled, and it was so pretty I felt my chest ache. "Oh, my God, that's even more adorable. I think you might be perfect, Damon Atwood."

I'm not perfect, but you are.

I couldn't stop the way I was staring at her with barely contained hunger. She seemed to become aware of it, because her smile faded, a more serious expression taking its place. Her eyes flittered all about, landing on the back of Alicia's head where she sat with Iggy a good number of rows in front of us.

"I've just realised I never told you about Julian's party," she said, her voice hushed.

"Oh?" I said, curious.

Rose looked down and fiddled with the sleeve of her top before answering. "I went to find Julian and bumped into Alicia leaving his bedroom. Her makeup was all smudged and her hair was a mess. It was obvious they'd just had some kind of fumble."

My eyes widened slightly at this news. I'd been under the impression that there was no love lost between Alicia and Julian. "That's surprising," I replied finally.

"I know," said Rose. "She acts like she hates him, but maybe she just hates the fact that she likes him. I don't know. People are strange."

"So said Jim Morrison," I quipped.

She studied me. "You're not upset?"

"Should I be?"

"Well, Alicia's been dead set on you for weeks. I mean, she was all over you at Julian's party even though she'd been secretly kissing the guest of honour in his bedroom."

I shrugged and replied simply, "She can kiss whoever she likes."

A few moments of quiet passed between us as Rose turned her attention out the window. The bus had just started the journey back to the city, and I found a certain peace in knowing I had two whole hours of her company. I could've spent the entire time just staring at her beautiful profile, but unfortunately, there were things we needed to discuss.

I touched her hand gently, bringing her attention back to me, and asked, "How are you feeling about Blake these days?"

It took her a while to answer, and the entire time I felt like I was holding my breath under water. "Better," she said at long last. "What Blake and I had will never be rekindled. I can even be around him now and not feel so…mixed up. Like I told you earlier, you were right. I needed time to get my head on straight, so thank you."

"And your head's on straight now?" I asked.

She smiled. "Yes, very much so."

"When can I take you to dinner, then?" I blurted, not even caring that I was being overly forward.

Rose laughed, and it was one of my favourite sounds. "When would you like to?"

"Is tonight too soon?"

She was still laughing as she shook her head. "How about next weekend? We move into the theatre this week, and everything's going to be a little hectic for a few days."

I nodded. "Okay. Next weekend it is."

I couldn't wait. Just thinking about being able to take Rose out for a meal and treat her like she deserved had my chest filling with pride. At the same time, I felt like a little boy on Christmas Eve, excited beyond words. It was ridiculous, the things this woman could make me feel.

Rose shifted in her seat, elegantly stretching her arms up over her head. I watched the movement with barely concealed fascination. Her body and the way she moved it was something of an obsession of mine.

"My shoulder's still a bit stiff," she explained, and my eyes traced the delicate arch of her spine, the way her hips flared out in an exquisite curve.

"It's a shame you fear the stage," I said without thinking, my voice low.

She looked at me, the comment taking her off guard. "Why?"

I moved closer so that my lips almost touched her ear. "Because a beauty like yours deserves an audience."

I could see her skin bead as a tremble moved through her. "Damon," she whispered, her hand going to my knee, the touch soft.

"What is it, petal?"

She exhaled a shaky breath. "You're the only audience I want."

Her response sent white heat shooting through my system, my adrenaline spiking as images filled my head. I saw Rose, naked and writhing beneath my sheets, my face between her legs as I tasted her wet sex, eyes never leaving her face as I soaked in her every reaction.

I took her hand that had settled on my thigh and held it in mine, my thumb brushing back and forth over the inside of her palm. Her breathing grew laboured, and I felt like my senses had been heightened. I could practically see the air leaving her, how the barest touch of red tinted her cheeks, the blood rising as she envisioned similar things in her own mind.

We gazed at each other then, the chatter of those around us filling the heavy silence that seemed to punctuate just how much I desired her. I could still feel her breast, full and lush in my palm, remember how her nipple pebbled instantly at my touch. I'd been dreaming of her tits for weeks, but I had no idea how touching them would totally eclipse that memory.

Rose shifted in place, her thighs pressing together, and I wondered if she was wet. It was all I could do to keep my cock in check, because she had a way of sending my blood south just by being close to me. The entire situation verged on the edge of torture. We had a long journey ahead of us with no privacy or route of escape.

In the end, Rose turned and rested her head on my shoulder. The affectionate gesture surprised me, made my heart thump harder, and I wondered if she could feel my pulse racing against her cheek. I lifted my arm and draped it around her, happy to just be there, quietly holding her. Her eyes closed, and after a little while I could see she'd drifted off to sleep. I was almost tempted to join her, but I didn't want to give up this time I had. I wanted to enjoy being so close to her after what felt like an eternity keeping my distance.

She only stirred when the bus finally arrived back in the city. I watched as she blinked a few times, moved her body, and then smiled when she remembered where she was and whose shoulder she'd fallen asleep on.

"Hey," she whispered, sitting up and pulling away to fix her hair. I already missed her, my arms feeling empty without her there.

"Hi," I murmured in response.

The bus pulled to a stop outside Iggy's studio, and Rose and I disembarked with the others. Out on the street, it seemed like we couldn't stop staring at each other. When we spoke, it was all at once.

"Want to share a taxi?"

"I guess I'll see you on Monday."

I'd been the one to offer sharing a taxi, but we both knew that wasn't a good idea. With how I was feeling, having spent the last two hours with her in my arms, all I wanted to do was carry her to my bed and keep her there for what was left of the weekend.

"I told Iggy I'd help him build this new chest of drawers he bought for his flat," said Rose, her cheeks colouring. I imagined she knew exactly why I'd been so eager to share a taxi.

"Okay, I'll see you Monday, then," I said, leaning down and placing a soft kiss on her cheek. When I stood back to my full height, I felt the weight of somebody's stare. Blake was standing just a few yards behind Rose, chatting with several other cast members. He wasn't speaking, though. His jaw was tight and his expression dark as he glared daggers at me. I continued staring him down, because fuck if I was going to be the one to look away first.

Finally, he turned his head, and I felt a small victory that I'd held my ground the longest.

A moment later, Rose said one last goodbye before going with Iggy. It wasn't often that I felt possessive of people or things, but Rose had sparked something inside me, something that made me want her like I'd never wanted anyone else before in my life. She was beautiful and kind, funny and caring, and now I could only move forward with the prospect of us being together as my goal.

I watched her walk down the street with her eccentric boss, knowing that if I had my way she'd be mine, and Blake would never put his hands on her ever again.

Eighteen.

Rose

It was Sunday afternoon when my phone rang. I put down the clean laundry I was folding as I watched the repeat of *Eastenders* on BBC1. Damon's name showed on the screen. My heart did one quick, hard somersault before proceeding to hammer away like a crazy monkey playing the drums.

The ride home from paintballing yesterday had been something else. I'd been so aroused, so near to him, yet with no choice but to keep my hands to myself.

I picked up after several rings, my voice expectedly shaky. "H-hey."

"Rose, are you busy?" he asked, sounding stressed.

"Oh, um, not really. What's going on?"

His next words flew out in one long stream of word vomit. Truth be told, it was probably the most I'd ever heard him speak all at once, so I knew something was wrong. "There are paparazzi outside the house, at least a dozen of them. One of them even climbed over the gate and tried snapping shots through the window. And Jacob called this morning to say Alicia and I have an appearance on a television talk show tonight to promote *Moulin Rouge*. He said he held off telling me because he knew I'd only stress out about it. Well, now I'm stressing even more since he's sprung it on me with barely any notice. I don't want to do it, but he said all promotional work is included in the contract I signed and — "

He would've kept talking if I hadn't cut him off mid-sentence. "Okay, okay, calm down. I'll be over there in a few minutes."

Damon exhaled. "Thank you, Rose."

Hanging up, I went to grab my shoes and handbag before realising I was still in my PJs. Damon had sounded so stressed, and I didn't want to leave him on his own any longer than necessary. With this in mind, I put on my winter coat, knowing it covered everything up, slipped into my shoes, and left the apartment.

When I reached Damon's street, I saw all the press waiting outside. They must have caught wind that he was going to be on this TV show tonight, and that was why they'd decided to pay a visit. I didn't want them to take any pictures of me going in, so instead I walked to the end of the street, then turned into the laneway that ran along the back of the houses. I found the gate at the rear of Damon's house blessedly unlocked and made my way to the back door, knocking a few times gently. A minute later Damon appeared, eyes darting in all directions.

"Rose, come in. How did you get back here?" he asked as I stepped inside the warmth of the house.

"Your back gate was open. Don't worry, it's locked now. I thought it best not to come in through the front door just in case those paps start splashing pictures of me all over *OK* magazine this week," I said with a hint of humour.

Damon grimaced and ran his hands through his hair. He wore loose-fitting jeans and a black T-shirt, his face sporting a light stubble. I tried not to stare when he lifted his arms over his head in agitation and a slim line of skin was revealed at his torso. "I didn't know who else to call."

I shook my head and told him gently, "Don't apologise. It's understandable that you're freaking out. How about a cup of tea? I always find it good for settling my nerves."

He exhaled, his panic fading a little. His mouth formed a smirk when I took off my coat to reveal my pale blue and yellow striped pyjamas. "Were you sleeping when I called?"

I went to turn the kettle on. "No, just having a lazy Sunday. If I don't have to work, then no way am I getting dressed when I could be wearing these."

Damon chuckled low, rubbing his jaw as he went to sit down at the table. "You're cute. And I think I feel better already."

I did a little curtsy and grinned. "Glad to be of service."

A few minutes later, I placed two cups of tea down on the table and took the seat opposite him. His eyebrows rose slightly as he looked at me, all expectant like he was waiting for me to unleash some sage advice.

"I'm not sure I'm the best person for you to be speaking with right now. You're nervous about being on TV, and I've suffered from stage fright almost my entire life."

Damon leaned forward on the table, clasping his teacup. I was momentarily struck by how out of place his big hands looked on the feminine china but shook off the thought. "Why is that, by the way?"

I let out a small laugh. "I thought we were supposed to be discussing your interview."

He shook his head. "Better to talk about you. It'll take my mind off things."

"You shouldn't be so worried, you know. This could be a good thing for you. You're going to be on stage six nights a week once the show starts up. Maybe facing your fears today will help ease you in."

"Stop diverting. Tell me why audiences scare you."

I took a sip and relented. "Fine. When I was little, I used to dance all the time. I'd camp out in front of the television and copy the dancers on screen for hours, never

225

caring if anyone else was around. Sometimes Julian would sit in and watch, cheer me on, and I loved his encouragement, even dreamed of a day when huge masses of people would cheer for me just like Julian did."

Damon smiled, and yeah, big, massive whoosh through the heart. "I bet you were a great kid."

"Not really. I was hyper and annoying. Too much energy, Mum always said. So anyway, you remember I lived in a house with all those other kids, Julian and Joanna's two daughters? Their names were Yvonne and Claudia, and they were a couple of years older than me. One day they noticed me dancing and for some reason thought it was the most hilarious thing ever. They rounded up all the kids who lived on our street and had them hide outside our living room window. Then, after I'd been dancing alone for a few minutes, Yvonne threw open the curtains, and they all began pointing and laughing at me. For months afterwards those kids would call me names and say my dancing was terrible whenever they saw me on the street. I wasn't terrible at all, but Yvonne and Claudia had put them up to it. Nothing but a pair of bullies. After that I stopped dancing in the living room, only in secret in my bedroom. I lost my desire for an audience completely. By the time I became a teenager and started taking lessons from Iggy, I still had this weird aversion to dancing in front of lots of people. I just wanted to be behind the scenes. That's where I'm happiest."

Damon was frowning as he listened to me speak. "Those sisters were probably jealous of your talent, but I understand how weird little things like that can give you a complex."

I nodded. "It's like when people have a fear of toothbrushes or toilet paper. Everyone thinks it's silly, but it usually stems back to some random traumatic experience from childhood. Now you know mine."

"I still feel robbed I'll never get to see you on stage. You were made to perform, Rose. Perhaps one day your desire for a cheering audience will return," Damon said kindly.

"You see me dance every day," I replied before motioning with my hands. "All you need to do is imagine a stage beneath my feet."

He didn't say anything, only stared at me over his cup as he took another sip of tea. A small moment of quiet elapsed before he let out an exhausted sigh. "Those photographers outside are pissing me off. I can put up with it for a day or two, but if they plan on being out there every day, I might have to move."

"Then they'll just find out where you're living the same way they discovered you were staying here. You know what I think? I think you should embrace it. Go out there, smile for the cameras, let them take a few shots, and then they'll leave you alone. It's the mystery that has them so eager to find out more, you know."

"Smile for the cameras?" he asked. "I can't see that going over well. I'll end up looking like a sociopath when it doesn't meet my eyes."

His dry tone made me laugh. "Then you just need to practice. Work it into your daily routine. Every morning after you've brushed your teeth, spend a couple minutes practicing your smiles in the mirror."

"I'm not doing that," he scoffed.

"All celebrities do it! How do you think they perfect those sassy poses they do in their designer dresses when they're walking the red carpet?"

"If I ever walk the red carpet again, I can guarantee you I won't be wearing a designer dress," he said, and I chuckled.

"Damon, be serious for a second. Practice takes away a good portion of your nerves. It's the powerlessness, the feeling that you don't know what you're doing that makes you anxious. Very few people have natural confidence. In most cases it comes from experience. Why do you think we rehearse and rehearse and rehearse for the show? It's so that once you go out there on opening night you'll be confident and prepared to dazzle the audience, rather than a nervous wreck hiding in the corner."

Damon wasn't looking at my face now; instead, his gaze was trained on my mouth as I spoke. I cleared my throat to garner his attention, feeling oddly aroused by how he lost concentration like that. His dark eyes met mine.

"Anyway, the most urgent issue facing us right now is getting you through this interview," I said as his focus returned.

He rubbed at his stubble. "Playing a part in front of a camera I can do. It's being myself that's the problem."

"Yes, I know. You've told me. This is why you need to forget about the audience and pretend you're playing a part. Pretend you're *acting* as an actor being filmed for TV."

"That could work," he said, his attention drifting to the clock on the wall. "It's not like I have another choice."

"What time are they picking you up?"

He grimaced. "In forty minutes."

"Crap. That doesn't leave us much time."

"I should just call Jacob and cancel. I can count about a million other things I'd rather be doing."

"Such as hiding away in this house and trying to ignore the press outside?" I said, lightly teasing.

A hot, sexy look passed over his features as he levelled me with an intense stare. It was a stare that said *challenge accepted*. "That... and maybe giving you head."

My mouth fell open as my pulse thrummed. I had no idea how to respond and wasn't entirely certain where that had come from. Sure, he'd been staring at my mouth all sexy-like just a minute ago, but never in a million years did I imagine *that* was what he'd been thinking about.

My voice came out all breathy and stuttering. "Damon...."

He cocked an eyebrow. "Rose, I won't apologise for wanting you."

"I don't expect you to, I just...." I closed my eyes for a second and tried to steady my breathing. "We haven't even gone on our first date yet." Why on earth I thought that was the most pertinent point to make in that moment, I had no idea.

Damon reached across the table, taking both my hands in his. "I'm not trying to rush you. But some days being around you is...difficult. You're so fucking sexy I can hardly breathe with it sometimes."

My eyes snapped open, and I just stared at him. We were locked in a moment for who knew how long when suddenly a loud, persistent knock sounded at his front door. He dropped my hands and stood, raking a hand through his hair as tension filled his body.

"That better not be those paparazzi again," he said, his jaw tight. The knock came a second time, and he walked out into the hallway. I followed and watched as he peeked through the peephole. His tension fell away somewhat as he opened the door and Jacob strode inside.

"Somebody's garnering quite the fan club out there," he commented before looking Damon up and down, his mouth forming an unhappy slant. "What's this? You're not even ready."

"I'm ready. You're early."

"You've got your shit in bucketfuls if you think that's what you're wearing," said Jacob, making a gesture of frustration with his hands before his eyes fell on me. "Rose! Thank God you're here. Take this man upstairs and find something in his closet that resembles a suit before I have a conniption."

I stifled a laugh and stepped forward, taking Damon's hand and leading him up the stairs. When we reached his room, I closed the door and finally let my laughter flow. "I don't think I've heard anyone use the word conniption in about a decade."

"He's being melodramatic. My clothes are fine."

"You're selling *Moulin Rouge*, Damon. You need to look the part. And Jacob's being melodramatic because this is his baby. I can't even imagine the amount of work it must've taken just licensing the score. If the show turns out to be a flop, then he'll be the one who has to live under the shadow of its failure."

"I suppose," he grumped, flopping down onto the bed.

"Did you notice he didn't even question my being here, nor the fact that I'm wearing pyjamas?"

"I doubt he notices much aside from his own reflection half the time," Damon commented wryly, and I smirked.

For a moment I stared at him lying there, one too many images flooding my mind. Damon cocked an eyebrow, like he knew exactly what I was thinking. I shook off the moment of sexy stupor, turned to his wardrobe, and opened it before flicking through the hangers. In the end I managed to find a nice plain white shirt and a navy suit jacket. There weren't any slacks, but his jeans could pass for designer. The look said laid-back Hollywood.

I handed him the clothes. "Go put these on."

Damon sat up, took both items, and proceeded to pull off his T-shirt. I stood there, having a *second* moment of sexy stupor, as his entire muscled torso was revealed to me. When he shrugged into the shirt, I stepped forward with eager hands. "Let me help with the…with the buttons."

His grin was wide, and it practically undid me. "By all means."

I silently did up his shirt, my knuckles brushing his skin. It was difficult to process the thought that soon I was going to start dating this man. And soon I could use his entire perfect body as I pleased.

"Will you watch the show?" Damon asked, looking down at me with his handsome brown eyes.

"Of course I'll watch it."

"If I know you are, then I think I'll be okay," he told me earnestly, and I stepped away, trying to stifle the urge to push him back down on the mattress. Being in his bedroom for any prolonged length of time probably wasn't a good idea. I'd have to remember that in future.

"Good. I always want you to be okay, Damon," I whispered in response.

***

"Hey!" Julian complained when I swiped the remote from his lap.

He was lounging on the couch, browsing Facebook on his tablet, and not paying a lick of attention to the television. I sat down beside him and flicked through the channels.

"Damon and Alicia are being interviewed in a few minutes," I said, and he perked up. I snickered. "Oh, now he's interested."

Julian let out a beleaguered sigh. "The starlet has been evading me of late."

"And there was me believing you when you said it was only a matter of time," I teased.

"Don't be cruel. I've got an itch that only a five-foot-nine redhead with double-D-cup breasts and a sassy attitude can scratch. Where else am I going to find such a rare treasure?"

"This is London. I'm sure you'll manage."

The show came on, and the host was just thanking the previous guests before he started to introduce Damon and Alicia. I gripped the remote, practically holding my breath as they walked out and shook the host's hand before taking a seat on the couch. Alicia wore a silver sequined dress and matching heels. Her hair was lavishly curled and her makeup done to perfection.

Damon, of course, wore the outfit I'd chosen for him, and something affectionate clutched at my heart to know I'd picked it out. But my God, the camera really did love him. Even though I could tell from his expression and posture that he wasn't at all comfortable, he still looked so handsome it was practically unfair.

He had the most perfect, flawless skin, with just a hint of a few lines around his eyes that pointed more to maturity than age. His carelessly tousled hair was effortlessly sexy, and the shape of his mouth had my mind tripping back to earlier, when he said he'd prefer to be giving me head than appearing on TV. Shivers overtook me at the visuals that flooded my mind.

"Well, Damon looks like he'd rather be having a flexi-cystoscopy right now," Julian commented dryly, his thoughts eerily mirroring my own.

I frowned at him. "Do I even want to know what that is?"

"It's when they stick a lens down your jap's eye to — "

Immediately I clamped my hands over my ears. "Oh, my God, shut up. Shut UP." That was way too much information. Typical Julian.

"Anyway, it's unpleasant, that's all you need to know." He seemed oddly pleased that he'd shocked me. We returned our attentions to the screen, where the host was currently talking.

"Damon Atwood, I'm delighted to have you on the show, as I'm sure our viewers are as well. It's been almost a decade since we've seen you on our screens, and now you've decided to take a stab at the West End. What made you choose the stage instead of film this time around?"

There was a pause as the camera panned to Damon. He swallowed, like his mouth was too dry, and all the while my heart was in my throat as I urged him, *Speak, Damon, speak. Pretend you're playing a role.* Finally, he answered, and I exhaled with relief.

"Well, I...um, it was all a matter of timing. My grandmother had always wanted me to act again, and it was shortly after she passed away that I was contacted by our director, Jacob Anthony, to audition for the part of Christian."

"I'm very sorry to hear about your grandmother," said the host. "But I am surprised that you had to audition. I thought winning an Oscar was the acting equivalent of getting tenure. You can have whatever role you want for life."

233

The audience laughed and Damon tugged on his shirt collar, eyes flicking from the host to the studio floor and then back to the host. Alicia let out a sweet chuckle.

"Oh, believe me, honey, no matter how long you've been in this business, sometimes you still have to audition. I had to do it for my last movie, *Saving Caroline*. The director wasn't convinced I could play a cop."

"Very true," said the host. "But in all fairness, you haven't got an Academy Award under your belt just yet, Miss Davidson." His tone was teasing, and again there was laughter from the audience. Alicia gave him a flirtatious angry kitten scowl. It was all a part of her persona, of course. When I glanced at Julian, I saw the barest hint of a smirk on his lips. He liked it when she put on the Marilyn Monroe façade. Though I imagined it was more because he relished the challenge of discovering whatever messy, emotional woman existed underneath it.

"I'm joking, I'm joking," said the host, raising his hands. "But let's talk about the show for a minute. How are you liking the West End, Alicia? Has it been a big change acclimatising to London after so many years in L.A.?"

"It's certainly been a learning curve. I'm still not quite sure what to order in restaurants sometimes," she giggled. "But it's all good, and I have such great people around me, especially my fellow actors," she went on, giving Damon a little nudge with her shoulder.

"Oh yes, of course, you both made your starts in Hollywood. You must have a lot in common."

"We really do," said Alicia. "Plus, there's the added benefit of Damon being British, so he can explain things when I get confused. This one time we were out for lunch and I saw a dessert item on the menu called Spotted Dick. I couldn't stop laughing, and poor Damon was mortified. Thank God he has the patience to put up with me."

I frowned at the screen, particularly since Damon was looking at Alicia like he didn't know what she was talking about. Had she just made all that up? Even though it was weird if she had, I still hoped so. I didn't enjoy thinking of them going out for lunch together, even if it was only as friends.

"It's certainly one of our more humorously named delicacies." The host grinned. "You two must be close, then?"

"Very close," Alicia answered. "I don't know what I'd do if Damon hadn't been cast as Christian. It definitely would've been a much lonelier experience leaving home to stay in a different country if he hadn't."

The host leaned closer, eyeing the two of them. "Am I sensing a romantic link?"

Alicia shifted and crossed one leg over the other, a very coy expression taking shape on her face. "Even if there was, do you think we'd tell you?" She smiled widely.

Again, Damon looked at Alicia like she was taking crazy pills. The host was too focused on the redheaded bombshell to notice, though I doubted the viewers at home would, either. I was attuned to him, and right in that moment I knew Damon was about as uncomfortable as if he were enduring that horrific medical procedure Julian had mentioned.

"They're not together. Why is she trying to pretend like they are?" I said, almost to myself.

"Because she's a shrewd businesswoman, Rose," Julian answered pointedly. "She knows how to pique people's interest enough to get them curious while still giving nothing away. Bet you a tenner the ticket sales for the show just went through the roof. People will go solely on the off chance that the two famous leads are getting it on behind the scenes."

"Yeah, but... but she can't just do that to Damon. He was already freaking out over this interview, and now she's making shit up off the cuff. It's going to put him off his game, and he's been doing so well."

Julian eyed me perceptively. "Answer honestly — are you really worried about Damon, or are you worried that what she's said might hold some truth?"

I gaped at him, upset now. "There's no truth to it. Damon's not like that. He's too honourable. If he and Alicia were together, then he'd tell me, and he certainly wouldn't be pursuing me like he has been if they were."

Julian's mouth tilted down in a frown, like he felt bad for what he'd said. There was also a hint of sympathy there, and I hated it. He didn't understand. He thought I was soft-hearted and naïve, falling for the charms of yet another actor. He didn't know the intense connection Damon and I shared, didn't know how it felt when we were alone together.

It wasn't that my heart was soft, it was that Julian's was too hard. He simply didn't understand. The problem was, though he probably hadn't intended to, he'd planted a seed of doubt.

I just hoped there was no water around that would encourage it to grow.

Nineteen.
Rose

I loved the smell of old theatres. Loved the faded grandeur of the velvet upholstered seats, the sense of history in the air, the echoing footsteps of performers long past. In this particular building, there was a cherub missing a foot and some sort of mythical creature playing a lute with no arm. I always liked to notice the things that for most people faded into the background. Sometimes you were so focused on the stage that you forgot to appreciate the aged beauty that surrounded it.

It was Monday morning, our first day of dress rehearsals, and I sat on the edge of the stage, staring out at the empty pews as I finished my cup of coffee. I arrived a little earlier than necessary, eager to get started, and lots of cast members were starting trickle in. There was also the addition of the orchestra musicians, who would be playing their instruments in the pit beneath the stage. There was just something about the music being live, loud and vibrant in your ears, that brought with it a whole new dimension to the experience.

Somebody came and sat down beside me, and my lips curved in a smile as I smelled Damon's woodsy cologne. Turning to look at him, I saw he was wearing his Christian outfit; black trousers, dress shoes, a white shirt with the collar undone, suspenders and a black hat.

"Good morning," he said as my eyes wandered over him.

"Morning. Nice threads." I didn't mention how hot he looked in period clothing.

His lips twitched. "Thanks."

A moment of silence elapsed before he asked, "Did you see the interview?"

I nodded, trying to keep a neutral expression. I'd been doing my best not to think about Alicia's sneaky tactics, trying to get people to wonder if she and Damon were an item.

"I did. You were great."

Damon let out a self-deprecating sigh. "You're lying. I was stiff and awkward, but at least it's over with now."

I turned my head to him fully and reached out to place my hand over his. "I'm not lying. I was so proud of you sticking it out even though you didn't want to be there."

"Aye, well." He paused before continuing, "I'm sorry about Alicia. I don't know where she got the idea to pretend there's something between us...."

"Don't worry about it," I cut him off. "She was just being savvy, getting people interested in the show." It was hard to say the words, but I forced them out. There was no room for any more jealousy between us. I didn't want there to be. And I trusted Damon, I had to.

His expression was tense as he rubbed the bit of scruff on his jaw. "The show should speak for itself. We shouldn't need to peddle false gossip to sell tickets."

I frowned. "No, you're right, but unfortunately it's the way of the world sometimes."

Glancing over his shoulder, I saw Alicia enter the theatre. We made brief eye contact, and there was something vaguely challenging in her expression. I tried to dismiss it, but it niggled at me. A moment later Jacob arrived, calling for Damon and Alicia to follow him to his office. Apparently, he needed a word. For a second I wondered what it was about, but I didn't think on it too much as I joined Iggy and we began the morning warm-up with the cast.

When Damon returned to the stage area, his expression was furious. What on earth had Jacob said to him to make him look so irate? Was he unhappy with the way the interview had gone yesterday?

Damon's anger was so virulent that it started to affect the mood of everyone else, and a tense atmosphere fell over the theatre. At one point when Iggy kindly asked him to stand on his mark, he snapped, telling him he'd stand wherever he bloody well pleased. The show of temper was startling, and I felt concerned. I noticed almost absently that Jacob and Alicia were standing off to one side, whispering to each other as though in cahoots.

When I managed to find a spare moment to go to Damon, I placed my hand on his elbow and asked quietly, "Is everything all right?"

His jaw moved, his mouth forming a straight line when he answered curtly, "Everything's fine."

I knew he was lying, but I didn't push him on it. When Iggy called for a break, I went to use the bathroom. At the end of the corridor, I stopped to take a quick drink from a water fountain, and when I turned around Damon was there, his gaze hot and needful. Without a word he took my hand and forcefully pulled me down the hallway.

"Where are we going?" I asked, a little on edge.

He didn't reply, and when we reached the room he was looking for, he pushed the door open before pulling me inside. I glanced around, seeing it was his dressing room. Damon let go of my hand, and I watched as he strode over to the dresser, his shoulders knit with tension. He let out an impassioned sound of irritation, raked a hand through his hair, then violently shoved a mug off the table in a fit of temper. It fell to the floor and shattered loudly.

I stood there, almost too nervous to speak, as he turned back to me. His gaze was dark – hungry – and when he started to advance on me, I backed up until I hit the wall. Damon stopped when he reached me, his chest flush with mine, and grabbed my face in his hands. Before I even had a chance to react, he planted his mouth on mine, kissing me like he was starving for it.

I instantly softened, my anxiousness melting away and another feeling building: arousal. There was something about Damon's kisses, something that made me want to open up to him completely. My lips, my arms...my legs.

His tongue swept inside my mouth, hard and frantic, and a small moan emanated from the back of my throat. He grunted, one foot kicking my leg aside so he could brace his knee between my thighs.

"Damon," I panted as he fumbled with the buttons on my blouse, flicking them open until my dark purple bra was exposed. Every tiny hair on my body stood on end when he moved his knee against the apex of my thighs, pressing down where a coil of desire lingered.

"I just need...." he began breathily but trailed off, too focused on what he was doing.

His mouth left my lips to trail across my jaw, down my neck and chest, until he reached the rise of my cleavage. There he pressed his lips to the tops of my breasts while letting out a deep rumbling groan.

"I just need to touch you." He finally finished his earlier statement. Right after he said it, his hand found the waistband of my leggings, slipping beneath to brush over the lace of my underwear. I mewled and moved my hips, desperate for him to go all the way. Touch me where I wanted him most.

His mouth returned to mine, his tongue sweeping in once more and tasting me like I was his favourite everything. When his fingers slid past the seam of my knickers, I sucked in a harsh breath. His touch was gentle at first, explorative, but I knew he had to be able to feel how wet I was. His thumb swept over my clit once, twice, three times, and I tilted my hips more to allow him greater access.

"Soft," he whispered huskily in my ear before sucking on the lobe. "Touching you gives me peace, Rose."

"Please," I begged, not entirely sure what for.

His fingers drew circles over my clit, and he stared down at me in fascination, his eyes glittering. They closed for a second, his mouth hanging open. When he opened them again, they practically scorched. "Only you, petal," he said, thumb pressing down on my clit as his fingers moved lower. He pressed one inside me, and I moaned so loudly I started to blush, my attention going to the door to make sure it was still closed. At the same time, I tried not to make any more noise for fear of someone passing by and hearing.

To this end, I bit my lower lip to stifle any sounds. Damon's erection pushed at my belly, and for a second I wished he'd undo his trousers so I could see. I wanted him inside me, wanted to feel what it was like to be joined with him completely.

His other hand went to the lip I was biting, pulling it free before slowly moving his thumb inside. It mirrored the movement of his thumb down below, making small, delicious circles in my mouth. I sucked on him then, feeling an orgasm building. He pushed another finger inside me,

241

and I practically came apart right there and then. I felt so full with him, couldn't imagine what it would be like to have him make love to me.

His thumb left my mouth to cup my cheek as he bent to kiss me once more. It was a deep kiss, full of unspoken need. Now his fingers were focused solely on making me come. I could tell he wanted desperately to see me orgasm because he seemed to grow more frenzied, every muscle in his body coiled tight.

"Oh, fuck, oh, God," I swore past his lips as a sharp, mind-blowing pleasure swept over me. My sex pulsed as I came and Damon continued to stroke me, but slower now, ever slower like he was matching the waves of my orgasm until they finally petered out.

Our gazes locked, and I couldn't look away. I saw a world of emotion in those deep brown irises as my brain sputtered and tried to comprehend what had just happened. He'd pounced on me for some unknown reason. There was a desperation about him, and I needed to find out its source.

We were still staring at one another, imprisoned in a moment, when a sound came from outside. The door knob turned, and someone began to enter the dressing room. We both froze, still entwined together.

"Damon? Are you in here? I wanted to talk to you about earlier — " Alicia's words came to an abrupt halt as soon as she saw us. No part of me was exposed really, well, except for my bra. But Damon's hand was still down my pants, so it was fairly obvious what we'd just been doing.

My pulse sped up, but I couldn't move, too mortified that Alicia had walked in on us mid…whatever that just was. Her mouth firmed, her eyes going steely and hard as she looked at Damon.

"I'm sorry. I'll come back later."

She closed the door with a loud, obviously pissed-off thud, and Damon let his chin fall to the top of my head. "Jesus."

"We should've locked the door."

"No, she should've knocked," he disagreed, sounding aggravated. I knew it wasn't directed at me, but my stomach still tensed at his tone of voice. A moment of quiet passed as Damon removed his hand from my underwear and wrapped his arms around me, holding me in an embrace.

"What do you think she wanted?" I asked softly.

He exhaled a long, weary breath before placing a kiss to my crown and moving away. I glanced at his crotch to find him still hard, but I wasn't brave enough to say anything about it. He went and took a seat by the dressing table, twisting around to face me. Self-conscious, I began doing up the buttons of my blouse. His eyes followed the movement.

"When Jacob asked us into his office, it was to inform us of the huge boost in ticket sales after last night's television appearance. He wants us to do more."

"Oh," I breathed, suddenly understanding. Julian had been right. "So that's why you looked so angry — you don't want to do any more publicity?"

Damon shook his head, both hands clenched into fists. "It's not only that. He wants us to...." He trailed off, jaw tight. "I can't believe he had the gall to suggest this, but he wants us to fabricate a relationship for the press. He wants us to pretend to be an item to sell more tickets."

My heart stilled, my mouth dropping open in disbelief. "What? He can't make you do that."

Damon scoffed. "He's not making me do anything. I told him to fuck off."

I gasped. "You told Jacob Anthony to fuck off? Oh, my God, Damon...." I paused for a second. "That's kind of badass."

He cocked one dark eyebrow at me, and I had to admit, it really was quite sexy. "The ticket sales haven't been living up to expectations. I told him I was already seeing someone, and then the bastard said I could continue having you hang about my house in your pyjamas as much as I wanted, so long as the press didn't catch wind. I don't care how good a director he is — the man is a fucking arsehole. I told him I'd quit if he kept pushing."

My hand went to my chest and rubbed, a touch of embarrassment hitting me at the "pyjamas" bit. I'd thought Jacob was so wrapped up in his own little world that he hadn't noticed my attire. Clearly, he had noticed; he just hadn't really cared.

Damon stood from his seat, coming toward me again and clasping either side of my neck. His thumbs rubbed into my tense muscles, perhaps in an effort to help me relax. "I won't let anyone interfere in what's between us, Rose. I promise."

"If you keep saying no, he'll try to have Iggy fire me just out of spite," I whispered. "I know men like Jacob. They hold a grudge."

Damon's eyes hardened. "If he fires you, then I really will quit. You're more important to me than this production."

Something in my heart literally snapped at that, and I felt emotion tugging at me. I didn't know whether I wanted to laugh or cry. Damon was so loyal and perfect and wonderful, and I didn't feel like I deserved him. I certainly didn't want him quitting his first acting role in almost a decade just for me.

"Hey," he said. "Get out of your head and stop worrying. Let me handle this. He's not going to win."

I stared at him, biting my lip again out of nervousness. I really needed to stop doing that. "Okay," I said finally, my voice tiny.

Damon's eyes flickered between mine, like he was trying to find any morsels of doubt so he could squash them. "Okay," he echoed, and then pressed one final kiss to my lips. His hand moved from my neck and he slid his fingers between mine, clasping my hand tight as a symbol of our solidarity.

***

Alicia was absent for the rest of the day. She was supposed to be there for dress rehearsals, but apparently she'd fallen ill and had to go home. I didn't think much of it, but suspected her illness was more sour grapes and anger after walking in on me and Damon *in flagrante*, or, well, halfway *in flagrante,* as it were.

I got to go home after lunch because the cast were working on dialogue. Stopping by the nearest supermarket, I picked up a few things for dinner before heading home. Everything seemed normal when I entered the apartment, and I went about putting away my groceries until I heard a distinctly sexual noise coming from the direction of Julian's bedroom – a feminine moan, to be exact.

It was afterwards that I noticed a pair of high heels strewn haphazardly across the living room floor, and there was a coat and handbag on the couch. Frowning, I knew Julian wasn't with a client, because he never brought them here. He only ever met up with them at hotels or their own houses. He liked to keep our home a home in that sense, but it was also for security purposes. Oftentimes, he might have a client become a little too attached, and if they didn't know where he lived, it ensured that they couldn't start stalking him. He also used a different name, and a special phone separate from his personal one to make himself even more untraceable.

So yeah, this wasn't a client. I actually found myself smiling after a minute, because it'd been a while since my friend had brought a woman home for sex, sex he wasn't being paid for. This could potentially be a good sign.

I went about my business, but put on my headphones to listen to some music and allow Julian and whoever he was with their privacy. About forty-five minutes went by, and I was just finished preparing a lasagne for dinner when his bedroom door opened. Soft footsteps sounded down the hall and I tried to play it cool, when really I was dying to check out Julian's new lady friend.

Any happy thoughts I'd been having immediately fled when I turned, spoon in hand, and came face to face with a very rumpled and very much freshly fucked Alicia Davidson.

Oh, Julian.

Bad choice.

Her gaze hardened, but she straightened up as though mentally putting on her armour. Yep, I was fairly sure this was a woman who wasn't going to let anyone shame her about her behaviour, least of all me.

"We really need to stop meeting like this," I said, my voice neutral.

Alicia gave me a contemptuous eye roll before walking into the living area and picking up her shoes. "You can save the holier-than-thou speech, Rose. I'm well aware that you're the perfect, sweet little flower and I'm the harlot out to seduce your handsome prince."

"That's not what I think of you," I said, putting down the spoon and bracing both hands on the counter as I watched her. "In fact, I don't blame you for wanting Damon. In all honesty, it's still hard for me to accept that he even knows my name, never mind enjoys my company."

She very slowly raised her eyebrows as she slipped on one dark blue heel and then the other. "Is that what they're calling it these days? It looked like he was more than enjoying your company today in his dressing room."

Ouch, that burned, no matter how much I wished it hadn't.

"Alicia, I never meant for you to walk in on that, but you have to know I'm not playing a game. I like Damon — I more than like him. And I'm pretty sure he more than likes me. We're just…seeing where things go between us." I shrugged and met her gaze evenly.

Some of the fight went out of her then, and she slumped down onto the couch. "I know that. I suppose I've known it from the start. The way he looks at you — that's special. He's just a really good guy, you know? He's an old-fashioned gentleman, the kind of man who'll treat you with respect and care for you until you're old and grey. I don't meet a lot of men like that in my profession. It was silly to think he'd be interested in someone like me." She paused to let out a joyless laugh. "My halo lost its shine a long, long time ago."

I was honestly shocked by her confession and moved away from the counter, going to take a seat across from her in the living area.

"That's not true. Good men would be lining up the block for a chance to go out with you. It's just this business — everybody's only out for quick, shallow connections.

I've been burned a few times myself. You need to look outside the pool of men who work in the industry."

She glanced at me then, considering me for a long moment. "Maybe you're right."

"You're beautiful, Alicia. You can have anyone you want."

Now one eyebrow rose, and she sighed sadly. "Obviously not anyone. Not Damon."

For a second I didn't know what to say. On the one hand, I wanted to tell her she probably could have him if he hadn't met me first, but on the other it felt wrong deep in my bones to even think it. There was something in me that truly believed it was fate that Damon and I had met, and the idea of him ever going with anyone else, even in an alternate reality, made me recoil.

"If you admire Damon so much, then why are you here with Julian?" I asked, my eyes going in the direction of his bedroom to make sure the door was still shut. I wouldn't put it past my friend to eavesdrop on this little conversation. Still, I had to ask the question. Although I may have felt some sympathy for Alicia and her inability to find a good man, I was still pissed at the idea of her using my friend.

She let out a humourless laugh. "Because I was lonely and he was available."

Now I frowned hard, because Julian didn't deserve to be treated like an object. Perhaps outwardly it wasn't so obvious to see that he was a good person, but if she knew him like I did, she'd know he was more than good. Seriously, sometimes before I went to bed at night I'd think about his childhood and just silently cry for the little boy he used to be.

"Oh, don't look at me like that, Rose," Alicia chided. "Julian's using me just the same as I'm using him. It's a win-win situation. No real emotions are involved so nobody gets hurt."

I grew stiff. "If you knew the real him you wouldn't say that."

Now she huffed. "That's where you're wrong. I know the real him all too well. The fact of the matter is that when I look at Julian, all I see is my own image reflected back, hard and world-weary and cold. I don't want another version of me. I want someone kind, someone selfless, someone who no matter how difficult I can be at times, will still love me anyway."

I stared at her, letting her words seep in. If that was how she thought of Julian, then she really didn't fucking deserve him. I could've slapped my friend for selling himself so short. He always did that and it broke my heart. I wanted him to find someone who could see his goodness like I could. And Alicia certainly wasn't that person; she was too wrapped up in her own wants and needs.

She rose then, picking up her handbag and coat. Her posture straightened, and then she took a few steps toward the door. I watched her go, but she paused for a second before turning back around. Her sharp, cat-like green eyes perused me.

"You might not believe this, but I like you, Rose, and I think if things were different we could have been friends. But know this — if I ever get my chance with Damon Atwood, I'm taking it, and I'll never apologise for going after the thing that I want."

With that she left, and I frowned at her retreating figure. Her words made me worry, because I knew that if anything were to cause me and Damon to drift apart, even for a moment, she'd swoop right in and steal him out from underneath my feet. But then I also knew that though he might be fooled by her, Damon would never love Alicia. Her words were far too revealing.

I'll never apologise for going after the thing that I want.

This was the difference between us. She saw him as a thing, another prized possession to have under her belt, something to make her feel good. I didn't see Damon as a thing — I saw him as a soul, a person, a being so vital he made the world a better place just by existing within it.

And I cared about his happiness, about how I made him feel, not just about how he made me feel in return.

Twenty.
Damon

I wanted to smile, watching Rose sit on a step. She was tying the laces on her shoes as we got ready to practice a routine. It was an odd sensation, because normally I was far too withdrawn within myself to want to do something as ordinary as smile at a woman I found beautiful.

So far I'd taken her out on two dates. One was dinner and a show at the London Palladium, and the other was a day out biking around the city. She knew every inch of the place, so I let her be my tour guide.

We were taking things slow, like we'd both agreed. We were still trying to remain friends and let things naturally progress to something more. I thought it was best, because we both had issues when it came to relationships, though I hadn't broached the subject of mine to her yet. There was this small part of me that thought she might be horrified, that the truth might scare her away.

Even so, I couldn't stop thinking about the time we spent in my dressing room. Making her come had been like a religious experience. I swore I could hear Beethoven playing in my ears when she fell apart on my hand. Time had moved in slow motion as I fixated on the tremors shuddering through her body and the way her breaths came out all choppy and uneven.

Jacob tried broaching the topic of me and Alicia faking a relationship a handful of times. On the third and final try, I lost my temper, telling him that if he didn't stop, I'd walk right out the door. An hour later he came to my dressing room and apologised, worried I really would up and quit.

Now we were halfway through the third week of dress rehearsals. One more week and we'd be opening the show to audiences. I was nervous about that, but also because I had a question I'd been wanting to ask Rose, a burning one that had been on the tip of my tongue for days now. Unfortunately, I hadn't yet built up the courage to get it out.

Alicia, who seemed angry after walking in on me and Rose together, had quickly forgotten the whole episode ever occurred. In fact, she was being even more friendly towards me than usual. I knew it made Rose edgy, the same way I felt edgy whenever Blake was within touching distance of her, but I could hardly avoid interacting with Alicia. We had to act together. It was unavoidable.

She came into the stage area wearing a glittery dress that looked like it was made entirely from silver beads, though admittedly I knew next to nothing about women's fashion. I did love how Rose dressed. It was understated but very feminine.

"Jacob," Alicia called to our director who was standing having a discussion with Iggy. "Is Farrah around? This dress is too long. I need her to take it up a little."

It didn't look too long to me. In fact, it looked a little short. But again, I knew nothing of fashion. Jacob pursed his lips, arched an eyebrow, and responded, "In my opinion, it shows quite enough leg already, Alicia dear."

She pouted. "It's not about showing leg, it's about being able to move efficiently. Every time I twist my hips, the stupid thing catches mid-thigh."

They continued to argue about whether or not the dress should be altered, and I knew it was going to take a while for them to come to an agreement, so I went to sit by Rose.

"If Farrah makes that dress any shorter, Alicia's going to be flashing her knickers at the front row," she said under her breath.

Letting out a quiet chuckle, I allowed my arm to brush against hers, and she inhaled sharply as colour warmed her cheeks. I found myself doing that a lot lately, finding new ways to touch her that weren't explicitly sexual. I particularly liked it when she inhaled like that, or when her skin pimpled into gooseflesh, because it was a sign she enjoyed my touch just as much as I enjoyed touching her.

"I just hope they don't spend all day arguing about it," I said, lips twitching.

"When Gene Kelly made *Singin' in the Rain*, there used to be all these rules and regulations about how much skin you could show on screen," Rose told me, going into another of her Gene Kelly anecdotes. I was particularly amused by the one about him purportedly donating money to the IRA in their struggle for Irish Independence. It was certainly a gutsy way to get in touch with your heritage. Over the last week or two, I'd quickly come to realise she was something of an encyclopaedia on the renowned actor, and could spout off fact after fact. It was very endearing.

"Anyway," she went on. "So there's this one scene in the film, actually it's sort of a dream sequence, and Gene's character performs this totally epic choreography with Cyd Charisse. She was a really famous dancer and actress of the time, which is phenomenal in itself, considering she suffered from polio as a little girl."

"Is that the scene with the woman in the white dress?" I asked, and her eyes lit up that I remembered it.

"Yes! She wore this short white dress with a long flowy scarf that they incorporated into the dance with a wind machine, which also made the dress blow up around her thighs. And you see, Gene really wanted to showcase Cyd's legs, because she had *amazing* pins, but the film censor would only allow a certain amount of thigh to be shown." She paused to let out an amused laugh. "Every time the censor came on set, Gene would quickly cover up Cyd's legs, and then every time he left he'd hike her skirt higher again for the cameras. If you go back and watch it, you'll notice how risqué it was for its time. You can even see a hint of arse cheek."

This last bit made me laugh, and I was aware of how much freer I was with my laughs around Rose. I was even relaxed enough to smile without feeling vulnerable. I trusted her implicitly.

"It's a pity Alicia doesn't have anyone to hitch up her dress," I commented, unable to help the affection in my voice. I loved how excited she got about these little Gene Kelly titbits.

"Perhaps they should employ someone for the job. Do you think many would apply for the role of skirt lifter?" she asked humorously.

That made me laugh more. "Aye, predominantly men…well, and lesbians."

Rose laughed, too, and when our gazes met, I had a sudden moment of courage as I blurted, "Come home with me this weekend."

Her eyes widened a small bit and her mouth opened, then shut. "You're going home?"

I nodded, my throat growing dry. "For the long weekend. I need to get out of the city for a while, been feeling a bit homesick. A few days back on the Island will see me right."

"Ah, I see," said Rose, and her expression turned sad as she studied me. "You never mentioned feeling homesick."

I shrugged and glanced away. "You don't need to be listening to me whining about homesickness."

Her cool, soft hand went to mine as she intertwined our fingers. "You never whine, Damon, and I like being the person you vent to. It makes me feel useful."

I moved my thumb, sliding it along the inside of her wrist, feeling gratified when I saw her tremble. "So, will you come with me? I don't want to be without you."

When she replied, her voice was quiet. "I'd love to…it's just, do you think it's a little soon for us to be going away together?"

Her question made something in my heart tug, because I knew what she really meant. She was nervous about spending the night with me. It was a big step, and, though I very much wanted to be inside her, I had no intention of rushing into anything.

"I don't think so. But Rose" — I coughed to clear my throat — "I have a spare bedroom you can stay in. This trip isn't about…sex," I said, almost feeling shy saying the word. God, what a pair we made. "I just want to spend a few days with you away from the city. I want your company, that's all."

She bit her lip, and my eyes followed the movement before she let out a small, nervous breath. "Okay, then," she said, mustering a smile. "I'll come."

My chest thumped wildly at her acceptance, and I squeezed her hand tighter.

"Thank you," I breathed, and I meant it. She had no idea the gift she'd just given me, no idea how appealing I found the idea of having her in my home, the only place where my heart felt whole.

***

255

Early on Friday morning we caught a flight to Inverness, and then I drove us to the island in a rental car. There wasn't a need to take a boat, as Skye was connected to the mainland by bridge. The entire journey Rose had her eyes glued out the window, fascinated by every new thing she saw. I couldn't blame her. We were in a very beautiful part of the world, a place that had always made me feel at peace ever since I was a child.

When I was a teenager and my life was turned upside down by fame and a selfish, out-of-control father, I'd come here for refuge and never looked back until the day Gran died. At the time I thought it might be a terrible decision to go to London, but looking at the beautiful, kind, amazing woman sitting next to me in the passenger seat, I now considered it one of the best decisions I'd ever made.

"I seriously can't get over this scenery. I feel like I'm in *Outlander*," she said with giddy excitement. I had the urge to lean across the car and kiss her, but restrained myself.

"Whatever did happen to Jamie and Claire?" I asked fondly. I hadn't listened in with her since that day we spent lunch together in the practice room, when I'd been so sexually frustrated I was sure twenty cold showers couldn't cool me down.

She cast me an exasperated look but smiled anyway. "*Sooo* much. There's no point even trying to catch you up. I'm already on book three. You'll just have to read them yourself."

"I think I will," I said.

"Oh, my God! Are those sheep on the road? Look how close they are to the car. They don't even care."

"You're such a city lass," I chided her. "You talk like you've never seen a sheep before."

Rose blushed. "I actually haven't. This is my first visit to Scotland. I never have much disposable income for holidays."

This news filled me with pride to be bringing her here for the first time, but also to be bringing her on what could be considered her first holiday in who knew how long. That's what I loved about Rose. Even though her upbringing had been just as unusual as mine, she wasn't jaded. She kept her sense of wonder about the world, and it was what made her special in my eyes.

"I'll have to make this trip a good one, then," I said low.

She looked at me as I concentrated on the road, and I could feel her studying my profile. "You seem different," she said at length.

"I do?"

"Yeah. There's this tension to you when you're in the city. It's not there anymore."

"Of course it's not. I'm home, Rose. No matter where my life takes me, Skye will always be my home," I said, glancing at her briefly.

She wore a slightly dazed expression. "I don't know why I find that sexy, Damon, but yeah, it's kinda hot," she blurted, and then seemed to think better of it. Her cheeks tinged with red.

"You're sexier," I said in an effort to soothe her embarrassment, my eyes tracing over her form. My words didn't have the intended effect, though, because she seemed to turn even redder and focused her attention out the window. I smirked. "What? No response?"

"None that's appropriate to be said in a moving vehicle when I can't act on it," she answered, shifting her thighs a little.

Now I was the one without a reply, my head swimming with the sexy-as-fuck image of her straddling me in the front seat. She might pull my belt free and sink her hand around my cock…. Fuck, I needed to think of something else. Sheep, I should think of sheep. Nothing sexy about sheep. Bloody noisy annoying bastards. They never shut the fuck up.

Ah, that did the trick.

After a few minutes of quiet passed, I finally spoke. "It feels good to get away from everyone. I like the cast well enough, but being around them every day was beginning to stifle."

Rose cast me a curious glance. "Even Alicia?"

"Especially Alicia," I said, placing extra emphasis on the words. She seemed content with that.

"I never told you about the day she walked in on us in your dressing room," she went on, almost absently, her gaze still trained out the window.

My curiosity was piqued. "No?"

Rose shook her head and turned her body to face me. When I put my hand on the gear stick, my fingers brushed her knee and she jumped a little. It was probably slightly perverse, but I enjoyed how reactive she was to even the simplest touch.

"When I got home that day, Julian had someone in his bedroom. From the noises I could hear, it wasn't too difficult to figure out what they were doing. Then a little while later his bedroom door opened, and out walked Alicia. I swear I couldn't have been more surprised if Mother Theresa had walked out of that bedroom."

I let out a laugh, taken aback. "You're joking."

"No joke. I think she went to Julian because she was feeling shitty about walking in on us. Now she's not returning any of his phone calls, and it makes me fucking angry because she was just using him. Julian deserves better. I mean, he's hardly broken-hearted over her, but I hate that this is the kind of behaviour he's come to accept. I just really wish a woman would come along and truly care for him, you know?"

I really wanted to emote, but because of my own experiences, I was slightly prejudiced towards Julian. However, I knew that if someone like Rose could love him like a brother, then he must have been a good person. There must have been a reason he made a living from sex.

"Has he ever had a girlfriend?" I asked, curious.

Rose sighed. "He had one serious girlfriend a couple years ago. She was an escort, too. It ended very messily, as you can imagine."

"Say if I'm being judgemental, but I can't see many women being okay with his profession."

Rose sighed. "No, you're right. I definitely couldn't do it. I guess I've just always held a hope for him. He has his reasons for how he lives his life, but sometimes I just wish he could love someone so completely that the very idea of sleeping with anyone else makes him feel ill. Is that horrible?"

"Not at all. You love him. You want him to be happy," I said.

A moment of quiet passed, and Rose began chewing on her lip. I could tell she wanted to say something more but was hesitating. Finally, she got it out.

"Can I ask you something? It's fine if you don't want to answer."

"No, ask me."

"The first day we met, when I told you about Julian, you said something that troubled me. You said you didn't have the best memories of sex workers...." Her voice trailed off, and my hands fisted reflexively on the steering wheel.

I coughed to clear my throat, which suddenly felt dry as a bone. My heart was beating double time, and a sick dread filled my stomach. I didn't want to talk about this. I didn't want her to be disgusted. In fact, I could hardly believe I'd said it at all, but it must have been a moment of weakness. I'd been so stressed that day, overwhelmed with leaving behind my island life and coming to work in London.

"I remember," I answered finally.

Rose seemed to hesitate again, and her voice was barely a whisper when she asked, "What did you mean by that?"

I lifted a hand and began to scratch my neck. I scratched so hard I was afraid I might leave a mark. "I told you about my dad, how he liked to spend my money on parties and booze, drugs, too."

Rose nodded but stayed silent. I summoned up the courage to keep going.

"I was just fifteen. Still a virgin, and, despite having worked in Hollywood for a number of years, I was still fairly innocent. Mum saw to that. I was even more sheltered than typical teenagers, because once I started acting, I was home schooled, so I wasn't around other kids much unless we worked together."

"Sounds lonely," Rose commented.

"It was, but then again, I've always been a natural loner. I mean, I like people, I just feel a bit drained if I have to be around them all the time. That's why I was so adamant about going home this weekend. I needed a break."

"Tell me about your dad," she prompted gently, obviously aware that I was veering off topic.

I exhaled heavily, feeling ill as the memory resurfaced. "We lived in a house he was renting in the Hollywood Hills – with my money, of course. The parties seemed to go on all day and all night sometimes, but I mostly kept to my room."

I paused, remembering that shy lad, the one who could put on another skin and make audiences feel a world of emotions, but then when he had to be himself again, he was painfully introverted. Self-conscious and timid. Still waters. Not much had changed, only now I wasn't so timid. I was stronger, more in control of my own destiny. Rose studied me sadly.

"After a while he got into hiring prostitutes," I blurted, and heard her shocked intake of breath. "It was easy to pay for things like that when you could afford it. I felt sick every time they visited the house, sometimes several of them at once. One Christmas when I got home after being on set, I found him in the living room with three scantily clad women.

"There were drugs scattered all over the table, and my dad was off his face. I tried going to my bedroom, but he was having none of it. Insisted I do a line to celebrate the holiday with them. I couldn't get away, and in the end he practically forced my head down until I snorted the white powder. Must've been cocaine, but really, it could've been anything. Next he announced that one of the prostitutes, I can't even remember her name, I was so traumatised, was to be my Christmas present.

"She climbed astride me on the couch and began taking off her clothes. It's such a weird thing to remember, but I have this distinct recollection of her talking about one of

261

my recent films, saying how sexy I was in it." I paused, gripping the steering wheel so hard my knuckles hurt. "I was a fucking child." I ground my teeth, angry at the memory, as Rose set a soothing hand on my shoulder.

"We can stop talking about this if it's too much," she said, her voice wavering like she was feeling just as emotional as I was right then.

I shook my head. "No, it's okay. If I don't tell you now I never will."

"All right," she whispered, keeping her hand on my shoulder.

"My...my dad took the other two women and went into his bedroom. I was left alone with that one prostitute. My head felt fuzzy from the drugs. I'd barely taken a drop of alcohol in my entire life, so obviously the coke hit me hard. Before I knew it, she'd taken my virginity. I can barely even remember because I was so high. The next morning, I woke up still in that same spot on the couch, my dad in the kitchen cooking breakfast and going on about me finally becoming a man. How he was so *proud*."

I fell silent then, letting the stark horror of the memory wash over me. I heard Rose hitch a small, watery breath before I continued. "I didn't touch a woman for two years after that, could barely even stomach the idea of sex. It all just felt like badness. In my late teens, just before I was granted my emancipation from my dad, I starting dating someone. Her name was Jennifer and she was an aspiring actress, but unlike me she was wild. Confident. I felt excited whenever I was around her, thought I was in love with her. In the end, it became clear she was only with me for my money and fame so I broke up with her. It was like Dad all fucking over again. I was so young, but at that point

I decided I'd never touch another woman again, and for a long time I stuck to it.

"Then about four years ago I met Lizzy here in Skye. She was a young widow with two small children, and she was very sweet to me. We struck up a friendship that slowly turned sexual. She knew about what had happened to me and was very patient. When we finally started having sex, it felt like I became obsessed. I'd abstained for so long, and then suddenly I couldn't get enough. In the end, it was my inability to trust that forced her to end it. She wanted to get married, but I just couldn't make the commitment. My experiences with Dad and with Jennifer meant I didn't trust anyone new. There was always this nagging voice in the back of my head telling me people only wanted me for my money, that as soon as I committed to Lizzy she'd change, start spending all my money and become a different person. This was why I could never give my heart to her, could never love her. She said I was just passing time with her and that she deserved to be loved completely. She was right. She deserved better than anything I could ever offer."

I stopped speaking then. Rose was being very quiet, but when I turned to look at her, I saw tears in her eyes. It shocked me to see her emote to my story on such a deep level that I had to pull the car over. I hadn't meant to upset her. Once I turned off the engine, I pulled her to me.

"Don't cry, petal. It's all over now."

She sniffled, her face pressed to my chest. "But you were so young, Damon. I can't believe the situation you were in. Your dad should be sent to prison for how he treated you, and that...that woman, what she did was tantamount to rape."

"I know that. I know," I said, petting her head and trying to soothe her, even though I was the one who'd been through the experience. It was odd, but in a way I felt a disconnect from it all. Now when I looked back, I didn't feel like that boy was me. I didn't feel like the sheltered, innocent lad who'd experienced that awful night. That had only been one thing amid years of neglect living with Dad, but it was the turning point. I might not have sought emancipation for another two years, but it was the details of my father's treatment of me coming out during the trial that had finally secured my freedom. A lot of the records were sealed, and I was glad. It would kill me to have people know about it. Some of the details were public, but not the most sordid ones. It was different with Rose. I wanted her to know. I wanted her to understand and accept me regardless.

"I'm getting snot all over your shirt," she said then, and I laughed tenderly.

"That's okay. I've got lots of clean ones in my suitcase."

She pulled away to look up at me, her eyes reddened from crying. "Damon, I can't imagine how horrific that must've been. It's the ugliest things that are the hardest to share, and I know how much courage that must've taken." She paused to suck in a breath. "But know this — it doesn't affect how I see you. I see you perfectly, and I like what I see. I always will. This only helps me to understand better, and for that I feel truly honoured. I feel honoured to be entrusted with your hurt," she said, whispering the last part. "So thank you."

I didn't know what to say. It was almost like she knew I feared her rejection and was eager to reassure me that it wasn't going to happen. "Thank you," I whispered back, repeating her words but with a different meaning. I ran a hand through her long, silky hair, my gaze tracing her pretty features. After a long while I hugged her with both arms wrapped around her shoulders, pressed my lips to the top of her forehead and murmured, "I'm so glad I found you."

Twenty-One.
Rose

It was early evening when we finally arrived at Damon's cottage. After our heart-to-heart in the car, I was still feeling very raw, still reeling from the things that had happened to him, things I couldn't change. I now understood so much, why he'd chosen a life of obscurity over fame, and why he was so resistant to letting people in.

But really, I felt honoured that he'd chosen to let me get as close as he has, even though I didn't really understand why he trusted me. The fact that he couldn't commit to this Lizzy woman was troubling, but perhaps he just hadn't been ready then. Perhaps he'd needed a few more years to get to that point. At least, I hoped.

Stepping out of the car, I breathed in the fresh sea air and just soaked up the scenery for a minute. Damon's cottage sat right on the coast, and there were barely any houses for miles around, just a small few scattered haphazardly in the distance. My hair was swept up with the wind, billowing around my head.

"It's so beautiful," I said, but Damon was busy getting our luggage from the boot and didn't hear me. I turned and started following him to the door of the cottage when the sound of a dog barking came from the distance. Glancing over my shoulder, I saw an older woman wearing a thick woollen jumper, heavy jeans, and Wellington boots making her way towards us, a golden German shepherd walking alongside her.

"Damon," she said in a thick Scottish accent, "it's so good to see you." She seemed pleased, but the dog seemed even more so, scarpering over to Damon and practically leaping on top of him. Seriously, the dog was so overjoyed to see Damon it was almost like he couldn't believe his luck.

"Charlie," said Damon, going down on one knee to give the dog's fur an affectionate ruffle. "How are you, boy?" The dog yipped and whined, like he couldn't contain his emotions. It was too adorable for words. When he licked Damon right on the face, I laughed, but he didn't even seem bothered by it.

"I've never seen him so excited," said the woman, chuckling.

Damon stood and introduced me to her. "Rose, this is my neighbour, Sheila. She owns a small sheep farm about a mile that way." He gestured to the right of his cottage. "And she's been taking care of my place while I've been in London. Sheila, this is Rose, a friend of mine from the city."

"Lovely to meet you, Rose," said Sheila, smiling kindly.

"And you," I replied, returning her smile.

"And this big handsome fellow is Charlie," Damon went on. "Charlie belongs to Sheila, but I steal him from her sometimes."

Sheila laughed. "That's an understatement. When you're home, he sleeps in your cottage more often than mine. I can't tell if he just likes you better or if he wants a break from all the sheep."

Damon chuckled softly. "I guess we'll never know."

"Well, here are the keys you left me, and your car is parked around the back. The tank is full if you're planning on doing any driving, though I see you've brought a rental. You can drop the keys back on your return to London. I've stocked the fridge with enough food to see you both

267

through, and left some clean towels and bedding in the cupboard."

"You shouldn't have gone to all that trouble, but thank you." Damon took the keys, and Sheila pulled him into a hug. He looked like he hadn't expected it.

"It's nothing. I can't tell you how happy I am to see your face again," she said before drawing away. "Ever since Maureen's passing, it hasn't been the same around here."

I surmised that Maureen was Damon's grandmother. He gave the woman a tender, understanding look as he said, "I know. I miss her every day."

Sheila sniffled a little before pulling herself back together. "Anyway, I'll leave you two to get settled. If you need anything, just pick up the phone. And it looks like Charlie's set on staying with you for the night, I'm afraid."

"No worries," said Damon. "His company is always welcome." He patted the dog again and Sheila left, walking back across the field that I assumed separated their houses.

I glanced up and found him studying me. "Sheila was a close friend of Gran's. She lived in a house just a couple of miles that way." He pointed in the opposite direction of Sheila's place. "Sheila's always been very kind to me," he went on, leading me inside the cottage. The dog, Charlie, sniffed at my hand. I petted his head, and he seemed to decide I was okay.

Immediately as I stepped inside I smelled a fresh citrusy scent. It didn't smell like fake citrus, though, like you get in chemical cleaners. When we went into the kitchen, I saw someone had placed several chopped lemons and limes in a bowl of water.

Damon caught me looking, shrugged, and explained simply, "Sheila."

"She must use them to freshen the air," I suggested, looking around. The interior was simple but homely. The floors were hardwood, and there were also wooden beams on the ceilings. It was all very rustic. There wasn't much in terms of interior design, but the place felt lived in and warm. I noticed the lit fire and thought Sheila must have seen to that, too.

"Do you pay her for doing all this?" I asked. It seemed like a lot of work to do just out of the kindness of your heart.

Damon sighed and raked a hand through his hair. "I've tried, but the woman takes offence whenever I bring it up. When you live in a place like this, everybody takes the time to help each other. That's why I don't like cities. There are too many people, and life becomes devalued somehow, taken for granted. Here, everybody appreciates one another, because they know how much we all need each other to survive."

I stared at him, speechless, and honestly, a little bit turned on. He was right, of course, but I'd lived my entire life in London. I was desensitised to the rush and the feeling of being just another one among too many.

I coughed to clear my throat. "Well, she seems like a lovely woman."

Damon nodded and lifted my suitcase. "She is. Come on, I'll show you to your room."

The spare bedroom was small, with just a bed, a closet, and a desk as furniture. Damon stood in the doorway after we both worked together to put fresh sheets on the bed. I glanced up and caught him staring at me, some kind of heat in his eyes. He didn't say anything, but seemed to shake himself out of it a second later.

"I'll, uh, I'll leave you to rest. The journey must have taken a lot out of you."

He closed the door and walked down the hallway, presumably to his own bedroom. My heart thrummed in my chest as I wondered what he'd been thinking just then. There'd been thick sexual tension growing between us all day, and I felt like I was just about ready to burst with it. I loved how he'd given me the window seat on the plane, and how he never let me carry my own suitcase, how he placed his hand on the small of my back in a protective gesture as we made our way through the airport. Alicia had been right. He was a gentleman.

I also couldn't get my mind off the fact that he had only ever really slept with a handful of women. There was something so sweet and lovely about it, because any woman would give her left arm for a night with a man who looked like Damon Atwood.

At the same time, it made me angry. No teenager should ever be introduced to sex the way he had been. There was a fierce need inside me to erase everything he'd been through. To make it better.

Letting out a long sigh, I opened my suitcase and changed into a comfortable jumper and some leggings. When I lay down to rest for a little while, I found myself unexpectedly drifting off to sleep. It was so quiet here, barely a sound to be heard for miles around. Perhaps that was why sleep came so easy.

I awoke to the smell of food cooking, and padded my way into the kitchen to find Damon by the stove, heating up a pot of what looked like lamb stew.

"That smells amazing," I said, taking a seat on a stool behind him.

He turned, looking sexy and relaxed in a grey long-sleeved T-shirt and lounge pants. His feet were bare, and there was something about the sight of his bare skin, any skin, that turned me on.

"It's all Sheila's doing. I found the pot waiting on the stove," he explained, sounding exasperated with the older woman's kindness.

"You really need to find a way to start paying her," I said, smiling and reaching my arms up to stretch over my head.

Damon's eyes followed the movement before he focused back on the stove. "Good nap?" he asked, voice a little strained.

"Yeah, I was pretty tired," I answered.

"Hmm," he said, the sound coming out quiet and contemplative.

A few minutes later, we were sitting down to eat the stew, paired with some thick, crusty bread and a glass of red wine. I felt comfortable and relaxed as Damon and I chatted, the wine helping me loosen up. I thought this was why I was brave enough to broach a new topic.

"Do you remember the day we first met?" I asked, chewing on a delicious piece of bread I'd just dipped in the stew.

"Aye," Damon replied.

"I've been thinking about it a lot. Back in the car you said the reason your relationship with Lizzy fell apart was because of your inability to trust. But that day, even though you were hesitant at first, you seemed to trust me without even knowing me."

Damon nodded, swallowing a bite of bread, elbows resting on the table. "You're right — I did trust you, but it's hard to put into words the reason why. It was just this feeling you gave me. You had the kindest eyes I'd ever seen, and this is going to sound strange, but it was almost like being offered help from a child. You had this way about you that made me feel at ease, like I didn't have to worry about you having ulterior motives because you just seemed so…so guileless."

His tenderly spoken words made me catch my breath as I held my spoon in midair. It felt good to know he'd had that instant level of comfort with me. And for a man like Damon, who had every reason to be wary of strangers coming into his life and trying to take advantage, that meant a lot.

"Oh," was the response I finally gave him.

Damon reached across the table to take my hand in his. His touch was warm and inviting. "The way I feel about you, it's unexplainable, but it just is. It's different from how I felt about Lizzy. It took me a long time to warm up to her, but with you I felt immediately endeared, curious even. I wanted to know you, but I'm just so bad at talking to people that you probably thought I had no interest."

"I could tell you were just shy. I'm not the most confident person in the world, either."

"Yes, but you're not closed off like I am. You're open to people — you even embrace them without question at times. I wish I could be like that, more open to new things."

"You are, you just don't realise it. The very fact that you accepted this role and came all the way to London proves it," I said.

He seemed to like the idea of being braver than he thought, because he gifted me a small but beautiful smile. My heart thrummed, and a warmth suffused my chest.

We ate the rest of our meal in companionable silence. Afterwards, we helped each other clean up, while Charlie scarfed down some of the leftovers. The remainder of the evening we spent in the living room. It had a large, panorama-style window that looked like it had been built more recently than the original structure. I wondered if Damon had completed the renovations himself. It perfectly showcased the view as the day slowly darkened to night.

There were two couches. I lay on one, listening to an audiobook and letting my eyes drift to the warmth of the fire. Damon sat upright on the other, his ankle crossed over his knee as he read a paperback of some crime thriller. I thought that in another life I could be happy here, happy to spend quiet evenings like these with a man like Damon.

It was late enough when Charlie came and decided he was going to join me on the couch. I chuckled and let him settle his big head on my lap, absentmindedly stroking his fur as I continued listening to my book. I noticed Damon watching us, a wry smile touching his lips. He said something to himself as he shook his head, but I couldn't hear because I had my earphones in. Still, reading his lips, it looked a lot like *lucky bastard.*

That made me grin, right before a ball of desire formed in my belly. I wanted to be with him tonight. I wanted to tangle our bodies together and have him make love to me until I fell asleep from exhaustion. Being alone like this only seemed to heighten the way I felt for him, and I wasn't sure I could last much longer not touching him.

When I felt sleepy enough for bed, I gently shifted Charlie off my lap and rose. Damon's eyes moved from his book to me. There was some kind of expectancy in his gaze.

"It's late. I think I'll hit the hay," I told him, and he stared at me for a long moment.

"Sleep well," he said at length, and I turned to leave. I swore I felt his eyes on me the entire time as I left the room.

In the spare bedroom, I pulled on a T-shirt and some shorts to sleep in, then climbed under the covers. I left the bedroom door open a little, hoping that Damon might interpret it as an invitation. Despite being tired, I tossed and turned until I heard his soft footsteps padding down the hallway. I practically held my breath when he reached my door, and my heart began pounding loudly in my ears when he paused, as though he'd noticed it was left open. What was really only a few seconds felt like an eternity, but then he gently closed the door and continued to his own room.

I knew he was probably just nervous. He'd told me this trip wasn't about sex, and he was trying to uphold that promise. Still, it didn't stop the bitter sting of disappointment from churning in my gut.

Twenty-Two.
Rose

The following morning, I woke up refreshed, despite the fact I'd felt just the teeniest bit rejected that Damon hadn't come to my room. It was this place. I couldn't help marvelling at how quiet it was, how at night the sky was pure black spattered with glittering stars. There was no smog, no yellow tinge of light pollution like you got back in London.

Rising from the bed, I went to pull the curtains and almost had a heart attack when I discovered a beast staring back at me. I yelped loudly in fright and practically leapt to the other side of the room, knocking into the closet and creating an awful ruckus. A second later, the door flew open and Damon burst inside, a look of concern on his face.

"Rose, what happened?"

I inhaled sharply and pointed to the window, trying not to fixate on how Damon was wearing nothing but a pair of navy boxer briefs. "I'm sorry. I just got a fright when I opened the curtains and that thing was looking in at me."

A moment elapsed as his gaze went to the window, then back to me, then back to the window. A second later he burst into laughter, his hands going to his stomach, he found my distress so funny. I was stunned because I'd never heard him laugh so loudly before, nor with such uncontained fervour. "That's not a thing, it's a ram. He must be one of Sheila's."

"A ram," I said, still breathing unsteadily. "Right. Well, you can stop laughing. I have every right to be scared when I open the curtains to find a creature with the horns of Satan staring back at me."

Now Damon laughed even harder as he came towards me and wrapped his arms around my waist, pulling me into a hug. He was smiling so widely it made my heart hurt. Nobody had a right being so flippin' beautiful. "Oh, God, I can't even...."

"Shut up," I huffed, fighting back a smile of my own. It was useless, though, and in the end I was laughing, too.

"Horns of Satan," Damon chuckled, his chin resting on the top of my head. "That's priceless. I have to tell Sheila. She'll be laughing for days."

"Come on, even you have to admit how sinister-looking those horns are," I said, resting my face against his warm, bare chest as our laughter died down. All of a sudden, the humour of the situation began to dissipate as a new feeling emerged. We were hugging, and Damon was practically naked. All I wore was a thin T-shirt and shorts, no bra.

He moved his hands, settling them on my lower back just shy of my bottom.

"I'm taking you into town today," he said in a low voice. "There are some markets we can visit, maybe go for a walk on the beach. Then I'll take you to my favourite pub to eat. They do the best roast dinner you'll ever taste."

"Sounds good," I murmured, turning my face and absentmindedly pressing a kiss to his collarbone. A shudder ran through his body at the contact. I kissed him again in the exact same spot and he drew me tighter, one hand sweeping over my bottom, the other pulling me close. My nipples were so hard right then they could cut glass, and I knew he had to be able to feel them.

I continued kissing him, light little pecks that had him letting out the most spine-tingling masculine groans.

"Rose," he said, his voice strained.

"Damon," I whispered, my hands smoothing over his shoulder blades. I stared up at him, his eyes flickering back and forth between mine, when all of a sudden a loud *baaaa* came from the direction of the window. We both glanced at the ram, who seemed to be enjoying his own little peep show – sheep show? Damon and I exchanged a look before proceeding to burst into laughter again.

"You can use the shower first. I'll make breakfast," he said, wiping a tear from under his eye. I nodded, disentangling from him and going to find some clothes. Once I was clean and dressed, I went into the kitchen to find a breakfast of sausage and eggs waiting for me. I dug into it all hungrily, loving the fact that he'd cooked for me.

A few hours later, we found ourselves walking around the nearby village as Damon pointed out places of interest. At one point he took my hand into his, and my heart did a little somersault. Neither one of us mentioned it, but we barely stopped holding hands the entire time we were exploring.

It was just as we'd emerged from a small coffee shop where we'd stopped to grab something to eat that I heard someone calling out to Damon.

"Damon! Is that you?" the female voice inquired, and I turned to see a pretty blonde approaching us. She was very petite, a few inches shorter than me, and had a little boy and girl with her. The boy looked to be about eight, and the girl was maybe four or five.

"Lizzy," said Damon in surprise.

"It is you. Hello! I hear you've been off in London acting again," she said kindly.

So this was Lizzy. I supposed it wasn't too surprising that we'd bumped into her, given how small the island was. Even though my first impression of her was one of pixie-like loveliness, I still found myself stiffening. This was Damon's ex-lover. She'd known him in ways I never had, and the sad fact of the matter was it made me maddeningly jealous.

"I have," he finally answered. "It's going well. Just back for the long weekend."

"Oh, that's good. I'm glad it's going well," she said, and a small quiet elapsed. Her two kids had wandered on ahead and were currently playing a game of chase.

"Thank you. This is my friend, Rose," Damon went on, pressing his hand to my lower back as he introduced me. "She works on the show with me as a choreographer."

Lizzy gave me an impressed look – a genuine one. I couldn't even hate her for being fake. "Wow, that must be very exciting."

"It has its moments." I mustered a smile for her.

"How have you been, Lizzy?" Damon asked, and the woman flushed with pleasure before offering her hand, where a diamond sat on her ring finger.

"Wonderfully! James and I tied the knot just last year."

"I heard," said Damon. "Congratulations."

Somehow, the news that she'd moved on to someone else after Damon and gotten married caused the pressure on my chest to lighten up.

"Well, I better get going before those two disappear on me," she said, eyeing her kids, who were halfway up the street. "You look good, Damon, happy. I'm glad you found someone." Reaching forward, she gave his hand a soft squeeze before hurrying after her little ones. I glanced at the man standing beside me to find him reddening slightly.

Was he embarrassed by what she'd said, assuming we were together in more than just a friendly capacity?

"I suppose it's only to be expected that you'd run into your ex when you live on an island," I said in an effort to break the silence.

He rubbed at the back of his neck, glancing wryly down at me. "I hadn't seen her in almost a year, actually. I heard she was seeing someone, though. I'm glad she's happy."

"She seems really lovely," I said as he took my hand again, leading me in the opposite direction Lizzy had gone.

"She is lovely. But she's not you," he said, as though trying to let me know he no longer had feelings for her. We walked towards the beach, sitting on the sand to drink our coffees and eat the pastries we'd gotten back at the café.

A few hours later, Damon took me to his favourite pub for dinner, and we both ate a massive meal of roast beef, gravy, and potatoes. I was fit to burst by the time some of the bar workers began setting up a stage area. Not long after that, a Scottish folk band arrived to play for the small Saturday night crowd that had gathered.

There were two fiddle players, an acoustic guitarist, a guy with a thin whistle, and another man playing the bagpipe. I was giddy with excitement, feeling like I was getting a real authentic experience as I clapped along to their set. At one point, several men and women got up to dance, and, after a lot of cajoling on my part, I finally managed to get Damon to dance with me. He'd had a few beers over the course of the evening, so he wasn't as stiff as he might've been. He was also far more confident in his dancing abilities now than he'd been back when we first met. In fact, when we stepped onto the dance floor, he pulled me to him, bringing our bodies flush together. I let out a surprised laugh, enjoying his forwardness as we started to dance.

"Why, Mr Atwood, is that a whistle in your pocket, or are you just pleased to see me?" I asked teasingly.

Damon smirked and glanced at the guy on stage with the whistle, then brought his mouth over my ear. "That's not a good comparison."

My eyes gleamed, merry with the beer we'd drunk. "No?"

He grinned, and it was the sexiest thing I'd ever seen. "Nah. You should've said didgeridoo."

I barked a loud, boisterous chuckle, loving how relaxed and flirtatious he was being. Sure, it was the alcohol, but I also thought it was being on the island. Damon was at peace here, and it made my heart swell.

The music was very vibrant, full of life and colour, and our movements were vigorous to match the speedy tempo. I felt sweaty and hot, but I loved every second. When one song came to an end and Damon ran his hand from my neck all the way down my spine, I shuddered. A familiar tight feeling returned to my belly as butterflies flittered all about. I loved it when he acted all manly like this, manoeuvring my body how he pleased.

"You're so beautiful right now," he said, lips on my ear.

I wasn't sure if that was the alcohol talking. My hair was sticking to the sides of my face, and my dress felt glued to my skin. The heat inside the pub had continually increased as the night wore on, especially now with lots of people up dancing.

"Are you tired?" Damon asked, his voice raspy.

I shook my head. "I'm never too tired to dance."

"Well, I am. We should head home." He was being insistent, but he didn't look tired. All of a sudden my pores tingled as I imagined why he wanted to leave.

"You're too drunk to drive," I said.

"Taken care of. I'll call for a taxi."

I was surprised that they actually had taxis here. In the end all I did was nod, allowing him to lead me outside, where the air was blessedly cool on my sweat-soaked skin.

The journey home was quiet and filled with tension. When we arrived back at the cottage, I got out while Damon paid the driver. Stepping inside the house, I felt a sudden bout of nervousness to be alone with him, and quickly muttered something about taking a shower before I locked myself away in the bathroom.

I could hear Damon talking to Charlie as I stepped under the spray, hoping the water might wash off some of my sexual frustration, but no such luck. Even when I was out and wrapped in a towel, I still felt edgy. The need for some kind of physical contact had me buzzing with adrenaline.

I went inside my room and put on some pyjamas, listening as Damon continued to restlessly potter around the house. I wanted to go to him, but I wasn't brave enough. Instead, I got into bed, flicked off the lamp, and tried to sleep.

It was useless.

My pulse was loud in my ears, too fast, my thighs practically quivering with unspent sexual energy. I heard Damon finally go inside the bathroom and the shower turned on. After a few minutes he emerged, the floorboards creaking under his feet as he went inside his room. I tossed and turned, trying to summon up the courage to go to him.

In the end I slid out of bed quietly, padded down the hall, and gently knocked on his door.

A loud, agonised sound came from behind it, my name a warning on his tongue. "Rose."

"Can I come in?"

"You probably shouldn't."

"Why not?"

Silence.

When he finally spoke, his voice was thick and gravelly. "Because I want to be inside you, and if I look at you right now, my restraint will break."

His words, though they were almost begging, spurred me on. Pushing the door open, I stepped inside and found him standing by the window. The curtains were still open and a pale sliver of moonlight shone over his body. He wore nothing but a towel around his hips, and I couldn't help letting my eyes trace the pleasing contours of his muscles.

His gaze was dark and full of uncertainty.

"Would it be so bad to break?" I whispered. "I want you, Damon."

That made something snap in him. Within seconds he was across the room, his hands sinking into my hair as he lowered his mouth to mine. I moaned into the kiss, needing it more than air. He began to move forward while I moved back until my legs hit the edge of the mattress. He never broke the kiss as he lowered me onto the bed, his towel falling off in the process. My pyjamas were thin, and I gasped into his mouth when I felt his hot, thick erection pressing into my bare thigh.

"Jesus, fuck," he swore, his mouth moving from my lips, over my chin, and down to my throat. He pressed his teeth to the tender hollow, growling as his hands gripped my hips.

"Damon," I moaned, tingles fluttering through my body. I was already wet when he reached down and slipped a hand inside my shorts. He touched me lightly, his fingers parting my lips as he tested my readiness.

"Perfect," he breathed, his mouth a gasp at my neck. The word seemed to echo through my skin, reverberating into my pores. My legs fell open as he started pulling my shorts and underwear down my thighs. Next he pulled off my T-shirt, baring my breasts to him. Even in the dark room I saw how his eyes glittered as he soaked in the sight of me. I felt nervous and exhilarated all at once.

I was naked, but so was he, and we both just sort of stared at each other. It felt surreal. I was here with Damon, about to cross a line that couldn't be uncrossed, and I'd never been more certain of anything in my life. Neither of us was drunk, but the alcohol was still vaguely present in my system, making me brave.

I reached out and gripped his neck, pulling his mouth down to mine. I slid my tongue along his lower lip and felt him shudder, and then I kissed him. We kissed for a long time, just drinking each other in. I loved the feel of his hard, bare chest pressed against my breasts. After a while I grew overly aware of his shaft rutting desperately at my inner thigh. I wanted it closer.

With one hand still on Damon's neck, I moved the other down between our bodies, gripping his hot cock, squeezing it lightly. He groaned noisily, the slide of his tongue in my mouth growing frenzied at my touch. I jerked him a few times, mostly just getting acquainted with the feel of him. Then, unable to wait any longer, I guided his tip to my clit and rubbed a slow circle. I gasped into his mouth at the same time his breathing turned erratic.

"Rose," he rasped. "*God, Rose.*"

"I want you," I whispered, continuing to move his cock over my clit. I could've come from that alone, but Damon grew more desperate, his hips jutting, seeking entrance. I let go, and the tip of his penis slid just the barest inch inside me. Damon grunted and withdrew. He held himself above me, just quietly panting for a few brief moments.

"I'll get a condom," he breathed, and I nodded, words failing me.

Just as he moved to get off the bed, I put a hand on his arm. "Wait," I whispered.

Damon froze, his dark eyes meeting mine in the moonlight. "What is it, petal?" he asked, reverence in his voice. I loved it when he called me that. He didn't do it often, only when he was feeling particularly fond. It made it that much more special, because it was so rare.

I swallowed for courage. "I don't want to use protection."

"Rose," he said, his cautioning voice almost a groan, his expression frustrated and torn.

"Just listen. I'm clean. Julian made me get tested after Blake. And I know you're clean, too. You said yourself the last person you were with was Lizzy, and that was years ago."

"Yes, but —" he started to protest, but I cut him off.

"And I'm on the pill. Please, Damon, I need this."

At that he laughed softly, running a hand over the stubble on his jaw. "You think you need this? You have no idea how much *I* fucking need it. But you don't have to impress me, Rose. I'll have you any way I can get you."

His last statement made my heart too full, the sentiment too lovely for words. "I'm not trying to impress you — I just want you," I murmured, staring at him meaningfully as I pulled his body back to mine. It was true. In that moment I had no reservations, none at all, even though I knew I probably should. Having sex with Damon skin to skin was going to make me fall in love with him, but I was too far gone to care.

His cock pressed between my legs again, and he cupped my face. I sucked in a breath as he just took a moment to stare at me. "You are, without a doubt, the most beautiful, kind, clever, and exceptional woman I have ever met," he said, completely sober.

He spoke openly, without any of his usual self-consciousness, and my heart pounded, emotion overtaking me. "And you...." I said, my voice catching. "You are the most remarkable man I've ever known." I felt like my words were weak and childish compared to his, but his expression transformed into one of absolute rapture nonetheless.

Climbing back over me, he kissed my lips, my chin, my neck and collarbone, before mouthing my breasts with a fierce hunger. He sucked on one of my nipples, and I let out a loud moan that seemed to echo into the silence of the cottage. Damon's cock nudged close, almost slipping inside me but not quite. Then he drew himself up, his eyes seeking mine as he pushed in. My breath caught in a gasp as he slowly filled me. He buried himself deep, and I felt myself clenching around him.

"Wow," he breathed, the word barely audible.

I could do nothing but gaze at him, a flush breaking out over my entire body from the sheer sensation of having him inside me. His hips started to move back and forth in a tantalising rhythm, his thickness hitting every sweet spot, the push and pull of him the most incredible thing I'd ever felt.

I arched my spine so he could go deeper, and a rough breath escaped him as his movements started to quicken. For a moment we both went so quiet, just completely lost in one another. All I could hear was his deep, uneven breathing, the slap of his body against mine. I reached up and sank a hand into his hair. It wasn't long by any stretch of the imagination, but it had certainly grown out since I'd taken him to get it cut all those weeks ago. I loved the silky feel of it, giving it a little tug as he continued to make love to me. A soft chuckle escaped him as he lowered his mouth to mine. I expected him to kiss me, but he didn't, not at first. Instead, he whispered against my lips.

"You like that?"

"Yes."

"Then keep doing it."

I pulled gently once more, and a low groan rumbled out of him. He caught my lower lip in his and gave it a teasing bite, the sharp sting sending a shooting pleasure through my belly. My hand left his hair to move down over his shoulder, feeling the dips and curves of his muscular back. I adored how his muscles moved, almost jumping under my touch. He was so sensitive to it.

He kissed me fully then, sliding his tongue along mine, our mouths melding as his hips thrust relentlessly in and out. We were still kissing when he reached down between our bodies, his deft fingers finding my clit and rubbing it in a way that had me curling my toes. He just seemed to know my body without having to learn it.

"Come," he urged me, his mouth dropping from mine as he rose up to watch me again.

I swallowed thickly, still panting as he hammered home. "I can't normally…when you're inside me, it's hard for me to…."

"You can," Damon grunted. "You can. Just *feel*, Rose."

I closed my eyes for a second, clearing all thoughts from my mind as I focused on the sensation of him filling me, of his fingers teasing at my nerve endings, coaxing me to a most heavenly pleasure.

"Your eyes, petal, open them," he begged me.

I opened my eyes, immediately losing myself in a sea of deepest brown. And that was how we stayed for the longest time, our bodies moving together, our gazes locked. Damon alternated between slow lovemaking and fast, hard fucking. His need for me was evident in every single thrust. It felt like he could go all night, like he enjoyed the feel of being joined with me far more than the orgasm he chased.

I felt how incredibly wet I was when his thumb pressed hard on my clit. It was that intense pressure that sent me over the edge, and I came more fiercely than ever before. Damon's movements stilled, his eyes finally closing as my sex convulsed around him.

"Jesus fucking Christ," he swore, as though unable to handle how good it felt.

I couldn't speak, far too exhausted from such an acutely intense orgasm. It felt like I'd been waiting for it my entire life. Damon bent to kiss me, and I was open to him in every way. I was soft and pliant beneath him, would have let him do anything in the world to me right then. He started to move again, and when he did, the sensation was intensified. I was tender after having just come, so the push and pull of his cock was unbearably pleasurable.

His lips were still on mine, our tongues tangled in an erotic dance, when his movements grew more frenzied. He thrust into me hard and fast, letting out the most sensual yet masculine sound as he came. I felt his wet heat fill me, my thighs clenching around his hips as he emptied himself. I purred at him, whispered incomprehensible, sweet little nothings as I sucked his bottom lip into my mouth.

Damon fell onto his side, pulling me with him as he dragged the covers over our sweaty, sex-soaked bodies. I curled into him, nestling my face in the crook of his neck as he placed a kiss to my temple.

"You feel like heaven," he said when we each finally caught our breaths. "And you taste like honey."

I let out a quiet, tender laugh and snuggled closer, savouring his heat. "Heaven and honey, I can live with that," I teased, and he palmed my breast, pinching the nipple as though in reprimand.

After that we just lay there, letting our exhaustion pull us under.

I woke in the middle of the night, still wrapped up in Damon, his scent and his warmth surrounding me. He was right about us being together feeling like heaven, because this was certainly as close as I'd ever gotten to a celestial experience. I ran my hands through his hair, and he stirred a little but didn't wake. His breathing was deep and even.

Staring at his beautifully masculine profile in slumber, I wondered if I hadn't already fallen for this man a long time ago, long before we'd ever known the sublime union of each other's bodies.

Twenty-Three.

Damon

I woke to sunlight and an empty bed. My sheets smelled of Rose, still carried the lingering warmth of her body as I ran my hands over the soft cotton. She hadn't been gone long. I could hear music playing from the kitchen as someone moved about, the clink of plates and utensils amid what sounded like "Across the Universe" by The Beatles.

Getting out of bed, I threw on some clothes and went to find the woman I'd spent last night making love to. There was a pressure right in the centre of my chest, a sense of urgency that was at the same time pleasant. It was the feeling of finally having my heart's desire mixed with the panic of being apart from her, even if we were only separated by a room.

It was a frantic sort of fulfilment. Everything was too new, too fresh, for me to feel at peace. Some old, forgotten instinct had me wanting to drag her back to my bed so I could sink inside her again and again.

Leave my mark.

I'd woken in the middle of the night to find her watching me. I didn't even ask her what she was doing, because I'd been so overcome by a deep and powerful need to have her again. I simply climbed atop her, kissing and licking every inch of her body until we were both breathless and sated.

When I stepped inside the kitchen, I found her humming along to the radio as she stirred some scrambled eggs in a pan. All she wore was one of my T-shirts. It was so long on her that it might as well have been a dress. Her hair hung like a mess of wavy silk down her back. I stepped close, reaching around her to take the pan off the burner before turning her body and wrapping my arms around her.

I couldn't wipe the smile off my face.

She startled a little at my sudden appearance, then smiled back.

"Morning," I whispered, bending down to steal a kiss.

"Good m-morning," she replied, the words a mumbled sigh on my lips.

I made a humming noise in the back of my throat as I took her in, keeping one hand pressed to the small of her back and lifting the other to slide my fingers through hers. Slowly, I started to dance. Her breath hitched as she stared up at me, neither one of us able to tear our eyes from the other.

John Lennon singing *Jai Guru Deva* filled the room. I joined him, singing to Rose that nothing was gonna change my world. I saw her bare skin prickle with goose bumps when she closed her eyes. I continued to serenade her, enjoying the way my voice made her weak.

After a moment she murmured, "I think this is the first time you've ever danced without having to be cajoled."

I hummed again, bending to kiss her neck. She shuddered. "I'm feeling unusually agreeable this morning." She sighed at the pressure of my lips on her skin. I let go of her hand and lowered to my knees. She peered down at me and I returned her gaze hotly.

Her breathing started to speed up as she asked, "What are you doing?"

I moved a palm over the outside of her thigh, pushing the hem of the T-shirt up to reveal her lovely bare flesh. "Making you feel good," I answered before pressing my mouth to her sex. She yelped and gripped my shoulders. I chuckled as her yelp transformed into a moan. I licked at her in long, even strokes, parting her lips and just revelling in her taste. I adored the sounds she was making, little whimpers and sighs.

"Oh…God…Damon," she panted, and I moved my eyes to hers. She trembled when our gazes met. I couldn't look away. I licked and sucked, finally moving to her clit and swirling my tongue around it. It had been so long since I'd done this to a woman, and I thought maybe that was the reason I felt so crazed. I didn't want to go back to London tomorrow. I wanted to stay here with Rose and make her come for weeks on end.

I massaged her thigh, moving my hand up until it met her wet heat. I slid two fingers inside her and she cried out, pressing herself to my face as one of her hands went to grip my hair. I loved it. Loved how I could make her lose her mind like that. Loved how she watched me all the while, never closing her eyes. She looked…enthralled.

I thrust my fingers in and out slowly, matching the movement of my tongue on her clit. She lifted a thigh, as though to grant me more access. I grabbed it and hitched it over my shoulder, finding I could eat at her deeper from this angle. Her entire body trembled at the depth. I could hear Charlie in the hallway, scratching and whining at the door to get in. It made me laugh, and Rose moaned before laughing, too. I was glad I'd had the forethought to close the door, and also that Charlie hadn't learned how to work the handle on his own yet.

I ate her out more feverishly then and felt her thighs tensing. She went really, really quiet, so quiet I thought maybe she wasn't enjoying herself anymore. I was wrong. The next time I circled her clit, she orgasmed with violent intensity right on my mouth. I groaned and continued licking until her tremors subsided and her body went limp.

I rose, pulling her into my arms as she sighed. "The eggs have probably gone cold."

I lifted her onto the counter, pulling her thighs around my waist and taking her mouth in a deep, erotic kiss.

"They haven't, but they will."

And then I proceeded to make love to her right there in the middle of the kitchen.

***

"Wear something warm today," I told Rose after I re-cooked breakfast and we'd both eaten our fill.

She cast me a curious glance. "Why?"

"Because I'm taking you out on my boat."

Her mouth fell open. "*Your* boat?"

I nodded, enjoying her surprise as I dried the dishes and put them away. "Yes. Remember the one I told you I worked on? I own it."

"You never told me that!"

I smirked. "I'm telling you now."

An hour or two later, we'd collected my car from where I'd left it outside the pub the night before, having been too drunk to drive home, and arrived at the harbour. It was a cool day, the air sharp and fresh. Salty sea air would always be something that reminded me of home.

"Is the fishing industry very big here?" Rose asked as we stepped aboard *The Angela*.

"It's declined a lot in recent years. Things are tough at times, but the men still manage to make a living," I answered as I led her to a spot near the front of the boat. I caught her elbow when she almost tripped over some netting, smiling because she seemed so out of her depth. Usually with us, I was the one who felt out of my comfort zone. It was a nice change to have the tables turned.

She glanced up at me with a sheepish grin. "I've never been on a boat before."

I wrapped my arm around her waist as we started to move off, some of the men calling greetings to us. "In that case, try to focus on the horizon so as not to become seasick."

She cast me a curious look. "Does that work?"

"Aye. It's a steady point to counteract the constant motion."

"Ah, right, that makes sense," she said, and snuggled close to me. I was on cloud nine having her be so openly affectionate. All those weeks I'd spent pining after her, wishing I could touch her in any small way, suddenly felt like a lifetime ago. With Rose I always felt this instant level of comfort, like she'd always been there.

I soaked up her reactions, excitement mixed with nerves as we made our way out to sea. She was fascinated by the scenery and by being on the water. I relished every tiny intake of breath or gasp of surprise. After a while, Danny, one of the crewmen, came and asked Rose if she'd like to watch as they hauled in a trap. She nodded eagerly, and we went to the other side of the boat where the men were hard at work. Acting out of instinct, I pitched in, the whole time sensing Rose's attention on me. When we finally had the trap on board, I stood back and let the crew take over.

Rose was quiet as I led her back to the spot where we'd been enjoying the view.

"Are you all right?" I asked, bending to place a kiss on her temple.

She nodded but didn't speak for a long moment. "I'm fine, just feeling a little like I want to drag you inside and do some more of the things we'd been doing last night."

"And this morning," I added, grinning like a fool.

"There's something strangely arousing about watching you work."

"I'm not afraid of getting my hands dirty," I teased quietly.

She laughed and shifted in my hold to ponder me curiously. "When did you buy this boat? More to the point, how does an ex-film star Oscar winner get into industrial fishing?"

I let out a small breath and stared at the water. "I was aimless for the first few months after I came to live with Gran. She had a friend who was a skipper. He had a large crew of men working for him and could always do with the extra help. Gran volunteered me, and at first I hated it, hated the men, the smell, the hard work. I never realised how pampered I was until I actually had to do a real job. After a few months, I started to appreciate the sense of achievement I got from the work. It hardened me, but not in a bad way. It made me appreciate the value of things. How the vast majority of people in the world have to work day in and day out just to make ends meet. There was a little bit of self-hatred that came with it, too, because I saw just how privileged a life I'd been leading, even if I did have my troubles with Dad. After a while, I wanted to use some of my acting money to buy my own boat, contribute to the local economy and create jobs, so I did."

"Seems like a very noble thing to do," said Rose. "Did you name the boat yourself?"

"Aye. After Mum."

She didn't say anything then, only laced her fingers with mine and squeezed my hand as we both stared out into the vast and unending waters that surrounded us.

A couple of hours later, we were home. Danny had saved us a small bag of shellfish that I started preparing for dinner, while Rose played catch with Charlie outside the cottage. I thought that perhaps it wasn't just I who felt more peaceful here. Rose had seemed even more beautiful to me this last day or two, more at ease, if that was even possible.

Glancing out the window, I saw Sheila approach. She ruffled Charlie's fur, then stood talking with Rose for a bit before heading in the direction of the cottage. She stepped in the back door, and I continued de-shelling the fish.

"Something smells good," she said, commenting on the broth I had simmering on a low heat.

"I took Rose out on the boat today. Brought home some produce, if you'd like to stay and eat with us."

She smiled and waved me away. "Oh, no. I won't intrude. I just came to check in and make sure you're enjoying your weekend."

"We are."

A moment of quiet ensued as Sheila eyed me. I almost told her to spit it out, but then she spoke, so I didn't have to.

"She's a lovely lass," she said.

I grunted and went to pull a dish from the cupboard. "Lovely" was too tame a word to describe Rose. She was stunning, ethereal, *incandescent*. Now, if only I could tell her all this in words, rather than simply thinking it.

"You're smitten."

I cast my eyes to the ceiling and shook my head. Sheila had a knack for making me feel like an embarrassed teenager with a crush on a girl at school. We didn't converse for a while, Sheila watching me work in quiet for a bit.

"What will happen, though, when you have to leave London?" she asked, voicing a fear I'd been pushing to the back of my mind for a while now.

I'll take her with me, I thought. *Wherever I go, I'll always take her with me.*

I tried not to ponder the fact that London was Rose's home. She'd lived there all her life. She was a dancer, and there weren't exactly many job opportunities for choreographers here in Skye.

I met Sheila's gaze and answered soberly. "We'll figure something out." There were lots of things we could do. Spend half our time in the city and half our time on the island, perhaps. I was sure that together we'd figure it out. Really, though, it was too soon to be thinking of these things. Last night was the first time we'd slept together. Everything was new. Fresh. I just wanted to enjoy it for a while.

Sheila moved to my side, giving my arm a decidedly solid squeeze for a woman of her age and stature. "I just don't want to see you setting yourself up for a fall, Damon," she said, her wise old eyes taking me in.

"I'll be fine," I told her gruffly.

Her gaze went soft. "Yes, I hope so. Anyway, I better be getting home. My Ned will be wondering where his dinner's gotten to. Like always, I'm only a phone call away if you need me."

I waved her goodbye as she went out through the back door again. Rose came inside, Charlie heavy on her heels. Her cheeks were pink and flushed from the outdoor air, and Sheila's dog seemed to be even more taken with her than I was. She sat by the counter and watched me cook, and afterwards we ate and spoke of our day.

296

Later on, as we were lying on the couch by the fire, Rose's head on my chest and a thick woollen blanket thrown over us, I felt completely at ease in the quiet. I could feel her soft heartbeat where my hand rested just below her collarbone. The longer we stayed like that, the more aroused I became. I was aware of every inhalation and exhalation, how goose pimples rose across the skin of her arms, showing me she was feeling it, too.

We shared a look.

I wasn't quite sure what hers said, but a second later she was moving to straddle me where I lay. I watched her movements with rapt attention, my eyelids at a lazy half-mast. Her hands went to the fly of my jeans, and I sucked in a breath. *Christ.*

Rose opened the button and pulled down the zipper, sliding her hand inside and cupping my already hard cock. I groaned and closed my eyes, saying her name like a warning.

"Rose."

"Just let me," she murmured, before pulling my cock free and lowering her mouth to it. I'd never experienced anything more erotic or frustrating in my life. She pressed her lips lightly to my tip, and I swore I felt it twitch. My balls drew tight, my cock begging for more. Whatever she planned on doing, I had no intention of stopping her.

"Take off your top," I ordered, the command husky. I needed to see her skin.

Her lips curved in a smile as she obliged me, first lifting off her pale blue shirt, then reaching around to unhook her bra. Her heavy tits fell free and I reached for one, moulding it tenderly with my hand.

"You're beautiful," I told her.

She blushed, wrapping her arms around her stomach, like she felt self-conscious all of a sudden. I pulled her arms away and brought her hand to my erection. "This is what you do to me. You're perfect. Never hide."

She sighed, her eyes going all big and soft, and I kissed her gently on the lips. She lowered her mouth to my cock again, this time licking up its entire length. I groaned so loudly it was a good thing I didn't have neighbours close by. And when she took me fully into her mouth, every muscle in my body drew tight. Her sweet, soft, wet little mouth moved up and down. I felt the barest scrape of her teeth, and it was agonisingly sensual. Reaching for her tits again, I took both in my palms, moulding and caressing them, pinching her tight little buds as she continued sucking me off.

I remembered what it felt like last night, when I sank myself inside her, how hot and slick she'd been, and almost came on the spot. Luckily, I had enough restraint to hold back. I didn't want this to be over yet. I wanted to savour the feel of her mouth on me for just a little while longer.

When she cupped my balls, my eyes rolled back in my head. My cock felt so hard right then that it was almost to the point of pain. She moaned around me when I pinched her nipples, and that was my undoing. I came with a low groan, emptying into her mouth as she continued sucking me. I felt satisfied, yet not. Her mouth had been perfect, but it only made me want more of her, and I knew without a doubt I'd be dragging her to my bed before long.

Rose lay back against me, her soft, lush tits against my chest. She kissed me on the pec, then let out a long, happy little sigh.

"This day's been perfect," I whispered as I pressed my lips to her earlobe, feeling her shudder.

"Of course it has," she said, letting out a soft chuckle. "All perfect days end with blowjobs."

I pinched her arm gently. "Don't give me that. Today was perfect, and it was perfect because I got to spend it with you."

She shifted to look at me, her eyes flickering back and forth over mine as some indecipherable emotion clouded her features. "I don't think I ever want to leave this place," she finally whispered, and I knew the feeling.

But we did have to leave, and that was the problem.

***

We arrived back in London on Monday evening, and by Tuesday morning we'd returned to the theatre for rehearsals. Opening night was on Friday, so everything felt even more of a rush than usual.

I caught Rose behind a screen that was part of the set and kissed her until her knees buckled. Now that we'd slept together, I felt like I wanted to be touching her constantly, finding new ways to make her burn for me. She giggled when I squeezed her arse, then gave it a light slap just as Jacob entered the theatre. I grinned at her retreating form as she scurried off to run an errand for Iggy.

Something drew my attention, and I looked up to find Blake staring coldly at me. My grin quickly fell as I held his gaze steadily. Rose was with me. He could try this intimidation tactic all he wanted. I wasn't backing off. Not now. Not ever. The fucker would just have to deal with it.

"All right, everyone, in the words of the infinitely wise and fabulous Noel Coward, just say your lines and don't trip over the furniture. We have three days to get this show polished for a live audience, and I want you all putting your best feet forward," said Jacob from where he sat in the front row. He now possessed a loudspeaker. A bit obnoxious, but

I supposed it made it easier for us all to hear his direction from the stage.

Today we were running the entire show from start to finish. I wore a white shirt, black slacks, and suspenders. I'd let my stubble grow in a little more than usual over the long weekend, and Jacob was quick to inform me I needed to shave.

My attention fell on Blake again, and I thought he seemed agitated. He was wearing a tailcoat, trousers and a waistcoat which was his costume for playing the Duke. Despite the debonair attire, there was something off about him. He kept scratching at his jaw, his eyes darting all about. I put it down to him being angry over Rose, but there was something about his twitchiness that rose my hackles.

He approached me right before we were about to start rehearsing the opening number.

"Damon. A word," he said stiffly, nodding to a quiet corner backstage. I schooled my expression, deciding I'd let him say his piece. Really, though, he needed to get it into his head that he and Rose weren't going to happen.

I didn't speak, simply folded my arms and waited for him to say something.

"Seems like you and Rosie are pretty close these days. I heard you both went away together this weekend."

"That's right," I answered, expressionless, giving him nothing.

He stared at me then, and something changed. He no longer looked pissed; now he appeared sympathetic. Towards me. What the fuck?

"Look, I'm being serious when I say I'd like us to be friends. I don't want all this animosity going back and forth. It's not good for the show."

"We're not friends, Blake, get it into your head. But I agree with you about the show. You and Rose are in the past. I won't bring it up again if you don't," I said firmly.

His blue eyes turned down at the edges, and he stared at me like I was the most naïve bastard he'd ever met. "But that's just the thing — it's not in the past," he said, and I blinked.

"Say again?"

He looked away, as though agonising over what to do. I frowned, not liking wherever this was going. He brought his attention back to me.

"We're not in the past. In fact, we were together just last week."

All at once my fists tightened, my jaw clenched, and I gritted my teeth. Every ounce of animosity I'd felt for Blake over the past few weeks came rolling back. I was two seconds away from losing it. "Elaborate."

"We've got history. Perhaps it was a moment of weakness, but she was lonely and she came to me. We fucked."

That was it. The final push to make me snap. Red clouded my vision. I punched him. His head swung sharply to the side, his body jerking as my fist met his face. It was like having an out-of-body experience — my anger overtook all rational thought. Before I knew it, I was fisting his shirt, practically hauling him into the air.

"You're lying," I growled, barely even recognising my own voice. "You're a fucking liar."

"I'm not lying. It's the truth. I'm trying to help you out here, m-mate," he sputtered.

I punched him again and enunciated each word slowly, "I'm. Not. Your. Bloody. Mate."

He groaned in pain and clutched his cheek. Red dripped down from where I'd hit him. I was vaguely aware that my knuckles were raw, but I was too overwrought to feel it. All of a sudden, Jacob was in my face and several cast members were dragging me away from Blake.

"Damon! What on earth do you think you're doing?" the director wailed.

"He assaulted me. I'm calling the police," Blake barked from somewhere in the background. I stared at Jacob blankly, my chest heaving with unspent rage, but I didn't utter a single word.

"You're not calling anyone. We'll settle this like grown-ups. Now please, will one of you tell me what's going on before I have a coronary. We're three days from opening the show, and you're attacking one of your costars."

"He's jealous because I fucked Rose," Blake spat, and I barged forward, going for him again. It took three men to hold me back, but only because I let them. If I'd wanted to punch Blake a third time, I would have. But no, my anger was morphing, turning inward as I wondered if I was a fool. Had Rose been lying to me all this time? Had she still been in love with Blake and using me as an amusement?

"Rose," Jacob tutted. "Your obsession with Iggy's little assistant is getting out of hand."

"It's not an obsession, I…." Trailing off, I tried to calm myself down, but it was no use. I wanted to hit something again. Preferably Blake. Somewhere vulnerable. The very thought of him with his hands on her made my skin crawl. She was mine.

She was….

I needed a minute.

Striding past Jacob, who was still wittering on at me, I walked away from all of them, suspicion and doubt filling my head. My trust issues rose to the surface, and in that moment I wondered if I ever should have come out of my shell, if I ever should have given Rose a chance to break down my barriers.

If I should have just stayed alone and lonely on my island.

Twenty-Four.
Rose

Something was off. When I arrived back at the theatre after rushing across the city on an errand for Iggy, there was a weird atmosphere among the cast. Several people eyed me curiously, and I even got a few hostile glances here and there. Jesus, you'd swear I just stole all the macaroons from catering.

I didn't get a chance to ponder it for long because Iggy pulled me aside, a beleaguered expression on his face that told me there was some kind of emergency.

"Alison's broken her ankle, the clumsy mare. We're a dancer down. I need you," he said, and I nodded, comprehension dawning.

"Of course. I can stand in for her during rehearsals until you find a replacement."

My boss sighed with relief. "You're a life saver."

"It's no problem," I told him, thinking that must've been the reason for the odd tension in the air. It didn't explain the hostile looks, but then again, theatre folk could be strange at times.

Alison played Nini, and was one of the foremost dancers in the show. She also sang in the chorus and had a couple lines of dialogue, but I wasn't too worried about that. I was no Damon, but I could hold a decent tune. Either way, it was going to be a nightmare finding someone to replace her on such short notice, but I was sure they'd manage somehow. About twenty minutes later I was in full costume, wearing a tight black skirt and corset, heels and a lacy shawl, my hair up in a bun.

"You should be ashamed of yourself," said Alicia spitefully as she passed me by.

I frowned, taken aback by her venomous tone. "Excuse me?"

She turned, wearing a long sequined dress. "I said you should be ashamed of yourself for what you did to Damon. The poor man is beside himself."

I stared at her, dumbfounded and unable to fathom what the hell she was going on about. "Are you on something? Damon's fine. I was with him just an hour ago."

Alicia eyed me and pursed her lips. "Well, a lot can happen in an hour. While you were off doing whatever it is you do, Blake had the good grace to inform Damon of your tryst. Honestly, Rose, could you not be happy with one of them? You really had to have them both?"

My heart raced, emotions flooding me as panic settled in. Blake. I knew something seemed strange about him today. He'd said something to Damon, and he was lying his black little heart out.

"I haven't been with Blake in months," I said, but she was already gone, being called to the stage by Jacob. All of a sudden Iggy was at my side, ushering me forward as we took our places for "El Tango De Roxanne." I was disoriented, confused, and perplexed as I looked all around, trying to find Damon. He had to know Blake was lying. After the wonderful, almost magical weekend we'd spent together, he had to know the purity in my heart, had to know that I'd never betray him like that.

Robert, the actor who played the Narcoleptic Argentinian, stood before me, ready for our dance. I knew the tango he and Alison performed during this number off by heart, but in the moment I was lost, could barely remember a simple two-step, I was so discombobulated.

The music started from the pit below the stage, the orchestra musicians playing the passionate tango as Robert said his lines, stamping his feet and striding around me with a fiery Latino temper. Iggy caught my eye from the side of the stage, mouthing furiously at me to dance.

I danced.

Some sort of emergency button went off inside me as my body moved on autopilot. Robert and I circled each other. He approached me and ran his hands down my torso. I was supposed to be the temptress, the harlot, the prostitute who sells her body, while he was the man obsessed with me. We acted out the emotions through our movements, and I was overly aware of art imitating life for a brief, fleeting second.

Passion.

Desire.

Jealousy.

Betrayal.

Anger.

Insanity.

Then Robert cast me aside, and several other male dancers surrounded me. I let them touch me, let them move me how they wanted, manipulating my body as the song continued.

And then I heard him.

Damon was singing.

The tiny hairs on the back of my neck stood on end. My throat constricted. My stomach twisted into knots.

I turned my head to see him striding onto the stage. He was all Christian, but his eyes were pure fire, every muscle in his body drawn tight, like a coiled spring about to snap.

All at once I was more overwhelmed than ever before, because as he sang about another man's eyes on my face, another man's lips on my skin....

It was all too much. The lyrics were too potent, too apt for our current situation, and though there was no truth to whatever Blake had told him, Damon looked like he'd just suffered the worst betrayal of his life. Was he acting? We'd rehearsed this number countless times before, but it never felt so powerful as it did now.

A second later the stage was full, rows upon rows of cast members dancing as the song went on and on. I slunk off to the side, glancing at Robert because it was part of the scene direction. Still, every chance I got, my attention when to Damon. And each time I managed to catch his eye, he looked like he didn't recognise me.

A lump lodged firmly in my gut and I wanted to be sick.

My heart started pounding, my body sweaty and my throat sore. I hated this limbo. I just wanted to go to him, but the scene wasn't done yet. When it finally ended, Jacob rose from his seat to give us a standing ovation.

"Oh, my God, that was amazing! I had chills. Chills, I tell you! Rose, you were a little stiff, but that's only to be expected. I know all this was thrust on you rather last minute, but I think you'll make a perfect Nini. The part is yours if you want it."

I stared at him, trying to discern what he was saying. This was the first time Jacob had spoken to me kindly since the whole drama with Damon and Alicia, insisting they pretend to be a couple. Then it finally hit me. He wanted me to be in the show. I couldn't. I wouldn't.

I was a behind-the-scenes girl. That was me. I created the dances, but I didn't perform them, not for audiences, at any rate.

Still...there was a tiny, minuscule, hopeful part of me that rejoiced, a part that wanted to be on stage more than anything else. It was my stupid fear that held me back.

I was about to respond, tell him I couldn't do it, when movement caught my eye and I saw Damon leaving the stage. Lots of chatter ensued, and Jacob seemed to interpret my silence as acceptance. I ran after Damon, calling his name, but he just kept on walking. Someone stepped in front of me, and I saw red when I realised it was Blake. Acting purely on instinct, I pushed harshly at his chest. He backed away by several feet, seeming edgy as he tugged on his hair.

"Look, Rosie, I can explain," he said, placing his hands in front of him like he had nothing to hide. What a crock.

"Don't call me Rosie! Who the hell do you think you are? How could you lie to Damon like that?"

"I'm going through a rough time at the moment, and I just, I saw you two together, you looked so happy and it pissed me off...."

"So you decided to ruin it? Do you need everyone to be just as miserable as you are? Is that it?"

"No, of course not, I just need you back. I *need* you. Please, Rosie, come back to me."

I paused to catch my breath, so angry I could've smacked him. I asked myself a question in my head, *Yard is to inch as quart is to...? Ounce.* I found that logical reasoning was always a great way to stem my anger. And then, when I looked at Blake, and I mean *really* looked at him, I saw everything I'd been too furious to see before.

There was a welt on his right cheek, and his eyes were bloodshot. I grabbed his shoulders and pulled him close to check his pupils. His eyes were almost completely black, the blue irises barely perceptible. He'd fallen off the wagon. Christ.

"You're high," I said.

"It was a moment of weakness. I'll get back on track tomorrow, I promise. Just give me another chance."

"For God's sake, Blake, another chance from me isn't what you need. What you need is to book yourself into a rehab facility."

He touched my face, and I reared away from his hand like it was on fire. "You can be my rehab. I'll lose myself in you, and then I'll be better again."

"You were using the entire time we were together, so we both know that's bullshit. I'm giving you a week to get your shit together. If you can't afford rehab, then you need to get into some kind of programme with meetings. If you don't, then I'll have no choice but to tell Jacob."

He looked miserable after I said it, but there seemed to be an understanding there, too. He knew I was right. The soft part of my heart wanted to comfort him, because I couldn't see someone suffer like Blake was suffering and not want to make them feel better, especially since there was a time when I'd had feelings for him. But no, he'd done something completely reprehensible and unnecessary, and he didn't deserve my comfort. I had to go and find Damon before he decided he was done with me forever.

When I reached his dressing room, I had a moment of complete and utter panic, drowning in anxiety. My hand was shaking as I raised it to gently knock on the door. When I got no answer, I knocked again and was met with a vitriolic growl.

"Whoever it is, fuck off," Damon shouted, and I heard something break inside the room. I couldn't leave. I had to see him. Summoning all my courage, I opened the door to find him standing by the dresser, a number of things knocked to the floor in temper. He looked wretched.

"Damon," I gasped.

At the sound of my voice he turned, his eyes dark with betrayal. "Get out!"

"Damon, he was lying. Blake was...."

"I don't want to hear his name, and I can't see you right now. Just...get out."

"No," I said, standing firm. "I'm not going anywhere. What he told you was a lie, and if you know me at all, then you should know that I would never betray you. What I feel for you is real. I have nothing to hide. And if you doubted me, even for a second, then you obviously don't feel for me what I feel for you."

At this he strode forward, his anger bubbling right below the surface. It made my heart pound, because I was terrified of seeing him unleash. My back hit the wall as he cornered me.

"Don't fucking...." He trailed off, struggling for words. "You're the one who...you're the one...." His gaze was frantic, his breathing erratic and uneven.

"I didn't do anything. All I see is you, Damon," I whispered. "*All I see is you.*"

We stared at each other for the longest time, communicating with only our eyes.

I'm hurting.

You don't have to.

But I am.

Some of the fight went out of him, his body slumping forward but still not touching mine. I braced myself against the wall, unsure of what he was going to do next. Our eyes stayed locked for who knew how long. It felt unnatural to see his beautiful brown eyes contorted with fury, to see his sensual, masculine lips drawn into a tight, angry line. I wanted to reach forward, smooth out all his tension, but I was too scared to move. Too terrified of breaking the moment.

At last he spoke. "I know he was lying," he whispered. "I know."

I startled in surprise at his confession. "Then why...."

"Because I doubted you, Rose. I *doubted*. I let all my issues take me prisoner, let them convince me you couldn't be trusted, that I'd been a fool to let you in. That's not right. I fucking hit him. I lost my shit when he said you slept together. That sort of anger is dangerous. I shouldn't want to hurt someone like that, no matter the reason."

"Oh, Damon," I said sadly, reaching forward to touch his cheek, but he flinched away. It hurt, cut me deep to have him cringe from my touch like that.

"Sorry," I whispered.

He shook his head. "No, it's not you. It's just...I'm feeling very raw right now. I need some space to sort my head out."

Again, that hurt. I didn't want to give him space. I wanted to take him in my arms and hug him close, kiss him until my lips were sore. The past hour had been the scariest of my life, and I just wanted it to be over. I wanted to reconnect with Damon, solidify the fact that we were together and none of Blake's lies could change that.

I looked down, noticing his reddened knuckles. He'd hit Blake. I couldn't believe he'd hit him. I remembered the red welt on Blake's cheek and knew it was true.

"Can I fix your hand? It's looks painful."

"No. I'll do it."

"Okay, I'll…I'll go, then," I said, my words choked, on the verge of tears.

I took a step towards the door, but Damon let out a noise of frustration. He came towards me and wrapped his arms around my shoulders from behind. My heart did one hard beat in my chest. He hugged me so tight it knocked the air from my lungs. I gripped his hand, squeezed it, and a long moment of quiet elapsed. Nothing was said, but so much was understood. I heard a runner pass by out in the corridor, knocking on dressing room doors and calling everyone back to the stage for the second half of rehearsals. I twisted in Damon's hold and looked up at him.

"Today's been rough. Let's just…let's take the night and talk tomorrow," I suggested, hoping he'd agree, hoping we were okay.

Some of the tension fled his body. He nodded, brought his lips to my forehead, gave me a tender kiss, and then I went.

***

That evening when I got home, I told Julian everything. He sat and listened to my woes, enfolding me his arms and reassuring me everything would be all right. When I'd gotten it all out, feeling exhausted and drained, I finally took a proper look at him and noticed he didn't seem so great himself. There were grey bags under his eyes, and his hair looked dirty and dishevelled. I also noted that I hadn't seen him go out to meet with a client in a while.

"What about you? How are you feeling?" I asked him softly.

He sighed, glanced away, and rubbed at one of his forearms. "I'm okay."

"I take it you still haven't heard from Alicia?"

He shook his head. "No, I haven't."

I gave him a sympathetic look. "She's not the one for you, Julian. She doesn't deserve you."

He let out a sad little laugh. "You're right, she doesn't. I wouldn't wish myself on my worst enemy."

"That's not what I meant and you know it. Alicia's a selfish woman. She has this obsession with finding a reliable, kind man who'll take care of her. That's why she's been so obsessed with trying to get Damon, but she only wants him so she can use him. You don't need a woman like that, Julian. You deserve someone kind, someone who'll love you the way you need."

"So I can ruin them?"

I stared at him, troubled. This sort of talk came and went with him, but he hadn't been down like this in over a year. We didn't talk about it much anymore, because he seemed to have found a balance in life and was doing so well, but he suffered from bipolar depression and took medication to keep his moods in check. It was another of the reasons why he didn't drink. Alcohol made him too wild and unpredictable.

"The only reason you'd ruin them is so they wouldn't get the chance to ruin you first. You're a pre-emptive striker. I've seen you do it."

"I don't know any other way to be."

"You say that, but it's not true. You think you wreck people, but you never wrecked me. In fact, my life's been so much better because you're in it. You make me laugh every day, listen to me whine about my relationship woes, help me whenever I need it. You'll find a woman worth loving, and it won't be Alicia. That one has enough issues of her own. And when you find her, Julian, you just need to love her the same as you love me…but you know, with sex and all that romantic stuff."

He laughed and waggled a brow. "You trying to tell me something, darling?"

I shoved him playfully in the shoulder. "You were always my first choice," I teased. "Unfortunately, you only ever saw me as a little sister."

He scowled, but a smile edged his mouth. "You're a dirty liar."

I grinned. "Hush! I'm trying to make you feel better."

We laughed and then grew quiet. I allowed my eyes to trace his pretty face and wondered if this whole thing with Alicia was indicative of a bigger change in him. Perhaps he was finally ready to find someone, someone to love who would love him in return. Suddenly overcome with emotion, I pulled him into my arms, squeezing him so tight I heard a little *oomph* of breath whoosh out. He didn't complain, but simply took my comfort willingly.

***

The following day I was eager to find Damon and see how he was feeling. I hoped beyond hope that he was over all the drama of yesterday and that we could just go back to how we were before. I needed to touch him, kiss him, absorb his scent. It was a fierce and disconcerting need, almost overpowering in its urgency.

I wasn't sure who had done it, but it seemed to have been spread around the cast that I wasn't the dirty cheater Blake had claimed me to be. That was one good thing at least. I even got a few commiserating looks. Making my way to Damon's dressing room, I found his door open, but when I stepped inside, Alicia was there. They were sitting by the table facing one another, and she was leaning forward with her hand on his knee as though to comfort him.

Oh, hell no.

"You've got some steel panties, showing your face," she commented as she eyed me cattily.

I narrowed my eyes to slits and glanced at Damon to find he was frowning at Alicia. "Rose is welcome in my dressing room any time she likes," he said sternly, and some of the tension left me. Alicia pouted and gave him a hurt look. It was as fake as her hair colour probably was.

"But how do you know she's not lying about Blake? I don't see why he'd say something like that if there was no truth to it," she said, like the little devil on his shoulder. Damon stiffened.

"He said it because he's got a drug problem," I interjected. "Yesterday he was high and feeling in the mood to cause trouble. *That's* why he said it. And anyway, you're one to talk. You used my best friend for sex and then dropped him as soon as you were done."

I couldn't tell what made me angrier, her constant attempts to steal Damon or the way she'd treated Julian. Alicia sat up straighter, her mouth tightening. If looks could kill, I'd be six feet under, because right then she appeared to want to throttle me for saying that aloud in front of Damon. Little did she know, I'd already told him all about her affair with my friend.

"Julian's a big boy. He can take care of himself," she said, eyeing me coldly.

I gave her a sharp, disbelieving laugh. "No, actually, he can't. In fact, you should probably be across town consoling him right now, rather than putting all your effort into Damon when he doesn't need it."

She sneered at me. "And why should I do that?"

I levelled her with a long, hard stare. "Because no one deserves to be treated like an object, and that's exactly how you treated Julian."

A moment of quiet ensued as we stared each other down. I couldn't be certain, but I thought I saw the tiniest flicker of remorse in her eyes. She glanced at the floor, then picked up her handbag, rifling through it as though searching for something. "What did he say to you?" she asked quietly, and I was surprised by the delicate catch in her voice.

"Why don't you go and ask him?" I suggested, not backing down.

She sniffled and stood, glancing at Damon one final time. "If you need me, come find me."

Her offer made me furious. I locked eyes with Damon, and he must have seen it because he told her coldly, "I won't need you."

She reared back like she'd just been slapped, and, without another word, turned on her heel and left the dressing room. The door slammed with a loud thud, and I felt a small moment of victory that Damon had stood up to her. We stared at one another for a long time. When he opened his mouth to speak, I thought he might say something about yesterday, about Blake, but he didn't. Instead, he surprised me with concern for my friend.

"Is Julian all right?" he asked, and I could tell he genuinely cared.

I stepped forward and gestured to the chair Alicia had just vacated. Damon nodded his permission for me to sit.

"He's okay. I just get so angry when stuff like this happens because he truly doesn't deserve it. Julian was never dealt the easiest cards in life."

"No?" said Damon.

I shook my head, struck with the sudden urge to tell him everything. I held Julian's pain in my heart daily. Perhaps sharing it with someone would lessen the burden, and I knew Damon would never tell another soul. I inhaled a deep breath before I spoke.

"When he was a little boy, Julian's mother was an alcoholic and would leave him alone in the house for days on end. She'd disappear with whatever man had caught her eye that week, and he'd have to fend for himself. But it was worse when she brought the men home, every one of them a new kind of scumbag eager to unleash abuse on the boy with a mother who didn't care what they did to him. He's suffered terribly with depression all his life because of it."

Damon stared at me sadly and asked, "Does he take any meds?"

"Yes. He's been on an even keel for the last few years, but I've been seeing troubling signs in him lately. I've even checked his pill bottles to make sure he hasn't stopped taking his medication. It all started with this ridiculous fling with Alicia. I told him from the start she'd only hurt him, but he wouldn't listen. Now I fear he might start back at his old habits."

Damon took my hand into his, his warm touch soothing to my frantic heart. "Old habits?"

I let out a breath and worried my bottom lip. "He started using heroin when he was seventeen. It went on until his early twenties, when I finally managed to convince him to go into rehab," I explained, feeling a little like history was repeating itself with Blake. "He's been clean ever since, but it was only a few months after he got out of the clinic that he started selling his services as an escort. He told me it was either sex or drugs, that he couldn't live without both. And I understood his reasons, knew he

317

needed the stimulation of at least one of those things to stem the horrors of his past. At least if he was smart about it, the sex wouldn't kill him like the drugs could have. It was the lesser of two evils."

Damon squeezed my hand as he surmised, "And you don't want him to go back to the greater evil."

"No," I whispered. "No, I don't."

"Come here, petal," he said, voice gruff as he pulled me over into his lap. I didn't resist, needing his warmth right then. Damon ran his hand up and down my back as I buried my face in his neck.

"I'm so sorry about Blake," I murmured after a time, voice watery. "I'm sorry he lied and you had to go through all that."

"Hush. It's over now," said Damon.

He held me for a long while, until one of Jacob's assistants gave a quick knock on the door, calling Damon to the stage to begin the day's rehearsals. Reluctantly, I crawled from his lap and we walked to the stage in quiet, lots of crew members passing us by, looking harangued with preparations for the opening night. When we arrived, the entire cast was sitting on the stage floor as Jacob stood before them.

"What's going on?" I whispered under my breath to Damon.

"No clue," he whispered back.

Apparently, Jacob wanted to give us all a pep talk before the show went to a live audience. On Friday the theatre would be packed with journalists and other press, all out to see if the stage adaption of *Moulin Rouge* was up to snuff. It hit me then that I still hadn't spoken to Jacob about finding someone else to play Nini. After he finished his speech, I got up and hurried over to him, but he was already surrounded by a number of people, so I had to wait for his attention. A familiar hand touched my elbow, and I turned to find Damon at my side.

"Are you all right?" he asked, eyes flittering across my face as he studied me.

"Yes, fine," I lied.

"You seem anxious."

"I'm fine, really," I lied again, not entirely sure why. I guess I just didn't want to start venting my worries about performing on stage to him, since things were still tentative between us. He eyed me closely, and seemingly my lies were pointless, because he saw right through them.

"You don't want to be in the show," he said, that perceptive gaze still on me.

I frowned and looked at my shoes, my lack of a response saying it all.

"I think you should do it," Damon went on. "I think you'll be wonderful."

His words reinforced my confidence slightly, but I still didn't fully believe him. "I can't."

"None of the other dancers will do the part justice like you can, Rose. I'm telling you, if I can go on live television to be interviewed in front of millions of viewers, then you can play this part. It's a waste if you don't."

I opened my mouth to speak, but he cut me off.

"Don't say anything. Just leave it one more night. If you still feel the same way tomorrow, then I won't get in your way when you tell Jacob. But please, just give it one more day. For me."

God, would there ever be a time when I could refuse this man? I stared at him, nodding my head before I even made my decision. "Okay, one more day."

He squeezed my elbow, a small smile gracing his lips. How I'd missed that smile. It had barely been twenty-four hours, but it already felt like a lifetime.

"Good. Now, can I ask another favour?"

"Of course."

"I'm have a radio interview this evening. They're sending a car over at five. Will you come with me?"

Again, I couldn't refuse, nor did I want to. I'd do anything to spend more time with Damon, to get back to the blissful place we'd been in before Blake decided to come along and ruin it.

"Yes, I'll come with you, Damon."

I always will.

Twenty-Five.
Rose

"Are you nervous?" I asked him as we sat in the back of the car on our way to the studio for his radio interview.

"Strangely, no."

I turned to face him, my eyes wide. "Really?"

He nodded. "Aye. There's less pressure with no cameras. I only have to worry about talking and not whether I look awkward or hostile or uncomfortable or…constipated."

I laughed loudly, unable to help myself. My knee knocked against his in the process, and butterflies flooded my belly at the simple touch. "Well, you wouldn't want that."

His answering smile was fond, and it made my insides flutter.

A quiet elapsed, and I fiddled with my hands in my lap. I felt restless. It was a pleasure to be this close to him, but an agony not to know if he'd let me touch him. If he wanted me to. Damon's leg moved so that his thigh rested fully against mine. I couldn't tell if he'd done it on purpose or if he just needed more leg space. He did have very long legs.

"They didn't ask Alicia along for the interview?" I queried, breaking the silence. Why on earth I thought it was a good idea to bring her up, I couldn't say. I was so bloody nervous it was ridiculous.

"No, just me," he answered.

"Oh."

More silence.

"Have those, um, photographers been around your house again?"

At this Damon smirked, turning his body to mine. "You're full of questions today."

"Sorry. I always ramble when I'm anxious." I clasped my hands more tightly in my lap.

His gaze traced the line of my nose before resting on my lips. "Why would you be anxious?"

I let out a shaky breath, and he started rubbing my knee. It felt too good. I loved how strong his fingers were, the magic they could work.

"Why would you be anxious, Rose?" he asked again, this time with his mouth a hair's breadth away from my ear.

"B-because I'm not sure where we stand."

"We stand where we always have," he replied. "Side by side."

His words made my breath catch, and in the next second he bent to take my earlobe between his lips and suck. It took all my strength not to moan and arouse the attention of the driver. I shifted in place as Damon's hand moved further up my thigh. I'd been starved for his touch, and now that it was happening I felt almost drugged on it. I twisted and buried my face in his neck. He let out a low, humming sound like he approved. I was just about to lift my head to kiss him when the car stopped and the driver announced we'd arrived.

My legs felt wobbly as Damon helped me from the car, so turned on I could barely see straight. The next half hour was a whirlwind of activity as we were welcomed into the studio and Damon was briefed on how the interview would run. All the while he kept his hand on my lower back, or on my elbow. At one point he even laced our fingers together, and I swore my heart flew right up to the ceiling in elation.

I was allowed to watch the interview through the glass windows of the studio. Damon sat on a chair across from the host as the audio was piped through speakers in the room I occupied.

Right off the bat, I knew the interviewer wasn't going to give him an easy time. The show allowed callers to phone in at the end and ask questions, so who knew what sort of stuff Damon was going to be faced with. Sure, he'd claimed in the car he wasn't nervous, but I felt nervous for him. I didn't want anyone asking him things that were too personal, like the stuff that had happened with his dad.

"So, you're doing *Moulin Rouge*, what's that like?" the interviewer, whose name was Troy Livingston, asked tartly. I could already tell he considered himself a funny guy, as well as edgy and post-modern. His voice held a hint of sarcasm, which got my back up. Damon, however, seemed to take it all in stride.

"It's a bit like having an acid trip in a turn-of-the-century boudoir while there's a burlesque show going on upstairs," he deadpanned, and Tony laughed. I exhaled in relief that he'd decided to go along with the tone rather than getting pissed. In fact, as I watched him sitting there, I noticed a difference in him. He seemed more at ease with himself, almost like when we were in Skye. I hadn't seen him this relaxed or confident around strangers before.

"Sounds like a party I'd like to attend. But, not to sound rude, we're all wondering if you can hold a tune. I think I can speak for everyone when I say nobody wants to suffer another Russell Crowe 'Javert.'"

"Are you asking me to sing?" Damon asked with a wry expression.

"If you want to belt out a few lines, I won't stop you," said Troy.

Damon chuckled, the low, husky sound incredibly sexy as it rumbled through the speakers. I shivered a little where I sat just beyond the glass window. "I think I'll leave your listeners guessing. If they're really curious, they can come and see the show."

Ha! Nice save. I was sure Jacob would be thanking him for the sneaky plug.

"Well, maybe that's for the best. People might start saying the only reason I do this job is so I can have grown men serenade me in the studio," Troy joked.

"It's not?" Damon asked dryly.

Troy only cast him an amused look before changing the subject.

"Ah, so here's a good one," he said, flicking through a few papers where seemingly a bunch of potential questions had been written down. "If you could star in the remake of any film, past or present, which one would you choose?"

Damon looked thoughtful for a moment. "If you'd asked me that a couple weeks ago, I probably would've said *Nil By Mouth*."

"Excellent!" Troy enthused. "I take it you're a Gary Oldman fan, then?"

"Oh, aye, huge fan."

"Didn't you star alongside him in that one film, the sci-fi thriller?"

Damon grimaced in self-deprecation. "I did. Admittedly, not my best work."

"Ah, come now. I don't think I can name a single successful actor who hasn't been in their fair share of stinkers."

Damon laughed, and again I shivered. He was becoming more free with his laughter, with his smiles, too, and it made me happy to see him opening up to people.

"True. Well, anyway, the other answer to that question is *Singin' in the Rain*."

Troy let out a big, boisterous chuckle. "For real? How do you go from gritty East End reality to a fluffy 1950s musical?"

Damon's expression was calculating. "I have a close friend who's crazy for Gene Kelly. As a challenge, I'd like to remake the film and have her admit I did better than the original," he answered, his eyes flicking to mine for a brief moment. They held a mischievous glint, and I knew he was goading me. *No way*, I mouthed at him as I shook my head. Gene was a mainstay in my heart. As far as I was concerned, remaking any of his films was sacrilege. Still, I couldn't wipe the smile off my face.

"That's some undertaking, but there's only one problem," said Troy, still chuckling away.

"And what's that?"

"You're too tall for a Gene Kelly role."

Damon smiled, and I swore it was my undoing. "If Hugh Jackman can play Wolverine, then I can play Don Lockwood."

Troy cast him a confused glance. "Who in the what now?"

"Wolverine is a five-foot-three Canadian played by a six-foot-two Aussie," Damon explained. "Anything is possible."

"I don't believe you," said Troy, glancing over his shoulder to call to his assistant. "Go Google if that's true."

The assistant came in with a tablet and handed it to Troy. He stared at the screen, scrolling through a web page. "Well, bugger me, you're right," he exclaimed. "Okay, I think this has been my favourite interview all year. We've gone from burlesque shows to gritty independent films to 1950s musicals to Marvel comics."

"I like to keep things interesting," said Damon.

"Well, goal achieved. So, how about we take a few questions from some callers?"

"By all means."

About fifteen minutes later the segment was over, and Damon emerged through the studio door. I gushed at him, telling him how great he'd been. He'd answered all the caller questions with finesse and charm, and I couldn't get over the change in him. If you'd asked me two months ago whether or not I thought he would've become so confident in his social skills, I'd have answered a definitive no. He'd come so far and I was so, so proud.

The car was there again to take us home, but on the ride I got a call from Farrah asking me to drop by her place because she wanted to measure me for a couple of costumes. I told her it was no problem before hanging up and proceeding to have a panic attack. Focusing on Damon and his radio interview had taken my mind off the impending doom of facing my stage fright.

His hand covered my shaking one as I slipped the phone back in my bag.

"Still feeling like you're going to vomit every time you think of Friday?" he asked softly, and I was surprised by how spot-on he was. Thinking of going on stage had me petrified and wanting to spew my guts up. Yes, lovely imagery.

"It's scary how you notice stuff sometimes," I said, and he gave me a warm look.

"I notice everything about you, Rose."

I blushed and glanced away. "Do you think the driver might be able to drop me off at Farrah's? She needs to take some last-minute measurements."

Damon moved forward and asked the driver to take a detour, and a few minutes later I was out of the car and waving him goodbye.

Once I was done at Farrah's, I got the tube home. When I arrived back at the flat the place was empty, so I assumed Julian had either gone out to meet with friends or he had an appointment with a client. The idea of it being the latter made me both relieved and disappointed. I didn't want him to be depressed, not ever, but at the same time I held out hope that this whole thing with Alicia might cause a change in him, make him want something different for himself.

I slept fitfully that night, waking up at around one or two to the sound of voices in the living room. It was Julian, but he was talking to someone. A woman. I crept out of bed and listened at my door, which I'd left slightly ajar. It only took me a moment to recognise Alicia's voice.

What the hell was she doing here?

I shouldn't have kept listening. I should've closed my door, climbed back into bed, and let them have their privacy. But for some reason, I just couldn't. Call it nosiness. Call it meddling. Whatever it was, I was glued to the spot like Mr Tumnus in Narnia when he was frozen by the White Witch as punishment.

"I never meant to hurt you," said Alicia. "In fact, from the first moment we met, I desired you. I desired you, but I hated myself for it, because I could see myself in your eyes. More importantly, I could see my father in your eyes. You were everything I always swore I'd stay away from."

Her words made me catch my breath. Had what I'd said to her in Damon's dressing room hit home? Was she here to apologise to Julian for messing him around?

"It sounds rather Freudian when you put it like that," said Julian in his usual glib manner, but there was a tenderness in his voice, one I rarely saw him use with anyone other than me.

"My father was a farmer. He was also a cheater and a gambler. I can't count the number of times I had to console my mom after another of his affairs came to light, or after he'd squandered all our money on the roulette table. Me and my brothers had to work our fingers to the bone just to scrape by. Nothing ever seemed like enough. The only thing that got me through was telling myself one day I'd be rich and famous, that I'd find a good, honest man to settle down with and be happy. A man who was nothing like him."

Julian let out a sigh I couldn't quite interpret. "That would be a beautiful life, Alicia, but perhaps beauty isn't always what you imagined. Sometimes an artist visualises his work but ends up with something entirely different when he puts paint to canvas."

"Am I supposed to be the artist in this analogy? Is my beautiful life the art that didn't come out the way I'd envisioned?" Alicia let out a jaded laugh. "Because yeah, it certainly didn't turn out like I planned, but it's far from beautiful."

"You are beautiful. Maybe that's all that matters. Beautifully flawed. Beautifully perfect. Beautifully strong. Beautifully fragile," he murmured, and I imagined he was touching her then, sliding his hand along her shoulder or fingering her silky red hair. "A dichotomy of contrasts."

"Don't," Alicia begged, her voice a coarse plea.

"I won't," said Julian. "Not unless you ask me to."

"And I won't ask."

Julian let out another long sigh, this one tired. "No. I know you won't. I know you don't want me, and I'm beginning to think I don't really want you, either. I don't know what I want. But I'd still like to be your friend if you'll have me?"

"I could use a friend," she sniffed.

"Then here I am. What's troubling you, dear friend?"

She let out a watery laugh. "You. Everything."

Julian laughed, too, soft and intimate. "I am trouble, this is true. Anything else?"

"Damon doesn't want me. He never did."

"If he doesn't want you, then it wasn't meant to be," said Julian. "You can't make someone love you, darling. That's just a fact of life."

Alicia let out a sound of frustration. "It just seems like nothing ever goes how I plan. My personal life is a mess, and on top of all that, I'm starting to feel like I've lost the connection with my character. Or maybe I never really had the connection to begin with. We open the show in less than two days, and I don't feel ready at all. I feel like I'm going to walk out onto that stage and nobody's going to believe me."

"They'll believe you. You simply have to find that connection, that spark. There must be something about Satine that you can relate to, something she feels that you feel yourself."

"I've tried, but I'm way too stressed out half the time to focus," Alicia said, sounding lost. In that moment, I felt for her. I forgot about all my jealousy and annoyance over her pursuit of Damon and simply saw her for who she was. A woman just like me, a woman who was scared.

"Well, let's think about her, shall we?" Julian began, his voice kind. "Satine is a French courtesan living in Paris during the turn of the century. She has luxuries and admirers, an adoring audience, but she isn't a part of normal society. In fact, if she were a real courtesan, Parisian society would've shunned her, barely acknowledged her existence. She lived in what the French termed the *demi-monde*, the half-world, a place of darkness and pleasure, but one not fit to be seen during the light of day. She was lusted after, lavished with gifts, her entire life endless parties and sex, but she was dying of tuberculosis, though syphilis probably would've been more likely. She had the world at her feet, or the half-world, if we're being specific, but she knew it was finite. She knew it couldn't last."

Alicia seemed taken aback, like she'd completely fallen under Julian's spell as he wove the tale of Satine's existence. "The poor woman."

"You see what you're feeling right now, hold on to it, don't let it go. This is your connection to the character."

"She must feel so alone."

"She does. Alone but surrounded. Loved hopelessly, but loved nonetheless."

"How do you know all this?" Alicia breathed.

"I read," Julian answered vaguely. Of course, I knew there was more to it than that. In a way, he was a modern-day Satine. He knew it because he read, yes, but he also knew it because he lived it. I heard him stand and walk across the living room.

"Here," he said.

"What's this?"

"It's a book I think you should read. *La Dame Aux Camelias* by Alexandre Dumas, *fils*." I knew the title

330

because it had sat for years amid our hodgepodge collection of dog-eared paperbacks. I'd never read it myself, but I knew it was one of Julian's favourites.

"What's it about?" Alicia asked.

"It's about a courtesan quite like Satine, the young Marguerite Gautier, though the character is based on a real-life woman named Marie Duplessis. She was a courtesan and the author's lover. The book tells the story of their affair. It's where they took the story for the opera, *La Traviata.*"

"Oh," she said. "I will. I'll read it." She sounded like she meant it.

"You can keep that copy. I have others," said Julian causally, but I knew he was lying. That was his only copy, and he'd had it for years. It meant something to him, and I wasn't sure if he should give it away so freely.

"Really? That's so kind. Thank you," she said, her voice still airy.

There was a quiet, and I thought Julian must have taken the book from her for a minute to flick through the pages, because the next thing he said was, "One of my favourite lines is in here." A moment of silence passed. "Ah, I've found it. *No matter how long I live, I shall live longer than you love me.* Have you ever heard anything more heartbreaking in your life?" he asked wistfully.

I thought Alicia sounded like she might cry when she spoke. "Why? Why would you pick that as your favourite?"

"Because, my darling, I know how it feels. I know what it's like to be constantly loved in a way that never lasts. And you, you know what it's like to fear the end of adoration, just like Satine. If your career ever ends, where will that leave you?"

"It will leave me with a nicely padded bank account and a life of leisure," she answered somewhat stiffly.

"Ah, but a healthy bank account is nothing if you have no one to share it with."

"Julian, *please*."

"I'm sorry. That was a horrible thing to say. Come here, let me read you a passage."

At this I couldn't listen anymore. They were both being too raw, too open with each other, and it wasn't my place to intrude. Even though I still didn't entirely trust Alicia, they deserved this moment, whatever it was, to be their own.

The following morning, I woke up to find Julian asleep on the couch. He looked wrecked. Alicia was nowhere to be seen, so I knew she must've gone home sometime after I'd gone back to sleep. Julian blinked open his eyes as I crawled in beside him, wrapped my arms around his shoulders, and held him close.

"Rose?" he said questioningly, his voice tired.

"I love you," I whispered, and squeezed him tight. There was a second where he simply did nothing, but then he finally hugged me back, his entire body sinking into the comfort.

"I love you, too," he whispered. "I love you, too."

Twenty-Six.
Rose

The phone rang several times before the director answered curtly, "Yes?"

"Hi, Jacob, um, this is Rose Taylor."

"What is it, Rose? I'm busy," he snipped.

"Yes, I know, and I'm sorry for interrupting you, but I really need to talk to you about this part you've given me."

"What about it?"

"I can't do it."

"Fuck off."

"P-pardon?" I stammered, taken aback.

"Something wrong with your hearing, dear? I said, Fuck. Off. Iggy might be happy to continue babying you, but I'm not. You're one of the most talented dancers I've seen in a long time, and yet you wallow in the background, never letting a soul see your talent. You're doing this show, Rose. If I have to drag you kicking and screaming, you're doing it. You can thank me when you're picking up your Olivier award."

And with that he hung up. I stood staring at the phone in my hand in both awe and panic, my gut churning. He wasn't taking no for an answer. He was going to make me do this.

And I was going to be sick. Again.

All morning I'd been in a tizzy, pacing around the apartment like a madwoman. Glancing at the clock, I saw I was going to be late to rehearsals if I didn't get my arse moving. I'd decided to call Jacob and tell him over the phone, because that way if he started berating me, I could hang up. Well, he did berate me – sort of. Only he was the one to hang up.

Was his particular brand of tough love what I needed? All I knew was that though his words were hostile, they'd bolstered me. He wasn't giving me a choice, and there was a certain freedom in that. I had to go on stage because there was no option not to.

I was going to do this. I owed it to the girl who used to dance so unselfconsciously in front of the television, not giving a care about anyone else's opinion. And I owed it to the woman I was now, the one who held her desires close, the one who secretly yearned for the excitement of the stage, of dancing in front of a live audience, but denied herself because of fear.

The entire day was a blur. Once I'd convinced myself I was going to be in the show, I put my all into it. I even stayed after hours to practice, making sure my moves were flawless. I barely saw Damon aside from when he was in character, and I was so bone tired after a day of nonstop practice that I could hardly keep my eyes open once I got home that night.

And then, almost in the blink of an eye, it was show time. I didn't feel like me. I felt like somebody else. Perhaps that was the point. It was fifteen minutes before they opened the doors to ticket holders, and I'd found a quiet spot backstage where I could have a nice little private meltdown.

I was experiencing heart palpitations. My skin was clammy with sweat even though I'd taken two showers that morning. I just couldn't seem to calm down, couldn't seem to stop thinking of the fact that soon there would be hundreds of pairs of eyes on me, waiting to laugh, waiting to point and snicker when I failed.

"God," somebody said from my right.

I turned to find Damon standing there in tuxedo pants and an off-white wife-beater vest. For a second I forgot all my panic, because there was no sight more delectable than Damon Atwood in a sleeveless top. He looked good enough to eat. I didn't say anything, just took him in as he approached. His gaze wandered over the skimpy outfit I wore: a black corset, lace stockings, suspenders, and a frilly skirt that rose up at the front. It didn't sound like a lot, but it actually covered up much of my body. My cleavage, however, was the focal point, and Damon couldn't seem to tear his gaze away.

His hand went briefly to his crotch, discreetly adjusting himself as his cheeks coloured. I was blushing, too. What a pair we made.

"You look incredible, underdressed but incredible," he finally uttered, his voice a husky rumble.

"I'm wearing more than a lot of the other dancers out there," I replied with a soft laugh.

"It doesn't feel that way. It feels obscene. Or maybe that's just my perverted mind's fault."

A moment elapsed, one laced with arousal and the need to touch. I cleared my throat. "So, how are you feeling? Ready for our grand opening?"

"I'm surprisingly calm. I wish I could say the same for you," he said, coming closer and taking my hand in his. "Rose, you're shaking."

"I know. I'm terrified."

"But you're so good. I couldn't stop watching you yesterday during rehearsals. Jacob should count himself lucky that the other girl was injured. You're so much better than her."

"Damon! Don't say that," I exclaimed, horrified but at the same time delighted with the compliment.

He chuckled. "I know, but it's true." His other hand moved over my bare shoulder, and my skin prickled at his touch, my body silently screaming for more. I turned to him, wanting to rest my face on his chest but fearing I might get makeup all over his costume.

"I miss you," he whispered then, his mouth so close I could practically taste him.

"Then why have you been staying away?" I asked.

I knew we were both on hectic schedules with preparations for the show, but I still wished he'd find a moment to come to me, a second for us to just be alone together. He was vital to my life now, and I couldn't do without him.

"Oh, petal, such reproach in your eyes," he murmured, taking my chin in his hand and tilting my head, preventing me from looking away. "But what beautiful eyes they are."

I swallowed thickly, my heart hammering. Between my stage fright and Damon's closeness, I was certain the poor beleaguered organ would soon give out on me. I stared at him. "You use that word like a weapon, you know. 'Beautiful' on your lips should be illegal, Damon Atwood. It makes me weak."

"I stayed away because I've been ashamed of my anger, of how I hit Blake," he confessed suddenly, taking me by surprise. "That's not the kind of man I want to be for you. Only the weak-willed succumb to their tempers like that."

"You had a right. If Alicia had come to me and told me she'd slept with you, I'm not sure she would've survived the conversation," I said with a hint of a smile.

Damon smiled in return, his face tilting curiously. "Oh, no?"

I shook my head. "I'd have scratched her eyes out."

He was moving forward, backing me into a wall. "No, you wouldn't. It's not in you, Rose. You're too kind-hearted. That's why I love you."

My gaze widened, my body froze, while my heart battered a frantic rhythm inside my chest. "Wh-what?" I whispered.

Damon seemed momentarily chagrined, like he hadn't meant to say that out loud. But then his expression transformed, his eyes shone with a fierce possession, and his strong arms surrounded my scantily clad body. All in that one meeting of our eyes, I knew he was telling the truth. In a heartbeat, every look we'd shared flashed through my mind, from that initial fleeting glance across the dance studio the first time I'd heard him sing, to this one. This one that told me I owned his heart, his soul, his *everything*.

He dipped his head down, his lips brushing mine as he replied emphatically, "I said, I love you."

One peck. Then, another. He licked across the seam of my lips, coaxing my mouth to open for him. So many feelings threatened to swallow me whole.

He said he loved me.

He said he LOVED me.

I was lost. Completely and irrevocably lost to him. His body melded itself to mine, pushing, seeking, grasping. I wrapped my arms around his neck, kissing him with every fibre of my being. He lifted my legs, and I wrapped them around his torso, our bodies flushed and heated.

I gasped a quick breath, momentarily breaking the feverish kiss to say, "I know this isn't the time, but I need you, Damon. I need you inside me."

He groaned, his mouth on mine again, his tongue hot and slick. We each began fumbling with each other's clothes, not giving a care to the fact we had to be on stage in a matter of minutes. He swore when he couldn't get to grips with my costume. Luckily, I easily got his fly down, sliding my hand inside his pants to palm his rock hard erection.

I jerked him slowly up and down, loving the silky feel of him. His hands fell away from me for a moment, his head dropping to my shoulder as a deep, rumbly sigh escaped him.

"Fuck, Rose," he grunted.

"I want you inside me," I whimpered, still moving my hand along his length. I swiped my thumb over the head and he hissed a harsh swearword, his jaw tight.

"And I want it, too, petal, I want it, too. But right now we have to get ready to go on stage."

"We have a few minutes," I murmured seductively. I was like a needy little sex fiend, desperate for a fix. In that moment, I was unable to think past the carnal need for contact, for the pleasure of his cock. Now that he'd told me he loved me, it was all I could think about. I needed to be connected to him on a most base and primal level.

"Yes, but if I fuck you, Rose, I won't want to stop. And if I fuck you, I won't be able to think straight when I have to perform with your scent all over me."

His sexual, heated words caused wetness to pool between my thighs. "Oh…Damon."

"Hush. We'll find time later. Right how I just want to know you're going to be okay through all this. You can do

338

this with your eyes closed. When you dance, imagine it's just you and I in the room. Imagine I'm the only one watching and the entire audience will fall completely under your spell. Just like I have."

I stared into his eyes, and somehow, all my earlier panic evaporated. I couldn't tell if it was his words or his unexpected declaration of love, but all of a sudden there was a calm inside me that hadn't been there before.

I nodded bravely. "I think I can do it."

His gaze flickered over my face, studying me as though to make sure I was telling the truth. I briefly wondered if he was afraid I might run off and abandon ship at the last moment. The stage manager came by then, giving us our ten-minute call. Damon pulled me into his arms, hugging me so tightly I felt entirely surrounded by him.

We stayed like that for a long time, just absorbing one another, but it all went by too quickly. Before we knew it, Damon was called to the stage, and I had to go join the other dancers at the back of the theatre. Jacob had arranged the show in such a way that the big club scene would play out both on stage and in the audience. The dancers would enter from the back, making our way down the aisles before finally finding our way to the stage. It was actually quite clever, because it meant the audience would truly get to feel like they were in the *Moulin Rouge*.

I took one last glance at my phone to find a message from Julian that made my heart warm.

Julian: *Break a leg. I'm sitting in the third row, centre stage. You're going to rock this daaaarlinnge!! Xxx*

Smiling fondly to myself, I slipped my phone to Iggy for safekeeping and watched as Henry took to the stage to sing the opening number: "Nature Boy." After the first verse, the spotlight shone on Damon as he sat by the prop typewriter to compose his tragic tale of lost love.

The final lyrics of the song hit me like a sledgehammer, seeping into my bones as a startling realisation took hold.

The greatest thing you'll ever learn is just to love and be loved in return.

Damon had told me loved me, but I'd never said it back. It seemed almost supernatural that the first words I ever heard him sing were the same ones that would help me see I was in love with him, too. My heart practically pounded out of my chest with the need to tell him, but the show had begun, and I wouldn't get a chance to be alone with him until it was over.

Somehow I just couldn't stomach the idea of saying it during a brief stolen moment between scenes. I wanted to make it special. *Later,* I reminded myself. I'd have all the time in the world later.

Before I knew it, I was taking my first steps out into the lavish auditorium, my first steps in front of an audience who could either love or loathe me...or worse, be indifferent. And though there were a few brief seconds where I thought I might pass out, I got through it. In fact, being on stage was far less scary than the anticipation of it. The more I danced with my fellow cast members, the more my nerves flittered away.

They flittered and flittered until I was no longer nervous at all, but exhilarated. The audience applauded after each big number, and catching sight of Jacob's overjoyed expression where he stood just behind the stage curtains, I knew the show was going down a storm.

Even Blake was pulling off his part with finesse, and I thought maybe he'd had a few drug-free days, because his eyes were clear and he didn't seem on edge like he had before. Alicia, of course, was her usual glorious self, in spite of the late night fears she'd expressed to Julian. When she was lowered down on the swing for "Sparkling Diamonds," I even heard a few awed intakes of breath. She looked like a sexy, diamante-encrusted, scarlet-haired angel, and I was certain Julian was more than enjoying the view.

And Damon, *God*, Damon was an entirely different person. He embodied Christian in every move, every dance, every beautifully sung line. It was difficult to focus on my own part, I was so enthralled by him. I thought back to his first day at the studio, when Iggy had bet me he wouldn't make it to opening night. Well, he had made it.

And he was shining for all the world to see.

The show went by in a flash, and I stood on stage with the other dancers as Alicia started to sing the final "Come What May" reprise. There were tears in her eyes, and in that moment I truly believed she was Satine. I wasn't sure if she'd read the book Julian had given her, or if she'd somehow clung to the connection she found as he created a story for the ailing courtesan, but the entire theatre was silent as she sang without any accompaniment from the orchestra.

Damon stood at the very back of the theatre, right among the audience members. Most of them didn't even realise he was standing there until he started singing, their heads whipping around in excitement and surprise as he belted out the lyrics, striding down the centre aisle towards Alicia.

The two met in the middle, still singing as Damon took her in his arms. Something happened when his eyes met mine. He sang the line that always hit me square in the gut,

341

and I knew it was meant for me. My entire body broke out in a fever of pinpricks and tingles.

I wished I could be the one in his arms right then.

Come what may, he would love me until my dying day.

Time stood still, my eyes, my heart, my entire soul was captured inside his. And then, the scene moved on, all hell breaking loose as a shot rang out and the audience gasped while the action of the story's finale unfolded.

We all walked out to several standing ovations when the show ended. I somehow found myself standing next to Damon, holding his hand while Alicia held the other. It wasn't supposed to be me. It was supposed to be in order of importance. He should have been holding Eddie's hand, Blake's, even. Definitely not mine. But there we were, standing together, skin touching skin, fingers entwined as the crowd roared their applause.

I'd worked on enough productions in my time to know that this one was a hit. I'd heard all levels of cheering, and in the words of Spinal Tap, this applause went up to eleven.

I was vaguely aware of Damon kissing me, his lips on the corner of my mouth before he was pulled away. Turning around, I found Iggy standing there, smiling like crazy.

"You were amazing," he said, beaming. "I'm so fucking proud of you."

I let him hug me, thinking this was the first time I'd ever seen my boss close to tears. He squeezed me tight, and then Julian was there, hugging me just as hard, telling me how well I'd done. Alicia passed us by, and I looked just in time to see Julian discreetly reach out and squeeze her hand. I wasn't sure what it meant, but I saw her squeeze back before she let go, moving on as a gaggle of people congratulated her on a spellbinding performance.

About ten minutes passed, and those clogging the backstage area began to trickle out. I looked over the tops of people's heads, trying to spot Damon, but I couldn't see him anywhere. Pushing my way past bodies, I sought him out, but then it hit me. I knew exactly where he'd be.

So I ran.

Twenty-Seven.
Damon

There were too many people.

They were smiling and telling me how great the show had been, but I still felt suffocated. Compliments were nice, but I just needed a moment alone to come back down to earth. Performing on stage for a live audience, one that had been rapt by the show from the very first song, had been exhilarating. Liberating. I honestly didn't know how much I truly missed acting until tonight.

The very second I got the chance to slip away, I did, finding solace in my blessedly empty dressing room. I sat in front of the mirror, my face sweaty and my hair going in all directions, the suit I wore rumpled from the show. I was exhausted. And tomorrow I had to come back and do it all over again. I was oddly looking forward to it – excited, even.

Every night a new audience.

Every night a new reaction.

I heard the door to my dressing open abruptly and turned my head to find Rose come inside, slamming it shut behind her and flicking over the lock. My pulse raced. She looked glorious. Her makeup was smudged, some mascara running down her cheeks. Like me, she was exhausted, but she'd never looked more beautiful.

"I love you, too," she blurted hastily, then clamped a hand over her mouth. Like she was shocked by her own voice.

Those four simple words gave me a feeling like no other, and though yes, there had been a part of me that was disappointed when she hadn't said them back, I knew it

344

was because she was drowning in the effect my own declaration had on her. Lust. Urgency. *Need*. I'd seen a fire light in her eyes when I told her I loved her, and her body had simply taken over.

I knew the feeling, because as she stood there, so messy and perfect and heavenly, I was struck by the desire to take her up against the wall.

"Come here," I said, the command guttural.

She ran to me, and I pulled her into my lap. "I love you, too," she said again, like there was a pleasure in the statement itself and she couldn't get enough of it.

"I know, beautiful. And I love you. Now, give me your mouth," I murmured, taking her face in my hands and slanting my lips over hers. She moaned when I slid my tongue inside, little gasps and whimpers escaping as she moved to straddle my lap. She felt so soft, her tits pushing into my chest where my shirt was unbuttoned, the sweet place between her thighs hot and welcoming against my thickening erection.

"I want to feel you fall apart on my hand," I said, the sinful words making her shudder. I loved how I had such a visceral effect on her. Reaching up, I pulled her hair out of its bun, the silky tendrils falling down, framing her face and shoulders. Christ, she was a sight to behold.

"You were so amazing tonight," she whispered, planting kisses along my neck that had my balls tightening. "I could hardly take my eyes off you."

"And I you. The way you move, it bewitches me," I said. "When you dance, when I sink inside you, when you come."

"Damon," she gasped when I pulled her corset free and grasped both breasts in my hands. "I can't wait any longer. These last few days have felt like a lifetime."

I knew what she meant. For me they'd been an eternity. I'd agonised over my reaction to Blake's lie, hated myself for being so easily manipulated. I didn't feel like I deserved her. But then, somehow, I realised that I did. We fit together perfectly. There was no one else for me. If I couldn't have Rose, I was condemning myself to a life of halves, and I wanted to live a whole one.

Her hands were at my fly, pulling my cock free, her soft palms gripping me. I let her take the lead, at the same time helping her out of her clothes. The door was locked, and I had no intention of seeing anyone until I'd had my fill of the woman I loved.

When she was naked and I was still mostly clothed, she rose up on her knees, positioned herself over my cock and then sank down on it. Slowly, so agonisingly slow. I hissed a strangled breath and gripped her waist. She was so wet, sheathing me with her heat, moving up and down as I stared at her in awe, mouth open, eyes hooded, completely entranced.

Bending forward, I took her nipple in my mouth, sucking it, laving it with attention before moving to the other. She whimpered at the contact, her eyes ablaze as she watched me go to work.

I fingered her clit as she rode me, feeling her thighs tense as she pushed toward orgasm. She bit her lip, her cheeks reddening and a lovely red sex flush spreading itself across her chest. The moment she came, trembling against me, I picked her up and carried her across the room. Setting her down on the small velvet couch in the corner, I positioned her on all fours, then pushed inside. Her sex pulsated around me, so wet and ready now that she'd come.

I didn't hold back, not for a second. She moaned when I gripped the back of her neck, holding tight as I hammered home. The sexy, beautiful curve of her arse drove me crazy, the sight of her before me, mine for the taking, was branded into my memory.

I watched as my cock moved in and out of her, loved the sound of her ample flesh smacking as I drove us both to dizzying heights of pleasure. It felt so good, but I didn't want to come like that. I never wanted to come inside Rose unless I was staring into the depths of her fathomless sea-blue eyes.

When I slid out, she whimpered her protest at the loss of me. I flipped her over, pulling her thighs around my hips as I sank back in, this time never taking my eyes off her. She inhaled at the new sensation, and I kissed her before she could let the air back out, swallowing her breath. I palmed her breast, moving my hand down, down, down, over her stomach, navel, and abdomen until I reached that sweet, sweet spot between her thighs.

"I can't," she rasped. "It's too soon."

"You can," I countered. "You can."

She could.

Rose came undone as I made love to her, the sensation of her sex clenching on my cock for the second time that night sending my head spinning. I lost it, unable to hold back as I spilled inside her. She petted at my hair, whispering sweet, soothing words to me as I tried to summon some form of intelligent thought. I had nothing. All I could do was lie on top of her soft, welcoming body, bury my face in her neck, and inhale her wonderful scent.

When I finally came to my senses, I lifted up on my elbows to gaze at her lovingly.

"Only you," I whispered, and she smiled so dazzlingly that my heart snapped in two and came together all at once.

"Only us," she whispered back, fingers still running soothingly through my short hair.

Twenty-Eight.
Rose

"We have to show our faces at the after-party," I told Damon as we lay there, basking in a post-coital bliss.

"After-party?" he murmured, his hand sliding over my shoulder and collarbone, my breast, before resting on the soft part of my stomach.

"Didn't you hear? Jacob organised it to celebrate our opening night. I doubt anyone will stay very late since we all have another show tomorrow, but it would be rude not to show up at all."

"I don't want to go," he grunted, moving down my body now to pull my thighs around his shoulders. I gasped when he pressed his face to my sex, inhaling deeply before licking a line right down my centre. "I want to stay here and eat you out for the rest of the night."

"As l-lovely as that sounds," I replied, stuttering because he was starting to tongue my clit in earnest now. "We really do need to go to the...party. I told J-Julian I'd be there, and Iggy, too."

"Don't care," he growled, his fingers finding me and slipping inside as his tongue went to work. I gripped the velvety fabric of the couch, moaning as I felt my third orgasm of the night building. Several people had knocked on Damon's door while he'd been inside me, but they must've heard my uncontrollable screams because the knocks stopped coming after a while.

I tugged on his hair and he looked up at me hotly, eyes dark as his tongue darted out and licked a long, wet line right down the centre of me once more. I shifted, a strangled cry escaping as his fingers moved in and out in a tantalising rhythm.

"I love you...so much," I gasped, and saw him smile as he continued to eat me out.

"We're not going to the party until I make you come at least twice more," he told me between licks.

I didn't even bother to argue. And he made good on his promise.

I knew I must have looked like a sex-flushed mess when we finally arrived at the wine bar for the after party, where our fellow cast members and stage crew were celebrating a successful opening night. I held Damon's hand, wearing a hastily thrown-together outfit of a black shift dress and heels. Damon wore jeans and a T-shirt with a casual navy jacket. Despite the lack of effort, he looked incredible. Or maybe I just thought that because I was so completely infatuated.

Every time he looked at me, every time we touched, no matter how casual, it had my heart doing somersaults and my stomach fluttering with happiness.

Stepping out of the cab, we were immediately met with the blinding flashes of cameras. I'd been so lost in a sea of Damon that I completely forgot about all the press who were covering our opening night. My stomach tensed when Damon's hand tightened around mine. I knew he didn't like this sort of attention and I didn't want him to become angry or upset.

Glancing up, I saw his jaw firm as he stiffly surveyed the wall of paparazzi that surrounded us. His eyes came to mine and I widened my gaze at him before mouthing, *just smile*. I could see from his expression that he remembered our conversation from weeks ago, when I'd told him that if he simply embraced the attention it wouldn't bother him so much. Besides, being photographed on a daily basis was part and parcel of the business.

It was as we silently communicated that his tension subsided. His shoulders relaxed, his jaw loosened, and he no longer held my hand in a death grip. His mouth moved and my heart leapt when I saw his lips slowly curving into a smile. The photographers called his name, asking how he'd enjoyed his opening night, who I was, whether or not he'd return to film after the show's run ended. All manner of questions. Damon didn't answer a single one.

But he smiled.

He embraced the situation instead of hiding, and that was how I knew he'd be okay. He might never love this side of the job, but he'd get through it, and that was all that mattered.

"Look at you, freshly fucked and ready to party," Julian whispered teasingly in my ear as soon as we entered the bar. Damon had gone to get us drinks.

"Shut your face," I said, biting back a smile. Trust Julian to be the first one to notice the signs of recent shagging.

"Oh, my God, I'm right, aren't I? I have to say, Rose, sex looks good on you. You're practically glowing."

I blushed profusely and elbowed him in the side. "I said, shut up."

Julian laughed as he lifted his glass of orange juice to take a sip, the move full of masculine elegance. "You know the more embarrassed you get, the more I'll just keep going. You need to own it. I'm glad you and the dashing Mr Atwood finally managed to reconnect. It was becoming downright depressing seeing you wallow around the flat like Bridget Jones after she broke up with Darcy."

"First of all, stop referring to him as 'the dashing Mr Atwood.' You make him sound like he should be in a Jane Austen novel, and secondly, I haven't been the only one wallowing." I eyed him pointedly, but he waved away the comment.

"Don't worry about me. I'm over the whole Alicia thing. We're friends now. It's all good."

"Have you spoken to her?"

"You mean since the night you eavesdropped on our little *tête-à-tête*?" said Julian nonchalantly. I opened my mouth to protest, but he held up a hand. "Don't even bother trying to deny it. The fourth floorboard from your bedroom door has a creak in it. I knew you were listening."

I frowned, realising he was right. I kept forgetting about that bloody creaky floorboard. "I'm sorry. Are you mad?"

"Of course not. I would've done the same thing. And besides, I'm eagerly awaiting the night you and Damon decide to do the dirty at our place. I'll have a glass up against the wall for that show, you mark my words," he quipped, and I slapped his shoulder.

"Don't you dare."

"You know I'm joking. Listening to you have sex would be like listening to my own sister, and even I'm not depraved enough to give incest a go."

I laughed loudly just as Damon returned with our drinks, his warm fingers skimming mine as he handed me the glass. He wrapped one arm around my shoulders and pulled me close before pressing a kiss to my temple. The show of affection had Julian doting like a drunk aunt at a wedding reception.

"Aw, would you look at you two, so adorable it makes me sick."

"You can say that again," came a familiar voice as Alicia appeared at his side. I stiffened momentarily, but then saw the friendly, open smile on her face and relaxed. "There were a couple of journalists wanting to interview you after the show," she said to Damon, a smirk forming. "Apparently Jacob's assistant tried your dressing room several times, but the door was locked."

"I was busy," Damon replied, like that explained everything.

"And you know what they say," Julian interjected cheerily. "If the boats a-rocking, be a dear and leave some cigarettes by the door for after."

Alicia chuckled, smiling at Julian like they were buds, before returning her attention to Damon. "Anyway, I did my duty and gave all the interviews tonight, but you can do them tomorrow. A girl needs her beauty sleep."

"I know something she needs more than sleep," Julian muttered past a sip of his drink, but Alicia let the comment slide, only casting him a vaguely amused flick of her emerald green eyes. Perhaps they really were friends now.

I felt someone pat my shoulder before I turned and found Blake standing behind me. Damon tensed almost instantly, but I sent him a reassuring look that said it was fine.

"Rose, can we talk for a minute?" Blake asked hesitantly. He shot a nervous glance in Damon's direction, and I thought he might be anxious he'd try punch him again. The nervousness was so unlike him. Normally he was confident to the point of cockiness.

Damon's arm around my shoulder tightened, but I turned and placed a kiss to the underside of his jaw. "It's okay. I'll be back in a minute."

He didn't seem too happy and only just managed to let his arm drop from me. For a second I thought he might tell Blake to fuck off, but he didn't, and I knew it had taken a lot of self-restraint. Stepping aside, I gestured for Blake to lead the way. I followed him to a small smoking area outside. He sat down on a chair and lit a cigarette, the plume of smoke billowing out as he exhaled. I took a seat next to him, and for a minute we just stared at the brick wall of the building in front of us. It was a chilly night, and my bare arms pricked with goose pimples from the cold.

"I gave Jacob my notice," he said. "He's got two weeks to find a replacement, and then I'm checking into the Priory."

I glanced at him in surprise. "Really?"

He nodded, sucking in another drag of his smoke, his other hand tucked in his pocket.

"Wow, that's great news. You're doing the right thing."

A small smile shaped his lips. He really was very handsome, even with the grey bags beneath his eyes and the perennially tired cast to his features. I could just imagine how gorgeous he'd be if he got healthy. "Yeah, well, it's nice to know someone cares."

"Of course I care. I'll always care about you to some extent, Blake. I can't be with someone and then just stop caring. It's not how I'm drawn."

He glanced at me, an intense look on his face as a silence fell between us.

"This role really is cursed. First Bob and now you. I bet Jacob's having a fanny fit as we speak," I said, smiling.

That solicited a small laugh from Blake. "Yeah, he wasn't too happy."

"No?"

He shook his head. "He basically tore me a new one, frog-marching me out of his office and calling me an ungrateful little prick. I didn't tell him about my addiction. Don't want it spreading around the industry, or I might have trouble finding work when I get out of rehab."

"I can understand that. The main thing is that you're doing this. And you don't have to worry about me. I won't tell anyone."

He shot me a look of thanks and sighed, raking a hand through his hair. "Good. That's a weight off my mind. It's nice to have an ex who isn't out to string me up by the balls for once."

I smiled at that. "Oh, believe me, there was a time when I wanted to, but I'm over it."

"Yeah, you've got Damon now. I really mean it when I say I'm sorry for trying fuck things up with you two. I wasn't in my right mind, but it's still inexcusable."

"Don't beat yourself up. It's all water under the bridge," I said, reaching out to give his hand a squeeze. We shared a look before I let go.

"He's a lucky son of a bitch, you tell him that from me," said Blake.

"She doesn't have to. I'm already well aware of it," came Damon's voice as he stepped out into the smoking area. His gaze wandered from me to Blake and then back to me. I stood and went to slide my fingers through his. A charged moment passed between Damon and Blake, like they were silently coming to an understanding. Then we told Blake we'd see him tomorrow before stepping back inside the bar.

"Did he behave himself?" Damon whispered, his breath tickling my ear. I shuddered and clenched my thighs, which were still sore from all the dressing room sex we'd just had.

355

"He did."

"Good," Damon said sternly, right before Alicia appeared in front of us. She glanced between the two of us before her attention came to land on me.

"Sorry to interrupt but I need to borrow Rose for a minute," she said with a smile.

I thought it was funny that Damon eyed her with almost the same amount of suspicion as he had Blake. She waved her hand in the air.

"No need to get your panties in a twist. I have nothing but pure intentions," she said as Damon continued to eye her. I let go of his hand and took a step toward Alicia, joking, "Seems like I'm quite the popular lady tonight. I'll come find you in a minute."

Damon nodded gruffly, kissed my cheek and then went to join Julian over by the bar. Alicia tilted her head for me to follow her to a small table in a quiet corner.

"So," she began as I took a seat. "I've got a couple apologies for you."

"You do?" I quirked a brow.

She nodded. "Uh huh. First, I just wanted to let you know that I've made my peace with the fact that you and Damon are soul mates. As much as it makes me want to barf, I understand now and I won't try to get between you again." She shot me a friendly grin and I smiled, rolling my eyes.

"And second, I'm sorry for how I treated Julian. You were right, he's an amazing person. He deserves someone amazing and I feel ashamed for my actions. I've already apologised to him and he's forgiven me. I just hope you can, too."

I shrugged. "If Julian's forgiven you then there's nothing else to say. Just...please don't string him along again. You were right when you said you were too alike. I've known him since we were kids, and I know he needs someone who's the opposite of him. *I'm* the opposite of him. It's why I'm the only person who's lasted so long in his life."

"And I need someone who's the opposite of me," said Alicia. "So we're all agreed. Here's hoping one day I find my reliable man and Julian finds a girl like you, but one he actually wants to have sex with." She laughed and I joined her.

"I'll drink to that."

A little while later, after I found Damon and we did our rounds, we both felt it was time to call it a night. Not least because of the fact that a heady tension still lingered between us.

I wanted him again.

When we got back to my place, Damon tugged me directly to the bedroom before quickly ridding me of my clothes. It was a long, long, deliciously wonderful night.

The following morning, neither one of us woke up before midday. I opened my eyes to find the bed empty and the delectable scent of bacon streaming in from the kitchen. Stretching my body out, I savoured the exhaustion in my muscles and bones, the wonderful ache between my thighs a mark that Damon had been there not long ago.

"Morning," he said, looking scruffy and handsome as he re-entered the room with a tray.

"Is this breakfast in bed? You do realise you already have my heart, right? You don't need to try steal it a second time."

He cast me an amused grin before joining me in bed and feeding me bacon. Did I mention how much I loved this man? It was just as we'd finished eating and Damon

357

started planting kisses down my body that a thought struck me. I sprang up, almost knocking him off the bed as I grabbed for my phone. Damon chuckled in amusement, perplexed as he watched me. He started running his hand up and down my back as he peeked his head over my shoulder.

"What are you doing?" he asked, voice tired and husky.

"I'm checking to see if there are any reviews of the show yet," I replied, scanning the search results before finding what I was looking for. "Ah! Okay, here we go, I've found one. Say a prayer it's favourable. I'm just gonna bite the bullet and read it aloud."

"Go ahead." Damon laughed softly at my antics, pressing a tender kiss to my shoulder. He didn't give a hoot about reviews, I could tell. He wasn't that sort of person. He didn't perform for praise. But I, well, this was my first ever performance. I knew I wasn't anywhere near being a focal point in the show, but I was eager to see if I'd gotten a mention.

"When I first heard that the esteemed Jacob Anthony was planning to direct a stage adaptation of Moulin Rouge, *I'll admit I was wary. So many questions entered my head. How will they re-create the frantic, surreal fast pace only modern film editing can achieve? Who will play the roles so synonymous with their original actors? And is it even possible to license such an extensive and varied score?*

"Well, let me just say here and now that the very moment the house lights dimmed and Henry Green stepped onto the stage in a bizarre representation of the legendary artist Toulouse-Lautrec, all those questions fled my mind. I was rapt from the very first song. In fact, I can't remember the last time I experienced such an all-consuming and visceral reaction to a performance.

"Anthony's Moulin Rouge *is a riot of colour, emotion, and charm. The cast are magnificently adept, from the lead actors to the chorus line. I was particularly moved by Damon Atwood's stage debut, whom we haven't seen in the public eye for almost a decade. Atwood was a stunning actor in his youth, but with the passing of years has transformed into a thespian of finest quality. His voice is unparalleled, often outshining the talent of those performing alongside him. There were several moments where you could almost hear a pin drop, the onlookers were so enthralled by his performance."*

I paused reading to glance at Damon over my shoulder and grin. He was trying not to let it show that he enjoyed the praise, but I knew it meant something to him to hear a faceless reviewer speak so highly of him. I returned my attention to the review.

"And then we have the much-beloved Hollywood star, Alicia Davidson, also making her stage debut as Satine. I was highly impressed both with her vocal chops and her ability to bring equal parts vulnerability and strength to a character who is ruthlessly ambitious yet behind it all hopelessly romantic. And let's not forget the fact that she's mighty fine to look at, too. The male members of the audience certainly weren't left wanting for eye candy.

"Last but not least, I must comment on the sheer magnificence of the production's choreography. I felt as though I were transported back in time as the dancers not only owned every inch of the stage, but every inch of the theatre, too. In a bold move, we audience members got to enjoy being surrounded by a bevy of be-frilled and be-corseted can-can dancers, making their way around the room like the entire building was their very own turn-of-the-century night club. In particular, the dancer who

played Nini Legs-in-the-Air was uniquely striking, especially during her performance of 'El Tango de Roxanne.'"

Damon wrapped his arms around my waist and squeezed tight as I stared at the screen of my phone, flabbergasted. I knew it was only one line, but I'd gotten a mention in the review. This was massive. One of the biggest things to ever happen to me. The review was on *The Guardian's* website. I'd gotten mentioned in a theatre review in the flippin' *Guardian*!

"I can't believe it. I can't believe I got a mention," I exclaimed breathlessly.

"And why not? You should've gotten more than just one line, but perhaps I'm biased," said Damon, kissing my neck. "Of course the reviewer noticed you. Your dancing is probably the best he's ever seen."

My phone dropped from my hand as Damon dragged me down and under his big, firm body. My legs straddled his waist as he bent to kiss me long and deep. I moaned into his mouth just as a knock sounded on my bedroom door. Julian didn't even bother waiting to be invited inside — he simply burst into the room, waving his tablet in the air.

"A reviewer in *The Guardian* mentioned you in his review, Rose! In *The Guardian*!"

Damon and I pulled apart as we chuckled at Julian's display. He hopped onto the bed, giddy as a child, and wrapped his arms around me. It was a good thing I had a T-shirt on, though I didn't have anything underneath. Damon wore only his boxers, but he was a bloke. Men could get away with that sort of thing. Anyway, it wasn't like Julian hadn't seen me in various states of undress countless times before.

It was only as Julian let me go that he cast a smirk in Damon's direction. "Christ, Atwood, at least buy me dinner first before you start waving that behemoth in my face. Go put some trousers on."

Damon flushed bright red, and I laughed so hard my stomach hurt. I loved how he could appear so big and dark and manly, yet get as bashful as a schoolboy sometimes.

"Piss off," he said, scowling at Julian, but I could tell he was trying not to smile. It made my heart sing to see the fondness in his eyes for my best friend, because I knew it had been difficult for him to accept Julian due to his past.

Julian rose from the bed. "Oh, wipe that blush off your face. You're family now. You'd better get used to my ways."

With that he took his tablet and left the room. I smiled so widely at Damon my jaw ached. I couldn't remember a time when I'd felt so happy, so content. He gave me contentment, and I loved him for it. There was emotion in his eyes. He was touched by what Julian had said.

"Family?" he asked, his voice catching a little. Since his grandmother died he'd felt alone, so I knew being accepted into my and Julian's odd little clan of two meant a lot to him.

I came and wrapped my arms around him, kissing him once lightly on the lips. "Yes, Damon. Family. Always."

Epilogue.

6 Months Later…

"I'm not wearing that. It's…it's yellow," I told the stylist as I stood in wardrobe, arguing over my costume. This was a tribute. It didn't have to be one-hundred-percent identical. There was room for artistic licence, for some modernisation.

"Canary yellow to be exact," the cranky faced woman corrected me, a stressed out slant to her features. "And Gene wore one just like this. The whole point of the scene is that it mirrors the original,"

"I'll wear a waistcoat, just not that one. Have you got it in black? Navy, even?"

She pursed her lips in annoyance but didn't say anything. I could tell I was getting on her last nerve.

Normally, I just took the clothes I was given and put them on. I wasn't an argumentative bloke. But I just couldn't get down with that waistcoat. It was going to make me look like a bloody banana.

"He's right," said Julian, coming to my rescue. "Shit like that flew in the 1950s, not so much in the 2010s."

I was relieved he'd decided to come visit us on set today. If it weren't for him backing me up, I feared the woman might have torn off my shirt and forced me into the blasted thing.

Someone had heard the radio interview I'd given, where I'd joked about remaking *Singin' in the Rain*. I'd only said it to get a rise out of Rose, but unfortunately, word had trickled down the proverbial grapevine. A producer responsible for heading a film celebrating Gene

Kelly's work during the twentieth anniversary of his death had caught wind. It was just after we'd completed the three-month *Moulin Rouge* stint that I got a phone call asking if I'd like to be involved. And, funnily enough, the scene they'd wanted me to re-enact was one with the dancer Rose had told me about, Cyd Charisse. Only in this scene she wore a green dress instead of white.

At first I'd declined. I'd just spent several months dancing, and I wasn't in much of a mood for more. But when Rose discovered the offer, she insisted I do it. I couldn't say no to that woman, so in the end I caved...with one catch.

I told the producer I'd do the tribute, so long as I could pick the dancer who starred alongside me. He agreed.

I picked Rose.

Let's just say, the night I told her she was going to re-enact Gene Kelly and Cyd Charisse's sensual dance with me was one I'll never forget.

After weeks performing in London, her stage fright was long defeated. She was over the moon at the chance to perform again, this time in front of a camera. The documentary and tribute was to be aired on the E! channel over in the States, but they'd made a special arrangement to come film our part in London. Our set was a trendy nightclub they'd rented out specially.

"Call me crazy, but I just had an inspired idea," Julian went on. The stylist folded her arms, eyeing him sceptically. "How about no waistcoat at all? What's the point of guns like yours if you can't show them off every now and again, eh, Atwood?"

The stylist's scepticism transformed into a giant grin, while my face morphed into a frown that said, *Not in a million years.* Unfortunately, I was outnumbered, and

Julian was determined once he got an idea into his head. That was how I found myself walking out onto the set in a pair of dress slacks, tap shoes, suspenders, a porkpie hat, and little else.

When I'd thought of modernisation, this wasn't exactly what I'd had in mind.

It wasn't too different from what I'd been wearing in *Moulin Rouge*, except for the little matter of being completely shirtless. Julian grinned over at me from where he stood by the stylist, thoroughly enjoying my discomfort. The thing was, his grin had this way of making others want to grin, too, and it didn't take me long to see the funny side.

I shot him a look that said I'd get him back one of these days.

His returning glance said, *Challenge accepted.*

It had been a long time since I'd been in front of a camera, but it was all coming back to me, the lights, the booms, the director' chair over in the corner, cables running back and forth over the floor.

It felt like getting reacquainted with an old friend.

I stood talking with the director, a short, dark-haired man in his late fifties, when my attention caught on something shiny. Rose walked into the room, looking a little hesitant but still eager. My mouth fell open. She wore an emerald green dress with lots of shiny bits…what were those things called? Tassels? All I knew was the dress was exquisite, and it moulded to every generous, luscious curve of her body. Her hair was up off her neck, fashioned in a way that made it look much shorter than it actually was. Her eyes were what caught me most though, such vibrant blue outlined by dark makeup.

She was like every wet dream I'd ever had come to life.

"Mr Atwood? Did you hear what I just said?" the director asked, dragging my attention away from Rose.

"Pardon?"

He huffed and repeated himself. I nodded along, still barely listening. Rose's dress was indecently short, her shapely legs displayed in all their glory. I want to fucking bite her right then, she was so sexy, especially in those shoes. I wasn't a man who knew much about fashion, but Rose wore some sexy-as-fuck shoes at times. Several set workers surrounded her, one woman dusting powder on her cheeks while another fussed with her hair.

Rose looked up then, perhaps sensing my attention, and a blush coloured her cheeks. We'd been together long enough for her to know what my looks meant. This one said, *I'm going to fuck you six ways from Sunday as soon as I get you alone.* I couldn't be sure, but I thought I even saw her tremble slightly.

My cock stirred, but I told it to stand down. We had a scene to shoot.

A few minutes later, it was action time. The dance began, and I performed the tap routine Rose had spent countless hours teaching me, the cameras following my every move. Before I knew it, I was bending down and kneeling before her as she held her foot in midair, displaying the entire length of her leg sheathed in provocative lace stockings. The hat I'd been wearing hung on the end of her shoe. It didn't take much acting on my part to look enthralled. Fuck, it didn't take any acting at all, especially when I saw the seductive gleam in her eyes.

I took the hat, flicked it onto my head, and then it was all her. I was no longer the focal point of the scene — I was a simple worshipper on the altar of her talent. I could tell by the slant of her mouth that she was amused by my attire, or lack thereof, but obviously she couldn't comment on it right then.

It was when I tugged her body close to mine, swaying her with me as our dance continued, that she managed to whisper, "Not that I'm complaining, but what's with the *Magic Mike* getup?"

I twirled her, letting her body slide sensuously down mine before pulling her back up again. "Julian's idea," I whisper-grumbled back.

The mirth in her eyes was almost worth the discomfort of showing off my bare skin. I hadn't failed to notice a few female members of the crew eyeing me up and down, which I found odd but not unpleasant. Anyway, it didn't matter. It wasn't like they could do anything about it. I belonged to Rose now, only Rose.

The scene was almost at an end. I held her close, intimating a near kiss before she pulled away teasingly. When the director shouted "cut," I caught her hand and swung her back to me, kissing her full on the mouth. Her little gasp of surprise made me grin into the kiss.

I couldn't wait for our planned trip back to Skye next weekend. We hadn't returned since our brief visit all those months ago, and I was eager to have her back in my home again. I knew our lives as they were couldn't exist in one place, and I'd grown to accept that. As we each followed our individual paths, we'd move around, but I had every intention of doing all that was in my power to ensure that where Rose went, I would follow.

Yes, I missed Skye, missed the quiet and peace of the island. It would always be my home, and Rose loved it just as much. We'd agreed that as often as we could, we'd go and spend as much time there as possible. But it didn't matter, because I'd changed. Home wasn't a geographical location on the map anymore, it wasn't a place set by four walls and a roof. Home now was a much more intangible, yet solid thing.

She was my home.

My beautiful, sweet, and forever enchanting Rose.

Some time later…

A Poem for Rose

I could write a hundred sonnets but barely breathe a word
I could sing to you 'til my lungs were sore but be silent when it ends
I could tell you a thousand things with a look but nothing with my voice
I could mould our story with my hands on your skin, but Christ, my useless mouth

I was closed
You were open
I was still
You moved
You opened me, you moved *me*

I saw you and there wasn't a choice
Your kindness gripped me, killed me, woke me
I acted, you didn't
I learned I didn't have to
Now there's comfort where my skin used to itch

You live
I love you
You breathe
I live
You dance
I breathe
I sing
You love me

Home isn't a place in the sky but deep inside your heart
Surrounding by thick walls made of flesh and blood and
soul
Say that you'll marry me
And you can live in mine

Forever yours,
Damon.

END.

About the Author

L.H. Cosway lives in Dublin, Ireland. Her inspiration to write comes from music. Her favourite things in life include writing stories, vintage clothing, dark cabaret music, food, musical comedy, and of course, books. She thinks that imperfect people are the most interesting kind. They tell the best stories.

Find L.H. Cosway online!

www.lhcoswayauthor.com
www.facebook.com/LHCosway
www.twitter.com/LHCosway
www.instagram.com/l.h.cosway

Books by L.H. Cosway

<u>Contemporary Romance</u>
Painted Faces
Killer Queen
The Nature of Cruelty
Still Life with Strings
Showmance

<u>The Hearts Series</u>
Six of Hearts
Hearts of Fire
King of Hearts
Hearts of Blue

<u>The Rugby Series with Penny Reid</u>
The Hooker & the Hermit
The Player & the Pixie

<u>Urban Fantasy</u>
Tegan's Blood (The Ultimate Power Series #1)
Tegan's Return (The Ultimate Power Series #2)
Tegan's Magic (The Ultimate Power Series #3)
Tegan's Power (The Ultimate Power Series #4)

Thank you for reading Showmance. Please consider supporting an indie author and leaving a review <3

P.S. Look out for Julian's book, coming in 2017!

CPSIA information can be obtained
at www.ICGtesting.com
Printed in the USA
BVHW01s1924310118
506884BV00001B/109/P